Also by Renee Ann Miller

Never Dare a Wicked Earl

Published by Kensington Publishing Corporation

NEVER DECEIVE A VISCOUNT

RENEE ANN MILLER

ZEBRA BOOKS
KENSINGTON PUBLISHING CORP.
http://www.kensingtonbooks.com

ZEBRA BOOKS are published by

Kensington Publishing Corp.
119 West 40th Street
New York, NY 10018

First Printing: June 2018
ISBN-13: 978-1-4201-4459-8
ISBN-10: 1-4201-4459-6

eISBN-13: 978-1-4201-4460-4
eISBN-10: 1-4201-4460-X

10 9 8 7 6 5 4 3 2 1

Printed in the United States of America

To John, for your love and support.
For family, far and near, whom I hold dear.

ACKNOWLEDGMENTS

This book wouldn't be possible without the support of many. Thanks to my family for their love and enthusiasm. Mom and Dad for always being there. Johnny, Becky, Bubby, and Adriana because you are special. To the extraordinary writers I've met on this journey that not only helped me, but became friends. To my fabulous editor, Esi Sogah, the Kensington team, and my agent, Jill Marsal, for setting this all into motion.

Chapter One

Bloomsbury, London
April 1877

Simon Marlton, Viscount Adler, stretched out on the bed next to his mistress. With a coquettish smile, Vivian fanned her ginger hair over the white silk counterpane and arched her back, drawing his attention to her body, visible through her sheer peignoir.

The movement should have excited him. It didn't. He knew what was coming next.

"Whom shall we play tonight?" Vivian asked, running her finger over his bare chest to the waistband of his trousers. "Romeo and Juliet or Antony and Cleopatra? We could be wicked and do an adaptation of *The Vampire*. You could be the bloodthirsty lord and I the poor dairy wench you seduce in the forest."

Simon gritted his teeth. He sorely regretted engaging an actress as his mistress, especially one between plays. He should have chosen a dancer, some limber woman who didn't feel the need to direct every sexual encounter, or plot it to death. And surely not one who screamed *Encore! Encore!* while she climaxed.

One more night of Vivian and he might play Cassius and throw himself down upon a sword. "When are you to begin rehearsals for your new play at the Lyceum?"

She twisted a shimmering tendril around her finger and pouted. "Sir Henry wants to do *Hamlet*. It offers few worthy female roles, though I would make a remarkable Ophelia." She sat up and dramatically flung her arms wide. "'O, what a noble mind is here—'"

"When will it begin?" he asked.

"Not for several months. I shall be bored senseless." She placed the back of her hand theatrically to her forehead and sank onto the pillows.

Good Lord, several months. Simon stifled a groan.

Vivian propped herself up on her elbow and lifted her glass of claret off the bedside table. "Adler, why don't you invite some guests to your country house? We could put on a play."

Eating pigswill held more appeal. How foolish to think the actress's company would settle the discontent plaguing him as of late. Perhaps a short reprieve from Vivian would put her in a more favorable light.

"How about a holiday in Paris?" he asked.

She sat up so abruptly, her wine spilled. Red droplets glistened on the pristine counterpane. She blotted them with the edge of her translucent garment, smearing the red into the bedcover. "How lovely! When do we set sail?"

We? Good God, no. He'd jump ship before they sighted land. "I have business to attend to in Town."

"I can wait so we can journey to France together. On the ship you could play Blackbeard and I the noblewoman you have kidnapped."

A nerve twitched in his jaw. "No."

"Redbeard?"

"There must be a ship leaving Dover tomorrow," he said, ignoring her suggestion.

"Tomorrow?" A small line formed between her thin brows.

"Yes, while there you could do a bit of shopping. Visit that Charles Worth fellow who is all the rage. Purchase yourself a few gowns."

Her hazel eyes widened. "Gowns?"

"Yes. My carriage will take you to Victoria station first thing in the morning."

Emma Trafford tapped softly on her sister's bedchamber door and inched it open. A single candle on a bedside table sent scant light into the dark room. Lily, dressed in a white cotton nightgown, stood before the window, her blond hair and slender twelve-year-old body illuminated by moonlight.

"Lily?" Emma whispered.

With a gasp, Lily spun around and tucked a pair of opera glasses behind her back.

Why, the little hoyden! If that gossipmonger across the street saw Lily spying upon her, the whole of Bloomsbury would know before daybreak.

"Are you watching Mrs. Jenkins?"

"Indeed not. One could expire from boredom observing her snooze all day."

Emma released the air in her lungs and glanced out the window. The London sky was absent its perpetual fog. Perhaps Lily had turned her mind to more intellectual pursuits. "Were you observing the constellations?"

"Ah . . . yes, indeed, the stars." Lily nibbled her lower lip.

One day, when they were old and gray, Emma would reveal to her sister that Lily always bit her lower lip when she lied. "No, you were not. Now confess."

Lily shuffled her bare feet. Even in the dim light, Emma could see the two red spots on her sister's porcelain cheeks.

"I'm observing the woman who recently moved into the town house next to Mrs. Jenkins. Have you seen her? She looks to be your age, perhaps a bit older. She wears feathered hats and gowns with huge bustles. Late at night, a fine carriage pulls up and an exceedingly tall gentleman enters the house."

"You were spying on them?" Emma tried to keep the shrill tone from her voice.

"Well, tonight they didn't close their shutters, and I was ever so curious."

Emma gasped. "Lily, that's scandalous."

"Ha! If you think I'm scandalous, you should see them. Do you wish to hear what they wear to bed?"

She did, but before Emma could lie and say no, her sister barreled forward. "The woman is dressed in a nightgown that barely hides her bosom. And the man, well, he's wearing just his drawers." Shock and titillation colored Lily's voice.

"Oh my goodness." Emma dashed to her sister's side and outstretched her hand. "Lillian Marie Trafford, give me those glasses. Now!"

Lily jutted out her bottom lip and handed over the opera glasses. "Em, the man has arms as thick as Titian's depiction of Mars. And he has the largest—"

Emma clapped a hand over her sister's mouth. She didn't know what Lily intended to say, but the child spent too many hours at the lending library examining books on Renaissance paintings, and Emma feared it wasn't a love of art that piqued Lily's interest.

"Not another word." Emma removed her hand.

"But he looks nothing like old Mr. Peabody when he drank too much punch at Mrs. Green's Christmas party and removed his shirt and trousers." Lily leaned close and spoke in a hushed tone. "He looks more like the paintings of the naked men on the ceiling of the Sistine Chapel. But larger. More powerful."

Oh my. Emma stifled the salacious images working their way through her mind.

"If you don't believe me, take a peek." Lily pointed at the window, her eyes bright.

The temptation to join her sister in wickedness tugged at Emma. She'd never seen a man wearing only his drawers. Well, except for Mr. Peabody, but his prune-like anatomy and pencil-thin legs hadn't impressed her in the least. And the one time she'd been intimate . . . that had been a debacle she didn't wish to recall. She set the opera glasses on a table and drew the curtains closed.

"Get under the covers, and promise me you will not spy on the neighbors again. Especially *those* neighbors." She pulled her sister toward the bed.

With a sullen expression, Lily climbed under the blankets and folded her arms across her chest. "I promise."

Emma pressed a kiss to her sister's cheek. "Now sleep well, dearest, and blow out the candle as soon as I close the door."

Across the central corridor, Emma slipped into her bedchamber and padded to the window. The curtain rings rattled on the rod as she pulled the material closed. Unable to resist, she parted the fabric an inch and peered out. The town house across the way glowed like a balefire in the dark night. Their new neighbors certainly didn't want for money.

She moved away from the window. After she changed into her white cotton nightgown, she settled between the sheets with a book of Tennyson's poems.

A half hour later, Emma stared blindly at a page. Doubtful the man across the way resembled Michelangelo's nudes. Men like that were only in artists' imaginations. She set her reading aside and turned down the wick on the bedside lamp, shrouding the room in darkness.

Boom! The bedchamber door flew open and slammed against the wall.

"Em!" Lily's frantic voice cut through the gloom like a shaft of light.

Heart pounding, Emma bolted upright. "What's the matter?"

Lily rushed forward, her pale face illuminated by the globed candle she held. "You must summon a constable."

"What's happened?" Emma tossed off her bedding.

Her sister's empty hand fluttered in the air. "The man. I-I believe he's killed the woman. He tore the thin material from her body, then settled under the sheets and climbed atop her. Her head thrashed back and forth while he . . . Oh, it was horrid. And when he was done, she just lay there not moving, eyes closed, with an odd expression plastered on her still face. *She's dead!*"

More than once, Emma had contemplated the joining of a man and woman—compared it to what she knew. Her single experience had left her sore, shamed, and ruined. But there were times she'd imagined a husband gently removing his wife's clothes in the dark. Or if they were daring, leaving a single candle lit. She'd never imagined all the lights on. Perhaps her imagination was lacking.

"Em!"

Lily's voice startled Emma from her torrid thoughts. "Lily, you promised you wouldn't spy on them."

"I know, but . . ."

Emma scooted to the other side of the mattress and lifted the blankets. "Get into bed."

Her sister's mouth gaped. "Aren't you going to summon a constable?"

She sighed. "Dearest, sometimes married men and women partake in activities in their bedchambers that girls of twelve should not be privy to. They . . . they play games."

"This was not a game! A game would be blind man's bluff or twenty questions. This was depravity. Murder. Just like the murders Inspector Percival Whitley solves."

Lily had a fertile imagination, and those penny dreadfuls she read about Inspector Whitley of Scotland Yard did not help. "Get into bed," Emma repeated. "I'm sure it was a game."

After setting the candle on the bedside table, Lily climbed in next to her. "If that is the type of amusement married couples engage in, I shall become a spinster." Lily grabbed Emma's hand under the sheet. "Is that why you didn't marry Charles? Because you knew once married you'd have to partake in such wickedness?"

Emma's chest tightened as shame overwhelmed her. Charles had asked for her hand three years ago, on her twenty-first birthday, a week after Papa died. She'd allowed Charles to convince her that they didn't have to wait for the sanctity of marriage to join with each other. He'd professed his love and told her he couldn't wait anymore. That madness might overtake him if he couldn't make love to her.

Three days afterward, he'd called and said his father was not in accord with the betrothal. How foolish she'd been to think a baron's son would marry out of his station, especially a portraitist with no fortune.

"We realized we didn't suit," Emma said, shoving aside the guilt over her reckless behavior.

"I'm glad"—Lily snuggled closer—"for I hate to think of you being forced to play such wretched games."

Charles had married last year, an earl's daughter, and his wife was now round with child. She dashed at the moisture filling the corners of her eyes. Silly to shed tears. She didn't need Charles or any other man. If she sold enough portraits, she could support herself and her two siblings all on her own.

Forcing a smile, Emma tucked the blankets around her sister's slender shoulders and kissed her cheek. "Goodnight, dearest."

The early sun shone through the morning room's windows, brightening the faded blue walls. Emma sat at her secretaire and perused the bills in front of her. Once she finished painting Mrs. Naples's portrait, she'd have nearly all the funds for Michael's boarding school tuition, along with enough to pay the coal merchant. Though not enough to pay what she owed Mrs. Flynn. The housekeeper continued to work for them even though Emma hadn't paid the woman her full salary in months. For all her gruff ways, Mrs. Flynn possessed a soft heart and a motherly tendency toward them.

The double doors swung open, and Lily stormed into the room with as much drama as the night before.

"I told you that man murdered the ginger-haired woman!" Lily grabbed Emma's hand and tugged her across the room.

"I do not want to hear another word about murder." Emma planted her heels into the threadbare carpeting.

Her sister stomped her foot and pointed at the window. "See for yourself."

The headache, which had begun as Emma looked at the bills, grew stronger. She pressed her fingers to her temples. "I insist you cease this spying."

"But Inspector Whitley says one must carefully search for clues, for they will always reveal the villain."

Emma attempted not to roll her eyes heavenward at the mention of the fictitious inspector. Setting a hand on the window's casings, she gazed outside. Two burly men were hefting a large trunk onto a dray across the street. "What is it I'm supposed to be witnessing?"

Lily groaned. "Don't you understand? The woman's body is stuffed in the trunk."

"You know no such thing."

"What else could it be?"

"They might be cleaning their attic."

A tall gentleman with broad shoulders stepped out of the town house. He was impeccably dressed in a navy overcoat and top hat.

"That's him!" Lily clasped Emma's arm, her fingers tight enough to leave marks.

The man lifted his hat and raked his fingers through shiny black hair.

Lily's warm breath puffed on the back of Emma's neck. "Criminals are always dark and dangerous in appearance. And if he isn't dastardly looking, I don't know what one would call him."

Emma swallowed. *She* would call him beautiful. The perfect subject to paint. His face all hard angles. His jaw strong and firm. His nose chiseled. He reminded her of a panther she'd seen at Regent's Zoo. Striking, yet if one were foolish enough to reach out to stroke its fur, surely they'd lose an appendage.

Her gaze shifted from his broad-shouldered body to the trunk. It was indeed large enough to hold a woman's body.

Oh bother. She was letting Lily's imagination play havoc on her own mind. "I will not make accusations against him." He looked not only dangerous, but also wealthy—a man financially capable of destroying them if they libeled him. "You have no proof."

"Proof? I told you what I saw last night. Now the trunk. What more do you need?"

"And I told you—"

"Yes, yes, a game. What balderdash."

The drayman's voice calling to the horses to *move on* drew their attention back to the window. A closed carriage with yellow wheels now stood in front of the town house as well.

"See," Emma said, pointing at the fancy equipage. "The woman is probably inside."

Lily bit on the nail of her index finger. "If you hadn't been arguing with me, I might have seen something. I'm going to go outside and peek in the carriage."

Emma grabbed her sister's hand. "You will do no such thing. Anyway, it has already started up the street."

Lily wrenched her hand free and pressed her nose to the pane of glass. "Drat, I know what I saw, and I shall prove it to you."

Chapter Two

Emma dipped her brush into the cerulean paint on her palette and lightly dabbed at the canvas. She stepped back and appraised her work. The portrait of Mrs. Naples and her dog, Alfred, needed a few more touches. A dab of white to highlight, a smidgen of gray to shadow, and the painting would be complete.

Thankfully, the widow and her pug no longer needed to sit for Emma. Mrs. Naples believed Alfred to be her late husband reincarnated. Emma hoped, if that were true, Mr. Naples had exhibited better manners than his namesake, who was the most flatulent animal Emma had ever had the displeasure to meet.

The tall longcase clock on the first-floor landing struck twelve times, resonating through the house. Stifling a yawn, Emma rubbed the back of her hand across her heavy-lidded eyes.

Midnight.

Surely, folly to continue when fatigue pulled at her limbs like leaden weights and the paraffin lamps burned low. She laid her brush down atop her palette and picked up a turpentine-soaked rag to scrub the paint off her tools and fingertips. The woodsy scent of the solvent filled her nose. Tomorrow she would finish the portrait, and most of the funds for Michael's tuition would soon be in hand. She set the rag into its bowl and glanced out the window. Blue moonlight illuminated the white stone of the town house across the way. The residence had stood silent all day. The servants, like their mistress, had all disappeared. A movement caught her attention. She set her hands to the glass and peered at a slim form dashing across the street.

Lily!

Emma sucked in her breath. The mint-drop slowly dissolving in her mouth flew down her throat. With a cough and an unladylike curse, she slipped the window's latch. By the time she threw the sash up, her sister had already opened the wrought iron gate of the darkened residence and was disappearing down the servants' steps.

Why had she told Lily she didn't have enough proof? She should have realized the child would devise some harebrained idea to ferret out evidence. Darting from the room, Emma wiped her hands on the loose white shirt and gray wool trousers she always wore to paint when alone. Garments her brother had outgrown.

She hurried down the stairs. In the entry, Emma grabbed Michael's knit cap off the hall tree and tugged it over her chignon. She opened the door, peeked out, and glanced at the neighboring town houses. Thankfully, Mrs. Jenkins would be asleep. The gossipmonger would weave horrid tales if she spotted either Lily or Emma scurrying about at such an ungodly hour, especially with Emma scandalously dressed in men's attire.

As she dashed across the street, cloudy tendrils of fog rose from the damp pavement to swirl around her ankles. A sense of foreboding moved down her spine like an icy-cold finger. She set her hand on the iron gate and swung it open. The hinges gave an eerie cry. She descended the steps, expecting to see her sister with her nose pressed to a pane of glass, but the gas streetlamp revealed an open window and a crate pushed underneath it.

This is beyond the pale, even for Lily. When she got her hands on her sister, she would drag her home by the ear. Then she would take an inordinate amount of pleasure in burning every Inspector Percival Whitley book Lily possessed.

She hefted herself up and swung one leg, then the other through the opening. Once inside, her eyes adjusted to the gloom relieved by the muted light streaming through the open window.

"Lily?" she whispered, moving to the stairs at the back of the kitchen.

Darkness filled the narrow stairway. Emma grasped the wooden handrail and ascended the steps to the third story, where the master's bedchamber would be, and hopefully Lily. A large mullioned window that overlooked the street illuminated a wide corridor with four doors. The one closest to the window on the right stood ajar. She crept into the dim room. The white dust covers draped over the furniture caused the tall pieces to loom like ghostly specters.

From the corner of her eye, she caught a movement. A white cat sprung from the darkness to land on the bed. Emma gasped and stepped back, pressing a hand over her pounding heart.

The cat meowed and craned its body toward her.

She reached out and rubbed the fur behind its ears.

Hooves clopping on the pavement echoed outside, shattering the silence of the street below.

Emma crept to the window and edged open one shutter. A carriage stood before the town house. The horses shook their heads, rattling heavy harnesses, and the breaths from their nostrils cut through the dark night with puffs of white.

A broad-shouldered man leapt from the carriage. His

long overcoat swayed against his tall legs, dispersing the fog swirling upward from the damp pavement. He lifted his head, and light from the lamppost slashed across his angular face.

She sucked in a mouthful of cool air. Earlier today, she'd thought the man beautiful, but without the sun to lighten his countenance, his face looked only menacing.

He strode toward the residence.

Her breathing quickened. With a hand fisted to her mouth, Emma spun away from the window and glanced frantically about. Where was Lily? Hopefully back home.

She ran into the corridor.

The front door opened, then slammed closed. Her limbs froze. The sound of her blood racing through her veins filled her ears with a *thump, thump, thump*. She dashed back into the bedchamber, dropped to her hands and knees, and crawled under the bed.

"Kismet!" The man's deep voice seemed to reverberate off the walls. Quick footfalls moved up the steps.

Emma poked her head out from under the mattress. The luminescent glow of the feline's eyes caught the moonlight as the animal slinked around the bedchamber. The cat moved into the corridor and meowed before dashing into the room and under the bed to join her.

"Kismet!" The gentleman moved farther up the steps.

Emma ducked back under the bed and blinked at the animal rubbing itself against her. "Are you Kismet?" she whispered.

The animal butted his head on her arm as though affirming her fears.

"Shoo." She pushed his furry body away and pulled her brother's knit cap farther down over her light-colored hair.

The man's footfalls grew louder. The floorboards near the threshold squeaked.

She clamped a hand over her mouth, hoping to muffle

her breathing as she dipped her head low and peered under the edge of the bed skirt. Light reflecting off the moon eased between the slightly parted shutters. A beam caught the shine of the man's approaching black shoes. Soft fur brushed against her arm, and the cat's purr rumbled in the room as though amplified.

"Ah, I knew you'd be in here." The man dipped to one knee.

His hand reached under the bed. Emma's heart pounded so loud, she feared the gentleman would hear it. She pulled her arms tighter against her body.

The pads of his fingers pressed against her shoulder.

Once.

Twice.

"What the hell!" he growled.

Long fingers wrapped around her arm in a bone-crushing grip, dragging her out from under the bed to hoist her upward. The man stood even taller than she thought. She tipped her head back and peered into his dark eyes. For a bizarre moment, she appreciated he held her upright, for her legs seemed incapable of the task.

"Lad, you picked the wrong house to pilfer."

Lad? She glanced down at her brother's clothing.

He gave her a shake.

Pain shot through her arms where his ungloved fingers bit into her skin. Panic squeezed her chest like a vise, and she rammed the heel of her shoe onto his foot.

As if nothing more than a pesky fly irritated him, his talon-like grip remained firm. "You wretch, give me one good reason why I shouldn't box your ears and drag you before the magistrate."

Her throat tightened.

"Damn you, answer me." He released her arm.

She tried to dart past him.

"No, you don't." His fingers clamped around her wrist.

Instinctively she fisted her free hand and swung.

He ducked. His white teeth flashed in the dim light.

Her brother had told her where to hit a man if attacked. Without further contemplation, she lifted her thigh and rammed it between the man's legs.

"*Owf.*" He fell to his knees like a sack of coal.

For several seconds, she stared at him as his breath heaved in and out. *Run*, a voice in her head commanded. Who will care for Lily and Michael if you are arrested? Eyeing the open door, she pressed her back against the wall and edged by his crumpled form.

She'd just made it by him when his large hand snaked out and wrapped around her ankle. She tried to shake herself free, but the man gave her leg a hard jerk, and she landed on her back with a heavy *thud*. A searing pain radiated from her tailbone to her shoulders.

Breathing unevenly, the man crawled over and sat atop her, straddling her body with thick, muscular thighs. His weight compressed her hips, imprisoning her. A shaft of moonlight slashed across his lean face, exposing his perfectly chiseled features and a crescent-shaped scar on his left cheek. Terror gripped her belly, but she couldn't tear her gaze away from the hard, beautiful angles of his face.

"Why, you misbegotten wretch. I was only trying to scare you, but now you've made me bloody well angry." He set his hand on her chest. His fingers flexed. His eyes widened. "Damnation, you're a woman!"

She knocked his hand away and bucked under him.

He leaned closer.

The scent of spicy male drifted off his heated skin, while his warm breath fanned against her ear.

Goose bumps scattered over her flesh.

"Why you little she-cat, I have half a mind to put you over my knee and spank you."

The low, almost seductive timbre of his voice sent a

frisson down her spine. Sparks exploded low in her belly. What was wrong with her? She should be frightened, but it wasn't fear that caused her pulse to beat faster. God, she must be mad.

The legs clamped around her eased. The man shifted, and his face tensed as if still in pain. "Now, if I get up, will you promise to behave?"

She wet her dry lips, opened her mouth, and snapped it closed as a shadow near the door slipped into the room. The slim form moved—shifted along the wall.

Lily. Gracious! Did the girl possess no sense? Did she wish them both to end up before the magistrate?

Emma wrapped her hands around the lapels of the man's coat and tugged his face to hers. She slid one hand behind his shoulder and motioned her sister to leave.

He jerked back. "What do you think you're about?"

"Repentance." Her voice sounded low and sultry, unrecognizable to her own ears. She slipped her fingers into the warmth of his thick hair and drew his mouth to hers. His lips held firm. Unresponsive. Obviously, she lacked sufficient skill to carry such a diversion to fruition. She was about to give up when his weight settled closer to her. The tension in his taut muscles uncoiled, shifting the air around them with a tangible force.

Uttering a deep, raspy noise, his mouth moved hungrily against hers. His fingers wrapped around her wrists. He pulled her hands off him and pinned them above her head. His tongue slipped into her mouth, tangled with hers before withdrawing, only to plunge again.

He tasted like brandy and sin, and the wicked way he kissed made her body heat. Everywhere. She fought the urge to arch against him. Failing miserably, she pressed her tingling breasts tighter to the solidity of his chest.

A floorboard squeaked.

Lily! Was the child still in the room? Watching? Not escaping as Emma hoped she would?

Emma slammed her palms into his shoulders just as a crash rent the air. Shards of pottery exploded around them like fireworks, and she pinched her eyes closed.

The man collapsed atop her, his body a dead weight. She opened her eyes to see Lily standing above them, holding the bottom of a broken vase.

"Lily, what have you done?"

Her sister tossed what remained of the vase on the bed and dusted off her hands. "Saved you, Em. He was about to kill you using the same method he employed against his other victim."

Oh my! Emma squirmed out from under the heavy weight of his body and held her fingers before his lips. The man's breath fanned against her skin. The knot in her stomach eased.

"Thankfully, you haven't killed him, Lily."

"I had to protect you. I couldn't let him—"

"Hush," Emma said, running her fingertips carefully through his hair to feel the back of his skull. A lump had already begun to form, but at least there wasn't any blood.

A ray of moonlight highlighted a gold ring on the unconscious man's right pinkie. Her sister crouched and touched it. "There's an emblem on it. What do you think it means?"

"I don't know. Leave it be." Emma gently brushed a lock of hair off the gentleman's forehead.

"It could be from some secret society of murderers. There was such a villainous group in Inspector Whitley's third book, *Blood on the Thames*."

A low moan eased from the man's mouth.

Emma shot to her feet.

Lily remained hunched over the gentleman, still inspecting his ring.

"Hurry." She clasped Lily's wrist and pulled her sister from the room. They raced down the stairs and moved to the open kitchen window.

"Em—"

She cupped her hand over Lily's mouth. "Shhh, his coachman awaits him. Climb out and wait for me."

With a nod, Lily hoisted herself out the basement window. Emma followed right behind. They crept to the top of the steps and peered at the man sitting on the carriage perch. His chin rested on his chest, and his snoring filled the night air.

Stealthily they tiptoed across the street and slipped inside their residence. Emma slumped against the front door and tugged off the knit cap.

"Em, you won't believe what I saw—"

With a finger that trembled, Emma pointed at the stairs. "To bed! Or so help me, I'm going to drag you up there by your braid."

Her sister's mouth fell open. "But—"

Emma pushed off the door and took a menacing step toward her.

Lily raced up the steps.

In the morning room, Emma opened the shutters and peered out.

If the gentleman didn't come out of his house in five minutes, she would have no choice but to tell his coachman he lay injured. Suddenly, the front door of the town house burst open. The man stumbled out, one hand holding his head, the other clutching the cat.

Pulling the shutters closed, Emma released the air held tight in her lungs.

In his club, Simon cracked open one eye and glanced at the expectant faces staring at him. He narrowed that singular eye on the crystal glass he held in his hand. Brown liquid congealed on the sides of the now empty goblet like horse dung on the bottom of one's shoe.

The corrosive concoction James Huntington had given him was going to put him in his grave. At least it would, if God had any mercy.

Simon pressed a hand to his throat. It burned as if he'd swallowed a flame-eater's torch. He leaned back against the leather chair. Why he'd spent the night at his gentlemen's club was beyond him. He should have sought comfort between the legs of a soft-spoken woman with hands that knew how to soothe. Obviously, that blasted vase had knocked all prudent thought from his brain.

He set the glass down. "That tasted foul."

Huntington grinned, a rare occurrence. At one time, he'd been the ton's darling—the man everyone wanted to be, but since his wife's death and the suspicion that fell on him, the marquess had fallen from grace.

Simon placed a hand to the front of his skull. Whatever he'd just swallowed wasn't alleviating the pounding in his head. If he ever got his hands on that little femme fatale, he would make her pay. Shoving her knee into his bollocks had been dire enough, but then to distract him with her warm mouth and supple body while her accomplice conked him over the head, well, that was unforgivable.

"Did it work?" Huntington pointed at the glass.

Julian Caruthers pushed his chair back from a baize-covered table and walked over to Simon. "Is your headache gone?"

The man's words reverberated off the mahogany paneling in the private room. "Could you extend a chap a bit of mercy and lower your voice?" Simon asked. "Whatever Huntington gave me is causing a slow death, and you're not making it a peaceful demise."

"Give it a minute, old chum," Huntington averred. "I swear on my grandmother's grave it works."

Caruthers's laughter filled the room. Simon assumed he found humor in the fact that Huntington's cantankerous grandmother was alive and well.

"I've rarely seen a man best you, Adler," Caruthers stated. "How many men attacked you last night? Five? Six?"

Simon glanced at one of his closest friends, Hayden Westfield. The only one with whom he'd confided that one of his attackers had been a woman who'd distracted him with her lush body and her promise of repentance.

"Yes, do tell us how many *men* attacked you." Westfield grinned.

Simon narrowed his eyes at Westfield. "Two *people* attacked me."

Caruthers blinked. "Just two! Hit you when your back was turned, eh?"

Westfield snorted a laugh before lifting the morning newspaper to shield his wide grin.

Damnation, must they all be so loud? Simon groaned.

"Where was your mistress while all this was going on?" Caruthers cocked a brow.

"I accompanied Vivian to Victoria station yesterday. She is holidaying in France."

"Her decision or yours?" Caruthers asked.

"Mine. I told her to go and buy herself some gowns in Paris."

"Ah, I see a pattern forming. You sent the mistress before Vivian there before you broke it off." Huntington sat at the card table.

Yes. That one, an opera singer, possessed a voice capable of shattering glass as well as eardrums. Simon sighed. "When Vivian returns, I'll probably buy her a pretty bauble and end it."

"How many mistresses does that make in the last year?" Westfield asked, lowering his newspaper.

Too many. Simon felt restless lately. Discontent. As if he lacked something that even his wealth couldn't buy. "Are you writing a biography on my life?"

"No, just concerned about you, old chum. Do you wish Dr. Trimble to be summoned?" Westfield rubbed at his chin.

"Why don't you have your lovely nurse-wife attend to him, Westfield?" Caruthers returned to his chair.

Westfield scowled at the man. "I'm not sure if he's moaning over the lump on his head or his bruised bollocks, and I'll not have Sophia inspect the latter."

Laughter erupted in the room again, and the pounding in Simon's head grew. He closed his lids and prayed for a quick death.

What seemed only minutes later, Simon opened his eyes and pulled his watch from his fob pocket. Nearly noon. Hell, he'd fallen asleep. While he'd slept, he'd dreamed of the she-devil's warm, mint-flavored mouth and soft body. He tipped his head to the left, then to the right. His headache had vanished.

Huntington and Caruthers played bezique while Westfield reclined in a chair and read. What was Westfield still doing here? He rarely spent time at the clubs since marrying. Unlike Huntington, who came to this private room to avoid all the whispers that perhaps he'd had a hand in his wife's death. A bloody lie.

Westfield flipped a page in his book and glanced at Simon, a concerned expression on his face.

Dash it all, what a mother hen the man had become. "Well done, Huntington," Simon called out, pointing at the empty glass.

The man looked over his shoulder and peered at him. "It worked?" He sounded shocked.

"Yes, what the deuce was in it?"

"Whisky, pickle juice, capsicum, oats, and—"

"Damn, Huntington, were you trying to finish him off?" Westfield asked, snapping his novel closed.

Huntington unfolded his tall form from his chair. "My valet swears it will cure any illness or strip the varnish off your furniture, if you prefer."

Simon cringed. He'd be lucky if he didn't end up with a hole in his stomach. He stared at the lighter band of skin on his left hand and blinked. Where was his signet ring? Had that bollocks-smashing vixen taken it? Or had he lost it during the scuffle? He jerked to his feet.

"Where are you going?" Caruthers asked.

"I have somewhere to be."

"I'm off, as well," Westfield said.

They stepped out of the room, and Westfield set a hand on Simon's shoulder. "Are you still coming for dinner tomorrow?"

"Of course. I haven't seen my godson in over a week. How is the little fellow?"

A smile turned up Westfield's lips. "He's crawling now. Perhaps it is time you married and started a brood of your own."

Marry? God, no. He'd witnessed firsthand how foolish falling in love could make a man. His stepmother was the devil's spawn. She'd poisoned Simon's relationship with his father, and his sire had gone to his grave believing everything that manipulating woman had said. No, he would not allow himself to be twisted around a woman's finger. "I enjoy my freedom."

The expression in Westfield's eyes looked too close to pity, and Simon realized he was trailing a finger over his scar. He lowered his hand.

"You need to learn to trust, my friend. Not all women are as manipulative as Julia."

"I trust women."

"Who? Your mistresses?" Westfield shot a disbelieving expression. "Even them you keep at a safe distance. A family would do you well."

He'd had a family, and he'd lost it in the blink of an eye, all because his father had taken Julia's words over his. "Your sermon on trust would have more impact if *not* preached the day after a woman tried to crush in my skull. Now I need to go. I have a little bird to cage."

"The woman from last night?"

"Yes." Like his stepmother, she'd sucked him in, then unleashed her true self. Simon clenched his hand, absent the weight of his ring. While he'd slept, the woman's sultry voice had whispered the word *repentance* in his dream. By God, if she'd taken his ring, he'd find her and make her pay.

Chapter Three

Lily paced the morning room floor. "I tell you, Em, moonlight highlighted the bed, and I saw red drops of blood smeared into the white comforter. You would have seen them if you hadn't entered the wrong room."

Emma turned away from the window. The town house across the street remained quiet. All morning she'd feared an army of constables would descend upon them, or at least question the neighbors, but so far nothing. She rubbed at her eyes. Unable to sleep last night, she'd risen and finished painting the portrait of Mrs. Naples.

Now, Lily's prattling threatened to drive Emma mad. "Have you studied your mathematics or started reading the book I gave you on geography?"

"Read? I'm too distraught. Do you realize I saved your life?"

Lud. She'd told the child, repeatedly, the man had not been murdering her. That in fact, *she'd* kissed him in an effort to distract him so Lily could escape. She closed her eyes and recalled the way the man's tongue had tangled with her own. Charles had never kissed her like that, or with such hunger. She ran the tip of her tongue across the top of her mouth. It didn't evoke the same sensations.

"Have you at least read the book of sonnets Aunt Henrietta sent you?"

Lily stared at the ceiling as though the water spot marring the white paint fascinated her.

"You are aware Aunt Henrietta will write and ask your opinion on them."

"Sonnets are as stimulating as conversing with Ronald Watts."

"Ronald cannot converse. He is only seven weeks old."

"Yes, that is my point." Lily crossed her arms over her chest. "I will read them if you return my Inspector Whitley books."

"I will not. You are fortunate I haven't tossed them in the grate and rendered them to ash. What you did was reckless. Unlawful. And God knows the condition of that poor gentleman."

"Poor gentleman? Pish! Dastardly villain, I say."

Emma strode to the secretaire, opened the desk's top drawer, and withdrew the brochure for Mrs. Hibble's School of Refinement. She turned the pages. "I still think this is an interesting school for young ladies."

"Egad, you cannot be serious. It's in Northumberland. The wilds of England. And the Geordies have a horrid accent. If you send me there, I shall return home speaking unintelligibly." Lily stalked toward the open door. She stopped and wheeled about, causing her long blond braid to whip in the air. "You would miss me, Em. With Michael away at school you'd be all alone."

She would never send Lily so far away, even if she possessed the funds to do so, but the threat always defused whatever tirade her sister fancied. "Mrs. Flynn is here, and I could invite Aunt Henrietta to stay with me."

Lily gaped. “Aunt Henrietta is in her dotage, sleeps half the day away, and when awake complains incessantly.”

“I would gain a small measure of peace and quiet while she slept.”

“Pfft.” Lily turned and continued her flamboyant exit. Her shoes stomped on the worn blue carpet as she stormed past the housekeeper entering the room.

Mrs. Flynn folded her thick arms over her ample bosom and frowned. “Mrs. Naples and *that dog* she thinks is her dead husband are here.”

Emma understood the housekeeper’s scowl. Not only did the pug have an excessive amount of flatulence, he’d also piddled on the carpet on his last visit. “Please show her in, Mrs. Flynn.”

Grumbling, the housekeeper exited.

A moment later, Mrs. Naples rushed into the room, the little dog trailing her as though the woman dangled a beef joint from the hem of her skirts.

“Emma dear, you have completed my portrait!”

How did she know? She blinked at the gray-haired woman.

As though she had spoken the question aloud, Mrs. Naples said, “Alfred told me during breakfast this morning.” She patted the pug’s head. “Didn’t you, dear?”

The dog gave two resounding barks.

“It is done, isn’t it?” the elderly woman asked.

Emma narrowed her eyes at the animal, and wondered, not for the first time, if Mrs. Naples wasn’t actually as loony as everyone thought. “Ah, yes.”

“I knew it. Alfred is rarely wrong.”

The dog barked again.

“Don’t be a braggart, Alfred. It is unbecoming.” Mrs. Naples leaned conspiratorially closer to Emma. “When we were first married, I couldn’t get a single word from him during breakfast, but now that he only wets the newspaper instead of reading it, he talks incessantly. Quite tiresome at times."

Alfred sniffed at the carpet. Mrs. Flynn would be livid if the dog piddled on it again. Emma set her hand on the woman's back. "Mrs. Naples, though the portrait is complete, the paint has yet to dry. However, I could show it to you and Alfred."

The woman excitedly clapped her hands together. "That would be lovely. Wouldn't it, Alfred?" The animal stood on his hind legs and walked in a circle.

In Emma's studio, Mrs. Naples held Alfred and stared at the portrait. The stillness of the woman, and her unreadable expression, caused a weight to settle in Emma's belly.

With a choked sob, Mrs. Naples placed her hand to her mouth and began to cry. Not a gentle cry, but a weeping-sobbing-shoulder-shaking cry. As if consoling her, Alfred nudged her face with his snout.

This doesn't bode well. The weight in Emma's stomach shifted upward, making her chest tight. If Mrs. Naples refused the commission, Emma feared she would cry more robustly than the elderly woman.

Suddenly, Mrs. Naples turned to her and grabbed her hand. "Oh, my dear, how wonderful. You've truly captured Alfred's soul. I can't thank you enough."

An hour later, Emma glanced around the grocer's shop. "Mr. Mays, I'll take a tin of Earl Grey tea as well." She tried to temper her smile, but since Mrs. Naples's visit, it seemed an impossible task.

When was the last time she'd felt so carefree? Not since before Father's passing. At present, she felt as if she floated on a cloud. How wonderful to feel so unburdened.

Mrs. Naples had not only given her a check for the agreed-upon commission, but three extra pounds. An unexpected boon! And if that hadn't been enough to set her spirits high, the fact the police had not shown up only added to her euphoria.

"Can I get you anything else, Miss Trafford?" Mr. Mays asked.

She pointed at the Keiller's marmalade. When Father was alive, the preserve of Seville oranges had been a breakfast staple, but she'd not purchased it in over a year. "I'll take a crock of marmalade."

The grocer, a short man in his early thirties with brown thinning hair, placed the container on the counter before he opened a large glass jar filled with pomfret cakes. He scooped several pieces of the licorice-flavored candies onto a piece of white paper and wrapped them up, then reached behind him for a round tin of peppermint drops.

He glanced toward the heavy drapes that separated the back room from the storefront. "Give these to Lily," he whispered, handing her the pomfret cakes. "The mints are for you. I know how you enjoy them so."

"Nigel!" a tight voice called from behind the curtain.

It appeared the grocer's overbearing mother stood guard, listening. Mrs. Mays held the misguided assumption Emma returned her son's affection. The woman had nothing to fear in that regard. Emma would not marry a man whose mother shadowed and dictated his every move. And she didn't need a man to take care of her.

"How thoughtful of you, Mr. Mays, but I insist on paying for them." She placed several coins on the counter and slipped the candies into her reticule. "I'll take the candy with me, but you may deliver the marmalade with my other groceries."

The grocer pointed to the packages Emma had set on

the counter when she'd walked into the shop. "Do you wish to leave your parcels here, Miss Trafford? It would be no trouble to deliver them with your order."

Emma glanced at the boxes. Before coming here, she'd purchased Lily a blue cotton dress and Michael a pair of gloves. Riding gloves, of all things. How utterly foolish. They'd sold their horse and carriage last year.

She ran her hand over the floral-patterned hatbox beneath the other parcels. She'd stood for ten minutes outside the milliner's shop, staring through the window at the cream-colored hat with its pink rosebuds and taffeta ribbons. Quite rash to purchase herself such finery.

"A most kind offer, Mr. Mays, but I shall carry them home with me." She was eager to show Lily the blue dress—and perhaps just as eager to try her hat on again.

Simon glanced out the window of his coach. The streets of Bloomsbury were filled with rattling drays, newsboys hawking papers, and the sweet aroma from a nearby bakery. Restless, he reached for his ring, momentarily forgetting its absence. He had a terrible habit of twisting it around his finger. He pulled out his silver cigarette case.

Empty. Blast it. He slid open the window behind the coachman's perch. "Hillman, stop at the tobacconist up ahead."

"Yes, m'lord."

The carriage pulled to the curb, and Simon leapt onto the pavement. He had only taken a few steps when a woman plowed right into him. His gloved hand shot out to grasp her elbow. "Forgive me, madam."

"No, no, it is I who must beg your forgiveness, sir." She started to peer around her packages, but the topmost one began to slip.

Simon released her elbow and steadied the parcel.

A grocer with a white apron tied around his waist darted out of a shop. The man flashed Simon a narrow-eyed scowl as he rushed to the woman's side. "Are you hurt, Miss Trafford? Do you wish to return to the shop and sit in the back room? I'm sure my mother wouldn't mind the company."

"Thank you, Mr. Mays, but it's quite unnecessary." The taut edge in the woman's voice clearly conveyed her distaste at the idea of spending time with the man's mother. However, the dull-witted chap's smile proved him oblivious.

Simon reached for the woman's purchases. "Madam, do you have a carriage I may convey these to?"

"Kind of you to ask, but I live a short stroll away. And it's such a pleasant day."

Simon glanced at the sky. It was a pigeon gray, and the sun had yet to make an appearance. Obviously, the woman suffered some visual deficiency. She appeared not only a detriment to herself but every pedestrian who walked Bloomsbury. He took her parcels from her delicate gloved hands.

The woman's gaze met his. She staggered backward and swayed like an off-balance toy top. Her golden-tipped lashes fluttered.

Dear God! Was she ill? He shoved the parcels into the grocer's hands and grasped the woman's shoulders to prevent her from tumbling to the pavement. Her stunning blue eyes turned unbelievably round as she focused on him.

"Madam, are you unwell?"

She opened her mouth, but nothing came out.

The grocer sighed. "I thought her so hale. Surely, Mother will not give her blessing now."

Simon narrowed his eyes at the foolish chap. "If you will give me her directions, I shall see her safely home."

The woman gave a frantic shake of her head and uttered a barely audible squeak.

The bell over the grocer's door jangled. A thin, prune-faced woman dressed in severe black moved to stand next to the grocer. "Come inside, Nigel. Let the gentleman handle this."

"But, Mama, we do not even know the man. He could be a blackguard. He could attempt to compromise poor Miss Trafford while conveying her."

Ignoring the bickering pair, Simon glanced over his shoulder at his coachman. "Hillman, take the woman's packages." He looked back at the grocer. "Her directions?" he snapped in an authoritative voice.

The color drained from the grocer's cheeks.

The old woman stepped forward. "Twelve Great James Street."

"But, Mama . . ."

"I-I'm fine, sir." The woman finally spoke, her voice a low unsteady whisper as if smoke scorched her windpipe.

Miss Trafford, apparently a neighbor of Vivian's, clearly wasn't fine. Her face was a ghostly shade of white.

"You cannot walk home in your current condition. And your packages are already in the trunk." Simon set a firm hand on the woman's back, ushered her inside his carriage, and sat across from her.

The vehicle swayed as Hillman returned to his perch, and then the equipage lurched forward.

Simon studied Miss Trafford's pale face. She possessed delicate features: a button nose and bow-shaped mouth that was pink and supple looking. Her blue eyes were darker than most, with nearly undiscernible flecks of gray circling her irises. Lovely. However, her blond hair brought his stepmother to mind. A knot twisted in his stomach, and he tossed thoughts of Julia aside.

He tugged off his gloves, set them onto the seat, and eyed the reticule that dangled from Miss Trafford's wrist. She probably carried smelling salts. Women who swooned usually did. "Are you feeling improved? Do you have a vinaigrette in your handbag?"

Miss Trafford shook her head, pressed her back into the corner like a mouse hiding from the kitchen cat, and stared at him as though he were the devil incarnate.

Perhaps, she wasn't ill. Perhaps it was . . . Briefly his fingers brushed against his left cheek. There were times when he completely forgot about his scar. Then there were times, like this, when he was more than aware of its presence.

When he was younger, the scar had stood out, a red ugly mark that drew attention. Unkind comments hurled at him from the lads at school had propelled him to use his fist on more than one occasion. However, after he'd bloodied a few noses, no one had spoken of it again. Time had mellowed the angry skin. Yet, Miss Trafford gazed at him as though he terrified her. Silly woman. He should have left her with the grocer and his crow-like mother.

"Madam," he said, attempting to keep agitation from edging his voice. "I assure you I mean you no harm."

"Where are you taking me?" Her shrill voice pierced his ears.

He forced what he hoped was an amiable expression. "Your residence on Great James Street. I'm not intent on ravishing you. Though you are welcome to complete our journey with your back pressed uncomfortably against the corner, I believe you will find the squabs more to your liking."

"Y-you are taking me home?"

Had he not just told her so? He nodded and resisted the urge to turn the door handle and shove her out. Where else did the daft woman believe he would take her? He lifted his hand and kneaded the knot of tension forming in the back of his neck.

"Yes. Allow me to introduce myself. Simon . . . Radcliffe." Best to use his mother's maiden name, not his title. It always brought about unwanted attention. The newspapers were fond of printing on-dits about him that were scandalous and *sometimes* true. Though most were lies perpetuated by some unknown source, most likely his stepmother, still trying to ruin his standing in society.

She needn't bother. His years of caring what society thought about him were long gone. However, if this woman had read any of them, she'd probably start trembling uncontrollably or leap from the moving carriage.

"And you are?" he asked.

She twisted her hands in the skirt of her plain navy dress. "Emma Trafford."

The vehicle stopped. "Ah, here we are." *Thank God.* The stimulating conversation could prompt a man to drink.

Hillman opened the door and lowered the steps. Simon alighted and offered his hand to assist Miss Trafford. She hesitantly set her fingers in his. A startling warmth seeped through her thin gloves as if they were skin to skin. As soon as her feet touched the pavement, he released her hand and took the packages Hillman had removed from the trunk.

"Thank you, Mr. Radcliffe." Miss Trafford reached for the parcels.

"No, madam. I shall carry them inside for you."

"Inside?" Her magnificent eyes widened. "I assure you, sir, I can carry them. You need not trouble yourself." The nervous edge to her voice grew sharper.

Ignoring Miss Trafford's protestation, Simon strode toward the front door. The woman fluttered beside him like a nervous goose. She opened the door and crept into the entry hall as if worried she might awaken the wild beast who slept within. She glanced around. Her tense body relaxed.

"Em!" a voice called from upstairs.

Miss Trafford stiffened.

A girl, wearing a yellow cotton dress and white stockings, slid down the balustrade, rump first. The child's bum hit the newel post. She swung off the railing like an acrobat at a fair and spun around. The girl peered at Miss Trafford; then her gaze swung to him.

The child shrieked—a most unpleasant sound that left his ears ringing.

The poppet resembled Miss Trafford. Same huge blue eyes, though her hair was a shade lighter. Sisters? Yes, and apparently as befuddled in the head as the elder Miss Trafford, for she turned to her sister and clearly mouthed the words *the murderer*.

I've stepped into a house of bedlamites. "Are you Miss Trafford's sister?"

Mouth hanging open, the child nodded.

He set the packages on the hall table with its chipped marble top. "Your sister nearly fainted. I conveyed her home because I believed it unwise for her to walk. Perhaps a physician should be summoned." Anxious to remove himself from the scene, he turned to the elder Miss Trafford. "Do you wish me to send for a physician? I know a Dr. Trimble on Harley Street. I highly recommend him."

She shook her head. A nervous little movement. "No, I-I feel quite recovered."

Simon wished he could say the same. The dashed bump on the back of his head once again throbbed, and a megrim hovered on the edge, threatening its full force.

"Well then, good day to you, Miss Trafford." He turned

to acknowledge the girl, who still gaped as though he stood naked before her. He inclined his head, pivoted, and left, hoping whatever ailed them wasn't contagious.

After crossing the street, Simon unlocked the door and entered the town house he'd purchased a few weeks ago. The residence stood quiet. Nothing seemed out of place. Like last night, white dust cloths still covered the furnishings. He dashed up the steps to the room where he'd found the she-devil intruder.

The broken vase crunched under his feet as he strode to the two front windows and folded back the shutters. Light streamed into the room, highlighting the shards of blue and white pottery scattered about. He scanned the floor for his ring, crouched, and moved several larger pieces of the broken vase around.

Nothing. Deep down, he'd known he wouldn't find his ring. The witch had stolen it. The devil take her. She'd find it hard to sell a signet ring with a nobleman's marking emblazoned on its bezel. She'd most likely pawn it to some bastard who'd melt it for the gold.

Hell and fire. It had been in his family for five generations. Every Viscount Adler had worn it. It was one of the few things, along with his title, his father hadn't been able to keep from him.

Anger tightened his gut. He walked to one of the front windows, slammed his palm against the casing, and stared out. A couple strolled up the pavement. The woman twirled her white parasol. Two laughing children ran up the street, a dog trailing them. How innocent they all looked, yet somewhere in this enclave of civility was a thief. The intruders had known the house stood vacant—that Vivian and the staff had left yesterday.

When he'd stumbled out onto the pavement last night, he'd not seen a soul. The she-devil and her accomplice lived close by. A neighbor most likely. He scanned the town houses.

Across the street, two people stood staring out the ground-floor window. Miss Trafford and her sister? Yes. Was it possible the woman's violent reaction to him had nothing to do with his scar? She stood about five-foot-six. Tall and slender, like the woman who'd kissed him.

Unlikely. His mystery woman had acted fearless. Ruthless. Miss Trafford was a timid creature frightened of her own shadow. No, the woman who kissed him was a sultry vixen with a warm, eager mouth. He stared at the shards of pottery. A bloody hell-cat that needed taming.

Chapter Four

"He's returned," Lily whispered as they stared out the front window.

"Yes," Emma replied, the disquieting tension in her chest razor sharp.

Her sister touched her own cheek. "Did you see his scar?"

"I saw it last night," Emma said, remembering the moonbeam which briefly highlighted Mr. Radcliffe's face.

Lily glared. "You didn't mention it."

"It is of no consequence."

Her sister released a heavy breath and set her hands on her hips. "If you read Inspector Percival Whitley's stories, you would know it is of great importance. Every villain has a distinguishing feature. An eye patch. A hook for a hand. Or a peg leg. In fact, in the last book, *Inspector Percival Whitley and the Crimson Lord*, the murderous baron had such a scar."

Emma sighed. "Indeed. What more evidence does one need? He must be dragged to Newgate and strung from the gallows."

"You may mock me all you wish, but I know a blackguard when I see one."

The child was hopeless. Perhaps Mama had dropped

Lily on her head when an infant. "Must I remind you again, that it was *you* who committed a crime?"

"Crime?" Lily snorted. "I'm conducting an investigation. Now, tell me exactly what he did. Do not withhold the slightest detail."

"He did nothing. I literally bumped into him outside Mr. Mays's grocery shop. I feared he would recognize me and summon the police. My chest tightened, a roaring filled my ears, and the space around me swirled, causing me to teeter. He offered to convey me home. Nothing more." Best not to mention the gentleman smelled as enticing as he had last night—like some exotic spice from the Far East.

"You're never dizzy. Or frail in the least."

"Yes, but *jail* has never loomed in my future, either."

"Obviously, he didn't see your face, and he won't involve the police. Criminals are not inclined to do so."

Across the street, a figure stepped up to the window of Mr. Radcliffe's town house. Emma shivered. He watched them. She felt it as clearly as she recalled the seductive slide of his tongue against hers. She clasped her sister's hand. "Come, dear. Step back. It would be best if we do not draw attention to ourselves. You must stay away from his residence. Do not take it into your head to snoop about again."

Playing with the tip of her long braid, Lily smiled angelically. "Em, would I do anything so reckless?"

"You already have, and you must never do anything so foolish again. And though you do not deserve it, there is something for you in the packages Mr. Radcliffe carried in for me."

"Radcliffe? So that's the blackguard's name." Lily tapped a finger against her lips. "I had expected something more sinister, like Mr. Lucifer."

God, give me patience. Emma retrieved the packages

and set them next to her on the faded yellow sofa in the morning room.

Rubbing her hands together, Lily plopped down next to her. “So what did you buy?”

Emma placed the top parcel with Michael’s gloves aside and handed Lily the larger box.

Her sister opened the package and lifted the dress out. A brief frown tugged the corners of Lily’s mouth downward.

“You don’t care for it?”

“It’s very pretty, Em. Thank you. I just thought you’d bought me some mystery books.”

“No, I think it best you refrain from reading them for a while.”

Lily’s shoulders slumped. She motioned to the milliner’s box. “You bought yourself a hat?”

“I did. I couldn’t resist.”

“Put it on.”

Unable to stop her smile, Emma lifted the lid and placed the delicate hat with silk roses on her head.

“Em, you look beautiful. Prettier than the Princess of Wales.”

Heat crept up Emma’s face. She took the hat off and carefully placed it back in the box. She shouldn’t have purchased it. It was an extravagance. Would the milliner allow her to return it?

The sound of Mrs. Flynn talking with someone outside drifted through the windows into the morning room. Emma’s heart stuttered in her chest before picking up speed.

“Do you think it’s Mr. Radcliffe?” Lily asked.

I hope not. Emma tiptoed to the window and parted the curtain an inch. Mr. Mays’s dray and horse were parked on the street. The man himself was carrying the groceries down the stairs to the basement entrance. Emma’s breath eased from her lungs. "It is only the grocer delivering my order."

"Mr. Mays?" Lily wrinkled her nose as if smelling bad fish.

"Yes. I forgot. He gave me some pomfret cakes to give you. Though I paid him for them."

Emma stepped into the entry hall, picked her reticule off the marble-topped table, and handed the candy to her sister.

Lily licked her lips, then frowned. "You aren't going to marry him, are you?"

"Who? Mr. Mays? Lord, no."

"Good. I'm going upstairs."

"Why don't you stay? I'm sure Mr. Mays intends to pay us a call." She didn't wish to entertain the man by herself.

"And watch him make cow eyes at you? No, I think I'll go read the geography book."

Ha! Doubtful. Lily probably intended on searching the upstairs for her Inspector Whitley books. She wouldn't find them. Not where they were hidden under the eaves in the attic.

As Lily moved up the steps, she pulled something shiny from the side pocket of her dress.

"What do you have there?" Emma inquired.

"Nothing." Lily nervously fumbled with whatever she held. The sparkly piece of metal tumbled down the stairs and landed by Emma's feet.

Emma glanced down at the gold contrasting against the red rug. Her palms grew damp. Her stomach tumbled within her. She picked up the ring with a lion and a swirling design emblazoned on the round bezel.

"Lily, please tell me this belonged to Papa. That you found it in his office."

"I did." Lily bit her lower lip.

Oh heavens, the child was lying. Emma swallowed the

lump of fear threatening to close her throat. "It's Mr. Radcliffe's, isn't it? You took it off his finger, didn't you?"

"I needed to. Don't you see the lion? Surely, it must mean something."

"Yes, it means you are not only a thug, but a thief."

The knocker banged against the front door. Clasping the front of her dress, Emma spun toward the sound. Mr. Radcliffe? Hopefully not. "Go to your room, Lily. And do not come out until you are twenty-one."

"May I have the ring back?"

The child had definitely been dropped on her head. "No!"

Lily stomped up the stairs.

Emma slipped the ring into the side pocket of her skirt and inched the door open.

Mr. Mays stood on the top step, a single red rose in his hand. She'd never been so relieved to see the man in her life. "Hello, Mr. Mays."

He doffed his hat and smiled so wide, she feared his jaw might lock in place. "Miss Trafford, you look much improved."

"Thank you. Do you wish to come in?"

"No, I promised Mama I'd be quick. I delivered your groceries, but before I left, I wished to give you this." He handed her the rose.

"Thank you, sir. How kind of you."

"You are most welcome." His cheeks reddened. "I wondered if you'd honor me with a stroll on Sunday."

Emma tucked her hand behind her back and crossed her fingers. She hated lying, but . . . "I fear I cannot. I've promised a portrait to a new client."

"Yes. Yes. Very understandable. Perhaps another time."

She forced a smile and nodded.

Across the street, Mr. Radcliffe stepped out of the town house. He looked so tall and powerful, and the expression on his face was fierce. A nervous bubble exploded in her stomach. She slipped her hand into her skirt pocket and curled her fingers around the weight of the ring.

"Is something wrong?" Mr. Mays asked. "You've turned a rather ghastly shade again."

"No, nothing."

He nodded. "Well, good day, Miss Trafford."

"Good day, Mr. Mays."

Mr. Radcliffe stepped to the curb and appeared to scan the pavement.

Lord, have mercy. He was searching for his ring.

She closed the door and slumped against it.

A half hour later, without waiting for his driver to lower the step, Simon leapt from his coach as it pulled up to his Curzon Street residence. He flexed his hand, still absent his ring. Doubtful he'd recover it. Anger tightened the muscles in his back.

As he stepped inside, Harris rushed forward to divest him of the overcoat slung over his arm.

He waved the gray-haired butler off. "I'm going upstairs, Harris. I'll give it to Baines myself."

Harris cleared his throat. "My lord, a messenger from Baring Brothers brought several documents over this morning. I've set them on your desk."

Blast it all. His warm bath would have to wait. The realization added to his foul mood. He handed the overcoat to Harris. "Give this to Baines, but have a care. There are slivers of broken pottery imbedded in the fabric."

The butler's bushy eyebrows pinched together. "Pottery, my lord?"

"Yes." Simon quickly strode down the corridor, trying to evade the barrage of questions Harris was in the habit of asking. Once inside his office, he shrugged off his jacket, rolled up his sleeves, and sank into the leather chair behind his desk. He rubbed at the knot in his neck while he perused the documents from his banker: a commercial loan amortization on a distillery that Westfield, Huntington, and he intended to purchase.

The sound of his valet screeching drifted down the corridor. Quick footfalls moved toward his office. Simon pinched the bridge of his nose.

Baines swept into the room, his round face florid, and his gray hair sticking up as though the valet had repeatedly raked his fingers through it in frustration. The ancient manservant outstretched his arm to exhibit Simon's overcoat, which dangled from the valet's thumb and forefinger as if it smelled like horse manure. "My lord, when you were barely out of short trousers I could tolerate your disregard, but this—"

"Can't you brush the shards out?"

"Indeed, a tedious undertaking, but I am more concerned with the smell." His valet inched the garment to his own face. His nose twitched. The man had the nose of a canine, capable of tracking down a scent from across the length of a cricket field.

"What bloody smell?"

The manservant shook a finger at him and tsked. "Such profanity, sir."

Simon took several deep breaths. "Baines, how old am I?"

"Thirty-one."

"Yet, you talk to me as though I'm still in leading strings."

"Do I?"

"You do."

"Well, a man of thirty-one *should* be aware that a fine

bespoke garment must be treated with reverence . . . as one would treat a treasured lover."

"If you can find a garment that can caress my bol—"

"My lord!"

Simon folded his hands atop his desk and forced a serious expression. The man would not leave unless he heard him out. "Speak your piece."

The elder man heaved an exaggerated breath. "Over the years, I've been required to remove wine, blood, and numerous unknown fluids from your garments, but I'm baffled as to how you have managed to get"—Baines sniffed the garment again—"turpentine on the lapels of your overcoat."

"I have no idea what you're talking . . ." A vision of his little femme fatale grasping his lapels last night halted his words. Yes, there had been an earthy pine scent on her fingers. His nostrils flared. How could he have forgotten the smell? That's right! He'd been conked over the head. Simon sprung from his chair. "What is turpentine used for?"

"What is it used for?" Baines echoed.

"Yes."

The valet blinked. "I believe varnishing."

The woman's palms had felt soft and her fingers free of calluses. No, he doubted she labored with her hands all day. "What else?"

Baines cupped his jaw. His eyes turned bright. "Artists use it to thin their paints and clean their brushes."

Simon snapped his fingers. Was that it? Did she paint with oils? He stared at the white band of skin where his ring normally was. Perhaps all was not lost. By Jove, if he was right, this clue offered a small sliver of hope that he might track her down. Recover his ring. He stepped around his desk and clasped his valet's shoulder. "Baines, you tiresome old goat, I could kiss you."

Wide-eyed, the valet stepped back. "Quite unnecessary, my lord."

"Harris!" Simon called, returning to his chair.

His butler stepped into the room.

"Harris, Baines, we are to take residence in Bloomsbury."

"Bloomsbury?" Harris echoed as though the location was as pleasant as a sip of soured milk.

"Bloomsbury?" Baines repeated with as much distaste.

One would think both servants were born and bred in Mayfair and not some rustic corner of Hampshire.

"Yes." Simon withdrew a piece of paper from his stationery tray and jotted down the address of his recently purchased Bloomsbury residence. He handed the paper to Harris. "Hire a cook and maid. No one else. You will inform them they work for Simon Radcliffe. I do not wish anyone to know I am Viscount Adler. Is that clear?"

Harris took the paper. "Yes, my lord."

"Are we to stay there long?" Baines's shoulders sagged.

He didn't know. Would he find his thief? Or was this nothing more than a futile expedition?

"Why must we go there?" Harris asked, his wrinkled face looking almost petulant.

Simon silently counted to five. Most men's servants cowered when their employers spoke, but the two older men standing before his desk had been in his family's employ since he had been knee-high. They seemed to think of themselves as his keepers more than his servants. He'd offered to pension them off, but the retainers were like annoying flies that wouldn't leave. And in truth, he'd miss the gray-haired coots.

"For God's sake, I haven't condemned you both to the gallows. Must you always question me?" He rubbed at the tension in his neck.

Neither man replied.

He raked his hand through his hair and flinched when his fingers brushed against his tender scalp. "That will be all."

The two men stared at him for a moment before they retreated, their heads bent close as they conversed. "He doesn't look drunk," Baines said in a voicc that most likely sounded low to a man of advanced years.

"Yes, but he's always held his liquor rather well," Harris replied.

Baines nodded. "Indeed, he has."

Simon leaned back in his chair, closed his eyes, and thought of the vixen's mouth pressed to his. Would he find her before she hawked his ring? This woman whose face he couldn't cvcn dcscribe. If he did, he'd take pleasure in bringing her to her knees.

Chapter Five

The following day, Simon had no sooner stepped over the threshold of Lord and Lady Westfield's residence when Celia, Westfield's nine-year-old daughter, came barreling down the stairs.

"Hi, poppet." He handed his gloves and top hat to the butler.

Celia leapt off the stairs and into his arms.

He whirled her about.

She giggled. "You're early, Uncle Simon. You're always early lately."

Was he? He set her down. How odd and unfashionable.

"Papa and Mama are getting dressed for dinner. You can come with me to the nursery to say goodnight to Vincent."

A nursery seemed as appealing as a gathering of debutantes and their overbearing mamas. But Vincent was a pleasant little tot, and his godchild, and as long as he wasn't required to hold the baby, what harm could come from it?

"Lead the way."

Celia grabbed his hand and they walked up the stairs. She stopped at the second-floor landing and headed down the corridor. "Vincent sleeps in Mama's bedchamber. It's the nursery now. Mama never used it. She's always slept with Papa."

That explained the perpetual grin on Westfield's face since he'd married Sophia nearly a year and a half ago.

They stepped into a room decorated with blue and cream striped walls. In the center was a white iron crib with an elaborate sheer canopy. A nursemaid sat quietly in a chair, her hands folded in her lap. She started to rise, but Simon held up a halting hand.

Celia ran to the crib. Standing on her toes, she peered down. "He's not sleeping yet. Come see." The child waved her small hand, motioning him closer.

Simon peered at Vincent, who possessed chubby cheeks, a mass of black hair, and dark eyes that seemed to absorb every movement. The baby grinned, and Simon experienced a jolt somewhere near his heart. No doubt, lingering indigestion from that deuced concoction Huntington had given him.

"He turned seven months yesterday," Celia said. "He crawls, you know. Right over Papa's chest when they play on the rug."

He set his palm on the baby's warm head. The child smelled like . . . Well, he wasn't sure, but it was rather pleasant. The urge to pick Vincent up and sniff him nearly overwhelmed Simon. As if burned, he jerked his hand away and touched the back of his head. Ever since that sod had cracked a vase over his head, he'd felt out of sorts.

"Why don't you have a baby, Uncle Simon?"

Throat suddenly tight, he coughed. "Best to have a wife first, dear."

"You could marry Papa's cousin Victoria. Great-uncle Randolph says he needs to find her a husband before she turns him gray."

Just then, Westfield and his wife, Sophia, laughed in the adjacent room. Neither Celia nor the nursemaid seemed surprised by the sound. The door leading to the other room swung open, and Sophia stepped over the threshold. She was an attractive woman with dark hair and olive-colored skin. Her steps faltered upon seeing him. Then her wide mouth turned up.

"Simon," she said, her hands outstretched to him. "How are you?"

At one time, their relationship had been uneasy, but he liked the woman, and it appeared the feeling was now mutual. He pressed a kiss to her cheek. "Well, Sophia, and yourself?"

She opened her mouth to reply, but Westfield entered the room. "Simon, I'll not have you wooing my wife before my eyes, you old s—Oh, Celia, I didn't see you there."

Westfield walked over to the crib and set a hand on Celia's shoulder while he stared at his son.

"He's a fine boy, Westfield," Simon said.

Smiling, Westfield glanced at him.

"Papa, do you think Uncle Simon should ask for Cousin Victoria's hand so they can have a baby?"

Westfield's smile evaporated.

Simon raised his hands, palms out. "Your daughter's idea, not mine. Nineteen-year-old debutantes are the last thing I'm looking for."

Westfield leaned over the crib and pressed a kiss to Vincent's cheek, then took Celia's hand, and moved to the door. "Let it rest, Celia. Uncle Simon will find a wife in time."

Sophia slipped her arm through Simon's. "If you could see your face, Simon." She laughed. "Such a lovely shade of white."

As soon as Sophia finished her dessert, she rose from the dining table. "Please excuse Celia and me, gentlemen.

I have promised to read Celia a bedtime story. We will leave you to your port." She held out her hand for the child to grasp.

Standing, Westfield kissed his wife and daughter.

Simon stood. His friend was fortunate; his new wife not only loved him, but genuinely cared for her stepdaughter. Perhaps that explained Simon's fondness for the woman. Sophia was the antithesis of his mercenary stepmother. He believed even if Westfield were a pauper, Sophia would love the man, unlike so many of the women Simon met who seemed only interested in his wealth and title.

"Mama is going to read *Through the Looking Glass*." Celia slid off her chair.

"Ah, one of my favorites," Simon replied.

"Truly, Uncle Simon?" Celia's eyes widened.

"Of course, but I am not as fortunate as you, for I must read it to myself at night."

The child giggled.

"After reading to Celia, will you join us in the drawing room, Sophia?" Westfield asked.

Something passed between them, some unspoken words.

"No, if you don't mind, I shall bid you goodnight." She turned to Simon. "Forgive me, but I feel a headache coming on."

He'd never known Sophia to suffer with headaches. There appeared to be something afoot. Something Westfield wished to convey in private. "Of course, Sophia. I hope you are much improved by daybreak if not sooner."

Celia and Sophia left the room.

"Is there a problem with one of our business ventures?" Simon asked.

"No."

"Surely, whatever you wish to say is not so dire that Sophia feels the need to exclude herself from joining us?"

With a tilt of his chin, Westfield motioned to the door. "Let's go to my study."

It appeared dire indeed, Simon reflected as he stepped into the study to find the grate lit, a whisky decanter, and two glasses already set out between the fireside chairs.

Sitting, Simon forced a laugh and attempted to ignore the knot forming in his stomach. "Out with it, old chum, the suspense is killing me."

Westfield took a long draught of the liquor and lowered his glass. "Your stepmother is in Town."

Julia. The discomfort in Simon's stomach intensified. With feigned nonchalance, he brought his glass to his lips and took a slow drink. He concentrated on the taste that filled his mouth before it slipped down his throat to warm his chilled body.

His longtime friend lifted the decanter.

Simon glanced at his glass. *Empty.* So much for portraying indifference—futile where his stepmother was concerned. "You saw her?"

"No, my sister did. On the Strand this afternoon. Julia mentioned she'd just arrived and is staying at the Langham Hotel." Westfield refilled both of their glasses.

The exemplary meal Westfield's French chef had prepared churned in Simon's stomach as memories of Julia flooded his mind. When he was sixteen, his stepmother had acted inappropriately toward him. Ha! *Inappropriate* was a kind word—she'd touched him and attempted to seduce him. And when he'd not complied, the witch had told his father he'd groped her and tried to force himself on her. Simon had contradicted Julia's story with the truth, but for naught. Father, so in love, had not believed him.

How kind he'd thought Julia when his father had returned from London with his young bride. At twelve, Simon had longed for a mother. Someone to fill the void his own mum's death had left. And at first he'd thought

Julia, though only nineteen, would fill that cavernous hole in his heart. She'd acted kindly toward him. Even championed him when his father scolded him.

In retrospect, he realized how Julia's motherly attention had made it even harder for his father to believe the woman a serpent in disguise. But Simon understood her now. Acting the devoted stepmother during those years had made it near impossible for his father to believe Simon's accusations. In truth, he doubted Julia ever really cared for his father. She'd all but admitted it, calling his sire pot-bellied, wrinkled, and old.

His father had tossed Simon out—paid for his schooling, but not welcomed him home again. His friends Huntington, Westfield, and Caruthers had opened their family homes to him. But as much as they'd welcomed him, he'd felt out of place, like the poor relation. So, he'd acted out at school, created trouble, hoping to be expelled and sent home. But his father's fat purse had always soothed the headmaster. It was a testament to the disdain his pious father felt toward him.

Simon turned the glass in his hand. The prisms from the cut crystal reflected the red embers glowing in the grate. "This is from the distillery you, Huntington, and I intend to purchase, isn't it?"

"It is."

"It's bloody awful."

"Yes, but potent."

Not potent enough. Simon took a deep breath, tried to release the pressure building up in him. He downed the remainder of his drink.

Westfield held up his own glass, seemed to study the color of the liquid within. "Do you control her purse strings?"

"A solicitor handles her finances. After our falling out, my father made sure I possessed little control where Julia was concerned. I had several barristers look over his will. The besotted fool must have known I would try to bring my wrath upon her; it's unbreakable."

Westfield nodded. "It's been seven years since your father passed. Why would she come to London now?"

Simon shook his head. Years ago, he'd given up trying to figure out Julia's twisted mind. "Most likely boredom."

"Will she call upon you?"

Simon stood and tried to tame the restlessness coursing within him. "I don't know. You saw her at my father's funeral. She put on a show. The bereaved widow who lamented her dead husband, all while acting the perfect stepmother." Simon remembered the nausea that had rolled in his stomach when Julia had touched his arm in that crowded room. He'd not even waited for all the guests to leave before ordering both her and her things brought posthaste to the dowager house. What a show she had put on, acting hurt for all to see. His father's old cronies and Julia's friends had thought him a cruel, heartless bastard.

Westfield's voice drew him from his thoughts. "Simon, don't do anything foolish."

Foolish? In truth, he'd thought about wrapping his fingers about Julia's neck more than once. He touched the scar on his face. His father and he hadn't spoken a single word to each other after Julia poisoned the man's mind against him. How terrible to be so in love with a woman that you believe everything she says—allow her to manipulate you. He would never put himself in such a position.

"I'm angry, Westfield, not mad. And as they say, time heals all." With a bitter laugh, he set his glass down. "Did you tell Sophia about Julia?"

Westfield shook his head and clamped a hand on Simon's shoulder. "I love Sophia. I have shared everything from my past with her. But this secret is not mine to share. You told me about your stepmother in confidence. I wouldn't break your trust, Simon. I only asked that Sophia give us some time alone to discuss something in private. Nothing more."

Sometimes Simon regretted telling both Westfield and Huntington, his closest school chums, what his stepmother had done. But after his father had all but cast him aside, their friendship had brought him through the darkest time in his life. "Thank you."

Westfield nodded. "Did you read the newest loan contracts Ned Baring sent over yesterday?"

"Yes, but I want to go over them one final time before signing them. I should head home and do that now." At the door, he glanced over his shoulder at Westfield, who was putting the stopper back on the decanter. "I forgot to tell you, I'll be staying at my Bloomsbury residence for a few days."

Westfield's brows drew together. "Why?"

"I wish to find that woman."

Westfield shook his head. "Why don't you let the police look into it?"

"Because I intend to handle this in my own way."

"Sounds like you're looking for trouble."

Simon jerked the door open. "No, trouble found me . . . I'm just going to return the favor."

Pain seared Simon's cheek as he stumbled backward from the blow to his face. Warm blood trickled down his skin. He bit back the pain and stared into his father's angry eyes. The man's fist remained clenched, as if he wished to strike him again.

Simon's gaze shifted to Julia standing in the corner of the drawing room. His stepmother's eyes shone with triumph.

With an explosive breath, Simon bolted upright in bed.

He set a hand to his cheek, expecting to touch blood from the impact of the signet ring tearing open his face.

His fingers slid across the healed, raised scar as he glanced around the dim room. He wasn't sixteen years old, nor was he at Adler Hall in Hampshire. He skimmed his damp palms over the silk sheets. He was in Bloomsbury—the residence he'd purchased for Vivian.

A nightmare, then.

He settled against the pillows. Sleep wouldn't come quick; it rarely did after that particular dream, yet it had been seven years since he'd had it. Not since his father's funeral. The last time he'd seen Julia. He reached for his signet ring.

Gone.

He should be glad, considering the scar on his cheek. For the hundredth time, he questioned why he'd not ducked or blocked his father's punch. He could have. Perhaps he'd felt it his due for trusting Julia so completely, for not realizing that a pretty face could mask an evil soul. The ring reminded him to be careful whom he trusted—that giving a woman your heart, as his father had, wasn't wise.

The small brass clock on the mantel chimed five times. With quick movements, he shoved the bedding off his naked body, allowing the chilled night air to bathe his overheated skin. He walked to the window. Great James Street remained quiet. He'd intended to come here in the morning. However, restless at his normal haunts, he'd found himself instructing his coachman to convey him to Bloomsbury near midnight.

Why? Had he hoped his little intruder would return tonight? That he would catch her?

Kneading the muscles in his neck, he moved back to the bed. Even in the subdued light, the red drops of claret Vivian had spilled on the bedcover stood out. He tugged the thick counterpane to the foot of the mattress and lay faceup on the sheets. He stared at the night's shadows dancing across the white ceiling while he took several slow breaths.

Baines and Harris, along with the cook and maid, were to arrive early today. He closed his eyes, hoping he might fall back asleep before the two manservants showed up and started another inquisition.

It seemed only minutes later when an annoying voice filtered through Simon's foggy head.

"You'll catch a cold sleeping like that."

Simon opened his eyes. Morning light bathed the room.

Baines stood at the foot of the bed staring at him. "Gave the new maid a fright, you did. Came in this morning to fill the grate and returned below stairs babbling like a fool."

Simon followed his valet's gaze. *Damnation, not a stitch of clothes on and his cock piss-proud to boot.* "Shocked her, did I? Have Harris offer her a year's wages, then send her on her way."

"Already done. Did you have trouble sleeping?"

Simon covered his eyes with his forearm and grunted his response. "What bloody time is it?"

"Ten." Baines rolled the cart with Simon's breakfast tray and freshly pressed copies of the daily papers closer to the side of the bed. "The arrival of your trunks and the staff early this morning has drawn quite a bit of attention by two old biddies who have repeatedly walked by your residence."

"I should stand at the window. Do you think my nudity would scare them away, Baines?"

"Might. Then again, might draw a crowd—or a constable."

Despite his weariness, Simon laughed. "I knew there was a reason I kept you around, you old curmudgeon. Must be your dry wit."

"My lord, might I ask if the woman who resides here is to return, or have you cast her aside?"

Baines acted as if he uttered the word *mistress* aloud, he'd combust. "Why?"

"The décor, sir, is beyond hideous. I've never seen so much pink, purple, and magenta, along with a green which looks like something one purged after a night of debauchery. The only room that is not godawful is this one."

The valet was right. Vivian's taste was abysmal. When he'd insisted no pink or gewgaws in the master bedchamber, she'd pouted. Sadly, he'd given her carte blanche in all the other rooms. A mistake of grand proportions.

When she returned he needed to cast Vivian off, but the thought of her theatrical reaction caused his head to throb. Simon swung his legs over the side of the bed. "Leave it be. Hopefully, we will not be here too long."

The man stared at him for several heartbeats, as if waiting for an explanation as to why they were here at all. He wouldn't give one, or perhaps he actually *couldn't* give one. This was a foolish venture, like looking for a needle in a haystack, yet his thief's sultry voice whispering the word *repentance* had once again replayed in his mind as he'd fallen asleep.

Baines continued to stare at him.

"What is it?"

"Your signet ring, my lord. I hesitate to ask what has become of it. Please tell me it wasn't lost at some gaming hell."

Simon touched the bump on the back of his head. He should be offended by the valet's question. He was a damn good card player. A sharper, many would say, who never bid more than he had at the ready.

After his father had all but disowned him, he'd used his skill at the tables to relieve those wealthier than he of their heavy purses. He'd invested those winnings wisely—

amassed a fortune greater than any his father had ever possessed.

"You know I'm skilled at the tables, and I wouldn't gamble the ring away. Now if you don't mind, I'd like to eat without further interrogation."

"Very well, my lord." At the door, Baines pivoted back. "Your name is mentioned in the *Globe*."

Simon reached for the paper and scanned the front page. Last week, he'd given a rousing speech in the House of Lords in favor of prison reform. He scanned the front page.

"The scandal page, my lord," Baines said.

Gritting his teeth, Simon flipped the pages.

> *It appears Lord A must have some Siberian blood. It's rumored the Scandalous Viscount was spotted rowing down the Thames wearing little more than a smile.*

What cock and bull. He'd gone rowing in Putney with three other members from his rowing club, but not nearly naked. Too bloody cold. One would freeze their bollocks off in this April chill. He sighed. The news that his father had all but cut him off, along with his own antics, had made him notable—the newspapers had made him notorious. And when there was nothing noteworthy to print, they published Banbury tales, titillating stories about the infamous Lord A, in an attempt to attract readers.

Most of the time, at least as of late, except for his string of mistresses, he was a rational man. When younger, he'd suffered some youthful indiscretions—acted the scamp. He'd drunk a bit too much in an attempt to anger his staid father, a man so in love he'd been blind to all that transpired right under his nose. But the man was dead and the memories . . . well, they were just that, memories. And like the sky, they appeared clearer on some days than others.

What was more damaging than the on-dits in the newspapers were the lies whispered about him throughout the ton. The word *deviant* had been mentioned more than once. He presumed Julia spread that malicious lie to discredit him, so if he ever told the truth about what caused his fallout with his father, the ton wouldn't believe him.

Mothers who truly cared about their daughters steered them away from him, leaving only those interested in his title and wealth. Simon blew out a breath in frustration. What did he care? He didn't wish to marry.

"I should have your tailor make you some long woolen drawers," Baines said, drawing Simon from his thoughts. An expression of reproof was plastered on the manservant's face.

"I don't need them. It's untrue."

"Of course, my lord." Clear doubt dripped from his valet's voice.

He narrowed his eyes at the man and pointed at the door. "Out!"

Two hours later, Simon exited his Bloomsbury residence. His feet had just touched the pavement when the door of the town house next to his flew open. Two rotund, gray-haired women, both dressed in dark lavender, rushed forward, their heels clicking a quick staccato.

"Halloo," the first matron called, waving a white handkerchief enthusiastically in the air.

Hell and fire. He could spot a gossipmonger a mile away, especially when they moved in pairs. There'd be no avoiding them.

"I am Mrs. Jenkins." She pointed a plump finger at the town house they'd sallied from. "We are neighbors." She imparted this information as though it were akin to a blood relation. "And this is Mrs. Vale." Mrs. Jenkins pointed at the residence next to her own. "She is your neighbor as well."

Simon forced a smile. "If I had known the beauty one could find in Bloomsbury, I would have taken residence sooner."

Both women tittered, and Mrs. Jenkins smacked him playfully on the arm with a force that would have knocked a less hearty man to his knees.

"I fear you are a flatterer, Mr. . . . ?"

"Radcliffe."

"Radcliffe." Mrs. Jenkins repeated his name as if he'd fed her a tasty morsel. "Will we have the pleasure of meeting Mrs. Radcliffe soon?"

"No, madam, I am not married." Obviously, they both retired early, if his late-night visits to Vivian had gone undetected.

"Was the woman who lived here a relation to you? We have not seen her in a couple of days."

"An acquaintance of mine, but she has gone on holiday, and I have taken over the residence." He took out his watch and flicked it open. His good friend Margaret, the widow Lady Griffin, having heard of Vivian's holiday, had invited him to call on her today for luncheon and lawn tennis, and a bit of recreation.

Smiling, both women nodded.

"It was a pleasure, ladies, but if you will excuse me, I am in need of my afternoon . . . constitutional."

"Oh, yes, of course," Mrs. Jenkins replied. She batted her lashes at him. "It has served you well."

"You are gracious, madam." He tipped his hat. "I bid you good day."

He thought himself free of their claws when Mrs. Vale

said in a small voice, "Mr. Radcliffe, I-I wish to invite you to a small gathering I'm having tonight."

Not bloody likely. "No, I'm—"

"Nothing too grand," Mrs. Jenkins added. "Just a few neighbors."

"I'm sorry, but I must decline your kind invitation." He tipped his hat again, took two steps, and stopped. These two tabbies probably had their fingers on the pulse, if not the jugular, of every resident on the street, probably all of Bloomsbury.

He turned back to them. They were both staring at him with crestfallen expressions. "Perhaps you lovely ladies could help me."

Their countenances brightened.

"I wish to purchase some artwork for my new residence. Do either of you know of any local painters that do landscapes?"

"There is Mr. Dubois," Mrs. Vale replied.

Mrs. Jenkins scrunched up her nose. "But he is French, and you know how temperamental the French are, especially artists. My niece does some lovely watercolors."

"I'm more interested in oils."

"There is Miss Madeline Smyth," Mrs. Vale said. "She does landscapes. Mostly of the English countryside."

Mrs. Jenkins scowled at Mrs. Vale. "But my niece's watercolors are more refined."

He turned his brightest smile on Mrs. Vale. "Miss Smyth? Does she reside on the street?"

"Indeed, she resides with her father at number three."

The door of the residence across the street opened and the child he'd met yesterday, Miss Trafford's younger sister, came out of the house with a trundling hoop. She stared at him for a long moment before she rolled the toy up the pavement.

Mrs. Jenkins narrowed her eyes at the girl. "Do guard your shins, Mr. Radcliffe. Those hoops are vile toys that the authorities should ban. Only last week, I heard one nearly maimed a horse. Why Miss Trafford allows her sister to engage in such an activity is beyond me."

Simon had never owned a hoop. His father, like Mrs. Jenkins, had thought them frivolous. "I shall, Mrs. Jenkins. You said her sister allows . . . am I to assume they are orphaned?"

"Yes, their mother died quite some time ago, and their father three years past. Miss Trafford does do her best to contain the child, but Lily's a bit of a hoyden."

He glanced at the girl. She was staring at him again. What an odd child. He looked back at Mrs. Vale. "Will Miss Smyth be in attendance tonight?"

"Yes," Mrs. Jenkins exclaimed.

"I might be able to alter my plans and attend."

Mrs. Vale's round face glowed. "Oh, how splendid!"

Mrs. Jenkins's hand settled over her rather ample bosom as she turned to Mrs. Vale. "Nine o'clock, right, Bea?"

Mrs. Vale nodded enthusiastically, sending a gray ringlet tumbling from her coiffure. "Yes, nine o'clock."

"I look forward to tonight, ladies," Simon replied, more than anxious to meet Miss Smyth.

Chapter Six

Bloody hell, I've been ambushed! Simon stifled a curse as he stepped into Mrs. Vale's drawing room. There wasn't another male in sight, and all eyes were on him. He felt like a mouse being dangled before a throng of felines.

Apparently, the scar on his face didn't evoke the same violent reaction from the matchmaking mamas of Bloomsbury as it had from Emma Trafford. Or, more likely, his fine equipage and the possibility he was a man of means overrode the deterrents of those more squeamish.

Mrs. Vale cut a path through the crush. The rose scent of her perfume added to the air already thick with every floral essence known to mankind. "Mr. Radcliffe, I'm so pleased you could make it to my little gathering."

Little gathering? They were elbow to elbow. It looked like every biddy, mother, and eligible chit from here to Sussex was crammed into the small room.

"Everyone is most anxious to make your acquaintance. Isn't that marvelous?" The corners of her lips turned upward, lifting her papery skin.

He forced a smile, wondering where Miss Madeline Smyth was, and how long it would take him to get an introduction to the painter.

"May I get you a cup of tea, Mr. Radcliffe, or a glass of lemonade?" Mrs. Vale asked.

Tea? Lemonade? Clearly, God wished to punish him for numerous misdeeds. "Neither, madam, though they both sound . . . refreshing."

"Mr. Radcliffe!" Mrs. Jenkins waved her handkerchief in the air as she fluttered toward him. "There is someone I wish to introduce you to." The woman grabbed his elbow and dragged him across the crowded room like he was a recalcitrant child. She stopped in front of a short little chit dressed in pink. "Prudence, may I introduce Mr. Radcliffe? Mr. Radcliffe, my niece Miss Prudence Langley."

The young woman giggled and shyly peered at him through lashes that were so fair they were nearly invisible. "Pleased to make your acquaintance, Mr. Radcliffe."

"Miss Langley." He inclined his head.

Red-faced, the girl twisted her fingers in her gown.

A movement caught Simon's attention. A young woman with loose brown hair rushed toward them like an Amazon, pushing the others aside as she approached. She ruthlessly bumped Prudence out of her way.

Caught off balance, the shy woman stumbled backward.

Mrs. Jenkins gasped, but quickly smiled as though nothing were amiss. "Mr. Radcliffe, this is my other niece, Miss Chastity Langley. Chastity is the one I spoke of . . . the one who paints watercolors."

Chastity was the opposite of her sister—darker in coloring, bold, and voluptuous. And the way she eyed him, it was clear her parents had not aptly named her.

"Charmed," she purred, thrusting out her bosom as she ran her tongue over her full lower lip.

Careful, old boy. Don't encourage this one. He kept his expression bland. "Miss Langley." He peered beyond her and inwardly groaned. Chastity Langley was the least of his troubles. A swarm of eager mamas and their daughters were forming a line to greet him.

An hour later, he'd met nearly every woman in the room. But not the one he'd come for. He turned to Mrs. Vale. "Is the painter Miss Smyth here?"

"Yes, I saw her earlier." Mrs. Vale stood on her tiptoes and glanced around the room. "There she is." The elderly woman lifted a plump finger and pointed to a slender woman who was a good three inches shorter than *his* thief.

Damnation. Clearly not the woman he sought.

"I shall introduce you, sir."

Simon inwardly sighed. It appeared he'd have to purchase a painting or at least pretend to be interested in the woman's art.

"Miss Smyth," Mrs. Vale said. "Allow me to introduce you to Mr. Radcliffe, our new neighbor."

The woman possessed a heart-shaped face, brown hair, and crystal-clear blue eyes. She offered a tentative smile and outstretched her hand for him to shake. "A pleasure to make your acquaintance, Mr. Radcliffe."

"Likewise, Miss Smyth." Simon shook her gloved fingers.

"Mr. Radcliffe is interested in purchasing some landscapes," Mrs. Vale explained. "Sir, did I mention that Miss Smyth's paintings are as lovely as any displayed at the Royal Academy of Arts?"

Miss Smyth's smile broadened. "You are too kind, Mrs. Vale. If you wish to see some of my work, you are more than welcome to call on my father and myself at number three. Just up the street."

Simon liked the artist. She wasn't flighty or pushy or, apparently, in want of a husband. "Thank you, Miss Smyth."

He glanced about the room, hoping to see a woman as tall as his thief. Several were of similar height. Perhaps if he heard their voices.

"If you'll excuse me, ladies. I think I see someone I know." A lie, but a plausible one.

Simon edged around the room, listening to the conversations. He stopped near a tall young woman who listened as a matron chatted about a vicious goose that chased her for a quarter mile while she was visiting her brother in Kent last month.

"I shall never return," the older woman exclaimed in a high-pitched tone that sounded like the screech of an injured bird.

Simon cringed. With a grating voice like that, most likely the woman's brother had trained the fowl, hoping for such an outcome.

"Geese are such vile creatures," the taller woman replied in a thick Scottish accent. Definitely not the she-devil he sought. He continued walking, stopping a couple yards shy of where Mrs. Jenkins stood. The older woman whispered something to the two matrons she conversed with.

All three women tittered like schoolgirls.

"Viscount Adler? Do tell, what wickedness did his lordship engage in now?" one of the women asked, fanning herself in an excitable manner.

Simon's ears perked up.

"Yes, do," the third woman said, her eyes wide.

Mrs. Jenkins paused as if wishing to heighten anticipation. Then, as though imparting a national secret, she glanced around the room.

Simon cocked his head closer.

"Did you read the on-dit in the newspaper about Lord A rowing on the Thames with barely a stitch of clothing on?"

Both women nodded.

"I saw the rascal. It *was* Lord Adler," Mrs. Jenkins said.

The lying old crow!

One of the women gasped. "You did?"

Mrs. Jenkins bobbed her head. "Indeed. The newspaper omitted some of the details."

"Yes?" the two biddies prompted in unison.

Mrs. Jenkins smiled like a cat with a wren in its belly. "He wore only a top hat and his trousers while waving the Union Jack at those on the banks."

What rubbish!

"How shocking," the third woman said. She didn't sound shocked at all; in fact, she sounded enthralled. "Where?" She wet her lips. "Do you think he will do it again?"

Her companions' gazes swung to her.

She flushed. "Well, I've never seen the man, and I've heard he is in possession of a fine physique. Though, they say his face is scarred. Were you close enough to see it, Mrs. Jenkins?"

"I was. It runs from his forehead all the way to his chin."

Another lie. Simon rolled his eyes.

"Did you notice our new neighbor's scar?" the second woman asked, obviously not realizing his proximity to her. "He looks rather piratical. All Mr. Radcliffe needs is a patch over his eye and a sword."

Mrs. Jenkins spotted him and rammed her elbow into the woman's ribs.

"Ouch! Goodness, Mrs. Jenkins. What are you about? I shall be bruised."

The gossip tipped her head in Simon's direction and arched a gray brow.

The woman turned around. The color in her cheeks dissolved.

"Madam," he said.

"M-Mr. Radcliffe, I-I hope you are enjoying yourself?" Her voice quivered.

"I am," he lied. God, was there anything worse than gossiping biddies? Yes. Mrs. Naples and her colicky dog were heading toward him. He looked for an escape. A green velvet curtain hung at a doorway not far from where he stood. On the other side, if fortuitous, would be a means to leave this tedious affair, if only for a brief respite.

Simon inclined his head. "If you'll excuse me, ladies." Mrs. Jenkins opened her mouth, but he turned away before she could forestall him.

As he moved toward the curtain, he noticed the gazes that followed him, both blatant and covert. He had nearly reached the curtain when the cacophony of voices grew. He peered over his shoulder to see a young man step into the room from the entry hall.

Fans fluttered and whispers grew as the women noticed the newcomer. Like vultures, several swooped closer, as if spotting a carcass. On careful examination, he realized the poor fellow looked no more than twenty-one. A veritable babe in the clutches of these predators. Poor unsuspecting sod.

Simon took the opportunity afforded him to slip behind the curtain. There was a narrow corridor and at the end of it a door. Salvation—if it led outside where he could enjoy a cigarette.

He made his way down the passage and stepped outside onto a back terrace. Most of the flagstones lining the ground were cracked and uneven with moss curling over them, making them treacherous to navigate. If the garden had ever been lush, those days were long past. It seemed doubtful any of the ladies would venture out here. He sucked in a deep breath of cool air, redolent with the earthy scents of spring.

The terrace was dark except for the light streaming from the set of French doors in the back of the drawing room. One of them swung open, and Chastity stuck her head out. He stepped back into the shadows between an outcropping of two chimneys.

"Mr. Radcliffe, are you out here?" the young woman

whispered. "Mr. Radcliffe?" She waited. When she didn't receive a reply, she uttered a blasphemy and stepped back inside.

He leaned against the building, reached into his inside breast pocket, and withdrew his cigarette case. He should return to Mayfair tomorrow. This was ridiculous. He didn't even know what his thief looked like.

The doors opened again, and two slender women moved carefully across the uneven stones, their heads bent close as they conversed.

Bugger it! He slipped his case back into his pocket and crossed his arms over his chest.

The shorter of the two women turned to her companion. The light from the French doors illuminated Miss Madeline Smyth's face. "I wondered if you had changed your mind about attending. I know you don't enjoy either Mrs. Vale's or Mrs. Jenkins's little neighborhood gatherings."

Clearly, the taller woman possessed a sensible mind.

"Maddie, you know I wouldn't attend at all if not for the fact I am looking for new clients."

"Mrs. Naples has been singing your praises. She is quite pleased with your work and has told everyone."

Simon nearly laughed aloud. Mrs. Naples believed her dog to be her dead husband. Not the soundest endorser, unless the woman was a psychic.

"I think it's your finest work," Miss Smyth said. "When others see the portrait, I do not doubt you shall have more clients than you could wish for."

Simon straightened. Portrait? The woman painted? Her height matched his intruder's. He narrowed his eyes and tried to see her face.

"I pray you are right, Maddie."

Miss Smyth shifted, allowing the interior light shining through the doors to illuminate the other woman's face. Good God, it was Miss Trafford. But he had already dismissed her as a possibility. The weak-minded woman couldn't be the she-cat he sought.

"Emma," Miss Smyth said, "perhaps our new, very virile neighbor would like to have his portrait painted."

Even from a distance, he noticed Miss Trafford stiffen. "Mr. Radcliffe? I hope not."

"Yes, he does exude a dangerous air. I'm not sure how Mrs. Vale persuaded him to attend, but it is a coup."

"Attend? He is here?" Miss Trafford's voice suddenly sounded like the high-pitched squeak he recalled.

"Yes, didn't you see him when you arrived?"

"No."

"But you have met him?"

Miss Trafford pressed her fingers to her temples. "Yes, and I made a complete cake of myself."

Simon nodded in agreement.

Miss Smyth moved to the French doors and peered inside. "I don't see him. He might have already left." She turned back toward her companion. "Do tell about your inauspicious meeting."

"Too dreadful to repeat."

"Really?"

"If only you knew," Miss Trafford replied.

Laughing, Miss Smyth pulled her shawl tighter about her shoulders. "Shall we return? It's too cold for me out here."

Miss Trafford shook her head. "You go ahead. I shall join you in a bit."

"Don't dawdle, Emma. Not if you wish to garner more business."

Miss Smyth opened the door. The cacophony from the room briefly seeped out onto the terrace before the door closed, muffling the sound.

As soon as Miss Smyth left, Miss Trafford paced the uneven surface. In the dark, her abrupt movements looked familiar—quite similar to his thief's. He shook his head. Impossible that such a timid mouse could be whom he sought.

She reached into her pocket, extracted a tin, and placed something in her mouth. Was she an opium eater? It would explain a great deal. She pivoted and started walking toward him. He pressed his back more firmly against the wall. Several feet from him, the woman's foot snagged on a lifted flagstone and she stumbled forward.

Damnation. He stepped out from the shadows to catch her.

Chapter Seven

If Mr. Radcliffe is here, I shall not return to the drawing room—was Emma's last thought before the toe of her left shoe slammed against a lifted flagstone.

She stumbled forward and collided with a hard chest. Strong hands grasped her waist, steadying her. Curling her fingers around the man's lapels, she glanced up into dark eyes.

"Miss Trafford," a smooth and masculine voice said.

A shiver raced down her spine. Even if the man hadn't spoken, Emma would have recognized Simon Radcliffe's spicy scent and impressive physique, along with the flash of his perfect white teeth.

"Mr. Radcliffe," she whispered, finding it difficult to speak with her blood pounding a steady rhythm in her ears.

The smile on his face faltered, and his eyes narrowed as though attaining some forgotten memory. His hold around her waist tightened. Painfully so.

Did he now recognize her as the intruder? The already rapid beat of her heart escalated. She swallowed the mint drop dissolving in her mouth. It slid down her throat like a lead weight. "Sir?"

"Yes." His low voice held a sharp edge.

"You're holding me too tight."

"Am I? Forgive me." His grip eased, but his warm hands remained on her waist. Unblinking eyes locked on hers, then slowly dipped to her mouth.

Unwanted heat flooded her body, and the air between them thickened, making it difficult for Emma to breathe.

The French doors leading from the drawing room to the terrace swung open. Mr. Radcliffe stepped back, setting Emma firmly on her feet.

Chastity Langley stood at the threshold. If Emma thought Mr. Radcliffe's gaze foreboding, Chastity's was ferocious. Possessive. She strode toward them, eyes narrowed on Emma.

"Mr. Radcliffe, I've been looking for you," Chastity said and slipped her arm through the crook of his.

Emma's years of painting faces had taught her to notice genuine expressions of pleasure. The smile he offered the other woman lacked sincerity. He looked like a feral animal thwarted in his hunt. A frightening thought, since Emma feared she might be his prey.

"Aren't you coming back to the drawing room, sir?" Chastity fluttered her lashes.

"Yes." He turned to Emma. "Miss Trafford, you are a portraitist?"

She couldn't lie, not with the other woman staring at her. "I am."

"Might I call on you to discuss a commission?"

The knot in her stomach twisted tighter. She wanted to say no, but what excuse could she offer? "Of course, sir."

"Then, I'll see you tomorrow. Is three o'clock agreeable?" The tone of his voice remained even, yet a warning seemed disguised in its civility.

"Yes," Emma said, trying to sound calm. She walked toward the French doors, forcing herself to move at an even pace, and not dart away like a scared child.

Inside, she searched for Mrs. Vale and Maddie. She wanted to say goodbye and run home as fast as her legs could move. She spotted both women talking with Mrs. Naples. Maddie was wrinkling her nose at Mrs. Naples's dog. The disgusted expression on her friend's face would have been comical, if Emma could dredge up a laugh, or even a smile. But she couldn't dislodge the fear clawing at her chest that Mr. Radcliffe had somehow recognized her as his intruder—the woman who'd kissed him in that dark bedroom. She glanced over her shoulder.

Mr. Radcliffe and Chastity stood next to the French doors. The man's gaze followed Emma like a fox closing in on a rabbit. Her pulse throbbed at her temples.

He knows. Nothing else could explain the intensity in his eyes or how firmly he'd held her waist. So tight, she'd thought his massive hands itched to snap her in two. She stepped next to Maddie and forced a smile at the evening's host. "Thank you, Mrs. Vale, for such a lovely gathering."

Mrs. Vale blinked. "You're leaving already? You just arrived."

"I'm not feeling well." Emma touched her temple, then her stomach, which still clenched with fear.

Maddie's expression turned concerned. "Oh dear. I hope you are not catching the collywobbles. Papa has been sick for days with it."

"No, just a megrim. I'm sure it will pass shortly." Only to return tomorrow when Mr. Radcliffe called. Maybe she could tell him she had contracted some hideous disease. But then she'd not be able to take on any new clients with him living across the street, watching. No, there could be no avoiding painting him if he wished it.

"I'll walk you to the door." Maddie slipped her arm through the crook of Emma's. "Not that I'm pleased you are unwell, but you have saved me. I was dying there. The smell. I'm not sure what Mrs. Naples feeds her dog, but it should be outlawed. Tell me, how on earth were you able to paint Alfred?"

"I held my breath a lot."

Maddie chuckled. "You poor soul. You deserved twice your commission, for that alone."

They stopped and Maddie hugged her. "Do feel better."

"I will." She just needed to be away from here. Away from Mr. Radcliffe's perceptive gaze. Oh, why had Lily taken his ring?

The hairs on the back of Simon's neck stood on end. The moment Emma Trafford had spoken in the dark, while her hands clasped his lapels, he'd experienced a feeling of déjà vu. And the scent of her minty breath only heightened the sensation. Was she his femme fatale? And if so, who was the man who'd hit him over the head?

Chastity's fingers skimmed up his arm, pulling him away from his thoughts. "Are you sure you wouldn't care for a glass of lemonade, Mr. Radcliffe?"

"I'm afraid I must take my leave, Miss Langley."

"Must you really?" Chastity's lips formed a pout.

"Yes."

"Before you leave, would you care to accompany me to my aunt's residence next door? I could show you my watercolors."

The clingy woman was on the hunt for a well-to-do husband. He didn't doubt that if he accompanied her, she'd lead him into a private bedchamber, and her aunt would walk in on them and insist he do the *honorable thing*.

"Thank you, but I really must be leaving."

Her lower lip protruded, and he thought she might stomp her foot. "Well, I do hope you might call on my aunt the next time I visit with her in London."

He nodded, keeping his gaze on Emma Trafford, who

was engaged in conversation with Miss Smyth. She stood near a wall sconce that highlighted her blond hair styled in a prim chignon. How innocent she looked in her high-buttoned dress of navy wool with its simple lace collar, adorned with only an ivory cameo.

As if she sensed his regard, she glanced at him, but quickly averted her gaze.

It didn't seem possible that this timid creature might be the vixen who'd kissed him with such abandon. She was either a consummate actress or she danced to the tune of an overbearing man, a scoundrel capable of leading her into thievery and violence. He would find out the truth, and if it was the latter he'd extract his retribution on the man, but if the former, Emma Trafford would pay for her misdeeds, especially if he didn't recover his ring.

Mrs. Jenkins rushed to his side. The twinkle in the elder woman's eyes reflected her pleasure at seeing her niece standing beside him.

"I must be going, Mrs. Jenkins. Where is our hostess?" Simon asked.

The elder woman's jovial expression faded. "You are leaving, sir?"

"Yes, I bid you a most pleasant night, Mrs. Jenkins, Miss Langley." He spotted Mrs. Vale across the room and strode to her. "Madam, you didn't mention that Miss Trafford is an artist, as well as Miss Smyth."

The woman tipped her head to the side. "But you said you wished for a landscape artist. Miss Trafford does portraits."

"Indeed, I did. I wish to thank you for inviting me. It's been a most entertaining evening."

"Mrs. Jenkins will host our next gathering in two weeks. You must attend."

He'd rather be thrown from a horse and trampled. He

lifted Mrs. Vale's hand and brushed his lips against her gloved fingers. "I shall try."

She blushed and tapped him on the arm with her fan. "Mrs. Jenkins is correct; you are a scoundrel, sir."

If she only knew.

He moved to the entry hall and passed Miss Trafford still conversing with Miss Smyth. He stepped behind her. "Until tomorrow, Miss Trafford," he whispered, allowing his warm breath to fan against her nape.

She turned to face him. Her blue eyes were large. Her cheeks flushed.

His gut tightened. She really was a remarkably beautiful woman.

"Y-yes, see you then, sir."

He nodded and made his way to the door, where a plump little maid handed him his overcoat. He stepped out of Mrs. Vale's house and walked the short distance to his residence. Both Harris and Baines were peering out a front window. They smiled and waved at him.

He didn't feel like suffering through another inquisition. He turned around and headed toward Theobald's Road.

His front door flew open. The two manservants rushed after him. "Where are you going, my lord?" Harris asked.

"To my club. I might get exceedingly drunk."

Baines tsked. "Have a care, sir. I've read liquor is a detriment to a man's health."

"Well," Simon said, continuing to walk as the two men followed him like two goslings trailing their mother, "then I might seek the company of a woman and convince her to do wicked things with me."

Both men gasped.

"I do hope you're not going to visit a house of ill-repute," Baines said, uttering the last word in a hushed tone. "You might catch a disease."

Simon stopped and peered at the two men. "If you continue to follow me, I'm going to insist you both accompany me. I'll get you each a young, frisky woman, perhaps two."

Both men pivoted, and as fast as their old legs could travel, scurried back into his house. The door closed with a heavy *thud*. Simon continued up Great James Street to Theobald's Road, intent on finding a hackney to take him to Mayfair.

Twenty minutes later, Simon sank into one of the two leather chairs set before a warm grate inside Hayden Westfield's library.

His oldest chum, standing next to a sideboard, motioned to a decanter. "Whisky?"

"No, I'm fine. Sorry to call you away from Sophia at this late hour."

"My wife is with our son. Rocking him. I was doing nothing more than watching them from the doorway."

"How is my godchild today?"

"Thirsty." Westfield grinned and sat in the adjacent chair. "You look in a fine mood. What brings you here? I thought you'd be at the club or at some card table."

"I think I might have found her."

"By *her*, am I to presume you refer to the woman who broke into your Bloomsbury residence?"

"Yes."

Westfield leaned back in his chair. "You sly devil. How?"

Simon waved his hand in the air. He didn't feel like explaining it all. "She is different than I expected."

Westfield laughed. "Foolish to stick your tongue in a woman's mouth in the dark. Did the light of day reveal a toothless hag?"

He envisioned Emma Trafford's lovely face—her bow-shaped lips, pink cheeks, and blue eyes with their long lashes. No, far from it. She looked innocent and sweet and unsoiled by life's darker twists of fate. Yet, he'd learned long ago, beauty could mask many sins. He remembered the first time he'd met his stepmother. How Julia had smiled and clasped his hands before hugging him and calling him *son*.

"Miss Trafford is quite attractive. She's a portraitist."

"A portraitist and a thief. What an interesting combination."

"I'm going to commission her to paint me."

A furrow formed between Westfield's eyebrows. "Are you mad? If this *is* the woman who robbed you, have you forgotten her accomplice tried to crack open your skull? Why don't you just go to some East End lodging house and flash a few banknotes about? I'm sure some guttersnipe will slit your throat if you're looking for trouble."

"I don't have a death wish."

"Wouldn't know it by the way you're acting. Dr. Trimble should have been summoned to attend to you. Obviously you're suffering some trauma from that blow to your head."

"I want my ring returned."

"Then have a couple of constables cart her down to the police station and question her."

"And my proof? What should I say? That I recognize the touch of her hands? The scent of her minty breath? It sounds dashed foolish even to my own ears."

Westfield leaned forward in his chair and laughed. "That's your evidence?"

Simon folded his arms over his chest. "Laugh all you want, you bloody sod, but I'm almost sure I have the right woman."

"I see there will be no dissuading you. Be careful."

Simon smirked.

"What do you find so humorous?" Westfield asked.

"You. At one time, you threw caution to the wind like a cat with nine lives. But now, you are truly a mother hen. You're as bad as my two manservants."

"What rubbish. No one can be as bad as Harris and Baines."

Simon stretched out his legs, clasped his hands behind his head, and studied his friend. The man had changed so much over the last year. He smiled more, and there was a look of contentment in his eyes. What would it be like to cherish someone as dearly as Westfield did his wife? To capture a woman's sincerest regard? Not because he purchased her whatever she wished for, but because of a strong affection. Because of love. Simon realized he was touching the scar on his face. He slowly returned his hands to the armrests.

"Simon—"

"I must be shoving off." He stood. God knew what type of comment his friend would make.

"Wait," Westfield said. "Did you read over the loan agreement from Baring Brothers again?"

"Yes. If you haven't signed the documents, go ahead. The financial terms are precisely what we want. We need to act fast. Get Huntington to read over the papers. Otherwise all of Finch's holdings will become the property of that bloodsucker he borrowed money from."

Westfield rubbed the back of his neck. "Finch's great-great-grandfather started that distillery. The old man must be turning over in his grave. I don't understand how Finch allowed himself to fall into the clutches of an East End moneylender such as Mr. Wolf. The man is ruthless and dangerous. He deserves his moniker, the Devil of Danbury Street."

Simon knew what it was like to lose nearly everything. "Should we lease the business back to Finch?"

"You know he'll only strip it raw of all the machinery

and start gambling again," Westfield said. "We didn't force the young buck into the gambling hells. In truth, we are saving him. After we buy his company, he'll have enough funds to pay off his debts and keep his town house. That moneylender would have left him with little more than a pot to piss in. He should never have borrowed from such a scoundrel."

"Yes, you're right. No, it's better this way," Simon said.

"The solicitor is sending me the final documents on the purchase tomorrow. I'll bring them over for you to sign right after. Then Huntington needs to approve them. Where will you be?"

"Bloomsbury. I've an appointment with my little painter."

Westfield shook his head. "Don't turn your back on the woman."

Chapter Eight

Leaning idly against the window frame, Simon stared out the mullioned glass of his bedchamber window in Bloomsbury. The afternoon sun, which had finally broken free of the clouds, shone bright on the row of narrow town houses that lined Great James Street. A short, plump woman with gray hair, wearing a white bibbed apron, fastidiously swept the steps of the Trafford residence.

"You wished to see me, sir?" Harris asked.

He glanced over his shoulder at his butler. "Yes. Our excursion to Bloomsbury might take a bit longer than I anticipated."

"Longer, my lord?"

Simon scrubbed a hand over his freshly shaven chin. "Yes. I want the morning room that overlooks the rear garden converted to my office. A desk will be delivered this afternoon."

Conveying his disappointment, Baines's sniffling floated out of the dressing room. He'd tasked his valet with packing the remainder of Vivian's clothing and retrieving more of Simon's garments from his Curzon Street residence.

"I have an appointment with one of our Bloomsbury

neighbors this afternoon. I might commission the woman to paint my portrait."

"A woman painter?" Harris echoed as though Simon had said *a gargoyle*. "Why? George Clayton is the premiere portraitist for members of the nobility."

Ignoring the man's question, Simon continued, "Lord Westfield will be calling here later with some documents for me to sign. If I'm not here, ask him to wait in the drawing room."

"Really, my lord, in *that* drawing room?" Harris said, as if putting Westfield in a place with purple-flocked wallpaper and pink pillows was tantamount to Simon's social ruination. "It's rather . . . garish." The butler's already razor-straight back stiffened. "My lord, if I might be so impertinent, I think it high time you settled down and found a woman of quality. I doubt you shall find her here or on the stage."

Baines poked his head out of the dressing room. "He's right, my lord, you should find yourself a suitable wife. Harris and I will not always be around to take care of you."

"I'm quite capable of taking care of myself, you old curmudgeons."

The clock on the mantel chimed. Three o'clock. Simon pushed away from the window. Time to visit Emma Trafford. Time to find out if he had the right woman, and if so, play with his prey a bit—set his claw on the mouse's tail before consuming it.

As Simon crossed the street, he noticed Miss Trafford's sister staring at him from a third-floor window. Hard to see, but he would have sworn she held a wooden stake as if he were a vampire. The girl was obviously twelve hot cross buns short of a baker's dozen.

He lifted the knocker and banged it against the door.

The plump older woman he'd spied earlier answered.

He handed her one of the calling cards he'd had printed this morning bearing the name Simon Radcliffe. "I've come to see Miss Trafford with regard to a portrait."

"Come on in, sir. She's expecting you." The woman gave him a jovial smile, turned the card over in her hand, and glanced back at him. "Simon Radcliffe," she read, her voice nearly inaudible. "I must say, you look familiar. Though I can't quite put my finger on where I've seen your face."

Simon held his breath. He'd had the illustrious privilege of having his caricature plastered in the newspapers for both political and social reasons more than once. Thank goodness, his features were usually exaggerated in the drawings, making it hard to recognize him from them.

"I'm sure we've not met." He averted his face and tugged off his gloves.

"No. Don't believe so, yet . . ." She tipped her head as if trying to recall where she'd seen him.

"Lovely weather, isn't it, madam?" Thankfully, her regard shifted from him to the transom above the door.

"Yes, finally feels like spring." She took his top hat and gloves, set them on the marble-topped table, and motioned to a sunny room to the right of the entry hall. "Please have a seat, I'll go tell Miss Trafford you're here."

Simon glanced around. The pillows and cushions on the yellow sofa and chairs sported faded coverings. A blue threadbare carpet covered the floors. Hard times had befallen the family. This would explain Emma Trafford's need for money. There were few opportunities for women in her tier of society—strictures dictated acceptable employment, but thievery wasn't one of them.

Emma Trafford entered the room, her hands clasped demurely at her waist. She wore a simple purple dress with a lace collar and a row of pearl buttons down the bodice.

Her blond hair was styled into a loose chignon and several tendrils fell about her face. As she stepped farther into the room, the sun streaming through the windows caught her eyes, making the blue color more intense. She looked like innocence personified, no more threatening than a playful kitten.

"Mr. Radcliffe," she said in a soft voice.

"Miss Trafford." He kept his tone even, camouflaging the anger he held toward her.

Her gaze, which seemed focused on the buttons of his waistcoat, lifted to his face. Her cheeks flushed. She was indeed worthy of the stage, acting the innocent. He would take pleasure playing cat and mouse with her. He motioned to the portrait of an older gentleman with gray eyes, which hung above the mantel. "Did you do this?"

She glanced at the painting. "Yes."

His knowledge of artwork was limited, but he could discern commendable pieces, and this portrait fell soundly into that category. Miss Trafford's face conveyed sadness as she stared at it. This was not the man he sought. This man was dead. "Your father?"

Distractedly she fiddled with the edge of her sleeve. "It is."

Something in her expression, the melancholy it revealed, tugged at him. He touched the lump on his head. No, he would not feel pity for her, no matter what predicament her father's passing had heaved upon her.

"He died three years past." She pinched her soft lips together, drawing his gaze to her plump lower lip.

"My condolences." He regarded the painting again. "You are gifted." A movement caught his attention. Lily peered around the edge of the doorframe.

"Good afternoon, Lily." He forced a smile.

The girl narrowed her eyes at him and ducked behind the wall.

"I appear to be a curiosity to your sister."

"I do apologize. Lily has an active imagination—along with an overabundance of inquisitiveness."

At least she'd put aside her stake, but he recalled how the imp had mouthed the words *the murderer* the first time he'd met the child. What was it about him? Simon lifted his hand, then realizing he was about to touch his scar, lowered it. "Just you and your sister reside here?"

"I have a brother who is attending school in Berkshire. But he hasn't been home since Easter."

Did she tell the truth? Odd that he believed her, but he did. Perhaps she had a lover and that was who had hit him. If so, surely she'd have painted or sketched the man. "Do you have a studio where I might examine your work?"

Miss Trafford nervously twisted a button on her bodice. "Yes, it's upstairs."

He motioned to the doorway. "Then, please, lead the way."

The sound of Lily's shoes clicking against the floorboards resonated as the strange chit ran down the corridor, farther out of sight.

Gathering her skirts, Miss Trafford climbed the steps before him. The feminine sway of her hips drew his gaze.

On the third floor, they entered a dark room redolent with the scents of paint and turpentine. She drew the heavy curtains open on the two windows that overlooked the street. Sunlight streaked through the clean glass, exposing a French daybed with green bolsters, a walnut armoire, two upholstered chairs in faded brown velvet, and an oak stool. An easel with a canvas covered by a cloth faced one of the tall windows and beside it stood a large round table—its surface scarred with splatters of paint in varying shades.

Atop the table were jars, rags, pigments, and a wooden palette. There were also three smaller tables set around the room with gas lamps on them.

The walls were dotted with several portraits of her sister and a boy who resembled them. Her brother? She'd painted both children at various ages. In the most recent portrait, the boy looked to be about seventeen. He favored both Miss Trafford's and Lily's coloring—same fair skin and blond hair.

"My brother," she said, as if reading his thoughts.

"Yes, I see the resemblance." There were no portraits of any other men.

There were also a few landscapes. The landscapes were different from the portraits. The lines not as crisp. The effect of realism discarded for a more abstract feel, which captured the sunlight and reflected off the subjects on the canvases. Though brighter in color, they conveyed a serenc restfulness.

The one of a family in a park caught his attention. He stepped before it. A woman pushing a perambulator strolled with a man while a young girl walked beside them. A bright blue sky hung above, and the grass and leaves stood out in vibrant greens. It brought to mind Westfield and his family. The tranquility his friend had finally attained in his life.

He glanced over his shoulder. "Did you do this?"

"Yes. A few months ago."

He lifted his hand, felt the raised paint, thick on the canvas's surface. He could imagine Emma Trafford toiling with her brushes, applying the layers. "I'd like to purchase it."

She blinked. "What?"

"I said I'd like to purchase it," Simon repeated.

"If it is a landscape you wish to buy, might I suggest

Madeline Smyth. Her works favor the style of John Constable. She's quite talented."

"Miss Trafford, I offer to buy a painting and you try to dissuade me. Is it for sale or not?" Agitation laced his voice.

"It's just—"

"A simple yes or no will suffice."

"Yes."

"I will send my man over for it. Set your price before he comes."

"You are purchasing it price unknown?"

"You are an honest woman, are you not?"

The color drained from her face.

"You look a tad pale, Miss Trafford." With a sweep of his hand, he motioned to one of the upholstered chairs. "You should sit. If you don't mind, I will look around."

"Of course," she replied, remaining where she stood. He scanned the room. If she had a lover, she kept his portrait in a private room, perhaps her bedchamber. He walked over to the easel and lifted the corner of the cloth draped over the canvas. She opened her mouth as if to halt him, but said not a word.

Was this what he searched for? He folded the fabric up. A portrait of a woman with intense blue eyes and blond hair, styled in a soft chignon, stared back at him. A self-portrait? No, there were fine lines around the woman's eyes and the corners of her mouth. There was also a carefree air to her smile, a gaiety Miss Trafford presently didn't possess.

"My mother," she said. "When I'm not engaged with a commission, I work on it." She opened a small drawer on the table next to the easel and pulled out a daguerreotype of a woman who looked to be about thirty-five. "This is the only photograph I have of her. I think our hair was of a similar color, but in truth, I cannot recall the exact shade. Sad how sometimes our memories fail us, even with regard to those dearest to us."

He glanced at the photograph. The resemblance between mother and daughter was unmistakable, except Emma's face was fuller, softer, and her lips more sensuous. More startling was how the painting mirrored the photograph, except the painting came to life with vivid flesh tones. It appeared a work of undying love.

"Where did you study, Miss Trafford?"

"I have never had formal training."

"This painting only confirms my belief in your talents."

Damnation, what was he doing? He had come here to find out who had tried to fracture his head; instead he'd purchased one of her paintings and was flattering her, and not for the sole purpose of extracting information. He pivoted on his heel, stepping away from the scent of rose water drifting off her warm skin. He needed to settle his mind on the task at hand—confirming Emma Trafford was the woman he sought, and discovering the identity of her accomplice.

"May I see some sketches you have completed?"

Emma pressed her palms to her stomach, hoping to stop its fluttering. The thought of being confined in her studio with Mr. Radcliffe held little appeal. Or perhaps it held too much.

Already the large space had grown small, as if the walls were closing in. She glanced at the painting he wished to purchase. The money she would ask for it would help sustain them for the next couple of months until she could find a new client—one that didn't make her stomach tighten, or that Lily hadn't unjustly hurt, and surely not one capable of sending them to prison if he found his ring hidden in the jewelry box in her bedroom.

She needed a way to get it back to him. If she could sneak into his house, she could toss it under the bed in the room where he'd kissed her. The sudden memory of his warm mouth moving hungrily against hers caused her toes to curl.

"Miss Trafford?" he asked, drawing her away from her lurid thoughts. "Your sketches?"

"Yes, of course. I have several." She needed to dissuade Mr. Radcliffe from giving her the commission. She wished he hadn't noticed her father's portrait downstairs or lifted the cloth and looked at her mother's. Why had she so foolishly shown him Mama's photograph?

Could she get him to believe her skill inconsistent? What did she have to lose? She opened the armoire. Her leather portfolio with her recent work lay on the top shelf. Emma removed several loose sketches from the bottom of the cabinet. She'd done them when younger before perfecting a grasp on proportions. The work looked amateurish at best.

Emma turned around and gasped as she nearly bumped into Mr. Radcliffe's chest. When had he moved behind her? She stepped back, rattling the armoire's doors as she banged into them.

"Careful." He reached out. His long fingers closed around her upper arms, steadying her. A spark of energy mixed with heat traveled from his hands and into her skin as if she sat too close to a roaring fire. His dark gaze held hers.

For a long moment, she couldn't look away. Did he know how dangerous he was to her composure? More reason he should go.

He stepped back, breaking the spell.

"Here." She handed him the loose papers.

He angled the drawings toward the sunlight streaming through the windows. His eyes scanned the top sketch of a horse whose ears were disproportionate to the rest of his head. Mr. Radcliffe's brow furrowed. "Interesting," he mumbled.

"Some days I'm more skilled than others," she said, trying to look contrite.

The next one was of a baby, most likely Lily, considering the yellowing of the paper's edges. Her sister's head looked misshapen, elongated like an egg. Emma had forgotten how horrid these sketches were. She bit the inside of her mouth to halt a smile.

Mr. Radcliffe tipped his head to the side and cupped his jaw. "Very flattering."

What? Was the man blind?

The last one was her father sitting behind his desk. It showed every detail, even several strands of nasal hair. Yes, this one would do the trick. "As I mentioned, sir, I am not always consistent in my work."

"Impressive, Miss Trafford. Your sketches have cemented my belief you are the perfect artist to paint my portrait. The commission is yours."

Emma nearly swallowed her tongue. Those drawings were abominations.

"Nearly as good as the portrait of your father in the morning room." There was a twinkle in Mr. Radcliffe's eyes. "Or the ones displayed here."

Ah. Clearly he was on to her and there would be no dissuading the man. Her stomach fluttered.

"When do we begin?" he asked.

"Well, I—"

"Tomorrow?" He handed her the sketches.

"I'm not sure I can fit you in."

"I was given the impression you are seeking new clients. Is there a *reason* you don't wish to paint me?"

Yes. Too many. "No, of course not, sir. Tomorrow afternoon would be fine. Is two o'clock agreeable?"

"Quite."

She motioned to the landscape. "Would twenty-five pounds seem a reasonable amount?"

"Twenty-five pounds?" A thin line formed between his dark brows.

Did he think the amount too exorbitant? She set the sketches down on the table. "If that seems too dear—"

"No. Not at all. I'm looking forward to this venture, Miss Trafford. It shall be . . . interesting." He grinned, flashing his perfect white teeth.

A nervous spark exploded in her belly, sending a tingling sensation to her limbs. This wasn't about his portrait. This was like a fox after a rabbit. And she knew in most cases the animal usually cornered its prey.

Chapter Nine

As soon as Emma closed the front door behind Mr. Radcliffe, Lily darted into the entry hall. "I can't believe you are going to paint him. You instructed me to stay clear of him, yet—"

"I know. But what was I to do?"

"You could have told him no!"

"What excuse could I give him? The man is already suspicious of me, and we could use the funds." Or was there another reason she'd accepted the commission? Did fear tempered with excitement feed some baser desire? If so, what addled her brain?

Emma inched the door open and peeked out. Three burly men were unloading a large desk and leather chair from a dray, while two older gentlemen dressed in black stood on the pavement. The one wearing a cutaway coat directed the movers.

Mr. Radcliffe began to converse with them.

Lily scooted in front of Emma. "Do you think those two old gents belong to the same society of murderers?"

Emma massaged her temple. "No. The one in the cutaway coat looks to be a butler."

"A butler?" Lily shook her head. "No one on Great James Street has a butler. He looks more like an undertaker, with his gloomy, pinched face."

"What are you two looking at?" a voice boomed from behind them.

Emma spun around. Mrs. Flynn stared at them while wiping her hands on her white apron. The housekeeper moved to the door, peered over Lily's shoulder, and made a little noise. The type Mrs. Flynn made when savoring one of her own lemon tarts. "What a fine buck of a man."

Emma agreed. Just his proximity caused a low hum to vibrate through her body. And he smelled clean and spicy, almost edible. She mentally smacked her palm to her forehead. Maybe it wasn't Lily Mama had dropped on her head when an infant.

"What?" Lily gave the elder woman a severe scowl. "He looks like a villain!"

"With that lovely sweet face?" Mrs. Flynn patted her gray upswept hair.

One could call Mr. Radcliffe's face arresting, but surely not sweet. "Are you referring to Mr. Radcliffe?" Emma asked.

The housekeeper shook her head. "He's an attractive man, but a bit too severe for my taste and a mite too young." She pointed at the man not wearing the butler's uniform. "'Tis the other man I refer to. Now that's a fine fellow." She glanced over her shoulder at Emma. "So has Mr. Radcliffe commissioned you to paint him?"

"Yes, he'll return tomorrow for his first sitting." Emma closed the door.

Mrs. Flynn tapped her index finger against her pursed lips. "I've seen him before . . . can't remember where."

"They've probably got his picture hanging in the rogues'

gallery in Scotland Yard, with all the other criminals," Lily said.

The housekeeper frowned. "Seemed a polite enough chap to me. A Savile Row gent, if I ever seen one."

Yes, his clothing spoke of wealth. Today he wore a navy frock coat, a silver waistcoat, and dark tailored pinstriped trousers. His clothes amplified the breadth of his shoulders, the length of his legs, and his lean build. Mrs. Flynn was right, he looked every bit the gentleman. Perhaps a successful merchant.

Someone struck the knocker.

Emma's body tensed.

Mrs. Flynn answered the door, and making an uncharacteristic cooing sound, tugged off her dirty apron and shoved it into the umbrella stand. Emma peered around the woman. The man they'd seen talking with Mr. Radcliffe—the one Mrs. Flynn fancied—stood on the top step. He appeared to be well into his sixties with a round, pleasant face and thinning gray hair.

The man nodded a stiff, formal greeting to Mrs. Flynn. "Madam, is Miss Trafford available?"

"Yes, do come in!" The housekeeper turned to Emma, her cheeks glowing with heightened color.

Emma stepped forward. "I'm Miss Trafford."

He gave a small half-bow. "Miss, I am um . . . Mr. Radcliffe's manservant, Mr. Baines. I'm here to collect a painting and render payment."

"I do apologize, Mr. Baines. I didn't expect you so soon." Emma motioned to the morning room. "Would you please have a seat while I wrap it?" She turned to the housekeeper, who practically drooled on the man. "Mrs. Flynn, will you bring Mr. Baines some refreshments?"

"That is quite unnecessary," the man said stiffly.

"But I baked a batch of lemon tarts this morning," Mrs. Flynn said, leading the man into the adjacent room.

Lily giggled. "I've never seen Mrs. Flynn make cow eyes before."

Emma smiled. Neither had she. Lifting her skirts, she dashed up the stairs. As she entered her studio, she noted how the light streaming from the window caught the painting Mr. Radcliffe was purchasing. It depicted a family taking a pleasant stroll through a garden with their children. Perhaps it did have some merit, though its simple oak frame did nothing much for it. She lifted the painting off the wall. Would it hang in a place of prominence in Mr. Radcliffe's house?

Did it really matter? The sale would put food on the table, coal in the vault, and help with Michael's tuition.

After wrapping the painting up in an old scrap of blanket, she tied it with string, and returned to the morning room. Mr. Baines sat on the sofa, while Mrs. Flynn stood staring anxiously at the man as he plopped the last bite of a lemon tart into his mouth. He rolled his eyes heavenward as though the mini-pastry was a decadent treat he wished to savor. A bit of lemon filling remained on his fingers and he licked it off and sighed.

"Ah, Mrs. Flynn." He stared at the housekeeper as if she possessed the power to pluck the stars from the sky. "I am all but speechless. Just the right combination of both tart and sweet, and the consistency of the lemon filling is like silk."

The housekeeper beamed; her cheeks grew pink. She pushed the tray of tarts, set on the needlepoint-covered ottoman, closer to him. "Mr. Baines, do have another."

Wiggling his fingers, he inched them toward the pastries. "Perhaps one more." He plucked a tart off the tray, took a large bite, and ate it hastily when he noticed Emma standing at the doorway. He stood and quickly moved to take the painting from her.

Emma glanced beyond his shoulder to Mrs. Flynn,

who looked crestfallen. "Do finish your tea, Mr. Baines," Emma said.

"No, really I must be going." With the painting tucked under his arm, he turned back to the housekeeper. "Thank you, Mrs. Flynn. Would you be kind enough to share the recipe?"

"Yes—"

"No," Emma interjected. "I'm sorry, but it is an old family recipe, and Mrs. Flynn has been sworn to secrecy. I'm sure if you would like, on another day she could make a batch for you to enjoy, along with her special tea."

The manservant moistened his lips. "No, I couldn't impose on your household, Miss Trafford."

"No imposition, sir." Emma smiled at the man.

"Only if you allow me to bring the ingredients," he said.

Mrs. Flynn's eyes sparkled. "Yes, that would be perfect. We need flour, sugar, butter, and a half dozen lemons. The other ingredients are the secret I can't divulge."

"Very well." Mr. Baines moved toward the door. He suddenly stopped, reached into the breast pocket of his coat, and extracted an envelope. "Lor—um, Mr. Radcliffe's payment."

Emma nodded and took it.

"Good day, Miss Trafford," he said as he left.

She closed the door and opened the thick envelope. The bills inside clearly exceeded twenty-five pounds. With a gasp, she braced a hand on the newel post.

"Did he cheat you, lovey? I don't care how handsome his manservant is. I'll set him straight, I will." Mrs. Flynn rolled up her sleeves, exposing her thick forearms, and stormed toward the door.

"No! It is not what you think. The amount within is too dear. I fear there has been some mistake." Emma slipped the envelope into her skirt pocket, grabbed her blue wool shawl from the wall hook, and stepped outside. A cool April breeze whipped across her face. She pulled the shawl tighter. As she crossed the street, the dray that had delivered the desk pulled away from the front of Mr. Radcliffe's residence. Behind it was a shiny black carriage. Did Mr. Radcliffe have company? She hesitated, but continued to his door, lifted the plain brass knocker and struck it twice.

The other man she'd seen earlier, the one dressed like a butler, opened the door. He appeared to be of a similar age to Mr. Baines, yet his face was thinner, more wrinkled, with wiry eyebrows that matched his gray hair.

"May I help you?" he intoned in a deep baritone.

"Yes, I'm Miss Trafford. Is Mr. Radcliffe at home?"

He held a silver tray out to her.

"I'm sorry, I don't have a calling card on me."

The butler's nose inched disdainfully in the air. The sound of a door closing echoed behind the haughty servant.

"Miss Trafford." Mr. Radcliffe stepped next to the man. "Thank you, Harris. That will be all."

The tall butler stepped back, inclined his head, and stiffly retreated down the corridor.

Mr. Radcliffe arched a dark brow. "Is there something we need to discuss?"

"Might I have a minute of your time?" Emma tried not to fidget.

"Yes, come in."

The entry hall was nearly identical in size to her own, though freshly painted in an ugly shade of green, with nary a crack in the plaster. She took the envelope of banknotes from her pocket. "Sir, I believe there's been a grievous mistake."

His eyebrow notched higher. "Really?"

She wished Mr. Baines had answered the door. "Ah, well . . . the amount in the envelope is far greater than twenty-five pounds."

As if she were a complex puzzle in want of solving, Mr. Radcliffe stared at her for a long moment, his dark eyes unblinking. "Miss Tra—"

A heavy bang from the adjacent room halted his voice. The walls rattled. The floor shook. He glanced toward the closed double doors. "My cat appears to have knocked something over."

Whatever had fallen sounded as heavy as a bag of mortar. "I do hope nothing of great value."

"Doubtful. There is *little* of value in that room." He sighed. "Miss Trafford, I have an appointment I need to get ready for."

"Forgive me." She held the envelope out to him. "As I said, there is more than twenty-five pounds in here."

"I believe the value of art rests upon whatever a buyer is willing to pay for it. Is that not true?"

"Yes, but—" Her words seized in her throat as he placed his warm ungloved hand to the small of her back and propelled her toward the door.

"Accept the payment. I wouldn't have given it if I didn't feel the painting worthy of such an amount. I will call on you tomorrow."

She glanced up at his hard, chiseled face.

Their eyes locked, and he inched a bit closer. His warm breath fanned against her cheek.

Her heart skipped a beat.

With a little cough, he straightened. "See you tomorrow."

"Yes, tomorrow, Mr. Radcliffe."

Simon closed the front door and flung open the double ones to his drawing room.

Westfield stood at the window peering out. "That lovely creature walking across the street is the she-devil who tried to relocate your bollocks? Surely, you jest."

Simon scowled. "You, of all people, should know an angelic face can mask a soul as dark as pitch. Have you forgotten about Adele Fontaine?"

"No. I will never forget what that madwoman did to my family, but for a thief Miss Trafford seems a bit too honest."

True, most thieves didn't try to return money.

Simon scratched his jaw. "I'm not sure what the deuce she's up to. She may be a better actress than Vivian."

Westfield laughed. "Not a hard feat. Though clearly your mistress's acting skills are not what enamored you to her. Nor her taste in décor." Westfield touched the back of a gaudy chair upholstered in purple-and-gold striped velvet with small pink flamingos stitched into the fabric.

Simon glanced about the room. He should never have given Vivian carte blanche. The purple walls and garish furnishings were enough to give one dyspepsia. And the baubles that filled nearly every inch, made it nigh impossible for a man to move about. The only tasteful piece was the blue china vase he'd given Vivian, but she'd seen fit to fill it with fuchsia-colored feathers.

He suddenly noticed the large bust of Shakespeare was absent one ear. "What the deuce happened to the Bard?"

Westfield grimaced. "Sorry, old chap. I bumped right into poor William. It's a bit tight in here. Do all these trinkets belong to Vivian?"

"Do you believe I'd have this much clutter by choice?"

"No, it's a bit nauseating." Westfield turned back to the window. "Are you quite sure Miss Trafford is the woman you seek? Perhaps you are mistaken."

Two days ago, Simon had not even considered Emma Trafford. Too timid a creature. But on the terrace at Mrs. Vale's, with dim light surrounding them, he would have sworn she was his femme fatale. The scent of her breath.

The feel of her in his arms. His own body's damnable, traitorous reaction to her.

"Not so sure?" Westfield asked.

"I have my doubts, but I'll find out. I might even attempt to seduce her to uncover the truth."

"Does retribution mean that much to you?"

"My signet ring was stolen."

His friend's gaze shifted to Simon's hand. "Why you wear the damn thing, I'll never understand."

"Because it is part of who I am."

"It doesn't matter that it is the reason you are scarred?"

"No. Julia manipulated my father so he'd not leave me anything besides what was entailed. That greedy witch *couldn't* take my title, my ancestral home, and she bloody well couldn't take my signet ring."

Westfield picked up the broken piece of the Bard's ear from the floor and set it next to the sculpture on its ornate Grecian-style podium.

"Might you have misplaced your impartiality because Miss Trafford's hair is close in color to Julia's? I know you have never been fond of women with blond hair." Westfield's lips pinched into a tight line.

"It has nothing to do with that." If his anger stemmed from anything it was most likely that he'd played the fool, allowing a woman to distract him with a searing kiss. He should have known better, yet he'd lowered his guard and once again been the recipient of a woman's treachery.

"If you seduce her and find out she is not your femme fatale, but an innocent, you might find your neck firmly ensnarled in the parson's noose. Tread carefully, my friend."

Yes, he'd be careful. Finding out the truth was of paramount importance, but marriage was the last thing he wanted.

Chapter Ten

"He's on his way, Em," Lily exclaimed the following day. For the last hour, the child had stood by the window, awaiting Mr. Radcliffe's arrival.

Attempting to ignore the rapid beating of her heart, Emma removed her mother's portrait from the wooden easel and set a newly stretched canvas on it. She wiped her sweaty palms over the skirt of her simple green day dress and straightened the sharpened pencils lined up neatly on the table by the easel.

"Lily, this would be a good time for you to read your book of sonnets before you practice the piano."

"As if forcing me to play the piano isn't cruel enough, now you wish me to read drivel. Even if disposed to such tedium, I wouldn't leave you alone with Mr. Radcliffe. I shall remain here and keep a keen eye upon the scoundrel."

Emma set her hands on her hips. "You will greet the gentleman with due respect. Your manners reflect us, and so far you have been most discourteous." She leaned closer to her sister and whispered, "Not to mention criminal."

Footsteps moved up the treads, along with Mrs. Flynn's cheerful chatter. Little currents of nervous energy exploded within Emma. With her hands pressed to her abdomen, she closed her eyes and took several deep breaths. When she opened them, Mrs. Flynn and Mr. Radcliffe were stepping into the room.

As usual, his charcoal-gray coat and cuffed trousers in a slightly darker shade, amplified his impressive physique. Today, he wore a grayish-blue waistcoat, a crisp white shirt, and a gray silk neckcloth tied in a four-in-hand knot.

Mrs. Flynn, whose nephew worked for Nick Minister and Sons, had mentioned this morning that Mr. Radcliffe's garments might be from that very tailor. Emma glanced down at her simple dress. She looked the pauper's daughter next to him, but he had dressed to have his portrait painted, whereas she had dressed to do the sketching.

"Mr. Radcliffe is here." The housekeeper beamed gaily at the man as he stepped past her and into the room. Emma remembered how he'd left Mrs. Vale's guests swooning in his wake. It appeared he'd tried some of his mesmerizing charm on the housekeeper today. Had none of them noticed that the man's easy smile rarely touched his eyes? He'd watched them like a constable seeking out his culprit. Or was it her guilt that made her feel this way?

"Mr. Radcliffe, how are you?" she said, attempting to keep the tone of her voice steady.

His intense gaze locked on hers.

A shiver trailed down her spine.

"Well, madam, and yourself?"

"Fine." If she didn't count the fluttering in her stomach, her sweaty palms, or the thundering in her chest.

"Miss," the housekeeper said, her cheeks a rosy pink. "Mr. Baines told Mr. Radcliffe he has never had such delicious lemon tarts in his whole life. Is that not true, sir?"

"Yes. In fact, he said one would be hard-pressed to find any comparable in all of Great Britain."

Mrs. Flynn pressed her hand to her large bosom. "Bless

his heart. Perhaps, miss, you and Mr. Radcliffe will wish to partake of some lemon tarts with your afternoon tea?"

Mr. Radcliffe's gaze, the scent of his skin, along with his very presence, unsettled Emma's composure. How could she bear to sit and eat pastries and drink tea with him? She forced a smile. "Yes, Mrs. Flynn. Thank you."

The man's attention shifted to Lily, and he smiled. "Hello, Lily."

Her sister folded her arms and narrowed her eyes.

Emma shot the child a warning look.

Lily sighed, and then swept into a deep curtsy befitting the Queen. "Mr. Radcliffe, I hope the day finds you well. I want to observe Em sketching you, but I must read a book of sonnets instead." She offered him a tight-lipped smile before asking, "Do you like sonnets, sir?"

The corners of his lips twitched. "Ah, I fear I have no great affection for them. Will you forgive my shortcomings?"

The pinched expression on Lily's face vanished, and she nodded. Whether Lily thought him a murderer or not, Mr. Radcliffe's *dislike* of fourteen-line poems written in iambic pentameter caused him to grow a bit higher in her esteem.

Lily spun toward the door, stopped at the threshold, and pivoted back. "If you need me, Em, just *scream* and I shall come running with Mrs. Flynn's rolling pin in hand."

Mrs. Flynn made a scoffing noise. "Come running? Rolling pin? What silly nattering, child. Can you not see Mr. Radcliffe is quality?" The housekeeper pinched Lily's ear between her pudgy fingers and tugged the child from the room.

"Ouch! Mrs. Flynn, you're hurting me!" Lily complained while the beefy-fingered woman dragged her down the stairs.

The smile on Mr. Radcliffe's lips disappeared as his gaze returned to Emma. Then, as if forcing himself to be congenial, mayhap even flirtatious, it quickly reappeared. "So, we are to be left alone?"

There was something dark and foreboding in his tone. A slight chill moved through her body.

"Yes." It would be for the best. She couldn't have Lily chatting about murder and mayhem. She pointed to a chair she'd set before one of the windows. "I thought we could do a portrait of you sitting, unless you desire a different pose."

"No, that's fine."

"If you will be seated, we will begin."

His fingers were long, and she immediately noticed the band of lighter skin on his right pinkie.

As if noticing the direction of her gaze, he said, "I normally wear a ring. Sadly, it was recently stolen."

The steady pattern of her heart skipped a beat. "How terrible."

"Yes, for those who took it. I intend to find out their identity and make them pay."

The way he peered at her reinforced her belief he suspected her. How? Her stomach lurched, but she forced a carefree smile. "I wish you well in your hunt, sir." She hoped her lie sounded authentic. "If it is of importance, and you recover it, I can add it into the portrait at a later date."

"Mark my words, Miss Trafford. I shall find those responsible. Do everything in my power to do so. When I was a lad, something of great value was taken from me. And I swore after that I would never allow anyone to take anything from me again without retribution. When I find the thieves, they will regret ever crossing my path."

The threat in his voice was as clear as a cloudless sky. She needed to find a way to get the ring back to him—make him believe he'd actually misplaced it. Trying to swallow the fear working its way up her throat, she motioned to the chair. "Please be seated."

As he sat, the material on Mr. Radcliffe's trousers tightened over his thighs. The memory of him sitting on her, those muscular limbs imprisoning her, caused the anxiousness already filtering through her body to be on high alert. She swallowed, picked up a pencil, and motioned to the canvas. "Today I'm going to be sketching your likeness. Please lift your chin, just slightly? Yes, yes, that's fine."

As she drew him, his dark eyes studied her every move. Her palms grew moist again, and the pencil slipped in her hand. Had anyone ever stared so intently at her? No. Not even Charles when he had asked for her hand and professed his love for her. Not even when he'd taken her innocence.

"Mr. Radcliffe, see that painting on the wall?" She pointed at a landscape of the Thames she'd painted from the Chelsea Embankment. "Try to keep your gaze directed on the painting."

"I'd much rather look at you, Miss Trafford. Really quite fascinating the way your blue eyes move as you study me and sketch. Such intensity . . . I feel quite exposed, as though even my soul is disclosed."

That made two of them. "I assure you, sir, I am only studying the angles of your face. You shall be relieved to know your soul remains quite obscured from my view."

A slow grin turned up one side of his mouth. "Would it be wicked of me to admit that fact relieves me?"

She didn't doubt that. She had a feeling, though a gentleman, Mr. Radcliffe was no saint. Especially since she'd learned he wasn't married. The redheaded woman who'd disappeared wasn't his wife. Wicked man. What would the two old biddies who resided next to him think if they knew the truth? If she told Mrs. Jenkins and Mrs. Vale, would they shun him? Would shame force him to leave Bloomsbury? No, she doubted that. He was on a mission to find his ring and have the thieves arrested, and she feared he cared little what others thought. Goose pimples prickled her skin.

As she sketched him, she marveled at his chiseled features—a strong jaw, dark, perceptive chocolate-colored eyes, topped by trim brows. Everything about him, including his wide, sensual mouth, which at times looked almost cynical when he smiled, was masculine.

The sound of feet trudging up the stairs broke into Emma's concentration. She finished sketching the hard, masculine angles of Mr. Radcliffe's jaw and looked up. Mrs. Flynn stood in the open doorway holding a freshly polished silver tray instead of the painted tin tray they normally used. The woman must have hidden it from Emma when she'd brought nearly everything of value to a pawnbroker.

"I brought the tea and lemon tarts, miss." The housekeeper turned her smiling brown eyes on Mr. Radcliffe.

"Thank you, Mrs. Flynn. I'm sure Mr. Radcliffe welcomes the opportunity to stand and stretch his legs." Emma had noticed his restlessness—the movement of his fingers, the rolling of his broad shoulders, along with the shifting of his feet. Such movements were not unusual in those required to sit for extended periods. But Mr. Radcliffe's restlessness reminded her of a large cat who sat for brief moments before the need to prowl—or worse, pounce—took hold.

Emma set her pencil down, and the housekeeper placed the tray on the table between the two brown upholstered chairs.

Mr. Radcliffe stood and rubbed the muscles in the back of his neck. "I must say, Mrs. Flynn, the scent alone is enough to make a man's mouth water."

The woman beamed at him as she exited the room.

Emma had to give the man credit, he excelled at flattery and sending a rosy hue to women's cheeks.

He moved to stand by one of the chairs and waited for Emma to be seated.

She willed her hands not to shake as she sat and poured the tea. "Milk or sugar?"

"Neither." He took the cup and saucer from her. His warm fingers brushed against her cold ones. "My goodness, Miss Trafford, your fingers are like ice." He set his tea down and reached across the table. The heat from his hands engulfed hers while his thumb swayed slowly back and forth over the nerve-filled skin of her wrist.

Her breath caught in her lungs. This was improper, yet if he didn't watch her so fiercely, she would have closed her eyes and savored the feel of his caress. *What a silly thought.* She pulled her hands out of his grasp.

"The tea will help." She took a slow breath and set a dessert dish with a tart before him.

Humor sparkled in his dark eyes. He knew he unsettled her. What type of game did he play? Did he think he could bring her to a place of complacency, and then get her to admit all? Surely, he thought her more intelligent than that. She filled her cup and added milk.

Taking a sip of the hot beverage, she peered at him over the edge of her cup. He lifted a lemon tart off the plate and took a bite. She couldn't tear her gaze away from his lips. He'd kissed her with that mouth in a way she'd not known—with his tongue. If he kissed her now would he taste like lemon custard? Distracted by her wayward thoughts, she took a sizable gulp of tea. Scorching liquid scalded her throat. A cough racked her body.

"Careful, love. It's hot."

Love? Her stomach fluttered. She squelched the sensation. Most likely, he called the serving girls in pubs by such an endearment. It meant nothing to a wicked man like him who appeared to be free with his affections. For a brief moment, she thought of Charles before shoving his image from her mind's eye.

"Baines is right, these are tasty. You're not going to have one?" He placed the remaining piece of tart in his mouth, motioning to the plate laden with a half dozen more pastries.

The thought of eating the sticky filling in front of him amplified the butterflies already fluttering in her stomach, and she doubted her singed palate would be able to discern the flavor. "No, I already had one earlier today."

Casually leaning back in his chair, he pinned her with his dark eyes. "So, Miss Trafford, how long does this process take, from sketching to the last stroke of your brush?"

"If you're diligent with your sittings—a few weeks. And I'm sure you'll be relieved to know, you won't be required to sit for me as the portrait nears completion. Have you ever sat for a painting before?"

"Once, when I was quite young. It was a long, drawn-out affair."

"Perhaps it only felt that way. I've painted my siblings, and anything exceeding five minutes seems a trial for them."

"You're probably right."

She stood, and he followed suit. "If you don't mind, I'll return the tray to the kitchen. You are most welcome to walk about the studio and stretch your legs."

"I am indebted for such leniency."

She grinned. "You make me sound like some cruel gaoler."

"Cruel?" he echoed. "No, a woman with such an angelic face cannot be anything but compassionate." The corners of his mouth turned up into a wry expression.

Warmth heated her cheeks. "I shall be back shortly."

* * *

As soon as Emma Trafford stepped from the studio, Simon moved to the large armoire. He'd seen a leather artist folio inside the cabinet yesterday, yet she'd chosen to show him old works that were far less refined than the paintings hanging on the walls.

What are you hiding, Emma? Might there be a drawing of the man who'd conked him over the head?

He glanced over his shoulder, and then opened the wooden doors. The shelves held glass jars of pigment, art supplies, and several paint-spattered cloths folded neatly. On the bottom shelf lay the older sketches and on the top shelf the leather folio. He lifted it down and opened it.

The drawings were mostly of children. He stopped at one, a sketch of three girls laughing as they circled ribbons around a Maypole. The children's faces conveyed exuberance—a sense of contentment and gaiety. The sketch was intricately detailed; he could all but hear their laughing voices and the song they sang as they danced about.

He flipped through the remaining sketches. The last one caught his eye. A woman, round with child, sat on a wooden bench. She held a parasol in one hand, while her other hand rested on the swell of her abdomen. He shook off the odd feelings the drawing evoked, snapped the binder closed, and quickly set it back on the shelf. The only men he'd seen in the sketches were Miss Trafford's father and brother.

Restless, he stepped into the corridor. Someone a couple of floors below pounded on a piano. The instrument sounded out of tune, and the pianist played with as much finesse as a drunk using his toes. He took the stairs to the first floor and moved toward the racket.

Miss Trafford's sister sat at a piano in the drawing room.

The child lifted and lowered her hands onto the keys with great force.

"What are you playing?" he asked, raising his voice above the clamor.

With a gasp, Lily peered wide-eyed at him. Thankfully, her fingers froze in midair, relieving the imminent possibility of ear bleeding.

"Bach," she replied.

Good God, the composer must be rolling in his grave.

She narrowed her eyes. "You shouldn't sneak up on someone. It is most disconcerting."

"You shouldn't play the piano like that, it's even more disconcerting," he replied.

The briefest of smiles touched her lips before disappearing. She tipped her chin in the air. "I don't wish to play, but Em insists I practice for an hour every day."

"And you play like that to dissuade her?"

The corners of her lips twitched again, confirming his suspicions.

"Apparently your sister is either tone deaf or has a firm constitution."

The child exhaled a heavy breath. "Indeed, I've been playing like this for what feels like forever, and Emma still insists I continue. Do you play?"

How long had it been since he'd played? Not since a gathering at Caruthers's country house several months ago. He'd regaled the mostly drunken crowd with broadside ballads and ditties about sailors bedding lasses with ample bosoms. "A bit."

"Then play something." Her tone implied disbelief.

"Another time, poppet. Your sister is most likely wondering where I've wandered off to. I need to return to her studio."

Lily's hand slid to something lying under the skirt of her dress.

Probably a rolling pin. God, the girl was a character. Shaking his head, Simon stepped out of the room, then pivoted back. "Your brother hasn't visited lately from school?"

"Not since Easter. But he might return home any day. And he is muscled and strong. Nearly as broad as you. No, he is larger." The child bit her lower lip. "One should be very frightened of him because he looks like that painting of Zeus. Not the one with that naked woman next to him, but the one where he is holding a scepter."

Simon tried not to laugh. In her odd way, Lily was as entertaining as a farce at the Vaudeville Theatre. "He sounds quite terrifying. I'm most interested in meeting him. I shall let you get back to your . . . playing."

He climbed the steps and had reached the studio's doorway when Emma darted out of the room and barreled straight into him.

Chapter Eleven

As Emma collided with Simon, he clasped her waist to steady her.

She glanced up, a panicked expression on her face.

"Looking for me?" he asked, his voice pitched low.

"Um, yes. When I returned and found you gone . . ."

Did she think he'd left the studio to search for his ring? The idea had crossed his mind.

Her delicate hands lifted to his chest as if to push him back, yet as their eyes locked, she froze.

Once again, holding her seemed familiar. Too familiar. Like a dream that replays in one's mind over and over. Though, unlike a dream, the scent of roses filled his nose, while the skin underneath his clothing grew warm where her palms touched him. His gaze shifted from her lovely blue eyes to her mouth. If he kissed her, would it confirm a memory, perhaps more tantalizing than reality? As if pulled by gravity, he leaned forward.

Her eyes grew wide. A small lump moved in her throat. Her tongue darted out to moisten her lips.

His damnable body reacted. Bloody hell. Not wishing her to realize the effect she had on that brainless appendage between his legs, he released her and stepped back.

For a long moment, she just stared at him.

Is she missing the contact as much as I am? What an odd thought. He shoved it into the darkest recesses of his mind. "Forgive me for wandering about. I heard piano playing and my curiosity got the better of me."

Straightening her clothing, she scrunched up her button nose. "You are too generous, sir. I would not call that racket playing as much as banging upon the keys. But if my sister thinks it will deter me from asking her to practice, she is quite mistaken."

"So you are aware of her ploy?"

"I am. If you find the noise unsettling and wish to terminate our arrangement . . . to find another portraitist, I completely understand." She smiled sweetly at him.

"My dear Miss Trafford, if I didn't know better, I'd think you were trying to dissuade me."

Red singed her already rosy cheeks. "No, not at all, sir. It's just this ruckus is enough to give anyone within hearing distance a terrible headache."

"I'll tell you a secret. When I was learning to play, I might have employed a scheme similar to your sister's."

"Somehow that doesn't surprise me."

Her honest comment startled him, and he found himself smiling. He forced his lips into a straight line. "Your sister seems rather leery of me."

"D-did she say something?" Her voice shifted an octave higher.

Was she worried? Did her sister know what he believed Emma did at night?

"Forgive her," she said, without waiting for his response. "She is strong-willed, and those silly penny dreadfuls she reads have made her imagine that danger and mayhem lurk at every corner."

Was that the reason Lily feared him? He remembered how she'd whispered the word *murderer* the first time he met her. Did he resemble one of the villainous characters the child had read about? He touched his cheek. "Perhaps my scar unsettles her."

"No, sir. Your scar is barely noticeable. And from an artist's view, you . . . you are quite handsome."

Damn her. He wasn't handsome. The scar on his face made sure of that. Emma lied with as much skill as Julia. Anger tightened the muscles in his back. "I have an appointment, madam. We will have to continue the portrait tomorrow, if that's agreeable with you." He heard the sharpness in his voice.

As if baffled, the conniver blinked. "Yes, that would be fine. Two o'clock?"

He nodded. "Good day."

Simon exited the Trafford residence, crossed the street, and stepped into his town house. He tossed his hat and gloves on the small side table by the door.

Harris rushed into the entry hall. "Something amiss, sir?"

Simon raked his fingers through his hair. He was an idiot who desperately wanted to believe Emma's softly spoken compliment. Hadn't he learned not to trust a lovely face unless he was paying the woman for her admiration?

"Sir?" The butler's gray brows knitted together.

Simon patted Harris's shoulder. "Ignore me, I'm in a wretched mood."

He stepped into the small drawing room off the entry. Baines was wrapping Vivian's plethora of gewgaws in newspaper and handing them to Nick, the young lad Harris had hired this morning to help box up the clutter.

The boy, who possessed shaggy brown hair and looked to be about fifteen, flashed a wide smile. "Good afternoon, guv'ner."

Baines heaved a heavy breath. "No. No. No. A proper servant does not address his employer as guv'ner."

The lad's face puckered. "Then whot's I to call him?"

"You will refer to him as *sir*. But there really is no need for you to speak to him at all."

Harris stepped into the room and handed the boy a broom. "Nick, go sweep the pavement in front of the house."

"Right-o, sir." The lad tipped two fingers to his forehead, took the broom, and headed out the front door, slamming it hard enough to rattle the walls.

Baines grumbled. "Where did you find him, Harris? The docks?"

Harris's spine stiffened. "He knocked on the door. Asked if we wished to employ a footboy. And we desperately need help packing up this mess." The butler blinked. "No offense, my lord."

"None taken." Simon plopped onto one of the ugly chairs with stripes and flamingos stitched into the fabric and stretched out his legs.

Baines harrumphed. "Harris, you should have known better than to hire a lad off the street."

Bickering, the two servants walked out of the room.

Relieved they were gone, Simon closed his eyes. The steady *swish, swish, swish* of the broom on the pavement outside lulled him into a groggy state. The memory of Emma Trafford's little pink tongue wetting her lips flashed in his mind. Draping an arm over his face, he shoved the image aside.

The rhythmic noise stopped. Simon leaned forward and peered out the slightly ajar window. Lily stood before Nick.

"What's your name?" she asked the lad.

A distrustful expression flashed on the boy's face. "Wot business is it of yours?"

Lily folded her arms and stuck out her chin. "You're not very sociable, are you?"

The lad braced his hands on the top of the broom's handle. "If you must know, it's Nick."

"I'm Lillian, but everyone calls me Lily."

Silence filled the air. Lily tapped her foot on the pavement. "A gentleman would say I'm pleased to make your acquaintance."

"I ain't no gent."

"No, but one day you might be."

"You thinks so, do you?" The boy's voice oozed disbelief.

"Oh, yes. I'm very intuitive. I think I might be clairvoyant."

"Clair whose aunt?"

"No, *clairvoyant*. It means capable of seeing the future."

Nick harrumphed. "And me mother's the Queen."

"I doubt that."

Simon bit back a laugh.

Nick pulled his flat cap off and swiped a sleeve against his damp brow. With narrowed eyes, he stared at the girl.

Lily reached in her pocket and withdrew something wrapped in a linen napkin.

Whatever it was, Nick's eyes widened.

Simon shifted closer to the window. The lemon tart in Lily's hand glistened under the sun.

"Do you want this?" She inched the pastry closer to the lad's nose.

The boy wet his lips. "Whot's I got to do for it?"

Simon wondered what indeed. The child appeared to always have an ulterior motive for her actions.

"Answer a few questions about Mr. Radcliffe?"

Simon stiffened. Why, the little imp. What the bloody hell was she about?

"Whot's you want to know?" Nick asked.

The chit tapped a finger to her chin. "What did he say when he hired you?"

"He didn't hire me. One of the old gents did."

Lily stepped closer. "The tall, pasty-faced one? The one that looks like an undertaker?"

Nick scratched his head. "Ye know, come to think of it, he does, don't he?"

"Yes, I thought so as soon as I saw him. So you've not noticed anything peculiar about Mr. Radcliffe?"

"Nothing. Seems a fine enough gent."

Lily's shoulders drooped, and she handed Nick the tart. "If you see anything unusual, let me know."

"Unusual?" Nick echoed. "Likes whot?"

"You know . . . Dead bodies, pagan rituals, graves in the basement."

Simon flinched. *Pagan rituals?* Did the child's imagination hold no bounds?

Nick scrunched up his nose before shoving the whole tart in his mouth.

Lily turned away and took several steps before pivoting around. "Do you read Inspector Percival Whitley's books? My sister took all mine away. I've searched high and low, and I cannot find where she hid them."

The lad brushed the crumbs away from his mouth and swallowed. Red suddenly heightened his cheeks. "Can't you see I don't have no time to read?"

Simon leaned back in his chair. He got the impression it wasn't a matter of time as much as ability.

Lily made a soft little noise, betraying her disappointment.

"I've got to go," Nick said. "That ole gent will get his trousers in a twist if I dawdle."

"It was nice meeting you, Nick." Lily crossed the street.

The front door of Simon's residence opened and banged closed.

"Nick," Simon called as the lad passed in front of the drawing room's doors. "Would you come here?"

"Yes, guv . . . sir."

"Do you know how to read?"

Nick peered down at his feet while his fingers tightened on the broom's handle. "No, sir, I ain't never learned to read well. But that don't mean I can't do the work asked of me here."

"I agree. However, would you be interested in spending an hour every morning with Mr. Baines, learning to do so? You'll get paid for your time. I'll admit the old goat's a bit short on patience, but he's a fine teacher. In fact, he was my tutor."

"You're going to pay me to learn to read?" Nick narrowed his eyes. "Why?"

"Because I employ quite a few clerks in my business, and in a few years, I'm sure someone will retire, and then I'll need a bright chap to fill that man's place."

The boy gaped. "You thinks I could be a clerk?"

"Of course. So should I tell Baines to expect you?"

The boy nodded. "Yes, thank you, sir."

After dinner, Emma made her way into her studio. Moonlight streamed through the window to highlight the white canvas with her unfinished sketch of Mr. Radcliffe. How fierce he looked in the drawing. His jaw firm. His mouth a serious line. Not boyish in the least, but when he smiled, his harsh face softened. She'd gotten the impression he'd been startled by her compliment. Didn't he realize the symmetrical beauty of his face? She could gaze upon it all day. Yet she needed to complete his portrait and send him on his way. The gentleman was on an expedition to uncover the truth, and with Lily about, he might find out what he searched for.

If she told him what Lily had seen, how the child had

misunderstood the situation, and returned his ring, would he refrain from summoning the police? She stared at the sketch—the intensity in his eyes. His words from earlier today played in her head. *Mark my words, Miss Trafford. I shall find those responsible. When I find the thieves, they will regret ever crossing my path.*

No, he wanted revenge. She mustn't allow the occasional softness in his expression and his blatant flirting to sway her. It was an act—a way to get her to lower her defenses.

With one last glance at the canvas, she exited the room and made her way down one flight to her bedroom. She closed the door to hinder prying eyes and lit the gas lamp on her dresser.

Mama's mahogany jewelry box, with a rose carved into the front panel, sat next to the lamp on the bureau. Emma opened the lid. The only items of true value were Mama's cameo, ruby necklace, and wedding ring. And she doubted the thin, plain band of gold was worth much. And, for all she knew, the ruby necklace could be paste, nothing more than cut glass. Twice she'd walked to the pawnbrokers with Mama's jewelry, intent on hawking the pieces, only to return home unable to part with them. But like the carriage she'd sold, they were most likely the next most valuable things her family had ever possessed. If Emma couldn't make a living with her portraits, she would have to pledge the jewelry to the pawnbroker.

At the rear of the box the velvet lining was loose. Emma reached between the mahogany and the brushed material and withdrew Mr. Radcliffe's ring. The light from the lamp reflected off the gold. Holding it under the illumination, she examined the swirling design with the image of a lion. Was it from some gentlemen's club or university?

As she slipped the ring back into its hiding place, her

fingers brushed against the rose Charles had given her after she'd accepted his marriage proposal. The vibrant red was now a faded wine color and the petals crisp to the touch. Why had she kept it? She should have burned it like she had her sketches of him. The man was married now with a child on the way. Emma walked to the grate and tossed the reminder onto the recently lit coals.

The tips of the dried petals smoked, turning them black before they caught fire and glowed. Orange flames licked upward, and then quickly died down. The reminder was gone, but not the memory. She didn't love Charles anymore, but the sense of not being enough for him had left a pain too close to her heart. And lately, she'd been wondering if Charles might have used her distress over losing her father to manipulate her. Perhaps he'd never intended to wed her at all.

Had she acted the gull? Been duped? As much as she didn't wish to admit it, most likely. Many members of the nobility lived scandalous lives. They were rakes. She should have paid more heed to what Mrs. Flynn read in the scandal sheets about their antics.

Now she was ruined. Soiled.

A tear leaked from her eye. Agitated over her moment of self-pity, she swiped at the dampness trailing down her cheek.

I don't need a man. But as the thought drifted in her mind, so did the memory of Mr. Radcliffe's kiss and the warmth that exploded in her belly during it. She shook her head quickly to dislodge her thoughts and moved back to the dresser to close the jewelry box.

The clapping of horses' hooves on the quiet street drew her attention. Emma parted the curtain. Simon Radcliffe stepped out of his residence and into the dark night. The moon and the streetlamp highlighted his tall form and broad shoulders to send a long shadow onto the pavement.

As if he sensed her watching him, his steps slowed and he glanced up at her window. She moved out of sight, pressed her back to the wall, and wiped the moisture on her palms against the skirt of her dress.

"Move on," the coachman instructed the horses. The clopping of hooves echoed into the night, and then faded.

She glanced at the jewelry box. She needed to sneak into Mr. Radcliffe's house and return his ring while he wasn't home. But not tonight. Too dangerous with his servants in residence. She must be patient and wait until the right opportunity presented itself.

Emma stepped from the room and made her way below stairs. She'd asked Lily to help Mrs. Flynn clear the dining table of their supper dishes, but she'd offered to dry them after they were washed. The sound of Mrs. Flynn squawking like a heron reached Emma's ears. Hastening her steps, she darted into the kitchen. The housekeeper's thick fingers were wrapped around a leaking plumbing joint. Water squirted outward, wetting the woman's face.

What else could go wrong? "I'll get Papa's wrench, Mrs. Flynn. I can tighten it," Emma said.

"You tightened it last time, dearie. What you need is a plumber."

No, she could handle this. Emma dashed to the corner cabinet and withdrew the large wrench.

Lily rushed over to the housekeeper, a pile of towels in her arms. She dabbed a dry one at Mrs. Flynn's cheeks. "Forget about me, child. Wrap them cloths around the pipe."

Water squirted on Emma's face as she clamped the wrench onto the leaking joint and applied pressure. The tool barely budged. Mrs. Flynn released the pipe to help Emma.

The two of them put their weight into turning the wrench. The flow of water trickled down to a slow dribble.

"This," Mrs. Flynn said, "is why you need to find a man and get married."

A man like Charles, who'd made promises he'd not kept. And as much as she'd loved Papa, he'd been little help to Mama, especially when Emma's younger brothers Samuel and Clyde died from influenza. Papa had buried his head in his books, leaving poor Mama to deal with the heartbreak alone. Emma could manage.

"We will be fine, Mrs. Flynn."

"Humph." Water dripped from the tip of the housekeeper's nose. Mrs. Flynn blotted her face with her apron. "I noticed the way Mr. Radcliffe stares at you, dear. I think he might be sweet on you."

Emma walked to the closet and pulled out the wet mop. She couldn't tell Mrs. Flynn that Mr. Radcliffe was more interested in sending her to jail than marrying her.

"And that scar on his cheek ain't so bad," Mrs. Flynn added.

Bad? Indeed not. His scar added character to a face almost too perfect.

"She cannot marry him," Lily exclaimed. "He is a blackguard."

Emma narrowed her eyes at her sister. "Hush, Lily."

"Fiddlesticks." Mrs. Flynn grabbed the mop from Emma and dragged it over the puddle on the floor. "He's a bit stern looking, but otherwise a strapping young man, I bet he . . ." The elder woman's voice trailed off as she glanced over her shoulder at Lily.

Heat warmed Emma's cheeks. She could imagine what Mrs. Flynn was thinking. Worse, she kept recalling the press of Mr. Radcliffe's lips and body against hers. Sadly, she also remembered how tightly he'd held her waist on

Mrs. Vale's terrace, and her impression that he'd wanted to snap her in two, along with his vow to catch the thieves who took his ring.

Worse, tomorrow he would return, and they'd be cloistered together with that odd tension as thick as fog between them.

Chapter Twelve

From outside the Trafford residence, Simon heard Lily banging on the piano. He cringed. How Emma Trafford and the housekeeper could stand the noise remained beyond his comprehension. He lifted the brass knocker and struck it soundly against the hard oak, hoping it resonated above the ruckus.

As if Mrs. Flynn had been standing on the other side waiting for him to arrive, the housekeeper flung the door open.

"Mr. Radcliffe. Come in, sir," she said, talking loud enough to be heard above the piano playing.

"Good day, Mrs. Flynn." He stepped into the entry hall and handed her his hat and gloves.

The housekeeper's gaze veered past Simon's shoulder to his town house across the street. She patted her gray bun.

"Do you know if Mr. Baines intends to call today?" Her fingers crushed the brim of Simon's hat.

He'd overheard Baines talking to Harris about purchasing some groceries. "Would you happen to be the reason he intends to buy sugar, flour, butter, and lemons?"

Her round face beamed. "Yes. Indeed. I offered to make him a batch of my lemon tarts."

"Ah, then that would explain his eagerness to go to market." Simon inhaled the sweet scent permeating the Trafford residence. His mouth watered. "Whatever you've already made smells enticing."

Mrs. Flynn's smile widened. "I just finished making shortbread biscuits for Miss Emma and yourself to enjoy with your afternoon tea."

"Madam, you tempt me to throw my bachelor ways aside and sweep you off to Gretna Green."

She blushed. "I'm old enough to be your mother, sir."

"Are you? I would never have thought that. Have you ever considered opening a bakery?"

She twisted her hands in her apron. "I don't have the funds for such a venture, and I wouldn't want to leave Miss Emma or Lily unless the older Miss Trafford weds." The woman stared pointedly at him, a mischievous gleam in her eyes.

Good Lord, did she mean to him? He had no interest in the institution. And if he did, it wouldn't be to a woman who might be a bollock smashing thief. He held up his hands as if to ward off an attack. "I only have eyes for you, Mrs. Flynn."

Blushing, she motioned to the stairs. "Miss Emma's waiting for you."

As Simon moved up the stairs, the sound of Lily's atrocious piano playing grew louder. Upon reaching the first-floor landing, he moved to the drawing room. Lily sat at the piano, banging her fingers against the keys as if she wished to cause permanent damage to the instrument.

"At it again, are you?" Simon asked.

The child whipped around so fast, she nearly toppled

off the piano bench. She frowned. "You're quite good at sneaking up on people."

"You would have heard me if you weren't creating such a hullabaloo. So, I take it your little plot still hasn't worked."

Her narrow shoulders slumped. "Emma *must* be tone deaf."

"She *must* possess a constitution of steel."

The girl's bow-shaped lips formed a genuine smile. One day she would break some poor fellow's heart—if she didn't snarl at him or drive him mad first. Lily brushed a few loose stands of hair that had escaped her long braid off her flushed cheeks.

"Did you ever think that actually practicing might involve less energy than banging so violently upon the keys?"

"No."

"Perhaps you should contemplate it." Simon motioned to the sheet music propped up on the music desk. "What are you *playing* today?"

"Chopin's 'Minute Waltz.'"

"Dear God, I'd never have recognized it."

"That's the point." She grinned. "So you're familiar with it?"

"I am."

"Then play it," she said as if he lied. She slipped off the bench.

Why not? Simon took off his coat and draped it over the back of a chair covered in faded blue damask. He sat and glided his fingers effortlessly over the keys, allowing the waltz to spring to life.

Lily's mouth gaped. "Blimey! You play even better than Em."

"You do," a soft voice said.

His fingers stilled. Emma stood at the doorway, wearing a sapphire-colored gown that made her blue eyes appear even darker. Curse his heart for skipping a beat. "Sorry, wandered off a bit."

"No need to apologize. I enjoyed listening to you tremendously."

"Keep playing, Mr. Radcliffe," Lily instructed. The child grabbed Emma's hands and pulled her to the center of the room. "My sister and I shall dance."

Emma shook her head. "Mr. Radcliffe is not here to entertain us."

Ignoring her protestation, he set his fingers to the keys and played a vivacious Scottish jig with a fast, carefree tempo.

Giggling, Lily twirled Emma about the room.

For the first time since meeting Emma Trafford, her smile appeared natural, not forced. Her pink cheeks glowed and turned rosy, matching the color of her lips. She tipped her head back and laughed. Unable to pull his gaze away, his blasted fingers stumbled on the keys.

Agitated by his damnable attraction to the woman, he rushed through the remainder of the song and jerked to his feet. As he slipped on his coat, he silently chastised himself. He had come here to learn the truth and recover his ring. He was allowing Emma's attractive face to derail him.

"That was beyond wonderful, Mr. Radcliffe," Lily said, her cheeks red from dancing.

"You are a master at the keys," Emma added. She arched one shapely brow at her sister. "Lily, if you practiced, you could play just as divinely. You have the talent to do so."

Lily harrumphed. "I'd rather listen to others play. Do you know any duets, Mr. Radcliffe?"

"Yes, a few."

"Papa and Em were so very good at them." Lily averted her face and peered out the window. When she turned back, her expression looked forlorn.

Emma draped an arm over the child's shoulders. The

affection the woman possessed for her young sister was palpable. If she was whom he sought, was that why she'd struck him? Was she desperate for funds? This room, like the morning room downstairs, was absent knickknacks and personal items, as if stripped bare. He gave himself a mental slap. He would not feel sorry for Emma Trafford. Not if she'd distracted him so her accomplice could attempt to crack his skull open like an egg. She could have killed him. He needed to remember that.

"What was that rousing song you and Papa used to play?" Lily asked her sister, pulling Simon from his thoughts.

"Brahms's Hungarian Dance number five. If you practice you could learn it. Then you and I could play it together."

The child sighed. "I do so long to hear it again. Do you know how to play it, Mr. Radcliffe?"

The normally brash child sounded melancholy and vulnerable—anything but resilient.

"I do."

"Would you be good enough to play it with Em? I'd be much obliged."

"Mr. Radcliffe's playing far surpasses mine," Emma said. "And I'm sure he doesn't wish—"

"I'd enjoy the duet." The words had flown from his mouth before he could halt them. What the hell ailed him? Why should he care about the child's melancholy?

For a moment, Emma's gaze met his. He thought she would refuse, but she strode to the bench. Her fingers plucked absently on the edge of her sleeve. "I have not played the piece in quite some time. I fear I might botch it up."

"I doubt that." He slipped his coat off again, and set his hand on the small of her back. Her skin felt overly warm beneath the thin cotton dress. An image of his hands gliding over her heated body, the swell of her breasts, while he settled between the softness of her thighs flashed in his mind.

"Mr. Radcliffe? Sir?" Emma's soft voice interrupted his wayward thoughts.

"Ah, forgive me. Did you say something?"

"I asked if you preferred to play the primo or secondo?" Emma motioned to the piano.

"Which do you prefer?"

"Father always played the low notes."

"Then I shall do the same."

Emma took her place on the bench, and he sat to her left. The scent of roses drifted to his nose.

Lily set the sheet music before them and stepped back.

He nodded at Emma, and they began. Her fingers danced across the keys. She played the piece well, but a bit too slow for his liking, and he picked up the tempo. She stumbled once or twice to catch up, but laughed. A light tinkling that complemented the sound of the keys. Unable to stop himself, he grinned.

They struck the last notes, and she turned to him. Her eyes shone bright with mirth; her rosy lips smiled. "That was quite wicked, Mr. Radcliffe, playing the piece so fast. What did you think, Lily?" Emma peered over her shoulder. "Oh, she's gone!"

Indeed, the girl was nowhere in sight. "Yes, it appears we were ill-used."

The pink on Emma's cheeks darkened. "My sister is incorrigible. I fear she concocted this plan so she could avoid practicing. I do apologize."

"No need. I enjoyed the duet." As much as he'd like to say it was a lie, it was not. How long had it been since something as simple as playing the piano left him feeling lighthearted? Was it the music or the temptress beside him?

Simon's gaze settled on her lush mouth. God help him, but he wanted to kiss her. He shifted closer.

Emma's eyes grew wide, turning her pupils into dark circles in a sea of blue, yet she didn't pull back.

Anticipation coiled tight within him. His jaded heart beat double time.

His lips were only inches from hers when the front door slammed closed.

Emma gasped and stood so fast, her hand knocked the sheet music onto the piano bench.

Gracious. Had she been about to let Mr. Radcliffe kiss her? Doubtful he would realize who she was from such an act, but she needed to be more careful. The man unleashed something in her that was beyond reckless. Without looking at Simon, she moved to the center of the room.

"Em!" Lily's fast footsteps moved up the stairs.

The legs of the piano bench scraped against the wooden floor, alerting her to Mr. Radcliffe's movement. The heat of his body almost singed her back when he stepped behind her. She should move away, but her feet felt glued in place.

His breath fanned against her nape.

Desire settled in her belly. She forced herself to take a step away from him.

Lily darted into the room.

Mr. Radcliffe moved to the chair and silently slipped his arms into the sleeves of his coat and shrugged it over his broad shoulders.

"Where did you go, Lily? You are supposed to be practicing," Emma said, pleased her voice remained even.

"I went outside to roll my trundling hoop. Then Mr. Radcliffe's tall, pinch-faced servant came out and peered down his long nose at me like I was an ant he wanted to stomp on. Scared the dickens out of me, he did." The child gave an exaggerated shudder.

"That's Harris. He's harmless," Mr. Radcliffe said.

The jutting of Lily's chin conveyed her doubt. "I shouldn't have left you alone anyway." Her eyes turned into tiny slits as she stared at Mr. Radcliffe.

Ignoring Lily's glower, Mr. Radcliffe motioned to the doorway. "Shall we go to your studio, Miss Trafford?" He looked impatient to get her alone again.

Emma's heart fluttered. She didn't trust him. Worse, she didn't trust herself.

"Of course." She walked to the ottoman and picked up the book on geography she'd borrowed from the lending library.

The heat of Mr. Radcliffe's gaze followed her like a low-flying hawk sighting a rabbit he intended to swoop down on.

She handed her sister the thick tome. "Lily, you will read this in my studio while I sketch Mr. Radcliffe. That way I can make sure you are doing as asked."

Lily frowned and exhaled a heavy breath.

A nerve visibly ticked in Mr. Radcliffe's jaw. For a long moment, he held her gaze. Then one corner of his sensual mouth hitched up.

Yes, Mr. Radcliffe, you scoundrel, I realize you're trying to lower my guard. You might have succeeded in momentarily turning my brain to mush, but I'll not allow it to happen again. The rabbit wasn't as stupid as he thought.

As they entered the studio, Lily dragged her feet on the wooden floor as if being forced to read about geography was tantamount to purgatory. With a heavy sigh, the child plopped herself on the daybed and opened the book.

Emma picked up her sketching pencil as Mr. Radcliffe

sat in the chair before the easel. She felt the warmth of his intense gaze. A tingling sensation filtered through her body.

"You must center your eyes on the painting hanging on the wall, Mr. Radcliffe," she chastised, attempting to veer her mind to the task at hand, not on the memory of his warm body next to her on the piano bench, and surely not on how she'd *wanted* him to kiss her.

Mrs. Flynn entered the room and waved an envelope in the air. "A letter from Michael just arrived in the post."

Excitement bubbled up in Emma. Letters from Michael were becoming scarce. She took the envelope with her brother's distinctive bold script. "Thank you, Mrs. Flynn."

"I've made some shortbread to serve with your tea this afternoon." The housekeeper smiled at Mr. Radcliffe.

He didn't seem to notice. His focus remained locked on the missive in Emma's hand as though it might be a clue to what he sought—her guilt.

"I love shortbread." Lily scooted back on the daybed and rested her head like she intended to nap.

"You'll get some after you read," Emma replied. "And tonight I shall quiz you on the Western Hemisphere."

Grumbling, Lily flipped a page.

"I'll bring your tea and biscuits in about an hour." The housekeeper exited the studio.

"Mr. Radcliffe, if you don't mind, I wish to read this letter from my brother now," Emma said.

"Not at all. Go ahead." He braced his forearms on his thighs and leaned forward.

She opened the envelope.

Dear Emma,

I hope both you and Lily are in fine health. I received your letter. I assure you all is well. I'm busy learning about Homer and the Greeks.

Thank you for the biscuits. The ones I brought back to school after Easter holiday barely lasted a week. The food here is abysmal.

Fondest regards,
Your loving brother, Michael

The letter was brief. Too brief. Her heart sank. Usually Michael gave a full account of how his classes were going. An unsettling sensation overcame her. Was he not taking his schoolwork seriously?

When home at Easter, he'd talked nonstop about Ernest Montgomery, a baron's son, whom he'd befriended at school. She didn't like the idea of him hanging around with the boy. The nobility lived by their own set of rules. She'd learned that firsthand, and when they acted wicked, society looked the other way. But Michael wouldn't receive the same treatment if caught engaged in some boisterous activity with the boy.

She sighed. She was overreacting—letting her own experiences with Charles color her perception of the situation. Michael was smart. He'd not partake in reckless antics. Surely, his infrequent letters and the brevity of this one reflected how busy he was at school, nothing more.

"Is there a problem?" Mr. Radcliffe asked, breaking into her thoughts.

She smoothed out her worried expression and forced a smile. "No. Everything is fine." She folded the parchment and set it on the table.

Mr. Radcliffe's gaze remained on the letter.

If he read it, he'd realize it contained nothing nefarious. And perhaps he could offer some insight. She picked it up and handed it to him.

He looked puzzled.

She glanced at Lily. The child was preoccupied, trying to balance the geography book on her head. "My brother's letter is very brief, and they have become less frequent. I'm worried something might be wrong at school. Might I ask your opinion?"

His bewildered expression deepened. "I'm not that familiar with children."

"Michael is nearly a man. Surely, you have some insight."

"Well, yes, I . . ." She'd never seen Mr. Radcliffe flounder, but her request to help with this family matter seemed to send him off balance.

He opened the missive and smiled. "He's complaining about the food. Definitely sounds like a typical lad at school. And quite understandable after enjoying Mrs. Flynn's cooking."

"Yes, I'm probably worrying about nothing." She returned his smile.

"Your brother is fortunate to have someone who worries about him while he's away." There was unmistakable sadness in his voice.

"Did you attend boarding school, sir?"

"I did."

"Were you homesick? Did you send letters frequently?"

His jaw tensed, then relaxed. "Sometimes I did long for my childhood home, but if I'd sent letters, my father wouldn't have read them."

His candid response startled her.

Sporting a bland expression, he motioned to her easel. But she could see the pain in his eyes. "Shall we get on with the painting?"

"Yes. Of course."

Two hours later, even after their afternoon break for tea and shortbread, Simon Radcliffe was as restless as a big cat in a cage. He'd acted that way ever since they'd conversed about family and his father.

"Em." Lily scurried off the daybed. "I need to use the water closet," she whispered into Emma's ear.

"I think we will call it a day, Mr. Radcliffe." Emma set her pencil down.

Bracing his hands on his thighs, he stood. His long fingers massaged the muscles at the back of his neck. The sight of his hand flexing against his skin made her body hum. The memory of how he'd acted only a few hours ago in the drawing room—like he intended to kiss her, replayed in her head. It wouldn't have created a problem if she hadn't *wanted* him to, but she did.

"Em!" Lily wiggled next to her. "I really have to go."

She didn't want to be alone with Mr. Radcliffe, but she couldn't make her sister wait any longer. "Okay, dear."

Lily dashed from the room. Her slippered feet thumped loudly on the wooden floor of the corridor and down the stairs.

Mr. Radcliffe gazed at Emma like a predator just released from his cage and let out to prowl for his dinner. She motioned to the door. "After you, sir."

He grinned. "No, after you."

She opened her mouth.

"I insist," he said.

As she moved by him, his hand settled on the small of her back, sending sparks through her body. She stepped away from him and descended the stairs at a less-than-ladylike speed. She needed to remember he was on a mission to find his thieves, not a beau interested in her.

Mrs. Flynn stood in the entry hall. "What is the matter, dear? You are moving like you've seen a ghost."

Not a ghost. Someone more dangerous than that—the man who could send her to prison.

Chapter Thirteen

Simon fought the urge to restlessly roll his shoulders as Emma painted his portrait. She'd been working on it for over a week. A few days ago, she'd put away her sketching pencils and brought out her palette, pigments, and brushes.

She bent and dipped her brush into her paint, and Simon took the opportunity to study her. She wore a high-collared dress in a drab shade of gray. This afternoon, he'd spent most of his time fantasizing about kissing her.

Confound it. Perhaps Mrs. Flynn added aphrodisiacs to the delectable treats she baked. It would explain Simon's wayward mind and his damnable attraction to Emma Trafford. He should go to Clapton's Boxing Club and allow some pugilist to knock the snot out of him. He inwardly shook his head, clearing his renegade thoughts. He was on a mission, and he needed to remember that.

As of yet, he'd not gained more knowledge than he had a week ago. During his sittings, no man had called on Emma, leaving him with little idea of who her accomplice was—if Emma was the woman he sought. Frustrated, he rubbed the back of his neck to loosen the sudden tension.

"Please, sit still, Mr. Radcliffe." Emma frowned.

He tried not to scowl. While painting, his timid little

mouse turned into a taskmaster. Another vision flashed through his mind—this one of him unclasping the tiny buttons that lined the front of Emma's gown and drawing one of her clean sable brushes over her naked breasts.

God, he was hopeless. He definitely needed a bit of afternoon recreation. He should visit his friend Margaret and see if she was interested in a game of lawn tennis . . . or something more stimulating. Yet as lovely as Lady Griffin was, the idea held little appeal.

"You're scowling, sir," Emma said, once again breaking into his thoughts.

"Forgive me."

She smiled, dimpling her rosy cheeks and swirled her brush in a jar of turpentine. Leaning over the table, she grabbed a rag and ran it over the bristles. "You seem rather restless, Mr. Radcliffe, and I've somewhere I wish to go, so we shall call it a day."

A spark of hope exploded in his gut. Was Emma about to meet the worm Simon hoped to unearth? The bastard who'd cracked a bloody vase over his head? He stood. "Very well."

"Can you return at two o'clock tomorrow?" She dipped another rag into the jar of turpentine and rubbed at the paint on her wooden palette. The scent of the solvent had now become as familiar to Simon as the rose water on Emma's skin.

"Yes, that will be fine." He moved to the door. "Good day, Miss Trafford."

A sense of excitement swirled through Simon as he crossed the street. Inside his town house, he entered the drawing room and watched the front door of the Traffords' residence, intent on following her. Impatiently he tapped his fingers on the window's casing.

"Something amiss, my lord?" Baines asked.

Simon turned around. The two old goats stood in the doorway staring at him.

Harris arched a bushy gray brow. "What are you staring at, sir?"

"None of your concern." Simon turned back to the window. Emma stepped from her residence, a parasol jauntily angled above her head, shading her from the bright April sun making an appearance on this brisk day. She'd changed out of her drab gray dress and into one similar in style, but in a muted blue color, along with a navy wool cape and a hat with roses on it.

"I'm going out."

"Out?" Baines echoed. "But you just arrived home, and I intend to make roasted chicken for dinner."

Simon stifled a groan. Two days ago, Harris had insulted the new cook's food, comparing it to gruel. In response, the woman had gathered her belongings, asked for her wages, and stormed out. Since then, Baines had decided he cooked as well as anyone they'd find at the local employment agency. Sadly, his valet was incorrect. Everything Baines prepared was overcooked and over-salted. He feared both Baines's and Harris's taste buds had mellowed with age.

"You two go ahead and eat it. I'm not sure when I'll return home." Simon snatched his walking stick from the umbrella stand and stepped out onto Great James Street.

Twenty-five minutes later, his walking stick tapped an even rhythm on the flagstones as he moved up Great Russell Street. Simon watched the feminine sway of the lithe figure walking a good ten yards before him. He'd been following Emma since she'd left her house.

Shc moved up the street at an efficient pace as though time was of the essence. Her steps had slowed only once, when she'd passed the gardens at Bloomsbury Square and observed several children frolicking about the park under the watchful gaze of a stern-faced nursemaid.

Emma stepped through the wrought iron gates of the British Museum.

A smile tugged on the corners of Simon's lips. The museum's expanse made it a favorite place for clandestine assignations. Did she intend to meet with the bastard who'd struck him?

She lowered her parasol and walked through the courtyard, past the colonnades, and stepped inside the building. With determined strides, she moved to the west end of the museum and entered the Elgin Room. Simon slipped into the shadowed perimeter behind a large Ionic column with an ancient vase perched atop, away from the light streaming through the skylights above. Emma's pace slowed as she perused several antiquities. Halfway down the expanse of the long room, she gracefully settled on a bench. For several minutes, she looked at the display before her. She withdrew a rolled piece of paper and a pencil from her reticule, and began to sketch.

Anticipation furled within Simon as he glanced around and waited for someone to approach Emma. Several times she paused, tipped her head to the side, and appeared to study the marble piece in front of her before her pencil moved again with quick strokes.

In her studio, from the corner of his eye, he'd noticed her doing the same thing when she sketched and painted him. And he'd been pleased his scarred cheek didn't face her. How foolish to care what she thought.

"Lord Adler," a man said, drawing him from his thoughts.

Simon turned to see Dr. Trimble standing to his right. He reached out and shook the man's hand. "Trimble."

The doctor gave a lazy smile. "Are you here to view the

Elgin Marbles or"—the physician motioned with a nod of his chin toward Emma—"something a little more warm-blooded?"

Simon glanced over his shoulder. Emma still sat with her head bent over her sketch. Her pencil continued to move across the paper.

He winked at the man. "The marbles, of course. What brings you here?"

"The Reading Room. A bit of research."

Simon nodded.

A somber museum employee walked up to them. "We're closing, sirs."

Closing? How long had he stood watching Emma sketch? Simon looked up at the skylights. Dusk was starting to settle.

"Guess I'll be shoving off." Trimble glanced at Emma and grinned. "Good luck."

After shaking the man's hand, Simon turned around. The museum employee chatted with Emma, his earlier somber expression replaced with a genial smile. A bolt of agitation slid down Simon's spine. Why should he care if the man flirted, or stood so close the scoundrel's legs practically touched Emma's skirts?

She nodded at the attendant, rolled up the piece of paper, and slipped it and the pencil into her reticule.

The visitors in the gallery moved toward the doorway, and a soft buzz of conversation filled the previously quiet space. Simon stepped back, waited until Emma passed, and fell in with the crowd vacating the room. She walked outside the museum and through the gates with the same steady pace she'd exhibited upon arrival.

On Great Russell Street two men moved past Simon. Both blokes appeared a bit worse for wear, as if they'd dined on gin. The taller of the two spoke loud, his words slurred, and the shorter man swayed like a seaman jostled on the prow of a ship faring a rough sea. Were they following her? Could either of them be the man he sought? The idea of her associating with such riffraff angered him even though he shouldn't give a flying fig.

A good thirty feet from the entrance, the taller man clasped Emma's upper arm and violently spun her around. "Whys don't you come with us, sweeting, and we'll shows you a grand time."

A streetlamp, a yard from where she stood, revealed her startled expression. She tried to shrug her arm loose. "Let go of me!"

Before he knew what he was about, Simon darted forward and grasped the man's wrist in a bone-crushing grip. "You heard the lady. Let her go."

The ruffian's face contorted with pain, and his cohort stepped closer.

Simon cocked a brow at the second bloke. "I wouldn't suggest it, chum."

The shorter man raised his hands, palms out, and walked backward.

Wincing, the brute released Emma's arm.

Simon applied more pressure before letting go of the scoundrel.

"We weres jush havin' a bit of fun with her," the taller man said, rubbing his wrist where Simon had clasped it.

"We best get going, dear." Simon offered Emma his arm.

She blinked, but wrapped her hand about his sleeve. They walked up Great Russell Street in silence.

"Thank you, Mr. Radcliffe," she said as they passed Bloomsbury Square.

"Think nothing of it, Miss Trafford." He felt her gaze on his face. They moved by a gas streetlamp. Her cheeks were flushed.

"How fortuitous you were close by. Were you at the museum?" The narrowing of her eyes was nearly imperceptible in the gloom.

Did she question the coincidence? Yes, she trusted him as much as he trusted her. Very little. "I was."

"Were you using the Reading Room?" She tipped her head to the side.

"No, just walking about. And you?"

Her expression softened; a muted smile formed on her soft lips. "My father was a curator at the museum. He even lived there before marrying my mother. Every Friday, an hour before closing, I'd walk there. Sketch a bit, then walk home with him. Old habits are hard to set aside."

"You miss your father?"

Her regard shifted from Simon to somewhere in the distance. "He wasn't around a great deal at times, but I do. We both shared a love of art."

He understood her loss—what it felt like to lose one's father, though he'd lost his long before the man had died.

She returned her attention to him. "What of your family, sir?"

"My parents died years ago, and I have no siblings."

Her hand on his arm tightened as though she wished to comfort him.

The contact not only sent heat through his veins, it lessened the discord speaking about his father always brought on.

"I got the impression that your father and you were not always close."

How did she know that?

His face must have reflected his bewilderment for she said, "You mentioned how he would not have read your letters while you were away at school."

Ah, so he had. Odd, he rarely talked about that part of his life. "We had a misunderstanding."

"It couldn't be resolved?"

"No. The rift was too great."

Once again, her grasp on his arm tightened. "I'm sorry."

He was, as well.

As they made their way to Great James Street, in companionable silence, the sound of voices behind them interrupted the steady cadence of Simon's walking stick tapping on the pavement. He glanced over his shoulder. The two drunkards from the museum were following them.

Bugger it. He took Emma's hand and quickly pulled her around a street corner.

"Mr. Radcliffe?" Her voice held an anxious edge.

Setting his hands on her upper arms, he propelled her backward into a narrow alley between two buildings.

Her blue eyes widened and her mouth parted as if she intended to scream. He pressed his finger to the plump surface of her lips. "The two men from the museum are following us. I want you to stay here while I continue walking up the street. Whatever happens, don't come out until I return for you."

Simon turned to walk away. Emma's delicate hand clasped his arm, halting his movements. She stepped close to him. The scent of roses filled his nose.

"But there are *two* of them," she said.

If she was his little thief, she probably thought him incompetent after what she and her accomplice had done to him. Doubtful either man would distract him with a kiss. "I shall be fine."

She nodded and released his coat.

He moved back to the pavement and strode up the street. He'd traveled a good five yards when the men's voices grew louder. The bounders turned the corner and were moving past where Emma stood. *Good, come on, chums, follow me a bit more. Yes, that's it.*

"Ish that him?" Emma heard a slurred voice ask. "Wersh the woman?"

"Are you looking for me, gents?" Mr. Radcliffe's voice sounded civil, almost jovial.

"Where's the pretty bird?" one of the men asked.

"Flown away," Mr. Radcliffe replied.

Footfalls grew louder. Emma's heart beat fast. Two shadows passed by the opening to the alley. Were the men going to engage in some misconduct? Even brawl?

A dull *thump* resonated in the air, followed by an *owf*, confirming her fear. Two against one wasn't fair. She couldn't stand idly by while they struck Mr. Radcliffe. She lifted her folded parasol above her head and crept down the narrow, stygian path. Another *thud* and *owf*. Then shuffling of feet and more grunts.

She neared the opening to the pavement when Mr. Radcliffe chuckled. She froze and lowered her makeshift weapon. Was she mistaken? Surely, a man pummeled would not sound so blithe.

"What fun this is," Mr. Radcliffe said in a lighthearted tone as if they were taking tea and playing a robust game of cards.

Someone grunted. Once, twice, a third time. *Thump*.

"Are you cozy now?" Laughter tinged Mr. Radcliffe's voice.

"*Hhrrmm. Hhrrmm.*"

"Well, yes, glad to hear it, then." Mr. Radcliffe chuckled again.

Goodness, what were they doing? She moved to step out of the alley. Someone appeared in front of her in the dark space. She gasped, lifted her parasol, and brought it down with all her might.

The person's hand shot out to halt her makeshift weapon's downward momentum.

"Damnation, woman, I told you to stay put. What do you think you're about?"

Mr. Radcliffe. Thank God! The air in her lungs eased through her teeth. "I didn't know what was going on. I thought you might need a bit of assistance."

"No. Everything has been tidied up quite well." He backed out of the alley and scooped up his top hat from the pavement. As he set it on his head, he picked up his walking stick, which leaned against the building.

Someone gave a muffled grunt to her right. She pivoted toward the sound, but Mr. Radcliffe stepped before her, blocking her view.

His eyes lit with mischief. He set his hands on her shoulders and turned her in the opposite direction. Stepping next to her, he offered his arm. "Shall we?"

The grunting continued. Her curiosity got the better of her, and she peered over her shoulder. In the gloom, she could see the two men tied together with their neckcloths. Some article of clothing was stuffed in their mouths. Both men's trousers were about their ankles, though they still wore their small garments. She sucked in a quick breath.

"I told you not to look," Mr. Radcliffe chastised.

"I didn't expect anything so . . ." Her face heated, and a small laugh bubbled up her throat. "You have a wicked sense of humor, sir."

"Yes, but they deserve much worse than the public humiliation they will encounter in the morning."

She twisted to glance over her shoulder again.

Mr. Radcliffe tsked. "Eyes forward, Miss Trafford. Eyes forward."

As they walked up the street, Emma studied Simon

Radcliffe. His presence filled her with a sense of safety. How odd, since she'd just witnessed the brute strength he could inflict. How had he learned to fight like that?

He glanced down at her. The moonlight caught his chiseled features. How handsome he was in a dark and dangerous way. Shouting caused them both to turn. A uniformed constable stood on the pavement before the two men. The shrill sound of the policeman's whistle rent the air.

"Dash it all." Mr. Radcliffe grabbed her hand and pulled her up the street.

"Shouldn't we stay and tell him what happened?"

"He may find little humor in my brand of justice."

"True, I had not thought of that," she said as they darted up the street.

"And if the men are arrested, we'll be dragged before the magistrate to testify. Sure to be a long, drawn-out affair, and I don't wish for the scrutiny."

"I see what you mean. Your business acquaintances might hear of it."

"Yes, indeed, my business acquaintances." He peered over his shoulder and slowed his steps. A broad smile spread across his face. "The bobby has given up his chase."

Breathing heavily, she nodded.

"Rest a bit, and catch your breath."

"No. I'm fine." She wished she could say the same for her parasol. The metal ribs were bent where he'd clasped it. The dashed thing would never open again. A small price to pay for his assistance. Thank God, Mr. Radcliffe had been at the museum—even if he'd been following her. Those dirty, drunken men had meant to . . . Without thought, she tightened her grasp on his hand.

He held her gaze for a moment, and then glanced at her parasol. "I shall buy you another."

"No need, sir. I appreciate you coming to my aid." The heat coming off his body warmed the cooling night air.

"Do you really think it wise to walk alone at this time of day?" Her hand was still clasped tightly in his. He released it and placed it atop his sleeve—very proper and all.

"I've never encountered a problem before, but maybe you're right."

"You should take a hackney home from the museum until the sun starts setting later in the day. Unless you walk with someone who can protect you." His dark eyes peered at her. "Do you have such a person?"

Was he fishing for information? Still trying to figure out who'd hit him if she was the woman who'd kissed him and stolen his ring? "No, I do not."

His lips formed a straight line, and they continued walking in silence to Great James Street. At the door to her residence, the entry lamp highlighted a visible red patch on his jaw.

"You're injured." As if of its own volition, her hand lifted and cupped the bruised skin.

His eyes widened.

She lowered her palm. "Does it hurt?"

"Not a bit. I've always thought I possess a jaw of steel." His gaze held hers, then lowered to her mouth. His body shifted closer, and his warm breath fanned against her cheek.

Her breathing quickened.

The front door flew open. Mrs. Flynn stood at the threshold. "Ah, I thought I heard voices." Red spots colored the older woman's cheeks. With her chin she motioned across the street.

Emma followed the woman's gaze. A curtain in the second story window of Mrs. Jenkins's house was drawn back and the glow of candlelight in the window revealed a person peering out. Mrs. Jenkins was a tattler of the highest order. The woman would gossip mercilessly about them if she thought anything untoward was happening.

"Dinner will be ready shortly. Is Mr. Radcliffe to dine with us?" Mrs. Flynn asked.

Dine with them? Emma's stomach twisted. "I'm sure he does not—"

"How kind. I'd love to."

Chapter Fourteen

The savory scent of beef stew with parsnips and carrots filled the small dining room in the Trafford residence. Simon glanced at Emma, seated to his left at the round table. The relieved expression she'd exhibited after he'd taken care of the two drunkards had evaporated. Now, she acted pensive, avoiding eye contact. Perhaps because he'd nearly kissed her before Mrs. Flynn opened the door.

Not for the first time, he'd wanted to. Wanted to taste Emma's mouth, and not just to see if her kiss felt familiar, but because of his damnable attraction to the woman.

Across from where he sat, a movement grabbed his attention. With her elbows propped on the table and her hands cradling the lower half of her face, Lily glared at him like he was a mouse caught nibbling the family's prized cheese.

"Lily," Emma said, "please sit straight, and remember people who glower run the risk of their faces freezing in a most unbecoming way."

The girl shot her sister a skeptical glance, but smoothed out her expression and draped a napkin over her lap.

Mrs. Flynn strode into the room, set a basket of rolls on

the table, and lowered herself onto the seat to his right. Simon quickly stood and helped the housekeeper with her chair. He'd never seen a servant join a family for a meal. Not true. When a tot, his nursemaid had eaten with him in the nursery, and later when Baines had been his tutor, the two of them had taken their meals together in the schoolroom.

"Would you care for a hot roll, Mr. Radcliffe?" A full smile wreathed the lower half of the housekeeper's face. She seemed the only one pleased he dined with them.

"Thank you, Mrs. Flynn."

Emma lifted the lid of a large white ironstone casserole. The full force of the savory stew's scent permeated the air. She passed it to him. His mouth watered. At luncheon today, Baines had served overcooked ham. Simon fed most of the rubbery meat to Kismet. Thank God, the cat didn't possess discriminating taste buds and ate nearly everything put in front of him.

"Do you wish me to serve you, Mr. Radcliffe?" Mrs. Flynn asked.

"Thank you, but that won't be necessary." Simon ladled the stew into his dish. "Smells divine."

The housekeeper's face reflected her pride. "Thank you."

He set the casserole dish next to Emma.

"We are quite fortunate to have Mrs. Flynn to cook for us." Emma smiled. "I fear we would be eating porridge if the task fell to me."

Mrs. Flynn tsked. "Now, dearie, you're a marvelous cook."

Lily snorted. "She makes everything taste like shoe leather or mush."

A soft *thump* resonated under the table.

Lily yelped and glared at Mrs. Flynn. "What did I do?"

The housekeeper scowled at the child before turning to

him. "Mr. Radcliffe, don't pay any mind to Lily. Her sister is a fine cook and any man would be blessed to have her as his wife."

Emma gasped. Two bright red spots appeared on her cheeks. "Mrs. Flynn!"

"'Tis the truth, child."

It appeared the older woman had taken on the task of a matchmaking mama. Realizing he was smiling, Simon sobered his expression.

Emma moved a carrot about her plate before she speared it with the tines of her fork. She glanced at him from her lowered lashes. "Mr. Radcliffe and I didn't venture to the museum *together*, by any means. We happened upon each other as we exited, and he was good enough to accompany me home. Thank you again for your kindness, sir."

Lily harrumphed, and all heads turned to the child. "Inspector Whitley says coincidences are few and far between." The girl flipped her long, fair braid over her shoulder and narrowed her eyes at him.

There was another *thump* under the table, and Lily yelped again.

"Sorry, dear, just stretching my legs," Emma said.

"I shall be black and blue before this meal is done," the girl grumbled. She plopped a heaping of parsnips into her mouth.

Simon forked a piece of beef. The meat practically melted against his tongue. He almost sighed out loud. After eating Baines's cooking, he wanted to kiss Mrs. Flynn—or possibly kidnap her. The woman's skill in the kitchen surpassed even his Mayfair cook's talents.

As they ate, the conversation moved to the mundane—the weather and the Queen's mourning wear.

"May I add more pepper to my food?" Lily asked.

The housekeeper glared at the girl as if she'd asked to eat her own hand. "It doesn't need more."

Simon agreed. It was perfectly seasoned.

"But I like mine spicy," the child said.

Emma sighed. "Yes. Go get the pepper shaker from the kitchen."

After Lily exited the room, Mrs. Flynn's scowl deepened. "Did either of you read the on-dits in the newspaper?"

Simon's spine straightened. Bloody hell, he hoped his name hadn't been bandied about in those ludicrous gossip columns today.

The housekeeper peered at Simon. "Though there was no mention of that *scandalous* Lord A, Mrs. Jenkins's housekeeper said that her mistress saw the nobleman boating shirtless on the Thames."

A nerve twitched in Simon's jaw. Was the harridan still spreading that lie?

"I think it doubtful," Emma said. "It was freezing cold most of last week. One would have to be a fool to engage in such an activity."

Either Emma had just championed him or called him a fool.

"Those scandal sheets are sometimes filled with falsehoods," he said, attempting to keep his tone even. "I doubt he actually went rowing without wearing a shirt."

"Oh, but he's a wicked one, Mr. Radcliffe," Mrs. Flynn said. "Rumor has it, even his own father wanted nothing to do with him when the old viscount was alive."

Emma glanced at him, and Simon realized he'd gone as still as a stone.

"Are you okay, sir?"

He nodded.

"Well," Mrs. Flynn continued, "Mrs. Jenkins also said that last month at some swanky Mayfair residence, the nobleman stood on the dining room table and sang a rather ribald ditty."

Now that is pure balderdash! He hadn't sung a ditty. He'd sung "God Save the Queen." And it hadn't happened last month, but years ago. That story seemed to resurrect itself every couple of years. And in his defense, he'd downed a bottle of vintage Perrier-Jouët champagne earlier, after his father had given him a direct cut at Tattersalls. Everyone at the horse auctioneers had noticed his father's refusal to talk to him, casting more speculation as to what had caused the rift. As if his stepmother's innuendoes that Simon was depraved hadn't already cut him off from the high sticklers. He'd become a leper in some circles. Persona non grata.

Emma set her fork down none too gently, drawing Simon from his thoughts. "Mrs. Jenkins is a gossipmonger and her stories are suspect at best, but I fear some members of the nobility don't hold the Queen's regard for morality. Let us not talk about such scoundrels."

It appeared Emma was *not* his champion. It also appeared she didn't hold certain members of the peerage, such as himself, in high regard.

"But what about Charles?" Lily asked, stepping back in the room and sitting. "One day, he'll be a baron, right? And if you had married him, you would have become a baroness."

The pink singeing Emma's cheeks darkened. "Hush, Lily."

So Emma had been engaged to a nobleman's son.

"That Charles Neville is a good-for-nothing." The housekeeper cut a piece of meat as though she were slicing off a piece of the man's anatomy.

Charles Neville? Lord Everly's son? He didn't really know the young man that well, though they both belonged to the same boxing club, but he thought Charles arrogant. While Neville's father, Everly, was a pompous blowhard. Hadn't Charles Neville recently married the Earl of Dalman's daughter?

Lily looked as though she wished to say more, but feared another swift kick under the table if she spoke again.

"No-good wretch." Mrs. Flynn stabbed her fork into a potato as if it were one of Charles Neville's bollocks.

"Did you see today's newspaper article about William Russell?" Emma asked, sounding eager to change the subject. "He's completed his book about the Prince of Wales's trip to India."

"The Prince. Hmm, another bad seed," Mrs. Flynn mumbled.

Emma shot the older woman a silencing look.

The housekeeper gave a clearly forced smile. "I mean how wonderful."

"I think it would be exciting to go to India," Lily said. "Inspector Whitley journeyed there in his novel *The Tiger's Eye*."

"I've never read any of the inspector's books," Simon said, thankful for the turn in the conversation. "I might have to purchase one."

Lily actually smiled at him. "I think you would enjoy them, especially *The Man of St. Giles*. It is about a fellow who works in a bank during the day. Everyone thinks him a fine gent, but he's really a murderer."

Emma narrowed her eyes at her sister, and Lily jerked her chair back as if expecting another kick to her shins.

"I've made roly-poly jam pudding for dessert." The housekeeper stood.

"That sounds lovely, Mrs. Flynn. Would you care for some, Mr. Radcliffe?" Emma asked.

"How could I refuse?" he replied.

Beaming, Mrs. Flynn left the room. She returned a minute later with two plates, each with a thick slice of the dessert on it. She set one before Emma and the other in front of him.

"Where's mine?" Lily grumbled.

"You and I are going to eat ours in the kitchen." Mrs. Flynn grabbed Lily's arm.

Emma's gaze snapped to the housekeeper. She opened her mouth, but Mrs. Flynn was already dragging the younger Trafford out of the room.

"I'm so very sorry, Mr. Radcliffe," Emma said after they'd left. "I'm not sure what Mrs. Flynn is about." Blushing, she lowered her lashes and brought the mixture of raspberry jam and pudding to her lips.

Simon's groin tightened. More than once, he'd partaken in debauchery that had included a sumptuous dessert. And the thought of engaging in such an activity with Emma Trafford appealed to him more than he wished to admit. *Good Lord, man, what is wrong with you?*

Needing a distraction, Simon mulled over what Lily revealed about Emma being betrothed to Charles Neville. Had the man found out she wasn't as sweet as she appeared? Simon recalled the pained look in Emma's eyes when Lily spoke of Neville, along with the way Mrs. Flynn had jabbed at her food, and Emma's own words about the nobility. Had it been Neville who proved untrustworthy? Hurt Emma? Simon shouldn't care, but the question clawed at him.

"So you were engaged to this baron's son, Charles Neville?" Simon knew it the height of impropriety to ask such a personal question.

The color of her already rosy cheeks darkened, and the fork in Emma's delicate hand, with a piece of dessert perched on its tines, stilled. "I was."

"Might I ask where you met him?"

She placed her utensil on her dessert dish and folded her hands on her lap.

"We met at the British Museum. As I told you earlier, I visited quite often while my father worked there. One day while drawing in the Elgin Room, Charles approached me and asked about my sketches. We struck up an acquaintance, and every Friday when I would go to the museum to wait for Father, Charles would show up. He'd sit on the bench beside me and watch me sketch, and we'd talk about art. At first it made me self-conscious, but I became used to seeing him there. I even looked forward to it."

"And he asked you to marry him?"

She lifted her napkin and dabbed at her lips. "You're as inquisitive as a barrister in court, Mr. Radcliffe."

He forced what he hoped looked like a sheepish expression. "Forgive me."

She stared at him with those dark blue eyes of hers and gave a weak smile. "I'm not sure why, but talking about this with you doesn't bother me. Yes, he asked for my hand after my father died."

There was melancholy in her voice, and Simon had a feeling this tale didn't have a happy ending for Emma—that there was more to her story. He knew what that felt like. Anger swelled inside him. "What happened?"

"When Charles's father found out his son had asked for my hand . . . Let us just say the man didn't approve."

"He breached his promise? Walked away?"

She nodded. "Some members of the nobility live by their own rules."

"You don't hold the nobility in high regard?"

"Some are not deserving of my regard." She drew in an audible breath. "Were you ever close to marrying?"

Yes, long ago. A marriage between him and Lady Alice

Granger of Yorkshire had been arranged by their parents when they were children. Alice and he had corresponded for years. She'd seemed willing to dismiss the gossip about him as balderdash. However, when nineteen, he'd traveled to the North Country to meet her. At the time his scar was still an angry red slash on his face, and he could see it repulsed her. "Once, but we drifted apart."

"Em!" Lily dashed into the room. The child's breath sawed in and out of her lungs. "Come quick. That deuced pipe in the kitchen is spitting water all over the place again, and poor Mrs. Flynn's trying to stop it."

"Oh heavens!" Emma dashed toward the door. "Mr. Radcliffe, I do beg your forgiveness, but I fear I must tend to this."

He stood. "Of course, but I shall accompany you to the kitchen. Perhaps I can fix—"

"Thank you, but no. This has happened before and I'm aware of what needs to be done."

Ignoring her assurance, Simon tossed his napkin on the table and followed her. She might know what needed to be done, but he'd not sit upstairs indulging in dessert while she worked on a plumbing leak.

In the kitchen, Mrs. Flynn stood near the sink, her beefy hands wrapped about an iron pipe spitting water through her fingers and drenching the front of the woman's white apron. "I cannot hold it much longer, miss!"

Emma rushed to a tall cabinet in the corner of the room and pulled out a large wrench. The weight of the tool pulled her shoulders down as she clasped it with both hands.

"Let me have that." Simon shrugged out of his coat and rolled up his shirtsleeves.

Emma peered at him. "No, Mr. Radcliffe, your clothing will be ruined. I assure you, I can handle this."

"I'm confident you can, but I wish to help." He took the wrench from her.

"Do you know how to use it?" Lily asked him, doubt in her voice.

He shot the child a haughty look and stepped up to the pipe. Mrs. Flynn released it and shifted back. Frigid water squirted outward, drenching his face and waistcoat. He set the tool on the joint and turned it.

The water leaking from the pipe increased like a geyser.

"Isn't he turning it the wrong way?" Lily asked the room at large.

Bloody hell! Of course I am! He didn't know a damn thing about plumbing. He set the wrench back on the joint and turned it the opposite way. The water became a trickle. Putting his weight into it, he gave it another firm twist.

The water ceased.

"Well done, Mr. Radcliffe," Lily exclaimed. "Em never gets the leak to completely stop. She usually just wraps some rags about it and puts a bucket underneath to catch the drips."

He grinned, some odd sense of satisfaction welling up in his chest.

Emma stepped up to him and softly dabbed a flannel across his wet face. Unlike so many women, her gaze stayed on his eyes instead of shifting to his scar. "Thank you, Mr. Radcliffe. How kind of you."

He stared into her blue eyes. They really were a fascinating shade, like bright sapphires.

Clearing her throat, Mrs. Flynn took the wrench from his hand. "If you take off your wet waistcoat, Mr. Radcliffe. I shall hang it by the stove."

"You really should remove all your clothes," Emma said.

"Really? All of them?" Amusement laced his voice.

Lily giggled.

As if suddenly realizing her words, Emma's cheeks turned red. "I mean, you should return home and change into dry clothes, so you don't catch a chill."

He supposed he should, yet he didn't want to go home. This house seemed so much warmer than his. And even though the piano needed tuning, he'd hoped to play it again. Simon tossed those thoughts from his head. Once again, he was forgetting his objective: to find out if Emma was his thief.

"Yes, I should get going. Thank you for such a lovely meal."

"I'll walk you to the door." Emma motioned to the stairs.

In the entry hall, she handed him his hat and gloves. "Thank you, Mr. Radcliffe, for your assistance with those two drunkards."

"Please call me Simon," he said.

"Simon," she repeated, her cheeks a lovely shade of pink. "And you may call me Emma."

Neither of them moved. Was she experiencing the same current toward him that he'd been experiencing for her ever since they'd stood in that dim alley? The same odd sensation he'd experienced when he'd kissed his thief in the dark. *His thief. Damnation, why am I continually losing my perspective on this situation?*

"You will return for another sitting tomorrow at two o'clock?" she asked.

"Yes, perfect." As if unable to stop himself, he stepped closer. His legs brushed against her skirts. The enticing scent of roses and soap filled his nose. He tucked a loose tendril of hair behind her ear, then skimmed the pads of his fingers across her neck to where her pulse beat. The steady patter picked up tempo, and a small lump moved in her throat as he lowered his head.

"Ahem."

Straightening, both their gazes swung to Lily standing near the basement stairs, her arms crossed over her chest.

"Goodnight, sir," Emma said, taking a sizable step back.

Simon opened the door. "Thank you again for a lovely meal."

As soon as Simon entered his residence, both Baines and Harris dashed up to him.

"You look like a drowned rat, my lord." The valet's gaze veered to the transom above the door. "Has it started raining?"

"I helped fix a plumbing leak at the Trafford residence." Simon heard the pride in his own voice.

"Are you sure you fixed it? Looks more like you stood under it," Harris said.

Simon scowled at the man.

"You know nothing about how to repair plumbing," Baines added. "And surely, it isn't something a gentleman should attempt. Perhaps you're feverish, sir?" The valet reached up as if to gauge the temperature of Simon's forehead.

Simon waved the man away. "I'm not feverish."

"Well, those wet clothes cannot be conducive to good health. Let's get you into some dry clothes," Baines said as if talking to a small child.

"I don't need your assistance." Ignoring Baines's protestation, Simon took the stairs two at a time. Inside his bedroom he strode to the window, and as he'd done numerous times before, he peered at Emma's residence. Though this time he didn't stare at the house hoping to learn something new. No, this time he stared at it wishing he was still inside.

Chapter Fifteen

Bright streaks of early morning sun cut through the window, casting a wide band of light across Simon's desk in his Bloomsbury residence. Restless, and finding sleep elusive, he'd risen earlier than usual. He stuffed his note to Mr. Marlow inside an envelope, along with several banknotes. Simon handed it to Nick, who stood patiently waiting before the desk, and tossed the lad a shilling.

Sporting a wide grin, Nick snatched the coin out of the air and slipped it into his tattered coat pocket.

"Not a word about this, especially to Lily. Are we clear?"

Nick nodded his head. "She won't get a word out of me, sir. Not. A. Word."

"Good lad."

The boy's stomach rumbled.

Simon doubted Nick had eaten. Every morning the boy showed up looking disheveled. Most likely his parents worked from dawn to dusk at some factory, leaving the child to fend for himself. Simon tossed him another coin. "That bakery on Theobald's Road sells hot cross buns. Buy yourself a couple."

"Thank you, sir. Do you want some too?"

An appealing idea. Baines would probably serve the same thing he cooked every morning: runny eggs, burnt toast, and bacon rashers as tough as a horse's hoof. He tossed Nick another shilling and winked. "You're a bright lad. Sneak me two."

"Will do, guv'ner. Will do." Nick darted out the doorway.

Harris walked into the office. Without a word, he placed the morning newspaper on Simon's desk, then exited the room as if it reeked of decomposing fish heads.

It appeared the man wasn't talking to him. He knew why. Last night Baines had walked into Simon's bedchamber to find him staring at Emma's house. The valet had accused him of being smitten.

Smitten. What poppycock. And when he'd refuted the claim, Baines had had the audacity to argue with him.

Simon *wasn't* interested in Emma Trafford. He'd nearly kissed her because he hoped to see if the kiss sparked a recollection. And his obsession was with the woman's home. It had more to do with Mrs. Flynn's cooking and the worn but comfortable furnishings that didn't have flamingos stitched on them. It definitely had nothing to do with Emma's smile, or the scent of her skin, or that she'd shown him her brother's letter and asked Simon about his own boyhood. Or that while he'd fixed the pipe, he'd felt like part of a family. And it surely had nothing to do with her hoyden sister.

Angry over Baines's gibberish, he'd threatened to banish the interfering man to the North Country. Now Harris was acting like Simon had kicked a beloved dog, and Baines was moping about as dejected as a wallflower at a ball.

Kismet, who sat on the windowsill, shot Simon a narrow-eyed glare.

"You too?"

The white cat jumped down and walked out of the room, his tail swishing in the air.

"It isn't like I'd actually do it," he called after the feline. Though at times the idea of sending both the old retainers away held immeasurable appeal.

You'd miss them, a voice in his head whispered.

Like one would miss a toothache.

Simon picked up the newspaper. As he read the political section, he noted the bent corner of another page. Damnation, the old coots had bookmarked something they found interesting. And usually what they found interesting pertained to Simon on the scandal page.

Gritting his teeth, he flipped to the dog-eared section.

> *It is rumored that the always scandalous Lord A drove through Hyde Park, dismounted his carriage, and took a leisurely swim in the Serpentine while fully clothed, shoes and all. He was accompanied by a woman with long, flowing red hair, who championed his strokes from the banks of the lake.*

Simon took a deep breath. Another Banbury tale. He hadn't driven through Hyde Park in months, but at least in this escapade he wasn't half-naked. Now that his stepmother had returned to London, was Julia up to her old tricks, spreading lies about him?

Harris walked into the office and dragged a dirty feather duster over the round table in the corner of the room, sending dust motes dancing through the sundrenched air.

Simon coughed. So this was how it was going to be. He

shouldn't care. The two men were servants. Yet in truth, he'd come to care for them as if they were two elderly, obnoxious uncles.

Family. The only family he had. They'd stood by him after his father had banished him. An unwelcome stab of guilt drifted through his conscience.

"How are you today, Harris?" Simon set the newspaper down.

"Well, sir," Harris replied in a clipped tone.

"Did Baines tutor Nick this morning?" He knew the answer. When Simon had walked by the drawing room, he'd heard the lad complaining about being taught to read using books meant for babies. But Baines had replied that one couldn't just jump into reading Charles Dickens.

"Yes." The butler's lips remained in a straight line.

"And what is Baines about now?"

"He's cooking breakfast."

The thought of eating the valet's food held as much appeal as walking on hot coals. He swallowed that thought and lied. "I'm looking forward to it."

The butler's lips twitched before he ruthlessly straightened them again.

Baines stepped into the room. His eyes looked tired. Had the valet slept poorly? Simon's guilt increased twofold.

"Sir, your breakfast is ready," the manservant said, his voice low and scratchy. "Do you wish to eat in the dining room or take your meal in here?"

Here would be better, since Simon could feed the food to Kismet undetected. He thought of how Mrs. Flynn had joined Emma and Lily for dinner. Maybe if he asked the manservants to join him all would be forgiven. "I would like us to eat breakfast together today."

Harris's bushy gray eyebrows shot upward. The man's

gaze veered to the decanter of whisky on the sideboard as though he feared Simon had drained it dry.

Wide-eyed, Baines wiggled a finger in his ear as if trying to dislodge wax. "Together, my lord?"

Simon sighed. "Yes. That's what I said."

"Most improper," Harris responded. The butler had the audacity to lean forward and try to sniff Simon's breath.

"Dash it all, man, I've not been drinking," Simon snapped. "Never mind. Just wheel the bloody cart in here."

The two old coots bowed their heads together. Baines cupped a hand to his mouth and spoke in his approximation of a whisper. "Do you think he's drunk?"

Harris shook his head. "No, I don't think so. His breath smells like the neroli oil in his tooth powder."

"Why must the two of you always presume I'm three sheets to the wind? Contrary to what those blasted scandal sheets say, I haven't been drunk in years."

The two manservants' faces flushed red.

"You heard us, my lord?" Harris asked.

"The neighbors most likely heard you. Even that old fellow up the street with the hearing trumpet most likely heard you. You were conversing in exceedingly loud voices."

"We were not, my lord," Baines replied, indignation in his voice.

Simon rubbed at his temples, fighting the urge to toss them both out of the room. "Do you wish to join me for breakfast or not?"

The two elderly men stared at each other, then Harris said, "We would be honored to break our fast with you."

The corners of Baines's lips turned upward. "Yes, we'd quite enjoy it."

Simon gave a succinct nod, wondering for the umpteenth time if that conk to his head had dislodged the circuits in his brain, or if there was something evil in the water in Bloomsbury. It seemed the only explanation for why he'd asked the two old goats to breakfast with him and why he couldn't stop thinking of Emma Trafford.

With a heavy sigh, Emma placed a postage stamp on the letter she'd penned to Michael. Even though she agreed with Simon that her brother's last correspondence wasn't that unusual for a lad at school, she still couldn't stifle the unnerving sensation that something was wrong.

As she stood from the secretaire in the morning room, the knocker tapped firmly against the front door.

She opened it to find a thin man with a long nose, wearing a green sack suit, bright red waistcoat, and flamboyant yellow bow tie. In his hand, he clutched a brown leather satchel. His attire, along with his prominent nose and overlarge teeth, made him resemble the illustration of the Mad Hatter from *Alice's Adventures in Wonderland*.

Without waiting to be invited in, the man entered the house like she'd been expecting him. He doffed his top hat. "Good morning, ma'am. Patrick Marlow, master piano tuner."

Piano tuner? "I'm sorry, sir, but I believe you have the wrong address."

He set his brown leather satchel down and removed a piece of folded paper from his coat pocket. "Miss Trafford?"

Had a neighbor summoned him, thinking that Lily's piano playing could be improved by tuning the instrument? A laughable notion indeed. The child was skilled; it was her attitude that was lacking. "Yes, but—"

"I'm on a schedule, ma'am. No time to dawdle. I've got several more calls to make in Mayfair." Impatiently Mr.

Marlow plucked his watch from his waistcoat pocket and flicked it open. The gold-faced timepiece looked costly.

Egad, what does the man charge for his services? "What will be the cost?"

He peered down his overlong nose at her, as if asking him such a question verged on vulgarity. With an exaggerated sniff, he tucked his watch back in his pocket. "The matter of payment has already been settled."

"I don't understand. You mean to say someone has already paid you? Who?"

"I'm not at liberty to say."

She glanced past the man's shoulder and beyond the open door to Simon's residence. A tall form stood at a second-floor window. "Did Mr. Radcliffe send you?"

"Mr. Radcliffe? I've no idea who that is. And as I said, your benefactor wishes to remain anonymous. Now might I inquire where your piano is?" He tapped his foot impatiently against the floor.

Lily's feet thundered on the treads as she ran down the stairs. Upon reaching the entry hall, the child stared at Mr. Marlow and abruptly stopped. Her head bobbed up, then down as her gaze traveled over the man's colorful attire. A grin lit up Lily's face, and she clapped a hand over her mouth and giggled.

"Lily," Emma said in a warning tone, fearing the child would say out loud that the man resembled a cartoonish illustration.

The housekeeper appeared in the entry hall.

"Mrs. Flynn, would you please show Mr. Marlow to the drawing room. He is here to tune the piano."

Without waiting for the older woman's reply, Emma grabbed her navy shawl off the wall hook and stepped outside.

As she strode to Simon's town house, she glanced up at

the window where she'd seen him standing. It was now vacant. Emma dropped the knocker against his door.

Harris answered.

"Is Mr. Radcliffe home?"

This time the stern-looking servant didn't ask for a calling card, but nodded. "This way, miss."

He led her to a room directly off the entry hall. Purple-flocked paper covered the walls. She glanced around, hoping to see the painting he'd purchased from her of the family walking in the park, but it was nowhere in sight. Emma blinked at the two purple-and-gold chairs. They appeared to have bright embroidered spots on them. She leaned close.

My goodness, are they flamingos? Yes, stitched in bright pink silk. It seemed inconceivable that Simon Radcliffe owned such silly looking chairs. A laugh escaped her lips.

Someone cleared his throat.

Emma spun around.

In all his harsh beauty, Simon stood in the doorway, dressed in a crisp white shirt with the sleeves folded up, revealing corded muscles. For a second, she found it impossible to pull her gaze away from his forearms and the scattering of dark hair on them. He stepped into the room. His tall, broad-shouldered body made the tight space feel even more closed in.

"Emma." The sound of her name on his lips, the familiarity in which he said it, caused a low hum to vibrate through her limbs.

"I wished to ask you something," she said.

"And what is that?" He closed the distance between them.

The exotic scent of citrus, spice, and male filled her nose, making her already strained senses snap to alert. "There is a piano tuner at my residence. Did you send him?"

"No."

She was nearly positive it was him. What type of game was he playing? "I'm not sure I believe you."

"Really?" He stepped even closer.

The proximity of his body pulled at her like a magnet. She fought the urge to erase the narrow distance that separated them.

Thankfully, Baines stepped into the room.

Simon's intense gaze shifted to where the servant stood. He took a deep breath, as if bolstering his patience. "Do you need something, Baines?"

The white cat that Emma had seen when she and Lily broke into Simon's house darted into the room.

"I was looking for Kismet," the manservant said, as if the excuse suddenly came upon him.

With its tail held high, the animal pranced up to Emma and rubbed his slinky body on the skirt of her simple green day dress as though Emma had rolled herself in catnip. She reached down and picked up the fluffy feline.

Kismet purred, craned his head, and smoothed his whiskered face against her cheek.

"That's odd." A furrow appeared between Baines's gray brows. "Kismet isn't normally so affectionate with strangers."

"Yes. It's like he's met you before." Simon's dark eyes pierced her.

Emma's heart skipped a beat. Her mouth grew dry. The cat nudged her hand. "Ouch! He bit my finger," she lied. Attempting to look in pain, she gave the cat to Mr. Baines. "You are correct. He isn't very fond of strangers."

"Really?" Simon said, an expression of disbelief etched upon his granite face. "I didn't see him bite you."

"He did," she averred.

Simon peered at her finger and his warm hand curled around her wrist to examine her fake injury.

Baines leaned over Simon's shoulder and stared at her finger as well.

Without releasing her, Simon said, "Baines, would you mind taking Kismet from the room before he *violently* attacks Miss Trafford again?"

The valet looked as if he didn't wish to leave. Did the manservant realize Emma's brain turned to mush when Simon stood near?

Simon cocked one dark eyebrow at the man.

Looking resigned, Baines nodded.

As the servant strode from the room, Simon called over his shoulder, "Close the door behind you, Baines, so Kismet doesn't run back in here."

The door clicked closed.

"I should go," Emma said, her heart picking up speed. "It might not look devastatingly painful, but my injury burns terribly."

"Really?" Simon lifted her finger to his lips and drew it into his mouth.

She gasped, but didn't step back, mesmerized by the sight. How wicked. Erotic. Her knees grew weak. She should slap him, but could do little more than stare as an odd sensation flittered in her stomach, while her breathing quickened.

He released her finger and blew on it, a light puff of breath.

The hairs on her nape stood on end.

"Better?" he asked.

Gosh, no. Wanton thoughts raced through her mind. She wanted to press herself against the hard surface of his body. Worse, she wanted him to blow on every inch of her skin to douse the heat now coursing through her veins. How naughty she was. Perhaps it hadn't been the melancholy of losing Father that had made her succumb to Charles. Might she possess an innate wickedness?

She shoved that unsettling thought aside. "Um, yes. I really should return home."

"Really?" There was a smile in his voice as if he could read her thoughts—knew what his touch had done to both her body and mind. He shifted closer, erasing the sliver of air between them.

Her heart beat fast, yet a frenzied anticipation swirled within her. She fought the desire to wet her lips.

The weight of his hand settled on her waist, each finger a separate point of contact. Heavy. Possessive. "I've been thinking of last night. Twice I wanted to kiss you, and twice we were interrupted. Have you thought about it, Emma?" He didn't wait for her response. His mouth touched hers and moved against it.

Heart still pounding against her chest, she parted her lips, inviting him to kiss her the way he had on that dark night in his residence, with a hunger that had left an undeniable mark on her memory—a wicked craving she'd *never* experienced before.

His tongue stroked hers.

More heat traveled through her body, reminding her one could get scorched playing with fire, and burned by one's own carelessness. Simon Radcliffe was on a mission. He would turn her life upside down, destroy her, if she let her guard down. Yet, she wanted to touch him again—to experience the feel of his hard body once more. She slid her palms up his shoulders. One hand continued its journey upward until her fingers combed through the hair at his nape, each strand warm and silky.

Uttering a deep moan, he cupped the back of her head,

while his tongue continued its erotic slide. His right hand shifted upward until his palm rested against the side of her breast.

Her nipples peaked. Her breasts tingled.

A knock rapped against the door, and Emma jumped back.

Chapter Sixteen

As the drawing room door opened, heat warmed Emma's cheeks. On wobbly legs, she took another step away from Simon.

His two elderly servants peeked around its edge.

"I'm going to strangle both of them," Simon mumbled, shooting both men a lethal look as they stepped fully into the room.

Thank goodness Lily wasn't here. If she'd heard Simon, her sister would once again start raving about him being a murderer. And by the unfiltered expression on his face, at this moment, Emma feared him quite capable of the task.

Ignoring Simon's glower, the stoic-faced butler held up a brown medicinal bottle. "Witch hazel for Miss Trafford's injury."

Emma peered down at her uninjured finger. The heat on her face traveled to her ears. "How thoughtful, but it feels much improved. Though I thank you for your kindness." *And your timely entrance.* Simon might brand the men as interfering, but Emma believed Harris and Baines to be her saviors—fairy godfathers protecting her from her own foolishness.

Without saying a word, Simon strode to the window and

shoved the lower sash upward. Either he was in need of fresh air or contemplating throwing both men out of it.

Though they seemed aware of their employer's discontent, the two servants appeared reluctant to leave the room. Were they worried about her virtue?

"Are you sure?" the butler asked, returning his regard to her.

"Yes, thank you." She peered at Simon's broad-shouldered back, remembered the feel of her hands on him, the exquisite heat of his body, and his knee-weakening kiss. "Mr. Radcliffe, I must take my leave."

He spun away from the window and stared at her as if commanding an explanation.

She cleared her throat. "Mrs. Flynn and Lily must be wondering where I've gone off to."

He nodded. "Then I will see you in a couple of hours for my sitting."

She didn't wish to spend the afternoon with him. Not after that kiss. Her body still hummed with something she could only describe as need, as though she'd been given only a sip of water after an arduous trek and needed more to quench her thirst.

"Sir, I fear I must cancel our sitting this afternoon."

His already dark expression turned stormy.

Emma had a feeling very few, if anyone, crossed this man's path when he stared at them as he did her now. She forced an amiable smile. "I must help Mrs. Flynn make bread."

One of his dark eyebrows arched as if he knew it a blatant lie.

"Then you must go." The cool tone of his voice sent a shiver down her spine.

"Good day." She nodded at him and his two servants, then strode to the door.

"Miss Trafford?" Simon said.

She turned around. "Yes."

"Will you resume working on my portrait tomorrow?"

She heard the challenge in his voice. Hopefully by tomorrow her foolish desire would be gone and her melting brain returned to normal. "Of course."

"Then I will see you then."

As she stepped out of Simon's house, Emma could feel him watching her. Trying not to run like a scared rabbit, she crossed the street and entered her house.

Mrs. Flynn stepped into the entry hall. "Where'd you rush off to, dearie?"

"I needed to speak with Mr. Radcliffe."

The housekeeper cocked her head toward the sound of the piano keys being struck, one at a time.

"Did he send that stuffy piano tuner here?"

"He said no." She was almost sure he had. Simon appeared capable of lying without even a hint of deception on his face. She needed to remember that, along with the fact that he was searching for whoever had broken into his house and stolen his ring.

"Then who sent him?"

"I believe he did."

A wide smile blossomed on the housekeeper's face. "I told you, dearie, he is quite taken by you."

Emma touched her still tingling lips. Realizing the action, she lowered her hand. "If he sent Mr. Marlow here to tune the piano, it is only because he seeks salvation for his ears."

Mrs. Flynn made a noise of disbelief. "Whatever the cause, I still say he's infatuated."

Pish. The man was up to no good. Most likely trying to confuse her and force her to lower her guard and confess.

"Did you see Mr. Baines?" Mrs. Flynn asked, breaking into Emma's thoughts.

"I did."

Pink heightened the woman's cheeks.

How lovely it would be if Mr. Baines returned Mrs. Flynn's regard. Though Lily, Michael, and she would miss the older woman dearly if the housekeeper got married and left. But Mrs. Flynn deserved happiness, and Emma wished that for her, more than anything.

"Do you intend to bake bread today?" Emma asked.

"Yes. Just about to start."

"I think I'll help you."

"Really?" The woman's eyes widened.

"Yes." Truthfully, Emma would rather paint, but perhaps if she helped it would ease her conscience about lying and distract her from what had transpired between her and Simon.

A twinkle sparkled in the woman's brown eyes. "We could send a loaf to Mr. Radcliffe, so he might see how skilled you are in the kitchen."

"Ha! I am not skilled in the kitchen and we both know that."

"Since the gentleman is in possession of a fine carriage and not one, but two manservants, he can hire me if he marries you, but it would serve you well to at least impress him with a few basic dishes."

Marry? Emma doubted Mr. Radcliffe was hunting for a wife. He was hunting for a thief, and mayhap a little enjoyment on the side. And she had been foolish enough to give it to him.

Simon watched Emma enter her house. He rubbed the knot in his neck. He'd known sending the piano tuner to her house would have her knocking on his door. He'd wanted to gain her trust. His kiss was meant to send her off balance. Instead he'd not only scared her away, he'd enjoyed the escapade.

He slammed his fist against the window jamb, rattling the glass panes. What the bloody hell was wrong with him? She would not thwart him. He would find out the truth. But what truth did he seek when he kissed her? Her guilt or innocence? Or nothing more than the press of her lips on his?

"Ahem." Someone cleared his throat.

He turned to see both Baines and Harris staring at him. He'd forgotten they stood in the room. "Go away," he snapped, trying not to scold them. He slumped into the flamingo-patterned chair by the window and waved them off like the pesky flies they mimicked.

"Are you to luncheon at home today, sir?" Harris asked.

"I am preparing lamb with rosemary and potatoes." Baines puffed out his chest like a proud peacock.

It will probably taste like cowhide. He needed to insist they hire a cook. Simon flicked an imaginary piece of lint off his sleeve while scouring his mind for the best way to word his request. He glanced back up. Baines appeared ready to explode with excitement.

Damn. Why he didn't wish to disappoint the man was beyond his comprehension. There was definitely something in the water in Bloomsbury. Something sinister, if it was turning him into a milksop. "Yes, that sounds . . . tasty."

"Very well, sir. Very well," Baines said, his voice elevated with pleasure. "When Nick returns with the fresh rosemary, I'll start seasoning the meat."

Simon's stomach made a noise.

"Ah, you are hungry," Harris said.

He didn't think it was hunger that made his stomach rumble—more likely fear.

"He didn't eat very much at breakfast," Baines said.

Not true. He'd eaten the two sweet buns Nick had brought him from the bakery, but he couldn't tell Baines that.

"I shall start preparing the meal, posthaste. Come, Harris, you can help me."

The butler sighed, but followed Baines from the room.

Simon closed his eyes and thought of the kiss he and Emma had just shared. That damned appendage in his trousers twitched and grew hard. *Get a grip on yourself, man. It was a bloody kiss, nothing more.* Though as tantalizing as the one he'd shared with his thief. His whole body had warmed like a heated grate. Merely a coincidence?

The front door opened and slammed closed. Nick stepped into the entry hall, carrying what looked like a bouquet of pine needles. Most likely it was the rosemary Baines waited upon. Without noticing Simon, the lad dashed by the drawing room's open doorway.

"Nick," Simon called out.

The boy's heavy footfalls stilled, then returned. Nick entered the drawing room and slipped off his flat cap. "Sorry, sir. I didn't see you there."

"After you give Baines the rosemary, I wish to speak with you."

Nick crushed the cap in his hands and shuffled his feet. "Did I do something wrong, sir?"

"Not at all. I wish to give you something."

Relief flashed across the lad's face. He nodded. "Be back in a wink of an eye, sir."

Simon stood and retrieved a copy of *The Crimson Lord*, one of the Inspector Whitley mystery books Lily enjoyed. Simon had sent Baines to buy two copies. One for himself and another for the lad.

Nick dashed back into the room.

"Baines tells me you are a quick study. That you're progressing quite rapidly with your reading."

The lad grinned. "I am, sir."

"I heard Lily speak of this author." Simon handed him the book. "I thought you might enjoy it as well."

"*The Cri-Crimson Lo-ord.*" The boy blinked. "This is for me? Thank you, sir."

An hour later, Simon leaned back in one of the chairs in his drawing room and grinned at a passage in *The Crimson Lord*. Surely, the penny dreadful wasn't meant to be humorous, but the way Inspector Whitley solved everything with just a quick glance at the evidence was more than amusing.

He lowered the book and glanced at Nick sitting on the other chair reading his copy. Nick's expression contradicted Simon's. The boy nervously bit his lower lip and flipped a page.

A noise outside the window caught Simon's attention. Lily, wearing a light blue cotton dress, matching hair ribbons, and flat-heeled button boots, squealed with excitement as she and two other girls rolled their trundling hoops up the street.

Nick lowered his book and glanced outside. The lad's expression reflected how he desperately wanted to join in the fun.

"Have you ever rolled a hoop before?" Simon asked.

Nick blanked his expression. "Nah, that's for babies."

"Really? I've always wished to try my hand at it. What do you say we see if Lily will let us give it a go?"

Excitement sparked in the boy's eyes, even though his face retained its bland countenance. Simon moved to the entry hall and stepped outside. Nick followed. As they approached the children, Lily glanced up and stopped. The two other girls continued up the street and turned onto Theobald's Road.

As he and Nick approached the chit, her blue eyes widened. She grabbed the trundling hoop and held it tight, as if fearing Simon intended to snatch it away.

"May Nick give it a go?" Simon asked.

The boy's shoulders sagged, as if Simon was forcing him to try something against his will.

Without uttering a sound, Lily held the wooden wheel and stick out to the lad.

A small, nearly imperceivable smile settled on the boy's face. He glanced at Simon. "If you insist, sir, I'll give it a try."

Nick placed the wheel on the pavement and smacked it with the end of the stick. It rolled a mere three feet, wobbled, and toppled over.

"You've got to give it a start with your hand." Lily moved over to Nick and took both items back. She tossed the hoop. It flew a few inches off the pavement before it rolled. She tapped it firmly with the stick as she ran beside it. "Don't use the end of the stick; hit it with the middle. The pressure must be even. Too much to one side or the other and it will wobble and fall."

Nick jogged next to Lily as she rolled the hoop.

"Here," she said, handing the stick to him. "Give it a go."

Nick hit it where she'd instructed, and it moved farther up the pavement.

"That's it. That's it!" Lily yelled, running beside the lad.

Though Simon couldn't see the boy's face, he could imagine the child's smile. Nick grabbed the hoop as he neared the crossroad and turned around. Indeed, a large smile lit up the child's face. Nick offered the toy back to Lily. She shook her head and said something. Nick's smile broadened even more as he set the toy back to the pavement and started rolling it to where Simon stood.

Mrs. Jenkins's front door swung open. "Be careful of your shins, Mr. Radcliffe! Those hoops are a menace!"

Silly old interfering crow. It wasn't even metal, and Nick maneuvered it like a champion. An odd, almost paternal, feeling tightened Simon's chest.

The children's footfalls and giggles grew louder. Bright-eyed, Lily and Nick smiled at each other as though they were longtime friends.

"Now your turn, Mr. Radcliffe," Lily said. "Nick told me you wanted to give it a go. You've never rolled a hoop either?"

"No, I can't say I ever have. And I doubt I'll be as skilled as Nick."

"You won't know until you try, sir," Nick said.

"True." Simon shrugged out of his coat and folded the garment over the wrought iron fence in front of Emma's house. He unclasped his gold cufflinks, slipped them into his trouser pocket, and rolled up his sleeves.

Nick handed him the toy. With a flick of his wrist, Simon tossed the trundling hoop; it landed several feet in front of him, wobbled, but didn't fall.

"Hit it," Lily screamed.

He did as instructed, and the wheel picked up speed. The children's fast footsteps, pounding on the pavement, and their laughter filled the air as they ran behind him. A smile turned up the corners of Simon's lips. He neared the crossway.

"How do I turn it?" he called over his shoulder.

"Slowly," Lily replied. "Take it off the curb and into the street. Make a wide turn, otherwise it will topple. You can do it. You've got enough momentum and no carriages are coming."

Simon gave it another firm tap with the stick. It moved at a fast clip off the curb with a little hop and wobbled, but didn't fall.

"Turn it. That's it. Hit it again," Lily instructed.

He did and it picked up more momentum.

Lily laughed, the sound infectious.

Grinning, Simon glanced up. Mrs. Jenkins stood on her step, her face puckered as if she sucked a lemon.

Harris stood at the door of Simon's residence, gaping. "Sir, you are in your shirtsleeves."

"Indeed, I am." Simon passed the gawking pair with the children running alongside him.

"That child has corrupted poor Mr. Radcliffe," Mrs. Jenkins huffed.

Simon laughed. The old prune would have an apoplexy if she knew his true identity. He had half a mind to stop and tell her, so he could watch her faint dead away. He looked at the children's smiling faces and spoke in a low voice, "Ignore the gargoyle, she wouldn't know fun if it bit her in the ar . . . um, toe."

Lily's mouth gaped, then she giggled.

Nick burst out laughing.

At the end of the street, Simon grabbed the wheel before it flew into the crossroad. Grinning, he swiped his arm across his forehead. "That was dashed fun."

Nick nodded, braced his hands on his knees, and took several labored breaths.

Air sawing in and out of her lungs, Lily tucked a long blond tendril behind her ear, which had fallen from her braid. "Capital job, Mr. Radcliffe! You've got the hang of it, and you're fast." She took a couple more winded breaths. "You'd drub Timmy Johnson in a race, and he's the fastest hoop roller in all of Bloomsbury."

"You would, indeed, sir," Nick added.

Simon handed the hoop and stick back to Lily. She set it on the cobbles and rolled it as they headed back. As they neared the Trafford town house, he noticed Emma standing on the pavement.

Lily sighed. "We're in trouble."

"It appears so. What offense have we committed?" Simon rolled his sleeves down.

"I'm not allowed to trundle my hoop in the street."

"Ah." He ran his gaze over Emma. She looked like she wanted to give him a tongue-lashing. A vision of her pink tongue traveling over him flashed in his thoughts, though he doubted that was what she had in mind. He shoved the lurid image aside. A dusting of flour colored her nose and cheek. Could it be she'd not lied and was indeed baking bread? "Is that flour on your sister's face, Lily? Is she helping Mrs. Flynn in the kitchen?"

Lily nodded. "Yes, but I doubt whatever she's making will be edible."

Next to him, Nick snorted.

Emma set her hands on her hips. "Lily, you know you're not allowed to play in the street." She settled her narrowed gaze on Simon. "And you, Mr. Radcliffe, should know better."

"I beg your forgiveness, Emma. I am solely to blame. Perhaps tomorrow I can make amends." A vision of their kiss flashed in his mind.

Her cheeks turned pink. Her eyes held his. Was she thinking what he was?

Oddly, he hoped so.

Chapter Seventeen

An hour after rolling the trundling hoop, Simon found himself in Clapton's Boxing Club. He needed a distraction from Emma Trafford, and a round or two in a ring would serve him well. The place was nearly empty, but the stench of cologne and sweat still mingled in the air.

He noticed Charles Neville standing near one of the rings. Though as tall as Simon, the ginger-haired man possessed a lanky physique common in younger men.

Lord Langford, another young swell, was assisting Neville with slipping on his boxing gloves. In here, members were held to the Marquess of Queensberry rules. Leather gloves softened the blows, and rounds were limited to three minutes. The politeness of it all was a stark contrast to the winner-take-all atmosphere of the illegal, more dangerous bare-knuckled brawls one could find in the basements of East End pubs or back alleys.

Simon remembered what Emma had said yesterday about her betrothal to the man. Something seemed off. Simon knew Neville's pompous sire wouldn't allow him to marry someone outside his station, and Simon was sure Neville had known that as well. The young buck was lucky she'd not sued him for breach of promise.

Simon nudged James Huntington, who was lifting dumbbells. He could understand Huntington's hesitation to go out. Everywhere the man walked, gazes and whispers followed him about his wife's death. Simon motioned to Neville. "What do you know of him?"

"More than I wish to," Huntington said. "He's a right bastard. Heard him bragging once about how all he had to do was mention he was the heir to a barony and most women all but dropped their knickers for him."

Damnation, I was right. The shite had conned Emma when she'd been at one of the most vulnerable points in her life, after the passing of her father. The cocky bastard had wanted something, and Simon had a strong suspicion what it was.

Simon suddenly wanted to hit something. No, not something. Someone. Charles Neville. The man would pay for his duplicity. Forcing a complacent expression, he strode up to the two young bucks. "Looking for a sparring partner, Neville?"

The boyish-faced man grinned and positioned himself in an upright stance, then crouching, he jabbed his gloved hands into the air in front of him. "Indeed, Adler. You think you're up for the task, old man?"

Old man? The smug little shite was about to learn how much Simon wanted to break Neville's perfectly straight nose. "Yes," Simon replied. "I think my old body can handle a couple rounds. Just let me get changed and put my gloves on."

Lord Langford's lips twitched. Unlike Neville, Langford had witnessed Simon's prowess in the ring, and knew him capable of inflicting a bone-crushing punch even when wearing gloves.

Ten minutes later, bare-chested, Simon slipped through the ropes and stepped into the ring were Neville stood with his back to Simon. The man hopped around like a kangaroo, punching and jabbing at the air in front of him as he bounced and shifted his weight from one foot to the other.

"Ready, Neville?" Simon asked.

The kangaroo swung around to face Simon. The cocky expression on Neville's face evaporated. He stilled as though gazing into Medusa's eyes. Obviously he'd believed Simon's broad shoulders were due to a tailor's skill at padding Simon's coats.

Looking like a rabbit who's just crossed the path of a hungry fox, Neville blinked. Simon was going to enjoy this.

Lord Langford struck the bell.

Without preamble Simon strode up to Neville and hit him with a quick jab to the face.

Wide-eyed, Neville stumbled back a few paces and shook his head. "I wasn't ready," he whined.

"You didn't hear the bell?" Simon arched a brow.

Neville shook his head and hopped around again. The silly fool would exhaust himself—already sweat beaded on the man's forehead. The young buck placed his gloves before his face, leaving his gut exposed, and stepped in front of Simon.

This is going to be too easy.

Neville drew back his arm, and Simon hit him in the stomach. Air swooshed from the man's mouth. He folded over and gasped. Simon moved back, giving him some space. He could have struck him again, but he didn't want it to be over yet.

Pale and unsteady on his feet, Neville straightened. He stepped up to Simon and swung wildly with his right, then left, then right, making contact twice with Simon's shoulder.

Simon hit him with an uppercut.

The young man's neck stretched as his head jerked backward from the impact.

"Jesus," Neville mumbled, shaking his head as if to clear the fog swirling about in his skull.

Neville swung again, another frenzied punch.

Simon ducked and planted a fist into the man's exposed ribs.

The man spun around and landed on the ropes.

Langford started counting. "One, two, three, four, five . . ."

Neville should have stayed for the count, but the idiot turned around and staggered toward Simon.

"Get on your knee, Neville, and admit you're beat, you fool," Langford called out.

"You wish to give up?" Simon taunted.

The younger man's face reddened and with his feet shuffling on the ring's floor, he stepped back to the center. Simon had known the taunt would work. Neville was a half-wit.

"Do you know a Miss Emma Trafford?" Simon asked, ducking another jab at his face.

The man's large Adam's apple bobbed in his throat. Simon could smell the fear on the young swell's skin. The bell rang, ending the first three-minute round, and Neville staggered to his corner of the ring.

When Simon reached his corner for the sixty-second break, Huntington tossed a towel at him. "I have a feeling by the way you're hitting Neville, you've an agenda."

Simon grinned. Huntington had always been smart. "Just a bit of poetic justice."

"Hit him on the brow. Once blood gets in his eye, he won't see very well."

"I intend to break his nose." Simon flashed a grin at Neville, who stood in his corner, wiping off his sweaty face. The young heir looked ready to climb the ropes and run for the exit. Simon had intended on drawing this out—going several rounds to extract a pound of flesh, but looking at the man made him sick. It was time to end this. The bell dinged and apprehensively Neville made his way to the center.

The man opened his mouth and before he uttered a word, Simon hit him with a quick combination to his face and gut.

With a *thud*, Neville fell onto his back, arms spread wide, out cold. Blood trickled out of his nose.

As if concerned about the man's health, Simon bent on one knee and gave Neville a none-too-gentle smack on his cheek. "You okay, *old boy*? Terribly sorry if I hit you a might too hard."

The man made a moaning noise.

Simon smacked him again.

The swell's eyes opened. He blinked.

Simon leaned close. "If you ever tell anyone what you did to Miss Trafford, I want you to know I'll track you down like a rat catcher does vermin and snap your neck. Have I made myself clear?"

The man grew even paler than he already was.

"Are we clear?" Simon repeated.

Neville wet his dry lips and nodded.

Simon leaned against the window casing in his drawing room and stared at the Trafford residence. One by one, the windows had grown dark, leaving only the two in Emma's studio lit. Then they'd darkened.

A new light appeared on the second floor. A slender form moved about in the room before drawing the curtains closed. Was that Emma's bedchamber? Yes, he could imagine her preparing to retire—how she'd pull the pins from her blond hair, allowing the heavy tresses to cascade down her back.

The light escaping the confines of the curtains faded, and the house stood dark.

He turned away from the window, tipped his glass of cognac to his lips, and drained it dry. A meager inch of liquid glistened through the cut-glass decanter on the sideboard. He poured the remaining brandy into his snifter and peered at the stairs beyond the open doors of the drawing room.

He should go to bed, attempt to conquer the nocturnal beast within, or be about Town. There was always some entertainment to be had. Yet he stood in the dark, staring at the Trafford residence, asking himself a question that continually echoed in his head like the bells in a church tower. Was the innocent-looking Emma Trafford the woman he sought?

Today when he'd kissed her, he'd not thought of revenge.

He'd wanted her. His hands skimming over her body, delving under her skirts to explore the silkiness of her skin. He wanted Emma in his bed. Under him. Straddling him. The possibilities seemed endless. He could still feel the sensation of her eager mouth and hear her little gasps of pleasure.

Hell, he was hard as a brick, and his balls were most likely a distinctive shade of blue.

He continued to lose track of his plan. Was he once again allowing a beautiful woman to connive him? Or was he chasing a ghost? Could Westfield be right? Had Simon displaced his anger onto Emma because she looked as innocent as Julia—convicted Emma on nothing more than circumstantial evidence?

Yes, they were both blond and beautiful, but Emma radiated kindness. She acted like a mother to her sister—cared for the child. Loved her. Julia only loved herself. He couldn't imagine his stepmother acting so caring and maternal unless searching for a means to an end.

He scrubbed his hand over his bristled jaw. Would Emma consider being his mistress?

Good Lord, where did that thought come from? Angrily he rubbed at the back of his neck. Bloody hell. What tomfoolery was he contemplating? He trusted the woman as far as he could spit. Simon slammed his empty glass down on the sideboard. Damnation! Once a fool, always a fool. He had to remember not to lower his guard.

A purr rumbled in the air, and Kismet rubbed his body against Simon's legs. He bent onto one knee and scratched the cat's neck. He'd brought the animal here after Vivian had seen a mouse. She'd detested the feline nearly as much as vermin. More so, since Kismet left his prized catches by the side of the bed for inspection.

Already restless, the cat darted into the room's shadows in search of new prey. Unlike Simon, the animal wasn't so easily detoured.

A movement outside the window drew Simon's attention. A shadow cut across the pavement as someone in front of his town house stepped under the lamppost. The slender man appeared to survey his surroundings before he tugged his flat cap lower on his head and crossed the street.

The hairs on Simon's neck prickled as the man slipped a key into Emma's front door and entered the residence.

Chapter Eighteen

Dressed in his shirtsleeves, Simon dashed out of his town house. In the short time it had taken him to drag on his shoes, the night's fog had thickened. No need to worry about Mrs. Jenkins spotting him through this pea soup.

As he crossed the street, both dread and exhilaration intertwined within him. Was the man he'd seen entering Emma's home the bastard who'd hit him over the head? He needed to know. Yet the realization that Emma might be as conniving as Julia knotted his gut. He stepped onto the pavement and peered through Emma's morning room window.

Nothing to see but darkness. Was the man upstairs in Emma's bed? A red, angry haze Simon didn't wish to examine flashed before his eyes.

Blast it. He would pound on the door and demand to know the man's identity.

Footfalls moved up the basement stairs, alerting Simon to someone's approach.

A tall, slender form stepped through the dark, foggy night to appear before him at the same time a cricket bat came into view, heading right at Simon's head.

"Bloody bastard!" a voice hissed.

What the hell. Simon ducked. The wood swooshed over him, making contact with the exterior wall of the residence. Shards of splintered willow flew in the dark air.

His attacker took a single step out of the shadows. Weak moonlight spilled onto his young face. A sense of having seen him before flashed in Simon's mind as his assailant cranked the bat back and swung it as if determined to knock the snot out of Simon.

He sidestepped as the wooden weapon whipped by his shoulder, scraping his arm. Burning pain seared his skin.

The momentum of the forceful swing brought the bloke's body sideways.

Ignoring the pain in his upper arm, Simon took the opportunity to grasp the bat's handle and jerk his attacker off-balance, causing the man to stumble. He grabbed his assailant's arm and twisted it behind the fellow's back. "Move and I'll dislocate your shoulder."

The front door swung open.

A gasp cut through the thick air.

Through the gloom, Simon zeroed in on Emma dressed in a white cotton nightgown and robe.

"Mr. Radcliffe! Good Lord, what are you doing to my brother?"

Brother? The paintings in Emma's studio focused in his mind. Of course, that's where he'd seen the lad's face.

Emma rushed to Simon's side and pushed at him. "Let him go, sir! Michael, are you hurt?"

Simon released him.

Breathing heavily, the boy turned around. "You know this bloke, Em?"

"Yes, he's our neighbor. A client of mine. What are you doing with that bat?"

"I thought he was . . ." The lad raked his fingers through his fair hair.

Emma clasped his arm. "Who did you think it was?"

"No one. Never mind." Her brother's voice sounded both sullen and defensive. Michael scowled at Simon. "That still doesn't explain why he was peeking through our window like a lecher."

The boy had him there. "I saw you enter the house. I became concerned since someone robbed me." There was some truth in that statement.

"Robbed?" Michael echoed. The startled expression on the boy's face seemed as genuine as his sister's had been.

"What are you doing home, Michael? Why aren't you in school?" Emma asked.

"I wish to pick up a few things."

"You need them so desperately that you decided to take the rail home and play hooky?"

"I thought you'd be pleased to see me." With a huff, the lad stormed into the house.

Emma blinked. "Something's going on with him." Her warm fingers touched his arm. "Your shirt is ripped. Are you hurt?"

"It's nothing." It was the least he deserved after coming over here half-cocked. He wasn't sure what had bothered him more, the possibility Emma might have played him for a fool, or that a man, other than himself, might be sharing her bed.

Emma shivered and wrapped her arms about herself.

Simon fought the urge to pull her into an embrace to warm her skin. He glanced at Emma's bare feet. "You should go inside, Emma. It's damp out here."

"Yes. I should see if I can convince my brother to reveal what's really going on. Thank you for your concern, and I'm sorry. Goodnight, Simon."

He waited until Emma returned to her house before he strode back to his own residence, unable to shake the feeling that Emma's was right—something was definitely wrong with her brother.

A short time later, Simon paced his bedchamber. The memory of Emma dressed in her simple bedclothes, a worried expression on her face, bothered him. And why should he care if something was wrong with her brother?

Blast it. He needed a distraction, and he knew what would work.

With only the moonlight guiding him, Simon lifted a pot on the back terrace of Lady Griffin's residence and removed the key to the rear door. Stealthily he made his way up the servants' stairs, as he had numerous times, slipped into her bedroom, and locked the door.

The glow from the grate revealed Margaret's dark hair and lithe form sleeping in her bed. He took three steps, massaged the back of his neck, and stopped. What was he doing here?

Damned if he knew.

He should go home. Yet his first thought wasn't of his luxurious Curzon Street residence, but his town house on Great James Street. Best to leave before Margaret heard him scurrying about and woke, but the thought of walking home or looking for a hackney at this hour held little appeal. He shrugged out of his coat and tossed it over a chair. Instead of moving to the tester bed, he stretched out on the settee. His long legs dangled over the arm of the short piece of furniture.

Damn uncomfortable. He closed his eyes and Emma's face floated in his mind as sleep overtook him.

"Simon, wake up."

Grumbling, he forced open his heavy-lidded eyes.

Margaret, dressed in a long cream nightgown, stood next to the settee, frowning. "What are you about?"

He didn't know anymore. Raking his fingers through his disheveled hair, he swung his legs to the floor, cringing at the pain in his stiff back and sore arm.

Margaret arched a brow, still waiting for an explanation.

"I thought we could . . . talk. But when I arrived you were sleeping."

"Talk?" She smiled. "Was that all?"

Initially, no. He'd come here to burn off the restlessness within him, and though he enjoyed talking with Margaret, it hadn't been the reason for his midnight visit. Yet after arriving, the desire to join her in bed had vanished.

"Who is Emma?" she asked, drawing him from his thoughts.

Simon's gaze swung to Margaret's. "Emma?"

Margaret sat next to him on the settee and patted his knee. "When I awoke you were saying her name. I presume she's the reason you didn't join me in my bed?"

What an idiot he was. Coming here and mumbling Emma's name in his sleep so Margaret heard it was beyond the pale. Like him, she was scarred, though hers were emotional, not physical, and he didn't wish to add to that.

Damn, he was an arse. "Forgive me."

"No need. We both know this relationship is based on reciprocal gratification, nothing more. No, that's not true. I consider you one of my dearest friends."

Simon slid his hand over hers and squeezed her fingers. After her marriage to that cheating rat-bastard Lord Griffin, Margaret trusted men very little.

"Do you love her?" Margaret asked.

Love Emma? How laughable. "Absolutely not."

She arched an eyebrow, clearly stating she didn't believe him.

"For all your charm toward women, I know the truth, Simon."

He frowned. *What truth?*

"You don't trust them. Not a one."

"What bosh. I'm here with you."

"Yes, normally sharing my bed, but have you ever confided in me? Told me what dark secrets you hold? Never. Have you ever done so with any woman?"

He thought of his conversation with Emma—how he'd revealed that he and his father hadn't been close. "I have."

"Her?"

Good Lord. He didn't blush, yet he felt his cheeks warming.

Margaret smiled. "I think I have my answer."

This was ridiculous. He didn't care for Emma. He wanted her in his bed. There was a difference. He would not allow himself to fall in love. Doing so left one vulnerable to manipulation.

Margaret stood, pulling him from his thoughts. "The maid who lights the grate will be arriving soon. And my servants are probably already buzzing about my house below stairs."

Simon glanced at the window. Muted morning light filtered through the sheer curtains. He should have left over an hour ago. He could withstand anything whispered about his antics, since there wasn't much that hadn't already been bandied around with regard to him, but Margaret's pristine reputation would be sullied if her servants witnessed him leaving her bedroom at daybreak. He stood and cracked open the bedroom door an inch. The sound of footsteps one flight below revealed he'd indeed waited too long to make his exit down the rear stairway.

Margaret's lips thinned into a straight line.

"Don't fret." He donned his coat, moved to the window, and pushed up the lower sash.

"Simon, you can't be serious. You'll fall and break your

neck climbing out my window. Then everyone will learn of it. It will cause a scandal."

He sighed. "I'm so glad you are as concerned about my demise as you are your reputation."

She laughed softly. "I am concerned about both."

"Indeed. No need to worry. Westfield and I became quite skilled at shimmying down drainpipes when at school." That memory brought his concerns back to Emma and her brother. Perhaps he should talk to the lad, see what was bothering him.

No, it was none of his concern.

Simon swung one leg out onto the ledge and reached for the drainpipe. The fabric of his coat stretched tight over his shoulders. A ripping noise reached his ear. Cool morning air filtered through the tear in the shoulder of his coat. Uttering a low curse, he wrapped his hands on the pipe, set the heels of his shoes against it, and slid down.

His feet silently touched the flagstone on the back terrace. Sludge from the pipe muddied the front of his clothing. He brushed it off as best he could, reached for his top hat to make a gallant bow, and realized he'd left it in Margaret's bedchamber.

My hat, he mouthed and pointed to his head.

Margaret nodded, disappeared for a minute, and returned. Leaning out the window, she tossed the top hat to him. It tumbled downward, fluttering like a one-winged bird. He caught it and placed it on his head before sneaking through the rear gardens and to the alley behind.

Best he return to his Mayfair residence and stay there for a few days. He needed to screw his head back on straight and remember his objective before returning to his house on Great James Street.

After a brisk walk, Simon stepped into his Curzon Street town house.

The under-butler, Samuel Pritchard, came barreling down the corridor. Upon seeing Simon in the entry hall, the man came to an abrupt halt and tugged down his waistcoat.

"My lord." The servant's eyes widened as his gaze raked over Simon's dirty clothes. He glanced past Simon's shoulders as if wondering where the two old retainers were.

"Follow me, Pritchard." Simon stepped into his office, picked up a piece of foolscap, and jotted a note to Harris and Baines, informing them he would return to his Great James Street residence in a few days. The two mother hens were probably pacing back and forth awaiting him.

He folded the note, wrote his Bloomsbury address on it, and handed it to the servant. "I wish this to be delivered. Harris and Baines are there."

"Yes, my lord. I'll send a footman right away."

Simon held up a halting hand. "No, I want you to deliver it, and you are not to tell anyone whom you work for. Understand? Especially a little blond-haired chit graced with an inquisitive nature. Do I make myself clear?"

"Most definitely, my lord."

"Take a hackney." Simon reached into his pocket and pulled out several coins.

"Very well." The under-butler dashed out of the room.

Simon slumped into the high-backed leather chair behind his desk. Mail was strewn haphazardly across his blotter. Harris would squawk like a chicken with a randy rooster on its tail if he returned to see the way Pritchard had tossed the post about. Harris had a system. Business correspondence in one pile. Social correspondence in another. Invitations in a third.

Simon sorted them. He'd just finished responding to every inquiry when he heard Harris's and Baines's voices. Inhaling deeply, Simon pinched the bridge of his nose.

Had he asked them to return? Of course not, but he should have realized they would.

The two servants stormed into the room. Baines wrinkled his nose. "You look like you slept in your clothes and rolled in a cow pasture."

For once he agreed with the man. "Thank you for making me aware of that. Now if you don't mind, I have—"

Baines gasped. "The shoulder of your coat is torn." The valet made a tsking noise and shook his finger at Simon. "I hope you didn't walk around Mayfair looking so bedraggled. It reflects poorly on me if you're seen about Town looking so disheveled."

"I did. In fact, I visited Marlborough House dressed this way. The Prince was aghast, and the Princess of Wales became so distraught by my dirty apparel, she swooned. She needed to be carried to her bedchamber and resuscitated with smelling salts."

The valet's color drained from his face. "Tell me you're jesting, my lord."

"I am. Now go away." With his hand, Simon motioned to the door.

Baines released a heavy breath.

"Where were you last night?" Harris withdrew a handkerchief from his pocket and handed it to Baines, who mopped at his damp brow.

"That is none of your business. Now would you both leave me in peace? I have work to do."

The two servants turned to exit the room.

"Wait." Simon tapped his pen against his blotter. "Baines, did you go to Miss Trafford's and inform her I would be away on business for a few days?"

"I did. Just as your note said, my lord."

"Good."

"Miss Lily answered the door. She is a very odd child."

"What did she say?" Simon scrubbed his hand over his bristled jaw.

The valet stared at Harris.

"Out with it," Simon prompted.

"She asked me if Harris moonlighted as an undertaker. The child clearly suffers from some disorder."

"She is fond of reading penny dreadfuls and has an overactive imagination," Simon explained, unsure why he defended the blond-haired imp. Hell, did he actually like the child? He recalled Lily's exuberant expression as she'd cheered Nick on as the lad wheeled the trundling hoop. Realizing he was smiling, Simon scratched his head and frowned.

It was time to accept the truth. That conk to his noggin had obviously caused some type of trauma to his brain. Nothing else explained his desire for Emma and his sudden defensiveness regarding her hoyden sister.

The carriage moved at a slow pace up Curzon Street. Impatiently, Simon leaned forward and braced his elbows on his knees while he ran a hand over his face.

The meeting with his banker in Bishopsgate had taken longer than he'd expected. Huntington and Westfield had grilled Ned Baring on the amortization of the loan and all the minute details, while Simon had sat, distracted. Bloody hell, distracted was an understatement. He'd almost snored through it all. Thank God, both his partners were astute businessmen and he needn't worry about the details they'd worked out.

Bone weary, Simon leaned back against the squabs and closed his eyes. Since returning to Mayfair two days ago, sleep had been elusive.

The rhythm of the horses' hooves clunking against the

pavement slowed as his carriage pulled before his Curzon Street residence. He'd reached the front steps when the door opened and a nervous-looking Harris stared at him.

"What's the matter, old boy?" Simon asked.

The butler's gaze shifted past Simon's shoulder.

Simon glanced behind him. A black carriage waited on the opposite side of the street. Simon leaned closer to Harris and whispered, "Baron Yules entertaining a bevy of loose women again?"

"No. You have a caller."

"An unfavorable one, by the distasteful expression on your face."

"Your stepmother, Lady Adler, arrived a short time ago and awaits you in the blue salon. I informed her you were out. However, she wished to wait."

Julia. Simon's stomach clenched as though a pugilist rammed his ham-sized fist in his gut. He should have known his stepmother would eventually pay him a call.

Clenching and unclenching his hand, Simon entered the drawing room and closed the double doors behind him. Julia, dressed in a light blue gown with a cream overskirt, stood behind the settee. Her hand lightly traced the fabric, a gentle sweep—back and forth. As her fingers moved, an unforgettable sense of discomfort settled in his belly. His gaze shifted from the movement to her face. Though nearly forty, her fair skin remained unblemished, and her blond hair retained its shine, yet he realized the color wasn't as golden as Emma's.

Without a word, he moved to the sideboard and poured himself a glass of cognac.

"You don't appear pleased to see me, Simon."

He gave a bitter laugh. "Julia, you've grown more delusional if you thought I would be awaiting you with open arms."

"We could be friends, Simon. Put our past differences aside."

Differences? Is that what she thought them? Her choice of words seemed almost laughable, if it wasn't so perverse.

He fought the urge to touch the scar on his face. "Madam, you are not welcome in *my home*."

She tipped her head slightly to the side and pursed her lips. "What will people say if we don't converse? They will whisper."

"Do you think I care? I've heard their whispers for most of my adult life. Everyone in the ton wonders why my father cut me from his life, and *someone* continues to spread malicious lies. I have become immune to their gossip." He walked to the tall arched window, glanced at a couple walking up the street, and took a sip of his drink.

He sensed Julia's proximity a moment before the scent of gardenias nauseated him. That old revulsion, which had started to ease, tightened—grew. He set his glass down on the sill, turned around, and forced a dispassionate expression. "If you are so concerned with gossip, return to Hampshire."

"I have rusticated in the country for far too long."

There was more to her tale than she was admitting. "What else, Julia?"

She sighed. "You were always so astute, Simon, unlike your father. I'm in need of funds."

"Good God, woman, don't tell me you've lost it all."

"I owe Lady Leeman ten thousand pounds."

Jesus. Lady Leeman was a skilled whist player who'd paupered several gentlemen after their wives had bet too deep.

Julia had the good graces to avert her eyes.

"I guess you will have to suffer the consequences. What a shame. I suppose the ladies in your inner circle will turn their backs on you if you don't pay your debt. Social ruin . . . how fitting."

"So you will not give me the money to pay off my marker?"

He cocked a brow at her. Was she mad? How could she think of asking him? "You thought I'd give you the money to pay off your debt?"

"Damn you, Simon. I am your stepmother. We are family."

His bitter bark of laughter exploded in the air like a gunshot. "Family? Do you even comprehend the meaning of the word?" For a brief moment, he thought of Emma and Lily. They acted like a family should. Loving. Caring.

She stepped close to him and placed her hand on his sleeve. "I do."

Simon jerked back. "You took nearly everything away from me with your lies, and now you have the audacity to ask me for money? I fear dementia has consumed your brain."

"That is unkind, Simon."

"Sometimes life is unkind. Strange how I learned that at such a young age."

She lifted her right hand and ran her finger over the scar on his cheek. "Poor boy. I told you not to tell your father. A man so besotted only hears what he wishes. And what man wants to learn his wife favors his son more than him?"

Simon knocked her hand away. "I'm not a child anymore, Julia. You would be well advised to never touch me again."

Somehow the truth of those words—that Julia could not hurt him, calmed the anger within him. She'd taken nearly everything from him—his father, his wealth—yet he'd survived. He picked up his cognac and strode to the mantel. He glanced up at the portrait of his father. The old man's dark eyes looked astute, as though they saw all, but the artist's depiction was an illusion. The man had been near blind when it came to Julia. Her beauty and angelic face masked a monster, and his father had lived in oblivion. He lifted his glass and saluted the portrait.

"Do you believe in hell, Julia?" Simon asked, not turning around.

She didn't respond.

"I don't wish to see you again. I suggest you return to Hampshire, for though I'm not a man who'd hurt a woman, you sorely tempt me to send you to the devil."

Her silk skirt rustled—announced that she moved toward the door. It opened and clicked shut. Simon lifted his glass to his lips and downed the contents.

Someone scratched at the door.

"Yes, what is it?"

Harris entered. "Is there something I can get for you, my lord?"

"No, but tell Baines tomorrow we return to Bloomsbury."

Chapter Nineteen

From her studio window, Emma stared through the night's fog at Simon's residence. No one appeared to be inside. Two days ago, Mr. Baines had visited and informed her that Mr. Radcliffe had been called away on business. The valet didn't know when his employer would return for his next sitting.

An hour after delivering this message, both Mr. Baines and Mr. Harris had hastily exited the town house and taken off in Simon's carriage. She'd watched the vehicle move up the street until it turned onto Theobald's Road.

Crestfallen, poor Mrs. Flynn now puttered around. The housekeeper wasn't the only one dejected. Nick, Simon's daily servant, had sat glum-faced for the second day in a row on the doorstep awaiting his employer's return. Even Lily acted downcast since the house across the way went dark.

Emma strode back to her easel. Restless, she'd removed Simon's portrait and replaced it with her mother's and resumed working on it. The black and white daguerreotype photo of Mama gave no clue to the shade of her gown, so Emma had painted it blue since it seemed to reflect everyone's mood. Even hers. Yet, she should feel relieved and pray Simon never returned.

She picked up her palette, mixed a bit of white pigment into the rich sapphire color, and added a few highlights to her mother's dress. Pleased with the outcome, she dipped her dirty paintbrush into the jar filled with turpentine and wiped it clean with a soft linen rag. She tossed the cloth into a bowl and brushed her damp fingers over the front of her trousers. Her mind drifted to thoughts of her brother, who'd left yesterday morning. He'd assured her that nothing was wrong except the examinations were challenging, but an uneasiness lingered within her.

Unable to help herself, she stared at Simon's unfinished portrait, which leaned against the wall. Somehow it comforted her.

Goodness, how silly. With quick, agitated movements, she lifted her palette, scraped the paint off, and cleaned it. After turning off the three gas lamps, Emma moved down the stairs to the floor below and tiptoed by Lily's door. Her sister had fallen asleep a couple of hours ago, as had Mrs. Flynn, leaving nothing but the sound of the clocks ticking to fill the quietness of the night.

Emma stepped into her bedchamber. The moonlight streaming through her window highlighted the objects in the room with a blue hue. A bolt of silent lightning flashed in the distance. Her gaze jerked to the window and Simon's town house. The empty residence afforded her the perfect opportunity to return his ring. If the basement window remained unlocked, she could easily sneak back in and place it on the counterpane, where he'd find it upon his return. She flipped back the hinged lid of Mama's jewelry box and wiggled her fingers between the torn velvet lining and the wooden sides. She plucked Simon's ring out and fisted it in her hand. The heat of her skin warmed the gold until it seemed to scorch her palm.

A nervous energy fluttered in her stomach as she slipped the ring into the front pocket of her trousers and made her way to Michael's bedchamber to get a knit cap and a navy sweater. On soft feet, she made her way down the stairs and drew the sweater over her head, then pulled the cap on and tucked her hair under the knitted wool.

Taking a deep, calming breath, she slipped outside into the night's fog.

The sound of hooves clopping on Theobald's Road broke the graveyard silence. Like a mouse in search of crumbs, Emma dashed across the street. In front of her, the white low-lying mist parted as she stepped through it to reveal the wrought iron gate that led to the area below street level. Unlike last time, the heavy gate swung on silent hinges. Holding on to the rail, she made her way down the steep steps.

Drat. The crate she and Lily had used to boost themselves up was gone. A gust of wind displaced the fog. Another flash of lightning lit the sky to reveal a person curled up in a ball in the farthest corner near the house. Heart beating fast, Emma moved to the stairs. As she took the first step, she glanced at the person, whose chest rose and fell, sending small puffs of white air into the cold night.

She stilled. Nick? Yes, she recognized his long brown hair, sticking out from beneath his flat cap. What was he doing sleeping here? Didn't the child have a home? She turned around, crouched next to him, and touched his hand, which felt as cold as death.

The lad bolted upright and grabbed something from his boot. The cold edge of a sharp blade pressed against her cheek. "I'll slit you like a rooster at Smithfield Market if you touch me."

"Nick," she croaked, trying not to move too much. "It is Miss Trafford. Lily's sister."

The boy rubbed a fisted hand against one of his heavy-lidded eyes and tucked the knife back into his boot. "I thoughts you were a man, miss. Your clothes."

"Understandable. I'm sorry to have frightened you." She pulled the knitted hat off. Her pinned-up hair came loose in several places and tumbled over her shoulders.

"What's you doing out here, miss?"

Standing, she slipped her hand into her trouser pocket to touch Simon's ring. She couldn't tell the lad the truth. "Um, I thought I saw Mr. Radcliffe's white cat roaming about. I came to fetch him. In this pea soup the animal could be run over by a carriage."

The child nodded. "Why's you dressed like a man?"

Her heart skipped a beat. She couldn't afford to have him repeat that he'd seen her dressed this way. "Sometimes when I paint I dress in my brother's old clothes, so as not to ruin my gowns, but I hope you won't repeat what you have seen. I'd hate to be gossiped about."

Another bolt of lightning lit the sky. The air held the scent of an oncoming storm. The child could not remain here during the cold, bone-chilling night. Emma wrapped her arms about herself. "What are you doing here, Nick? Don't you have a place to sleep? A home?"

Nick stood and smacked the dirt off his trousers. "I was waiting for Mr. Radcliffe and the old gents to return. They told me they'd be back in a few days."

His averting her question answered it as clearly as if he'd affirmed it. The child was homeless. Thunder rumbled in the distance. "You cannot stay here. A storm is about to split the sky open, and you'll end up drenched. You might take on a chill and get sick. My brother, Michael, is away at school and you may spend the night in his bedroom."

The lad blinked. "You are inviting me to sleep in your home?"

"Yes, of course, come."

He shoved his hands in his pockets and rocked on his heels.

Several small drops of rain fell from the sky. Pulling the knit cap over her hair, Emma climbed up the narrow stairs. "Nick, if we wait much longer, I fear we will get caught in a deluge. We must hurry."

"I ain't lookin' for no handouts. If I go, I need to earn me keep."

"You shall. In the morning after we eat eggs and bacon, you will have to sweep the doorstep and help Mrs. Flynn in the kitchen scrub the pan she used to bake the warm muffins in. You like buttered muffins, don't you?"

Nick licked his lips and nodded.

Emma smiled to herself. "Then we have a deal."

The following morning, Nick shoveled three hardboiled eggs into his mouth in quick succession. Obviously, the boy hadn't eaten much since Simon left.

Lily wrinkled her nose and opened her mouth.

Emma shot her sister a warning glance.

Little good it did, for Lily asked, "Do you always eat so fast, Nick?"

Nick wiped his sleeve across his chin and drew back his shoulders. "I'm a man. Men eat faster and more than women." He squeezed the small muscle in his upper arm.

The expression on Lily's face didn't bode well. Emma gave Lily another don't-you-say-a-word glare, again to no avail.

"Mr. Radcliffe doesn't eat like that, and he's broader in the shoulders than any man I've met. I bet he could catch a cannonball, like that strongman John Holtum does."

"Yes, but Mr. Radcliffe is older." Emma nudged her sister's foot under the table. "Nick's body is still developing at a very quick pace. He needs to eat more at his age. Might I ask how old you are, Nick?"

"Fifteen, miss."

"Yes, that's what I thought. Fifteen is a most important age for eating." Emma shoved the plate with the last rasher of bacon toward the lad. "I'm not in the mood for bacon today. You are more than welcome to eat mine."

Mrs. Flynn frowned. "You not feeling well, miss?"

"I am quite well, thank you." Emma picked up a muffin and spread marmalade on it.

After the dishes were cleared away and washed, Mrs. Flynn handed Nick a broom and sent him outside to sweep the doorstep.

Emma followed him. The money Simon had paid for the painting he'd purchased, along with what she would charge him for the portrait, had eased her financial burdens and put food in their larder and cupboards. Surely, enough that she could offer this poor lad a place to stay in exchange for a job, though if he continued to eat like a growing boy did, her money would run out sooner than she hoped. "Nick."

He turned and looked at her as though worried she was about to send him on his way. "I'm sorry, ma'am, if I ate too much, but Mrs. Flynn is a fine cook. And I'll work hard to earn that food. I'll even shimmy down your chimney to clean it, if you wish."

"Oh heavens, no. I would never ask you to climb up on our roof, and you are too large to scoot down the chimney.

You might get stuck. And I'm not displeased. In fact, I was thinking . . ."

The sound of hooves on the pavement and the appearance of a grand equipage with yellow wheels turning onto Great James Street made Emma's stomach heave upward as though it wished to take residence in her throat. The familiar carriage slowed and stopped in front of Simon's residence.

A smile wreathed the bottom of Nick's face. "Mr. Radcliffe has returned."

"So it seems." Emma placed her hand over her queasy stomach as pleasure and nervousness battled for precedence within her.

The carriage lurched to the side as an occupant disembarked. Simon's tall form appeared on the pavement. He made his way around the back of the vehicle. He wore another fashionable gray suit, a crisp white shirt, and a silver four-in-hand tie, but no hat. His dark hair shone under the morning sun. The unreadable expression on his face as he crossed the street made her question whether their heated kiss had been an erotic dream brought about by a fever she didn't recall. No, it was real—another ploy by him to lower her defenses.

He stepped before her and bowed his head congenially. The way his gaze took a leisurely path down her body, evaporated any fanciful idea that she'd dreamt of his touch or the pleasure it bestowed on her.

"Emma, how are you?"

"I am well, sir."

"Is your brother still visiting?"

"No, he stayed only until the morning after he arrived."

"Were you able to find out what's bothering him?"

"He assured me it's nothing. Just the pressures of school and examinations, leaving him a bit on edge."

He glanced at Nick holding a broom. "What are you about, lad?"

Nick stared at his feet. When he glanced back up, his cheeks were red. "Miss Trafford offered me a bed and a meal if I done some work for her."

"A bed?" Simon asked, his regard returning to hers.

"Nick," Emma said, sensing the boy's discomfort, "would you ask Mrs. Flynn if she will be good enough to make me a list of groceries she needs this week?"

"Yes, ma'am."

The door clicked closed behind the child.

"He has no home?" Simon's dark eyes held hers.

She shook her head. "I don't believe so."

"And you have taken him in?" Simon cupped his shaved chin.

"Yes, for the night in exchange for him completing a few chores. I was about to offer him a live-in position when you returned."

A furrow creased the smooth skin between his dark brows. "Why?"

"Why?" she echoed.

"Yes, why are you willing to take him in?" Again he held her gaze as if he couldn't comprehend her actions. Understandable, since he believed she'd robbed him.

"Because I think he's an orphan. And he's not much older than my sister. I cannot fathom what it would be like to live on the streets. To sleep in the cold and worry where one's next meal is coming from. He sat on your step for two days awaiting your return."

Simon's jaw tensed. "Blast it. I did not know. He told Harris he lived on Theobald's Road. But I should have realized something was wrong. I shall offer him a permanent position."

Simon Radcliffe was compassionate. And that knowledge made her heart squeeze in her chest with the same nitwit longing she'd felt for him while he was away. "He'll be pleased. Will you be sitting for your portrait today?"

"I will. Is two o'clock a convenient time?"

"It is."

He leaned close. His masculine, heady scent filled her nose. She tried but failed to stop her toes from curling in her shoes. His gaze dropped to her mouth. Like the quickness of the storm last night, she remembered the feel of his lips on hers. The heat of his skin. And the wicked way he'd touched her. And she wanted to experience it all again.

Simon Radcliffe was dangerous in more ways than one.

"Then I shall see you at two o'clock." She turned on her heel and entered the house, her stomach full of butterflies and anticipation.

Chapter Twenty

"You're going to wear a path in the rug, my lord," Baines said, sticking his head out of the dressing room off Simon's bedchamber.

Simon shot the valet a narrow-eyed scowl and slumped into the upholstered chair by the window. Bracing his forearms on his knees, he scrubbed his hands over his face. Emma Trafford was a quandary—a puzzle in need of solving. Everything about her residence, from the threadbare rugs to the faded furniture, proclaimed misfortune had settled on her household, yet she'd been about to take Nick in. How could such a woman be his she-devil? She was the antithesis of how he'd expected the woman to act.

Emma was kindhearted. One only had to witness how she loved her sister. In fact, she should be canonized for the patience she bestowed on the child.

You're wrong about her being your femme fatale, a voice in his head whispered. Was he? Or was she just that sly? He recalled Westfield's comments about Simon's evidence being shoddy at best, and if he was honest with himself, Simon would agree. And he'd not seen any man call on Emma, except that bumbling grocer. Doubtful that fool was her accomplice.

Simon thought of that dreadful book he'd been reading about Inspector Whitley. The man had an innate sense of who his suspects were—a gut feeling. And everything within Simon felt he had the right woman. Everything, but his common sense.

"Bloody hell," Simon grumbled.

Baines appeared in the doorway of the dressing room again. "Did you say something, my lord?"

"No, just talking to myself."

"Oh dear," Baines mumbled.

"What?" Simon narrowed his eyes at the man.

"My first employer, Lord Hutten, started talking to himself. And we all know what happened to him. Dreadfully sad when a gentleman of sixty-five insists he be dressed in short trousers and wants his maids to spank him while proclaiming him a naughty boy. He was mad, and it all started after he began talking to himself."

"Once again, Baines, you are a comfort to have around. And Hutten wasn't mad, he was perverse and sexually frustrated."

"Might that be your problem, my lord?" Grinning like a sly fox, the man strode back into the dressing room.

No, that wasn't his problem. Or was it? In truth, Simon couldn't step within three feet of Emma without feeling some damnable reaction. He was like a bloody dog in heat. He should get in his carriage and return to Mayfair. Forget about finding his ring. And forget about Emma, her warm smile, and the odd contentment he had begun to feel every time he entered her house. He touched the back of his head. The lump had vanished, but he was sure that blow had done something to his brain.

Releasing a heavy breath, Simon stood and strode to the painting Emma had done of the family walking in the park. Harris had set it on the mantel. Simon ran the fingers of his left hand over the painted surface and touched the woman's likeness. She was blond like Emma and the gentleman dark-haired. As if unable to stop himself, his fingers drifted to the baby sitting in the wicker perambulator. The infant, with full cheeks, wore a white dress and lacy bonnet. Simon thought of Westfield's son and how the toddler smelled. Would this infant smell the same way?

My God, he *was* going mad. This was a painting. Nothing more.

Baines said something.

Simon glanced over his shoulder. The valet stood in the dressing room doorway again, one of Simon's coats draped over his arm. "What?"

"I said, Miss Trafford is quite skilled."

"Ah, yes. Quite. I think I should have the painting reframed."

"I'm sure Lord and Lady Westfield would appreciate that."

"Westfield?" Simon echoed.

"Didn't you purchase it as a gift for them?"

Had he? He rubbed the back of his neck. "Yes, of course."

"So should we pack it up? Send it to be reframed and delivered to their residence?"

Simon turned back to the painting and centered it better on the mantel. "No rush. Maybe I'll give it to them for Christmas."

Baines chuckled.

What the deuce did the man find so funny?

Usually Emma enjoyed afternoon tea as a break when painting.

Not today.

Over the rim of her porcelain cup, she watched Simon, who sat across from her at the small table in her studio, finish his slice of Mrs. Flynn's Victoria sponge cake. He licked a bit of raspberry jam off the tip of his finger.

Emma's stomach clenched. She couldn't look at his sinful mouth without thinking of the kiss they'd shared the other day, or how he'd drawn her finger into his warm mouth. Throughout the afternoon, the memories had continued to insinuate themselves into the forefront of her thoughts. The days they'd spent apart hadn't cooled her desire for him. It seemed to have strengthened it.

Lud, I need to find a way to return his ring to him, finish this painting, and send Simon Radcliffe on his way. She cleared her throat. "This afternoon, I intend to do some shading. I don't believe it should take more than an hour at most, so I shall not keep you very long."

Instead of looking relieved, a crease dissected the smooth skin between his brows.

Was he disappointed? Had he missed her? What silliness to contemplate such a thought. *You are a ninny, Emma Anne Trafford. A bumbling fool.*

Simon nodded. He stood and offered her his hand.

Not wise to touch him. Without taking it, she stood. The heat of his gaze warmed her back as she strode to the easel. He watched her like a hawk setting his sights on his prey. Was he once again trying to throw her off balance? All day, he'd been glancing at her as if she were a specimen in a jar.

As he passed her on his way to the chair, he leaned close. "Is something the matter, Emma?"

There seemed to be genuine concern in his eyes. "No, but I was wondering the same thing. Is something bothering you?"

His brows drew together. "Of course not. Might I ask why you'd think that?"

Because you've been staring at me, more intensely than usual, she wanted to say, but she bit the inside of her mouth to halt the words.

"Emma?"

"It's nothing. Now please sit, so we might resume your painting."

Over the next hour, Emma worked on Simon's portrait, shading in the hard angles of his face, the hollows below his high cheekbones, and the line of his jaw, slightly darker than his face. It seemed no matter how close he shaved, it didn't remove the shadow of his bristles, which added to the look of danger he exuded.

Piano music drifted into the room. Not the harsh banging she'd become almost immune to hearing, but an enchanting sound. Emma placed her brush down and moved to the doorway. Setting a hand on the casings, she leaned into the corridor and cocked her head toward the lyrical notes.

The music, the skill with which the pianist struck the keys, as if an extension of their hands, made her breath catch.

She felt the warmth of Simon's body as he moved to stand behind her at the doorway.

"Lily?" he asked.

It could be no one else. Mrs. Flynn was a skilled baker, but she didn't know how to play the piano. "Yes. It must be. Though only nine when our father died, this is how she played before his death. I remember the first time she sat and started tinkling with the keys. She'd barely learned to talk, yet she had this innate ability."

A waltz sprung to life and drifted upstairs.

Simon gave a slow shake of his head, as though amazed. "She's a prodigy."

"She is." Without thought, Emma set her hand on his arm. "I must thank you, Simon."

A frown darkened his already intense face. "For what?"

"I believe it is having such a finely tuned piano that draws her to play it again. Or nothing more than hearing you play so well that makes her long to play with comparable skill."

"But I told you, I wasn't the one who sent Mr. Marlow."

"Really? Then you must be a psychic, sir, for I do not believe I revealed the piano tuner's name."

A slight smile curved up one side of his mouth. "Ah, got me." He extended his hand to her. "Then, as my thanks, I request this dance."

She didn't wish to dance with him. To feel his body close to hers for any length of time was unwise, yet she set her hand in his. He curled his fingers around her right hand, and placed the palm of his other hand on her back. Gazes locked, Simon slowly led her around the room with a skill she should have realized he would possess.

As they danced, the waltz Lily played picked up tempo.

Simon wrapped his arm tighter around Emma's waist, pulling her closer to him. She luxuriated in the heat coming off him and the strength of his arms holding her. He spun her so fast, she slid her hand over his nape to keep in time with him.

The corners of his lips turned upward.

A laugh escaped her mouth.

The hard, powerful muscles of his shoulders flexed under her hand. Her skirt brushed against his legs, while the tips of her breasts touched his chest—a light brushing that made her nipples peak under her corset. The contact was decadently delicious.

His steps slowed. They suddenly stood perfectly still as if chiseled from marble. The music seemed distant compared to their breaths coming fast, mingling in the scant air between them.

Under her palm, the muscles of his shoulder bunched and moved as though breaking free of the constraints that momentarily froze him. Simon lifted his hand and drew the pad of his thumb over her lower lip. The urge to draw the tip into her mouth, as he had her finger, nearly overwhelmed her. She now understood Adam's weakness when Eve offered him the apple. Wanting what you know is forbidden might be the greatest test of all. *Sin, seduction, recklessness*. The words drifted through her mind like the sweet song of the devil tempting her. Before she could stop herself, her tongue lightly touched the pad of his thumb.

The sight of his eyes widening added to the heat warming her nerve endings. She enjoyed shocking him—knew it was a rarity, and the knowledge that she'd done it thrilled her.

His large hand cupped the back of her neck, and he dipped his head. The silky texture of his lips brushed hers. The contact grew firmer, more possessive as he coaxed her lips open. His tongue slid sensuously against hers, tangled, and withdrew.

She whimpered, longing for more.

His tongue returned—slid against hers. This kiss hungrier than the last.

Her legs felt weak, her head dizzy, and her desire immeasurable. She centered her senses on the feel of Simon's mouth—the way it moved against hers. How his tongue withdrew, then plunged again, along with the warmth of his body touching hers. The scent of his spicy skin, added another layer to the overpowering sensations. Like that night in his dark house, she couldn't stop herself from arching into him, a silent request for more of his tantalizing touch.

His hand on her waist slid up to capture the weight of her breast as his mouth trailed a path over her neck, nipping and kissing. His breath fanned against her ear. The sharp pinch of his teeth bit into the tender flesh of her lobe.

She bit back a moan. Realizing the music had stopped and Lily could walk into the room, Emma jerked back. She spun away from Simon and pressed the pads of her fingers to her tingling lips. Dancing with Simon Radcliffe might be as dangerous as playing with matches in a hayloft. She gave herself a hard mental slap. Hadn't her time with Charles shown her that she was too easily seduced? Yet, Emma had never wanted Charles like she wanted Simon. Never felt such a hunger claw at her. The kisses he'd bestowed on her had never made her heart beat erratically. And their joining . . . Goodness, the man had done nothing more than lift her skirt, undone the fall of his trousers, and thrust himself into her. The pain had brought tears to her eyes. He'd not even kissed her during the act or touched her breasts like Simon had just done.

The warmth of Simon's hand settled on her back. Emma fought the desire to close her eyes and lean back against the solidity of his hard-muscled chest. She took a deep breath, and without looking at him, she stepped out of the room and into the corridor.

"I think you should go, Mr. Radcliffe." Though her voice started off firm, his name quivered on her lips.

"Emma—"

"Please, Simon."

He rubbed the back of his neck and nodded.

She watched him make his way down the stairs and listened to the sound of the front door closing.

A mere fifteen minutes later, the clopping of horses' hooves drew her to the window. Simon's carriage stood in front of his residence. He strode out and onto the pavement. For a moment, he stared across the street.

Did he intend to march back over?

Her chest grew tight. Tense seconds passed. He climbed into his carriage and the vehicle drove off.

The air in her lungs swished out. Relieved, she finished cleaning her tools and made her way downstairs. On the marble-topped table in the entry hall lay the post. Two bills. With the mail clutched in her hand, Emma walked into the morning room. Slumping onto a chair, she tossed the bills aside and leaned back in the chair, closed her eyes, and recalled what had transpired after Simon and she had danced a short time ago.

What had she been thinking, letting him touch her so intimately? She wasn't sure. The only thing she knew was that being in Simon's arms while they'd danced had felt perfect.

Simon leaned back in his seat in the Royal Court Theatre in Sloane Square. After leaving Emma's town house, he'd stepped into his own residence only to get a whiff of whatever Baines was burning in the kitchen. Hungry, along with disgusted by the turn of events during the afternoon, Simon had headed to his club in search of a half-decent meal and an evening of entertainment.

He feared if he lounged about his residence in Bloomsbury, he would spend the remainder of the day staring at Emma's town house while he pined for her like a lovesick lad. What had happened? He still wasn't sure. One moment they'd been dancing, and the next kissing. And not because he wanted to whittle information from her, but because he couldn't help himself.

Blast it all! What addled him? While he kissed her, his cock had grown as hard as an anvil, and he'd realized he'd once again lost the train of his thoughts—become derailed from his quest to find out the truth.

It appeared that once a fool, always a fool.

Seated next to him in the box, Caruthers laughed at the antics of a performer on the stage, drawing Simon from his thoughts. He glanced over his shoulder at Huntington, who lounged in the back row, looking glum-faced. Who could blame the man? It seemed all eyes were on him, not the stage. Huntington's marriage had been an unhappy one, but how could they think he killed his wife?

As if Caruthers's thoughts ran parallel to Simon's, the man turned around in his seat and gave Huntington a sympathetic look. "Do you wish to leave?"

Huntington shook his head.

Caruthers frowned. "Bastards. The ton isn't happy unless they have something to gossip about."

"I don't wish to discuss it." Huntington's voice was firm, unbending. He looked close to losing his patience. Caruthers knew to clap his mouth shut. The marquess had a devil of a right hook, and the man looked primed to using it at the moment.

Caruthers nudged Simon's shoulder and pointed at the box opposite theirs in the theater. "Hey, old chum, isn't that your stepmother sitting with Lord Jarvis?"

Christ, yes. Simon grunted a confirmation. So the witch had not returned to the country. Her blond hair was piled loosely on her head, making her look younger than her true age, and the blue gown she wore displayed her breasts to their full advantage.

"I'd heard Lady Adler was back in Town," Caruthers said. "If I might say, she's held up quite well."

Unlike both Huntington and Westfield, Caruthers was unaware that Julia's malicious lies had caused the rift between Simon and his father, though his friend knew Simon held little affection toward the woman.

Simon's gaze shifted to the man sitting beside Julia. Lord Jarvis was in his sixties and in poor health. The widower had only one heir. If Simon's memory served him right, the boy would be close to seventeen. Was the woman up to her old tricks? Would she alienate this man from his son, suck the boy into a state of trust, only to accuse him of the unspeakable at a later date? Then drain Jarvis's coffers dry?

A knot tightened in his gut. He'd bet his last farthing

Jarvis was her next plump pigeon—a way to pay off her gambling debt. Simon's hands curled into tight fists.

The curtain on the stage fell and the gong announced the intermission.

Caruthers stood. "I'm in need of refreshment. Either of you blokes want anything?"

Simon shook his head.

Huntington, who looked like he'd not slept or eaten in days, briefly opened his eyes. "Nothing for me."

"Suit yourselves," Caruthers said, and left.

Across the theater, Lord Jarvis stood, leaving Julia alone in the box.

Simon jerked to his feet.

He knocked Huntington's foot with his own. "I need you to accompany me."

Bleary-eyed, the marquess stared at him. "Where?"

"Do me a favor, James. Don't ask questions."

His friend and business partner stood and straightened his damask waistcoat.

As Simon made his way to the other side of the theater, Huntington quietly followed him. When they neared Julia's box, his friend asked, "What do you intend to say to her?"

The man might be sleep deprived, but he was one of the most astute men Simon knew.

"I'm not sure."

"Just don't toss her over the balcony."

Simon's gaze swung back to his friend. He would never do such a thing, but the idea of sending Julia to the devil still contained an unwise appeal. Probably why he'd asked Huntington to accompany him. No, he knew the true reason. He feared in such a public place, Julia might rip her own bodice and accuse him of molesting her, then ask for a sizable amount of funds to not scream and draw all eyes to them. With the gossip, along with the fact his father had cast him out, the ton would believe her. Simon opened the door to the box, and he and Huntington stepped inside.

Smiling brightly, Julia turned around in her seat. Her beatific expression fell upon seeing him.

"You bloody witch," Simon said. "Are you determined to ruin another family just to pay off your debts?"

Her cheeks flushed before a catlike gleam lit her eyes. "I have no idea what you refer to, Simon."

"I'll tell Lord Jarvis what you're up to."

"Do you think he'll believe you? I'll tell him the same thing I told your father. That I scorned your advances. Who do you think Jarvis will believe? A man who doesn't follow society's rules, or me?"

Curse her. She hasn't changed.

Julia's gaze shifted to Huntington. "Must the marquess stand here while we discuss this?" The woman had the nerve to look down her nose at Huntington like he was no better than rubbish.

"Yes." Simon drew in a slow breath. "I might reconsider paying your debt, Julia."

One of her delicate eyebrows lifted. She knew there would be a stipulation.

"Yes, my dear stepmother, there is a catch. If I pay off your marker, you must agree to leave Great Britain. I don't care where you go. Be it France or America. But if you ever return, I will make the loan payable immediately."

"You can't ask that of me. What about the dowager house?"

"What about it?"

"It is my home."

"And it sits on my land." The reason he rarely went to his country house.

She fisted her small hands. "I won't do it."

He couldn't allow her to ruin Lord Jarvis's life, nor the man's son's. "I will include a yearly stipend."

Julia's eyes widened. "How much?"

"Five thousand."

A smile lit her face. "I'll do it for six thousand."

"I'm reducing the offer to four."

"What?" she hissed like the snake she was.

"If you ask me for an increase again, I'll reduce it to three."

She blanched. "B-but—"

"You have five seconds to accept, otherwise the deal is off the table. Five . . . four . . . three . . ."

"Damn your eyes. Yes, I'll go to France."

Simon forced his expression to remain bland. He opened the box's door, eager to be away from the witch. "My solicitor will draw up the contract and be in touch. Once you sail for Calais, the marker will be paid and the funds for this year sent to you. But remember, the ten thousand pounds will be set up as a loan, payable on your return to Great Britain. Have I made myself clear?"

"Yes. I'll sign your damn papers. Better than bedding another old man."

As Simon and Huntington made their way back to their box, the marquess peered astutely at him. The man cocked one of his dark brows. "Why did you pay her debt? You have every reason to hate her."

Simon thought of Emma and her sister and what it meant to care for the members of one's family. The bond he'd not experienced in over a decade. "Because I don't wish Jarvis's son to be cast aside when Julia sets her plan for the young heir in place. I'm all too familiar with how that feels."

Huntington clapped a hand on his shoulder. "Let's gather Caruthers up and get the hell out of here. I think we both deserve to get pissing drunk."

Chapter Twenty-One

The sound of hail hitting Emma's bedchamber window woke her. The tapping against the glass stopped. Good. She dreaded the thought of venturing into the attic to empty the buckets placed under the leaks in the old roof. She pulled the counterpane tighter about her shoulders and closed her eyes.

The noise started again. *Tick. Tick. Tick.*

It didn't sound like hail. She tossed off her bedding and slipped from the warmth. As she padded to the window, the cold of the wooden floor seeped through the threadbare rug and added to the chill traveling down her spine. She parted the curtain slightly and peered at the clear moonlit sky, then below at the street. A tall figure with a top hat stood on the pavement like an apparition rising from the low-clinging fog.

Her heart skipped a beat before it strummed hard against her ribs.

The man tipped his face up, allowing the moonlight to travel past the brim of his hat to disperse the shadow on his face.

Simon? His arm moved and another scattering of what might be pebbles tapped against the windowpane.

What madness bedeviled him? She drew in a slow breath, grabbed her white cotton wrapper, and slipped her arms through the sleeves. Avoiding the treads that creaked, she made her way down the steps and inched the front door open.

Her unexpected houseguest swept off his hat and gave a flamboyant bow. "Emma."

"What are you doing out here, Simon?"

"Taking an evening stroll."

His breath smelled of spirits. Was he drunk? "It is far from evening." She peered over his shoulder to Mrs. Jenkins's residence across the street. Thankfully the windows remained dark. "You will wake Mrs. Jenkins and draw attention to yourself if you don't lower your voice and return home."

"Home," he echoed. "Somehow, at the moment, it doesn't appeal to me as much as the warmth of your house."

For a second, his harsh face looked vulnerable. And then the softer expression vanished, making her question whether it had been nothing more than a figment of her imagination.

A light appeared in one of Mrs. Jenkins's third-story windows.

Lud. The gossipmonger was awake. Emma seized Simon's hand and pulled him inside. She closed the door, barring not only the tattler's view, but the glow from the streetlamp, leaving the entry hall bathed in only the streaks of moonlight streaming through the transom above the door.

In the dim space, shadows cut across Simon's angular face to highlight the dark stubble shading his firm jaw. How she'd love to paint him like this, his face dark and troubled. It seemed a glimpse into the real man—the man who not only frightened her but warmed her insides and made her daydream wicked thoughts.

"Em, you shock me, dragging me inside your house." His thumb swayed against the thin skin of her inner wrist. "Is it the cloak of darkness that makes you more daring?"

A chill crept down her back. Did he refer to that night? The already heavy beat of her heart escalated. He might suspect her of being the woman who'd kissed him, but he had no proof. She needed to remember that.

"I have no idea what you speak of." She released his hand. "I think you are inebriated, sir. I have pulled you inside because Mrs. Jenkins is awake. That tattler will whisper words of impropriety if she sees you at my door this time of night."

"Ah, smart move. We can't have the old bat telling stories, can we?"

Emma should be vexed at him, but she smiled. "No, we cannot."

She peered down the corridor at the steps that led below stairs to not only the kitchen but Mrs. Flynn's bedchamber. Thank goodness, the woman was a sound sleeper, but if Simon woke Lily there was no telling what her sister would say or do.

"Is everyone asleep?" he asked.

Of course they were. It was nearly two in the morning. Emma pressed her index finger to the warm surface of Simon's lips. "Yes. Now shhh. I don't wish you to wake my sister."

His mouth parted, and his tongue touched her finger before he gently bit the tip. Like the last time he'd done the same thing, heat exploded in her belly.

"You like that, don't you?"

She did, but she'd not admit it to him. She shook her head.

"Let's try it again and see, shall we?"

"Behave," she chastised, trying to sound stern even

though her body craved his touch. Needing to distance herself from him, she spun on her bare feet and moved to the morning room. Emma parted the shutter an inch and peered at Mrs. Jenkins's house. The light still glowed from one of the gossipmonger's windows, silhouetting a figure standing before it.

The squeak of the floorboards and the warmth coming off Simon like a hot grate alerted her to his presence behind her. Goose bumps prickled her skin.

"Trapped like a fox during the hunt," he said, his breath touching the crown of her ear.

Did he mean him or her? She turned around. A foolish move . . . only inches separated their mouths. Terrified of what she would do, Emma scurried by him. He needed to leave. And fast, before she did something reckless. She grabbed his hand and led him down the dark, narrow corridor to the rear door.

"You'll have to go out this way," she whispered, releasing his hand.

He leaned against the wall in that lackadaisical way that made him look harmless when he was anything but. His dark gaze traveled the length of her body. Her nipples peaked. She grabbed the open edges of her robe and wrapped the fabric tighter about herself to hide his effect on her body.

With a determined glint in his eye, Simon stepped close and set his broad palms on the wall behind Emma—one on each side of her shoulders.

That heat his body exuded engulfed her again—a near tangible flame. He smelled spicy and male, more enticing than one of Mrs. Flynn's desserts.

"I've thought about kissing you all day, Em." Slowly he lowered his head.

The scent of brandy teased her nose. And curse her for

wanting to taste it on her tongue. He pressed his lips to hers. A gentle kiss that turned urgent as his mouth moved hungrily against hers. Molten heat flooded her body. Everywhere. As if of their own volition, her hands lifted to his shoulders. She forced them to return to her sides. Was he playing a game of seduction again, trying to lower her defenses?

He pulled back. "Come now, Emma, I know you can do better than that."

"You are drunk, Simon. You cannot come into my house in the middle of the night and kiss me so wickedly."

"Wicked?" he repeated, as if she'd laid down the gauntlet and challenged him. "Really, my dear Emma, that kiss didn't even skirt the edge of wickedness. Now the kiss we shared that night you snuck into my house . . . now that was wicked. Two strangers. In the dark. Do you ever dream about it, darling? I must admit I do."

He didn't sound intoxicated anymore. No, he sounded quite sober. The dark, almost predatory look in Simon's eyes set the nerve endings in Emma's body on alert.

"Tell me you don't think of it. What is one more lie between us?"

"I don't know what you refer to."

"Really? Let me see if I can refresh your memory." He lowered his head and set his firm lips against hers, coaxing them open as he deepened the kiss. He tasted of liquor and desire. His mouth skimmed over her cheek. His tongue touched the rim of her ear.

She heard her own whimper. The place between her legs grew damp. And, not for the first time, Emma wanted this man to teach her everything he knew about carnal pleasure—to dislodge the memory of her and Charles's encounter, which lacked tenderness and had only inflicted pain. As if drawn by an undeniable force, she slid her hands over his hard chest.

She would have sworn his muscles quivered under her touch, but most likely that was nothing more than an illusion brought on by her own need and the fog of desire clouding her head. While his tongue continued to stroke hers, his left hand settled on her waist and skimmed upward. The tips of his fingers left a trail of heat on her back, while his thumb traveled over the front of her ribs until he reached the underside of her breast.

Don't stop. Please. She whimpered in frustration.

As if he understood her discontent—her need—his thumb swayed against the thin material of her nightgown, stroking her peaked nipple. Her breasts grew heavy, tingled.

His mouth shifted to her ear. "Do you like that?"

What a wicked question. She shouldn't answer him. "Yes."

She felt his smile against her neck. His hand cupped the weight of her breast and squeezed. Gently at first, before applying more pressure. Her bare toes curled against the wooden floor.

This was wrong. Well, at least it was wrong to stand so close to the basement stairs. If Mrs. Flynn came up the steps, she'd see them. Emma might not be thinking straight, but she was lucid enough to know the precariousness of the situation. The housekeeper would take a frying pan to Mr. Radcliffe's head.

"This way," she whispered. She took his hand in hers and pulled him back into the morning room off the front entry hall. Quietly she closed the double doors and locked them. With the front shutters drawn, only scant moonlight cut into the dim room.

Her eyes adjusted to the darkness.

Simon stood close, watching her. What was he thinking? God, what was she thinking? She should have asked him to leave, not dragged him into this room, but ever since the first time they'd kissed, she wanted Simon to show her what it felt like to be loved properly.

As if submerged and coming up for air, her conscience buoyed to the surface. Intent on opening the door and sending him on his way, Emma grasped the handle.

Simon's fingers settled over hers, stilling her movements.

Then it all happened so fast. She was in his arms again. His mouth on hers. Almost frantically, she slipped his coat off his shoulders. He shrugged out of it, then his fingers gathered the front of her robe and drew the garment down her arms. The soft material brushed against the backs of her calves as the robe fell to the floor. Cool air filtered through the thin material of her nightgown—a welcome reprieve from the heat scorching her skin. She worked at the buttons of his waistcoat. It landed on the rug, adding to the pile of garments by their feet.

"If we don't stop, Emma . . ." His voice trailed off. His jaw tensed.

She didn't want him to stop. She got on her toes, pressed her open mouth to his neck, and tasted the salt on his flesh.

"Good Lord," he mumbled. He lifted his fingers to the buttons that lined the front of her nightgown, but hesitated.

Did he feel the heavy beat of her heart? Construe it as fear? It wasn't. She was beyond analyzing her thoughts. Goodness, every kiss, every touch, every stroke made her desire him. She wanted this. And that knowledge freed something within her. She'd let Charles take her innocence because she'd been frightened after Papa's death. Grief, and the uncertainty of her siblings' lives and her own, had sent her into a place she thought too dark to find her way out of by herself.

Perhaps she'd never truly loved Charles. Only gravitated

to him because he seemed an anchor in a chaotic storm, allowing her to confuse her grief with another powerful emotion. But this act between her and Simon was something she craved.

Fear didn't precipitate it, and that understanding empowered her. She gave a slight nod of her head.

It seemed all he needed. He undid the buttons of her nightgown. The soft cotton brushed against her skin as it slithered over her shoulders, hips, and legs, landing in a puddle by her feet. Simon's hungry gaze traveled the length of her naked body.

"You're lovely," he mumbled. "Perfect."

She wasn't perfect. But she didn't wish to contemplate whether his words were false flattery aimed at one goal.

He lifted his shirt over his head. Moonlight settled on his taut skin to reveal the muscles that shaped his masculine form. As an artist, she'd always thought the male body lovely. She'd studied it. Simon's eclipsed any she'd seen on canvas or in life. He was beautiful in every conceivable way, honed smooth, and contoured as though set on Earth by a master sculptor. Once again, she was struck with how she wanted to paint him. Not sitting in a chair with his fine bespoke garments, but in dim lighting, his body unclothed, and moonlight reflecting off his skin.

His hands shifted to the fall of his trousers.

Emma stifled the nervous laugh working its way up her throat. Instead, she concentrated on the intensity of Simon's eyes and the way the muscles in his shoulders flexed as he removed the garment.

He tossed his trousers, along with his drawers, onto a nearby chair. Her gaze dipped to the rippled muscles of his abdomen. Then lower to the thin line of hair that trailed below his navel to a bush of hair and his jutting manhood.

Gracious me. She swallowed. She might not have seen Charles's shaft before he'd ruthlessly thrust it into her, but she doubted it had been so large. A sudden fear overcame her. Would it hurt again?

She'd little time to contemplate it all. Simon pulled her into his arms. Her breasts pressed against his firm chest—a tantalizing meeting of skin on skin. Each point of contact an overwhelming heat that dissolved her questions, leaving only desire.

With her face cupped in his hands, he set his lips to hers and gave her a deep, intoxicating kiss. His hands traveled down her body, cupped her bum, and lifted her. The hardness of his erection nudged the spot between her legs.

One minute they were standing, the next lying on the threadbare carpet. It didn't offer much softness, but that seemed of little consequence to either of them. There was a frenzied need to their movements, as though if they didn't hurry some catastrophe would forestall them.

A burst of lightning lit the sky outside, sending an illuminating flash between the edges of the shutters. The streak of light touched Simon's skin, making him glow as if an illusion. Would she awake in a tangle of sheets to find this was nothing more than a dream?

No, the scent of his skin, the hardness of his muscles, and the heat between them was more than a dream could conjure. This was neither dream nor illusion, and in the morning she would suffer the consequences of her actions, but she didn't care. She was already ruined. Really, what difference could this make? Except she was about to allow the enemy to have his way with her, but Simon seemed too far removed from that part of him she feared. It appeared they'd both laid their differences aside for this one glorious moment of passion.

Lying on his side, he pulled her next to him. Simon stroked the tip of one of her breasts with his tongue before drawing the pebbled peak into his mouth. He made a noise—appreciative in its tone, like a gentleman experiencing the finest brandy on his palate.

Unable to help herself, she watched his mouth moving against her flesh. A low moan eased from her lips. The desire to touch him overwhelmed her. "May I touch you?"

"I'd be disappointed if you didn't." He cupped her hand and placed it on his hard length.

She slid her hand down the silky shaft to the base.

Simon's eyes drifted closed. The muscles in his neck tightened. She doubted the fierce expression on his face reflected pain. No, he enjoyed her touch as much as she enjoyed his.

While she touched him, his palm ran over her inner thigh and settled on the most private part of her body, where she was wet. A pulse thrummed where her legs joined. She arched into his hand. Her breaths came fast.

Shifting, he settled between her legs. The firm pressure of his hips spread her thighs wider. His dark gaze held hers, and she felt the tip of him pushing into her. Slow at first, as if he thought it would hurt her, but there was no pain, just a stretching, and then he was in her. Hard and thick. There was no burning like last time. Only a fullness that seemed perfect.

For a minute, he stared at her. Did he know the truth? That she was already ruined?

His mouth came down on hers. Fierce. Demanding. Was there anger in the act? No, she didn't believe so, just desire. She felt the play of muscles in his shoulders as he cupped her bum and lifted her slightly. He moved his hips, then pulled back, never breaking the contact, and then filled her again in a slow, erotic way that built up anticipation for the next stroke of his hard flesh. She arched against him, drawing him in farther.

He moaned, a low, primal noise, and pressed himself so tight against her, the pulse between her legs exploded. Once, twice, three times, gaining intensity. The odd sensation left her breathless. The intensity slowed, leaving her both sated and drowsy.

His once slow movements picked up speed. He drew back and thrust forward. Uttering a blasphemy, he pulled out. His warm seed spilled on her thigh.

"Forgive me," he said, his voice raspy. He reached for his coat, withdrew a handkerchief, and cleaned her.

Thank goodness Simon had enough sense to think of that. Charles had pulled out a sheath of some kind. Anger stirred in her. The bastard *had* set out to sleep with her. She would not think of it now—not let it ruin the contentment Simon's lovemaking had caused within her.

Another flash of lightning illuminated the room. Beside her, Simon lay on his back, his eyes open, his breath labored.

Rain begun to tap against the windowpanes, and she suddenly realized how cold the air was. She wanted to cuddle up to Simon and absorb the warmth coming off his body. As if he was thinking the same thing, he pulled her into the crook of his arm. She set her head on his chest. The beat of his heart was fast, like hers, yet everything within her felt calm, relaxed.

For long minutes they lay together, their bodies warmed by each other's. Content, Emma fought the urge to close her eyes and drift off to sleep.

Simon's stomach rumbled.

"Hungry?" she asked with a small laugh.

"Famished. Baines is a dreadful cook."

"That bad?"

He chuckled. "Yes."

Simon appeared to be a man accustomed to only the best.

So why did he continue to eat Baines's terrible cooking? "Are both your manservants related to you?"

Simon grinned. "No, but I must admit I care for the two old coots like family." He moved as if to touch his ring and, not finding it there, visibly stiffened. He ran his index finger over her bare arm. "I need to ask you something."

Emma knew what it was, and, for a moment, her heart stopped.

Chapter Twenty-Two

The beat of Emma's heart, which had slowed after their lovemaking, resumed with a wicked force. She knew what Simon wished to ask her. *Are you one of the thieves?* She could all but read the question in his eyes. The problem was, she didn't know if she trusted him. Their joining had been fueled by a rash desire that neither had wanted to deny—not love, and surely not trust. That might be a bridge they never ventured across.

Simon shifted sideways. His gaze locked on her. "Do you remember when I told you about my ring having been stolen?"

Finding it nearly impossible to talk, she nodded.

"The thieves who broke into my house across the street, hit me unconscious and took it. I've been on a mission to find those responsible."

"A mission?" she echoed, stalling for time as she pondered what her response would be. If she told him the truth, would he forgive her? She wasn't sure.

"Yes." His sensual lips thinned into a straight line. "I need to know. Were you somehow involved, Emma?"

The vulnerability in his handsome countenance tore at

her. Tears pressed at her eyes. Lying to him went against every fiber in her being, but the fear inside her over-shadowed all else. She'd trusted Charles and that was the most foolish decision of her life. Would trusting Simon be as reckless?

She forced a carefree laugh. "Me? You believe I entered your home and stole your ring?"

"I've considered it."

The tautness in his face reminded her of the man who'd entered her house an hour ago, not the one who'd just made love to her. Emma took a deep breath. In truth, she hadn't taken it. *Lily had.* "I swear to you, I did not steal your ring, Simon. I swear on my sister's life."

His eyes widened.

Yes, that got his attention. He realized she loved Lily—knew she wouldn't say such a thing if untrue.

"You're telling the truth, aren't you?"

Unable to draw a breath through the guilt clogging her throat, she nodded again.

If ever Simon had wanted to believe someone, it was now as Emma stared at him with an innocent expression on her lovely face. More than once, he'd questioned his belief she was involved. Westfield was right. Simon needed to admit that his evidence against her was practically nil. So why had he all but convicted her? Had he wished for a reason to explain the damnable attraction he felt for Emma?

The sound of someone moving down the stairs pulled him from his thoughts.

"Emma! Are you downstairs?" Lily called out.

Eyes huge as saucers, Emma scrambled to her feet. "Yes, dear. I'm . . . reading."

The footsteps drew closer. The handle turned. "Why is the door locked?"

Simon tugged on his trousers as Emma slipped on her nightgown and hastily buttoned it. "I must have turned it by mistake. Go back to bed. I'll be up in a minute."

"I've got two pairs of socks on my feet, and I'm still freezing," Lily said. "May I sleep with you? I promise I won't take my socks off and rub my cold toes on your legs in the morning to wake you up."

"Yes, climb into my bed. I'll be up shortly." Emma slipped her arms through the sleeves of her wrapper.

Lily's slow yet heavy footfalls echoed as the child made her way back up the steps.

Emma turned to Simon. "Can you let yourself out the back door?"

"Yes, of course." He snatched his shirt off the floor. As Emma dashed by him, he couldn't resist clasping her hand and pulling her warm body against his. Reluctant to leave, he kissed her for a long moment. When he released her, unshed tears filled her eyes, but before he could say anything, she pulled her wrapper tight about her body and dashed from the room. Simon fought the urge to follow her and ask what was wrong, but he knew the answer.

He was an arse. He'd all but accused her of thievery. Only minutes after they'd shared the intimacy of their bodies. And being with Emma had felt unequaled by anything he could recall. Her soft sighs. The way she'd looked at him with her beautiful blue eyes. It had been perfect before he'd opened his damn mouth.

He was an idiot, but tomorrow he'd make it up to her.

The following day, Simon leaned back in his office chair, propped his feet on the desk, and opened the velvet-covered jeweler's box. The afternoon light streaming through the window caught the blue topaz pendant that dangled from a gold chain. He brushed his thumb over the large stone. After leaving his boxing club this morning, Simon spent over an hour at Hancock's, on the corner of Bruton and New Bond Streets, choosing the necklace for Emma, settling on this one because the brilliant stone made him think of her lovely eyes. Then he'd bought Emma a new parasol to replace her damaged one, Lily sheet music, and Nick a trundling hoop.

He'd hoped to give Emma the necklace during their sitting this afternoon, but returned home to find a missive canceling their appointment. Once again, she stated she was baking bread. She was avoiding him.

A knock sounded on the door.

"Yes. Come in."

Harris entered. The smoke filling the corridor drifted into the room, along with the scent of burnt food.

It appeared Baines's most recent attempt at cooking was as futile as the others. Simon stifled a groan. He didn't think he could force himself to eat another abysmal meal. This morning the toast resembled coal and the rashers were nearly as dark. In an effort to save not only his palate but his stomach, Simon had dined at a chop house for luncheon.

Bushy gray eyebrows cocked high, Harris walked over to the desk and peered at the necklace. "Very nice, my lord. Is it for Miss Trafford?"

"It is." Simon snapped the box closed and slipped it into his top desk drawer.

Harris pointed at the frilly pink parasol set on the corner table. "Is that for her, as well? Or are you to use it?"

Simon ignored the question and the silly smirk on the butler's face. "What is Baines burning?"

"A beef roast."

"I think I shall dine at my club this evening."

"He's called in the cavalry, my lord."

"Cavalry?" Simon asked.

"Mrs. Flynn. After she finishes baking bread, she has agreed to help Baines resuscitate dinner."

It smelled beyond hope, but if anyone could salvage it, Mrs. Flynn could. Simon stood. "Was there something you needed, Harris?"

"Yes, Baines wishes to know if you'd prefer béarnaise or port sauce?"

"Whichever he decides, is fine."

"Very well, sir." Harris strode to the door.

"Do you know if it is Mrs. Flynn's half day?" Simon asked.

Harris turned around. "I believe so."

Perhaps if he invited Emma and Lily to dine with him, Emma would accept, and he could give her the necklace. Simon removed a piece of parchment from his paper tray, penned the invitation, and handed it to Harris. "Please deliver this to Miss Trafford and wait for her reply. I've invited her and Lily to dine with me."

The butler's lips curved ever so slightly. "Miss Trafford and her *sister*? How domestic, my lord. Are you finally considering taking a wife?"

Marriage? Lord, no. So few of them were successful. He need only look at his own family. His father's and Julia's marriage had been a sham. And what of poor Huntington's union? A disaster. No, he didn't intend to marry. Marriage wasn't something one should take lightly, like his stepmother had. It required commitment. Love. He shook his head.

As Mrs. Flynn enthusiastically mixed flour, yeast, and water into a glutinous glob in the hot and humid kitchen, Emma dragged her sleeve over her forehead to wipe away the perspiration prickling her brow. They'd been making bread for nearly two hours.

With a sigh, she kneaded the mixture on the wooden board. The moist dough stuck to her palms like glue. The scent of yeast, which at first seemed pleasant, had lost its appeal over an hour ago.

Fast footfalls thundered on the stairs. With a broad smile, Lily stepped into the room. "Em, Mr. Radcliffe has bought Nick a trundling hoop. Do you want to come and see it?"

It shouldn't surprise her that he'd bought the boy a gift. Simon might try to hide it, but he was kind. She thought of how he treated his two manservants and the extra money he'd given her when he'd purchased her painting of the family in the park.

"Em, do you wish to see it?" Lily repeated.

Was Simon outside, as well? She both craved seeing him and feared it. The task at hand suddenly seemed a godsend. "I wish I could, but"—she lifted her flour-incrusted fingers and wiggled them—"as you see, at present I'm engaged in helping Mrs. Flynn make bread."

Lily scrunched up her face. "Why would you ever wish to do so?"

Indeed. She'd asked herself the same question, repeatedly. She knew the answer. She wished for a distraction—something to steer her mind away from what she'd engaged in with Simon last night. An impossible task. Her body still hummed. Her lips tingled. And a tiny pulse beat between her legs when she recalled the pleasure of Simon's body joining with hers. But all of it was tempered by the fact that she'd lied to him.

"I thought making bread today would be enjoyable." Foolish thought, that.

"Not for those who must eat it," Lily mumbled.

The child was right. Emma's loaves always ended up hard as bricks on the outside and too mushy on the inside.

"Now you go on outside," Mrs. Flynn said. "And leave your sister be."

After Lily left the room, Emma glanced up at Mrs. Flynn. "She's right. I'm hopeless in the kitchen."

"That means you can only improve. And you will."

Obviously, the fumes from Emma's paints and turpentine were affecting the woman if she thought Emma would ever be a skilled baker. Emma pressed her fingers knuckle deep and continued to work the sticky dough.

"It's too wet, dearie," Mrs. Flynn said. "Add a bit more flour."

Emma scooped a measure of flour out of the crock and dumped it over the dough. A cloud of golden powder drifted into the air. Coughing, she turned her face into her shoulder and sneezed.

The housekeeper snorted.

Emma's own laugh took hold of her. She licked at the flour on her lips and dusted off her face.

Still chuckling, the older woman opened the oven and took out several baked loaves. Mrs. Flynn's bread looked perfect, symmetrical, and golden in color. They were most likely light and airy inside. Emma's, on the other hand, looked misshapen, crusty, and all around unappealing. Lily would insist they give them to St. George's parish as alms for the poor. But with their money dwindling, they couldn't afford to do so. Perhaps Mrs. Flynn would use Emma's to make bread pudding.

Lily's fast footfalls pounded on the stairs again. She dashed into the kitchen and waved a piece of paper in the air. "Mr. Radcliffe has invited us to dine with him tonight."

Emma's heart stuttered in her chest. "At his house?" The words came out like a squeak.

"Of course at his house. He says he wishes you to experience Mr. Baines's cooking firsthand."

Even though nervous about seeing him again, she couldn't help her smile.

"Don't worry, dearies," Mrs. Flynn said. "I'm going to help him cook the meal."

"Can we go?" Lily anxiously shifted from one foot to the other. "His pinched-faced butler is awaiting your reply."

A wide grin took up the lower half of Mrs. Flynn's face. "Say yes, dearie."

She would have to see Simon sooner or later, and seeing him with her sister would be safer. And it might be the perfect opportunity to place his ring somewhere in his house so he'd find it. Or perhaps it was time she trusted Simon and told him the whole story about that night in his house. "Tell him we would be honored."

Chapter Twenty-Three

Simon paced the floor of his bedroom and let out a slow breath. Why was he nervous? It wasn't as if he'd never dined with a beautiful woman before. Though he couldn't recall ever inviting one's sister. Not true. There was that one time in France, but they'd been twins, dancers, and his reasoning a bit wicked.

He stepped in front of the mirror in his dressing room, buttoned his blue silk waistcoat, and straightened his gray tie, a shade lighter than his trousers. The only thing good about Baines taking over the kitchen was the tranquility of dressing without the valet hovering over Simon like a doting nursemaid.

Releasing another slow breath, Simon shrugged into his charcoal-gray coat and stepped out of his bedchamber. The pleasing scent of savory and sweet cooking filled the air. God bless Mrs. Flynn. As Simon took the last step into the entry hall, the knocker sounded against the front door. Harris, standing by it, reached for the handle.

"I'll get it." Simon waved the butler away and rushed forward.

The man blinked. "Really? I must say, sir, you appear as

anxious as a cat about to be bathed. Are you sure you're not more enamored with Miss Trafford than you realize?"

"Go away!" he snapped, realizing the man touched on an emotion Simon didn't wish to examine.

The butler grinned.

Trying to control the scowl on his face, Simon opened the door. Lily peered at him with a mischievous expression, while Emma offered a slow, hesitant smile.

A place close to his heart clenched.

His gaze drifted over her blue silk gown. Unlike the high-collared dresses she normally wore, this gown revealed more of her luscious skin. He wanted to drag Emma upstairs and nibble every inch of her soft, rose-scented body.

As if she could read his wicked thoughts, her pink cheeks darkened.

"Hello, Emma, Lily. Welcome." He moved aside and they stepped into the entry hall.

Emma, still looking uncomfortable, held her sister's hand like a lifeline. "Good evening, Simon. We thank you for the invitation to dine with you."

"I should be thanking you. Mrs. Flynn is a godsend. My house hasn't smelled this good since . . . Well, I cannot recall it ever smelling this wonderful." He winked. "But don't tell Baines that."

Lily turned and saw Harris standing behind her. The child jumped back and squeaked.

Simon bit back a laugh and motioned to the drawing room. "Please have a seat. I'm sure dinner will be ready shortly."

Inside the room, Lily stopped in front of one of the chairs and rubbed her finger over the embroidered flamingos, then giggled. "You like birds, Mr. Radcliffe."

Those damnable chairs. "Not particularly."

Emma shot her sister a stern glance. "Lily, please sit."

Exhaling a heavy sigh, Lily strode to the settee. The child squealed with delight as she passed the table with Simon's copy of Inspector Whitley's *Crimson Lord*. She snatched it up, plopped down on the cushions, and started flipping the pages. "Did you read it, Mr. Radcliffe? Isn't it wonderful?"

Wonderful wasn't the word he would use to describe it. "Whitley certainly has a flair for the dramatic."

Lily nodded enthusiastically.

"Good gracious." Emma peered at him, the pensive expression on her face replaced with mirth. "Don't tell me you're reading that drivel, as well."

Simon grinned. "I was curious."

Harris stepped into the room and cleared his throat. "Dinner is ready."

Lily sprang to her feet. "Good, I'm starved. Can I bring the book with me?"

"No, you may not. Please leave it here," Emma said.

Simon offered Emma his arm, and she rested her hand on it. A jolt of warmth shot through his body. Strong. Powerful. Disconcerting.

As they stepped down the corridor, Emma leaned close to him. "Simon, after dinner I need to speak with you."

That pensive expression returned to her face. His gut tightened. "Is something wrong? We can step into my office and you can tell me now."

She nibbled her lower lip. "No, we will talk after dinner."

Something was definitely troubling her. Perhaps she was still worried over her brother.

Lily scrunched up her nose when they stepped into the dining room.

Understandable. The wainscoting was a putrid green and the upper half of the walls were done in pink and orange stripes. He'd have it painted. He could ask Emma to suggest a color. Simon frowned. What was he thinking? He owned a lovely home on Curzon Street. Did he intend to stay here?

"You sure like pink, Mr. Radcliffe, and this green looks like pea soup," Lily said, drawing Simon from his thoughts.

"Lily," Emma chastised.

Simon chuckled. "No, she's right. It does look hideous. What color would you both suggest?"

"I like emerald, and Emma's favorite color is blue." Lily glanced nervously at Harris as the butler pulled out a chair for her.

"Is blue your favorite, Em?" Simon asked, thinking about the necklace he'd purchased for her as he pushed her chair in.

She glanced over her shoulder and smiled. "Yes."

The door to the dining room opened and Baines walked in carrying a silver tray and soup tureen.

Hopefully, Mrs. Flynn had made whatever was in it.

Emma leaned close and grinned. "You look almost as green as the walls."

"You think yourself a wit. You won't be laughing if Baines made it," he whispered, returning her cheeky expression.

"Oh, now you have me frightened."

"You should be," Simon replied with a laugh.

Baines lifted the lid and the scent of rosemary and thyme floated through the room.

"I think that smells like Mrs. Flynn's herb soup," Emma said, a hopeful tone in her voice.

Baines nodded. "It is, miss, but I added a few additional spices to it."

Everyone seated at the table stiffened.

Without thought, Simon slipped his hand over the white tablecloth and grasped Emma's fingers briefly and gave them a squeeze. Somehow sitting next to her felt right, even with Lily staring at him like she wanted to stick her fork in his hand.

The warmth of Simon's fingers grasping Emma's made her heart beat a little faster. She'd experienced the same flutter when he'd answered the door. Guilt continued to plague her over lying to him. She slipped her finger into the pocket of her gown and clasped the warm metal of Simon's ring. After dinner, she would tell him everything—trust him. If he cared for her, he'd understand. Her stomach knotted. It was a leap of faith, but she needed to take it.

Baines stepped next to her with the tureen. Emma pulled her hand from her pocket to ladle herself some soup. "It smells wonderful, Baines."

Smiling proudly, the man finished serving, set the tureen on the sideboard, and exited the room.

"You try it first," Lily said to Simon.

Tentatively Simon dipped his soupspoon into the creamy broth and brought it to his mouth. The tense expression on his face eased. "It's delicious."

Lily tasted it. "Mmmm."

Emma lowered her spoon into the soup. Raised voices in the corridor stilled her hand.

"See here, miss, you can't go in there. The master is entertaining," Harris said in his stiff baritone.

"We'll just see about that, we will, you clodpoll," a woman screeched. The sound of glass shattering rent the air, followed by fast-moving footsteps.

Simon paled. Mumbling a blasphemy, he stood with such force, his chair toppled backward. With a white-knuckled grip, he caught it before it crashed against the floor. The dining room door burst open. A redheaded woman, wearing a costly gown of sea-green silk with layers of tasseled fabric, stood on the threshold.

"Vivian," Simon said.

Lily sucked in an audible breath. Her hand clutched Emma's arm. "She's not dead," she mumbled.

No, not dead, and the woman's hurt expression, anger, and obvious confusion clearly stated Simon had not severed his relationship with the redhead. Emma's stomach rolled. A strong wave of nausea followed. She'd been foolish once again.

The woman, whom Simon called Vivian, set the back of her hand dramatically to her forehead. "Simon, what is going on? That lummox at the door tried to stop me from coming inside and . . ." The woman's gaze shifted to Emma before falling back to Simon like a pendulum. The redhead's shoulders stiffened, and her eyes shot daggers. "Is this why you sent me on holiday? You rutting dog! Has this scrawny light-skirts taken my place? A bloody dancer, no doubt!" The woman looked at Lily. "And this one's no more than a child!"

Heat colored Simon's high cheekbones. His hand flexed. "You think I would touch a child?"

As if oblivious to his anger, the woman continued, "Where are my things? Have you packed them away?" Before Simon could answer, the woman plucked the ladle from the soup tureen and threw it at him.

He sidestepped. The ironstone utensil clacked against the wall and tumbled to the floor. Soup splattered around the room.

Emma lifted her napkin and wiped her cheek.

Grinning, Lily used her sleeve. "This is better than one of Inspector Whitley's books."

Something bumped Emma's leg. She peered under the

table to find the cat cowering beneath. Kismet's ears were plastered down on his head. His hair stood up straight on his back. The animal made a mad dash out of the room and past Harris, who stood gaping like a beached fish.

It seemed like a comedy—a farce one would see on a rowdy East End stage, yet the unsettling sensation that Emma had been nothing more than a diversion to Simon while his lover was away rendered laughter impossible.

Mrs. Flynn and Mr. Baines appeared in the doorway. Their startled gazes traveled from Simon to the enraged woman, then to Emma.

Without a word, Simon moved to the redhead, set his hand on the woman's back, and ushered her to the doorway. Mrs. Flynn, Baines, and Harris parted like the Red Sea before Moses.

Simon glanced over his shoulder. A nerve twitched in his jaw, a steady tattoo. He stared at Emma for a long minute. Or was it no more than a couple of seconds? Time had grown sluggish. "Carry on. I shall be but a moment."

Carry on. Was he mad? His lover had returned and he expected her to sit here and eat soup.

He strode from the room. The woman shrieked in a tone painful to one's ears. Baines and Harris followed.

"I knew all along he'd not murdered her. Simon is *too nice* to be a true villain," Lily said.

It appeared her sister was as poor a judge of men as Emma was.

"Come, Lily. I think it best we return home." Emma stood on wobbly legs and clasped her sister's hand.

"But Simon said to wait," Lily complained. The child's eyes grew round. "Do you think they left to engage in those wicked games again?"

The thought made Emma's eyes burn.

Mrs. Flynn dashed to Emma's side. "Who is she? What's happened?"

"I believe his paramour," Emma whispered into the woman's ear.

The housekeeper gasped.

Still holding Lily's hand, Emma moved down the corridor. The butler and the valet now stood outside the drawing room, their ears pressed to the closed doors. They straightened upon seeing her.

Inside the room, the woman was sobbing in earnest.

"Vivian," Simon said. "Stop crying and let me explain."

The scoundrel was trying to talk his way out of this mess. *Vivian* was more than welcome to him

"Explain?" the paramour yelled. "I should have known a scoundrel like Lord Adler could not be faithful to one mistress! I should have accepted Lord Fairmount's offer."

"Lord Adler?" Emma repeated, her heart beating so fast she feared it would cease from exhaustion. She peered at the two manservants. They both flushed like truant schoolboys caught playing in the park.

"Is it true?" Emma heard herself ask in a small voice.

The red on Baines's cheeks deepened. "Well, um, yes."

Suddenly looking paler than normal, Harris nodded.

"Gorblimey," Mrs. Flynn said. "I knew he looked familiar. I've seen his caricature in *Punch* magazine."

"Lord Adler," Lily mumbled as if still processing it all.

"Come, dears." Mrs. Flynn wrenched the front door open.

"You're leaving?" Baines asked, looking like he wanted to weep. "But we still haven't served the roast and parsley-topped potatoes."

Mrs. Flynn narrowed her eyes and jabbed her index finger into Baines's chest. Once, twice, three times. "I hope Lord Scandal chokes on it."

Harris stepped up to Emma. "Please wait, Miss Trafford, I believe his lordship has a gift for you."

A gift? For services rendered? What a fool I've been. Again.

"He can take his gift and shove it up his . . . nose," Mrs. Flynn said.

Lily dug her heels into the entry hall rug. "I wish to stay. I want to know where the woman has been."

"It's none of our concern." Emma pulled her sister outside. The cool air felt too thick to draw into her taut lungs.

"Come, dearies," Mrs. Flynn said, prompting them to cross the street.

Once inside her house, Emma slumped against the closed door.

Mrs. Flynn stared at her but said not a word.

"Can you believe it, Em?" Lily said. "He's a nobleman . . . just like Charles, and he was living right across the street from us."

Just like Charles. The words felt like a perverse taunt. Tears filled her eyes, then trailed down her face.

Lily's eyes grew wide. "What's the matter, Em?"

"Come, child." Mrs. Flynn took Lily's hand and drew her down the corridor and below stairs. "Let's leave your sister alone for a bit. You can help me make dinner. She'll feel better with a bit of food in her stomach."

Emma couldn't eat. The thought of food intensified the nausea gripping her stomach. So it seemed they had both been keeping secrets. She reached into her pocket and clasped the ring. Goodness, Lord Adler. A favorite subject of Mrs. Jenkins's tattles. And if the gossipmonger spoke the truth, his lordship was a libertine who'd possessed a bevy of mistresses. And none had lasted very long.

A pounding on the door startled Emma. She straightened.

"Emma, open the door!" Simon yelled.

"Go away, *Lord Adler*. I do not wish to speak to you right now."

"Open the door, Emma, or I'll break it in."

The sharp tone in his voice implied he wasn't kidding. She squared her shoulders and grasped the door handle. It was time they both revealed their secrets.

Chapter Twenty-Four

The fierce expression on Simon's face made Emma regret opening the door. He stood on the top step, his coat brushed back, his fisted hands on his lean hips, a nerve jumping a steady beat in his strong, chiseled jaw.

A movement beyond him drew her attention. Simon's carriage stood before his residence. Was his lover inside? The vehicle pulled away, and Emma noticed Mrs. Jenkins and Mrs. Vale had exited their homes. The two old women watched the goings-on with rapt interest. Emma wouldn't allow the gossipmongers a front row seat to whatever spectacle would commence. She stepped back, allowing Simon to enter.

Footfalls dashed up the basement steps—the rapid pace proclaimed them Lily's. Face pensive, her sister stepped into the corridor. "Em, is everything fine?"

Before she could reply, Simon spoke. "Your sister and I need to talk, poppet. Can you give us a moment?" The calm tone of his voice contradicted the storm in his eyes.

Mrs. Flynn came up the steps and stood behind Lily. The protective woman clasped her heavy wooden rolling pin like a billy club.

"You have no need for that, Mrs. Flynn," Simon said.

"You know I would never do anything to harm Emma. I only wish to speak with her."

The housekeeper narrowed her eyes. "I know Simon Radcliffe wouldn't harm a blessed soul in this house, but I'm not so sure about Lord Adler."

"As you now know, madam, we are one and the same." Simon's low voice sounded infused with steel. "And not different in many ways."

The housekeeper narrowed her eyes. "That's what worries me."

"As I said before, everything you've read in the scandal sheets isn't always true, madam. Please give Emma and me a few minutes alone."

Lily's and Mrs. Flynn's gazes shifted to Emma.

She wiped her moist palms on the skirt of her dress and nodded.

Still looking unsure, Lily and the housekeeper turned away and made their way below stairs.

Simon clasped Emma's hand and pulled her into the morning room. He closed the doors behind them. The sound of the lock clicking into place caused her heart to skip a beat.

"I wish to explain . . . about Vivian," he said.

"No need. It all seems rather clear. Vivian is your current mistress." She arched a brow at him, daring him to deny the blatant truth.

"She *was* my mistress, but not any longer."

"Dismissed like all the others. Poor woman. If the gossip is true, you've had a harem of them, *Lord Adler*."

"Emma . . ." He strode forward.

Holding up her hands, she stepped back.

Yet Simon kept moving toward her, erasing the distance between them. When a mere two feet separated them, he stopped. "Let me explain."

"No need, my lord. Though I do wish to ask you one question, if you don't mind?"

"Anything." His hand curled about her elbow, sending warmth not only to her arm but the rest of her traitorous body.

"Do high-born gentlemen like you and Charles Neville sit around your fancy clubs discussing your conquests—the foolish women you've ruined?" She needed to know if she wore a scarlet letter. Was an easy mark. The possibility made her stomach twist.

"What?" Simon flinched as if she'd cracked her palm against his cheek. "Good Lord, you don't really think that."

Warmth heated her cheeks. "I don't know what to think. I've had two liaisons. Both with men of noble birth. And I'm nothing more than a portraitist, and a struggling one at that. It seems a rather strange coincidence."

He released her elbow. "Emma, you know I didn't set out to make love to you. It happened. There was no plan. And I'm disgusted Neville breached his promise to marry you. But I'm not him."

"Do you know him?"

His jaw visibly tensed.

"Do you?" she repeated.

"Yes. I know him. He's a fool."

"Well, at least he pretended to want to marry me. What do you intend to do? Ask me to be your next mistress?"

"Would that be so terrible?" His hand settled on her waist and he shifted closer. "I could take care of you and your family. You wouldn't want for anything."

"Until you tired of me. Like Vivian?"

She'd never seen Simon blush, didn't think him capable of it, but red singed his high cheekbones. "My relationship with Vivian was nothing more than an arrangement. With no promises. Those tears she cried today weren't for me, but for my financial support. We never loved each other.

Whereas, you and I . . ." He raked his hands through his dark hair. "We share a connection that cannot be denied."

A connection? He meant lust. Not love. And the desire between them would fade when it wasn't so new to him. Hadn't she learned that firsthand from Charles? How fleeting desire could be. And being a nobleman's mistress was not what she aspired to. She wished to be an example to her sister. She tipped her chin up. "I'm not interested."

"Just think about it. You could paint all day without worrying about money, and at night you and I could . . ." His gaze held hers. The air between them grew thick, charged with the passion neither of them could deny. He cupped her face and angled his mouth over hers. His kiss was fierce and demanding. He coaxed her lips open, his tongue plunged, and tangled with hers.

She melted against him. She wanted him like a drunkard craved another bottle of gin, knowing it was nothing more than a short reprieve from the insidious thirst that would return with a vengeance. But she wouldn't become his lover just to be discarded. That would be worse than what happened between her and Charles. That would be social ruin. Everyone would know. And how would her neighbors like Mrs. Jenkins and Mrs. Vale treat her after Simon cast her off? Worse, she might get with child. Any children they had would be bastards. A nobleman's by-blows. And despite their father's blue blood, society would scorn them.

It was time to put an end to this. And she knew just how to do it. She pushed him away and took several steps back. Fearful she'd change her mind, Emma quickly reached into the pocket of her skirt, pulled out Simon's ring, and held it in her outstretched palm.

His gaze narrowed on the shiny metal. He blinked, as if trying to dislodge an illusion, then stepped back as if kicked in the gut.

Swallowing the lump in her throat, she struggled to find her voice. "We've both had secrets, Simon."

If she'd thought him angry before, it was nothing compared to the fury in his eyes now. She could almost taste the betrayal swirling within him, more powerful than her own.

"You lied?" His hands clenched like he wanted to shake her until her teeth rattled.

"I did." She fought the urge to explain it all to him, sensing he would forgive her, but that wouldn't send him away. And right now she feared herself more than him. Feared if he kissed her again, she'd say yes to his proposal.

"I guess the game is up." Casually, as if it meant nothing, she tossed the ring toward him.

He didn't even try to catch it. It bounced on the rug and landed by his feet. "I could have you arrested."

"But you won't, will you, because it would just be another sordid tale in the scandal sheets." Panic tightened her airway. She hoped her assumption was correct. "Isn't that why you didn't involve the police in the first place? You might pretend you don't mind your name in the scandal sheets, but I think you do."

The slight clenching and unclenching of his jaw proclaimed she'd guessed right.

"Tell me the name of your accomplice. The bastard who hit me."

"I will never tell you."

"Good Lord, Emma, you could be arrested if caught. Are you willing to risk your freedom for such a blackguard? Do you love him?"

"Yes."

His hands flexed.

"Go back to your fancy house in Mayfair, my lord. I've enjoyed our little game, but I think it is time we put an end to it." Emma tried not to blink, fearing if she did she might cry.

Without picking up the ring, Simon turned around and strode from the room. He closed the front door so hard, the walls shook.

And only then, did Emma allow her tears to fall.

"Full house," Caruthers said, a broad grin dimpling the man's left cheek.

With a flick of his wrist, Simon tossed his pair of fives facedown onto the table.

"Distracted, eh, my friend?" Caruthers swept up his winnings and meticulously stacked the coins.

Simon picked up his glass of whisky and took a long sip. He glanced around the private room in the gentlemen's club. Once again, he wondered why he'd come here after leaving Emma's residence instead of seeking out female companionship. Most likely, because he intended to get pissing drunk. And if the way he was letting Caruthers rake him over the coals was any indication, he was already halfway there.

Caruthers snapped his fingers in Simon's face. "Day-dreaming again, old chum?"

"Damn, you, Caruthers. Just deal the bloody cards." Simon downed the remaining contents of his glass in one gulp and glanced at Huntington. The marquess sat at an adjacent table in the private room, writing something on a sheaf of paper. Probably a tally of all those that had turned their backs on him since his wife's unfortunate accident. Poor bloke.

"Simon!" Caruthers snapped.

"What?" Simon straightened in his chair and peered across the table.

"I said it's your bid." Caruthers tossed his cards on the

table. "Bloody hell. There is no joy in winning when you aren't even paying attention. How about we go to Ferguson's Music Hall?"

"In Spitalfields? Why?" The rookery in the East End wasn't one of their normal haunts.

"I hear there is a new songstress, Eliza Bird, who's been blessed with breasts large enough to suffocate a man."

Without looking up from his writing, Huntington snorted.

Simon wasn't sure that was the way he wanted to die, but he needed a distraction, and there was always a fight to be had if one looked hard enough in the East End. He placed his cards on the table and stood.

"How about you, old boy?" Caruthers eyed Huntington. "Care to join us? I hear the songstress is looking for a wealthy protector. And if anyone needs a good tupping it's you, my friend."

For the briefest moment, Huntington appeared to be considering it. The perpetual motion of his pen stopped, then moved again. "Go bugger yourself, Caruthers," Huntington said.

An hour later, Simon and Caruthers weaved through the throng of patrons in the smoky East End music hall. The shabby concert-room was a far cry from the opulent Alhambra or any West End venue. This place boasted sooty lamps and gold-colored wallpaper that had lost its sheen years ago.

Nevertheless, there were few vacant tables. And most of the empty seats were along the back and side walls. Simon spied one unoccupied table a stone's throw from the stage. As they moved toward it, several men, already seated and laughing heartily at the antics of the comedian on stage, shifted in their chairs and gawked at them. The tailored attire Caruthers and he wore proclaimed them persona non grata—as welcome as a rat in one's larder. This Spitalfields establishment catered to laborers, dockhands, and the petty thieves who lived here and in the neighboring rookeries. Tonight, the mostly male crowd appeared a bit rougher than normal.

Upon reaching the table, the low hum of voices escalated around them. "Bleedin' nobs," one grungy man seated at the adjacent table hissed. "Go home. We ain't want ye kind 'ere."

A second, oversized bloke, seated at the same table, stood and reiterated that opinion before spitting into his beefy palms and rubbing his chafed and reddened hands.

"Sit your arse down, MacDonald, or I'll sit it for you." A tall, redheaded man approached the table, a wooden cudgel thicker than a policeman's billy club in his hands. "I'll be havin' no ruckuses in me establishment."

The man named MacDonald shot Simon a contemptuous look before slumping back into his chair and picking up his muddy-colored pint of ale.

A plump serving girl with a pretty face, who looked no more than sixteen, approached them. "What can I get ye?"

"I'll take a pint of ale," Caruthers said.

"Make that two," Simon added.

Her eyebrows rose. A frown settled over her freckled face. "I bet me cousin two pence ye was going to order champagne."

"Did you now?" Simon asked.

"I did," she responded, looking vexed.

"Do you serve champagne?"

"Gorblimey, no."

"Then how is he to know that initially we didn't order it?" Simon asked.

Her eyes narrowed, furrowing the smooth skin between

her brows, and her face brightened. "Well, I'll be. Ye make a fine point."

She marched to a tall, lanky lad wearing a soiled white apron who stood by the bar. She spoke to the boy before setting one hand on her hip while extending the other, palm up. The lad shot both her and them a severe scowl before placing the coins in her hand. She all but tossed her hair in his face as she walked away, a definite spring in her step.

The comedian left the stage, and the crowd applauded heartily. The serving girl returned and placed two pints of dark ale on the table. "That'll be a threepence each."

Simon reached into the pocket of his damask waistcoat, withdrew a sovereign and a sixpence, and handed it to the girl.

She stared at the coins for a moment before a broad smile wreathed her face. "Thank ye, sir." She bobbed up and down.

The movement drew the attention of MacDonald at the next table. "Are you daft, girl? Wot you be doin' that for? He ain't the Queen."

Shoving the coin into her dress pocket, the girl turned fully toward the man and flashed him a defiant expression. "I'd lick the man's feet, MacDonald, at this very moment, if 'e be askin' me to. So never ye mind."

Pressing his palms to the top of the table, MacDonald shifted as if to stand, but glanced toward the cudgel-wielding proprietor standing near the stage. "You's got a saucy mouth, Molly. I knows for a fact your father wouldn't be lookin' so kindly upon you at this moment catering to the likes of those men."

"Shows what little ye knows, MacDonald. Me da is goin' to be as pleased as a doxy spotting a group of sailors on leave when I show him this shiny canary in me pocket."

She gave Simon and Caruthers another flamboyant curtsy and stomped off.

Simon leaned close to MacDonald. “Fine lass, full of spirit, is she not?”

The Scot narrowed his eyes and flexed his fingers into a fist. “I’ll be seein’ you after Eliza’s performance.”

He acknowledged the threat with a grin. Exactly what he wanted. A good round of fisticuffs might stop him from replaying the day’s events in his head like a kineograph and lessen his dark mood.

Several men at adjacent tables craned their heads. “Bleedin’ nob must have a death wish,” someone muttered.

“Ay, the Bull’s got a good three stone on the swell,” another added.

Indeed, the man they called “the Bull” looked capable of sending one to meet his maker, but if he thought Simon would be an easy win, he was about to learn differently.

A sudden hullabaloo of feet stomping, hand clapping, and cheers commenced. A voluptuous woman with a mop of curly flame-colored hair stepped onto the stage. One could not call Eliza Bird pretty, but Simon presumed many of the men in the concert-room didn’t look any higher than her neck and the short costume made of French tulle which exposed her silk stockings, garters, and the cleavage of her overripe breasts.

“My God,” Caruthers mumbled. “They weren’t lying. Asphyxiation is indeed a possibility.” Caruthers stuck two fingers in his mouth and let loose an ear-splitting whistle.

The saucy songstress winked at them.

Caruthers leaned back in his chair. “Christ, I think I’m in love. What do you think, Simon?”

He shrugged one shoulder. At the moment, the only woman he could think of had distracted him so a thug could attempt to crack his head open like a coconut. He should just stand still and let MacDonald knock some sense into him.

Throughout Eliza's performance, the predominantly male audience whistled, clapped, and verbally haled the woman's mediocre voice. After she sang several ballads, she exited the stage to a round of hearty applause and boisterous cheers. When it became apparent she wouldn't take to the stage for an encore, several patrons filed out of the hall at a fast clip. The numerous bordellos that dotted the local streets appeared to be in for a profitable night.

Caruthers slapped Simon's back. "Damn fine show."

"Yes, if one is tone deaf." Simon peered at the table next to him. MacDonald eyed him like a finely cooked joint.

"You weren't thinkin' of slithering away, were you now?" the man asked.

No, he'd thought of Emma throughout the songstress's performance. A few rounds with the Scot would suit him well. "What, and miss a chance at rearranging your not-so-pretty mug?"

The hostility seemed to slip away from MacDonald's countenance and he grinned. "You ain't no milksop. I'll give you that."

Simon, Caruthers, MacDonald, and the men at his table stepped into the melee that was the exodus and made their way to the street.

"I'll wager my friend will be victorious. Do I have any takers?" Caruthers shouted.

"I'll bet you a threepence," said one grizzled man, who looked as if he didn't have a pot to piss in.

"Believe me, old man," Caruthers replied, "you'd do better to wager on my friend's side than against him. He's a leftie with a mean uppercut. And I believe he's pining over a woman and in a rather foul mood. The man's primed to hit something."

Simon narrowed his eyes at his friend. "Sod off."

Caruthers laughed.

The elderly man raised a bushy eyebrow. "A woman's got under his skin, huh?"

"Indeed. Nothing else explains his poor mood," Caruthers replied.

The old man grinned. "A woman will do that to you. I say threepence the nob wins!"

"I'll take that wager," another man shouted.

MacDonald slipped off his tattered sack coat and handed it to the bloke who'd sat next to him in the hall.

Simon followed suit, passed his frock coat and top hat to Caruthers, and loosened his tie. However, before he'd finished removing the garment, a hard right struck his jaw. He stumbled backward. Regaining his balance, he flashed MacDonald a smile. No Marquess of Queensberry rules here.

Tossing his neckcloth to Caruthers, Simon stepped toward MacDonald and ducked when the other man tried to strike him with another jab aimed at his face.

MacDonald was about to learn fighting wasn't solely about brawn; one had to think, to react, and predict an opponent's moves. Simon knew when it came to those who were heavier, as MacDonald was, that if he ducked and weaved, his opponent would tire. He'd also learned that quick combinations were the most successful in downing a man. A milling crowd formed a circle around the two men and became as boisterous about the fight as Eliza's performance.

Simon landed a firm uppercut against MacDonald's chin, sending a spray of spittle into the air.

His opponent answered with a sharp left; however, Simon quickly moved and MacDonald's fist clipped his ear.

After several minutes, MacDonald's chest heaved up and down, while his feet dragged on the pavement. At this point the Bull had struck more blows, but most had hit

Simon's arms and chest, whereas he'd caught the man twice squarely in the face, and a gash on his brow was dangerously close to splitting open and trickling blood into the man's eye.

MacDonald hit Simon squarely on the jaw. Flashes of light blinded Simon for a minute. He blinked to clear his spotty vision. Jesus! Now he understood why they called him the Bull.

The man dipped his head, charged like an enraged animal. Simon sidestepped and the man stumbled into the crowd. The Scot emerged with his face red and fist cranked back.

Unbidden, Emma's words from today rushed back into Simon's head. Red-hot anger bubbled to the surface. Simon blocked the punch, rammed his fist into the man's abdomen, and planted a facer on him.

Arms flailing, MacDonald stumbled backward, taking several spectators to the pavement with him.

"Jesus, Mary, Joseph," one of the Bull's cohorts said. "He's out cold."

The grizzled old man took his flat cap off, waved it into the air, and whooped.

Simon looked at his red knuckles. "Drinks are on me," he said, shaking his hand in the air to remove the sting.

The crowd cheered and rushed back into the music hall, except for the two men who stayed to lift MacDonald off the ground.

The bare-knuckled brawl hadn't made Simon forget about Emma, but perhaps getting drunk would.

Chapter Twenty-Five

"It's been a week since Lord Adler left. Do you think he will ever return for his portrait?" Lily asked, stretching out on the daybed in Emma's studio and rubbing her eyes.

"I don't think so, dear," Emma replied as she added highlights to Simon's likeness. Without forethought, she pressed her free hand to her chest, where, hidden underneath her dress, Simon's ring hung from a blue satin ribbon. He might not return for the painting, but surely he would return for the ring. Wouldn't he? She was starting to doubt it.

"Then why do you continue to work on his portrait?"

Emma wasn't sure. Perhaps it was penance. Looking at it made her heart ache. Twice during the week, she'd contemplated going to Simon's residence in Mayfair and telling him the whole truth about that night she and Lily had entered his house. But what good would it do? It might prompt him to make the same offer, and she wasn't sure she'd say no to becoming his mistress. It was better to stay away from him. Better he hate her.

"He *might* return for it." Emma forced her voice to remain even.

"I miss him and Nick," Lily said, propping a pillow

under her head. "Mr. Radcliffe . . . I mean Lord Adler, was topnotch at rolling a trundling hoop, and I was hoping he'd trounce that braggart Timmy Johnson in a race. And Mrs. Flynn misses Mr. Baines. She says she's angry at him, but I think if he came back, she'd say all was forgiven."

Emma didn't wish to talk about it anymore. Tears were already welling up in her eyes as she thought of the empty house across the street.

The room grew shadowed as the sun began to set. She glanced at Lily, who'd grown surprisingly quiet. Her sister appeared to have drifted off to sleep. Quietly Emma washed her tools and moved to the water ewer to clean her hands, only to find it empty.

She draped a blanket over Lily and exited the room with the pitcher. As she descended the steps, the knocker struck the front door.

Simon? Her stomach fluttered. Emma set the ewer on the entry hall table and took several deep breaths. She smoothed her skirt with her damp palms and opened the door.

Two men in wrinkled plaid sack suits stood on the top step. The tall one sported a wide moustache and muttonchops. The setting sun reflected off the man's hair, slick with pomade. He flashed a gap-toothed grin.

The other caller was shorter, with several days' worth of stubble and a metal toothpick clamped between his teeth. Without smiling, his gaze traveled a leisurely path down Emma's body. A licentious grin turned the corners of his lips upward.

Wretched man.

She folded her arms. "May I help you, *gentlemen*?"

The man with the muttonchops combed his fingers through the coarse hair on his jaw. "Indeed, you may," he replied with a thick cockney accent. "Is this the residence of Michael Trafford?"

What could these two men want with her brother? "It is. May I ask what this is about?"

The second man scraped the toothpick between his two front teeth. "Is 'e 'ome?"

"No, he's at . . ." An unsettling feeling gripped her stomach as she thought about Michael's odd behavior. Best not to reveal where Michael attended school. "No, he's not, but if you leave me your calling card, I'll make sure he receives it."

The fellow with the muttonchops stepped closer to her. The scent of strong cologne and perspiration wafted to her nose. "Now you wouldn't be lying to us, would you?" He motioned to the man next to him with a jerk of his thumb. "Me friend 'ere don't take kindly to liars."

The shorter man plucked the toothpick out from between his lips and ran the sharp, pointed edge down the left sleeve of her dress, applying enough pressure that the edgc scraped her skin.

Fear gripping her, Emma started to close the door. The taller man set his hand against the wood, halting its progression.

Mrs. Flynn's heavy footfalls moved up the steps from below stairs. She strode into the back corridor, which ran from the front door to the rear of the residence. "Who's at the door, miss?"

Emma swallowed. If Mrs. Flynn thought these men meant Emma any harm, the elder woman's protective claws would come out, and she doubted the housekeeper was a match for these two brutes. "They have the wrong address. I'm giving them directions. I'll be downstairs in a minute."

The houscckeeper's retreating footsteps made the air held tight in Emma's lungs exit on a heavy exhale.

The man lowered his hand from the door and flicked a

piece of lint off his sleeve. "Tell your brother we'll be back, and he best have the money, 'cause Mr. Wolf ain't take kindly to those who don't pay 'im back."

Her throat too tight to speak, Emma nodded and slammed the door closed. Knees wobbling, she slumped against the hard surface. What type of man had such unsavory characters working for him? And how had Michael come to owe the man money?

A noise jerked her gaze to the frosted glass window at the end of the corridor. A dark, shadowy figure stood outside, trying to wrench the lower pane up.

Heart pounding fast, Emma pulled Papa's old walking stick out of the umbrella stand and raced down the corridor.

The lower sash slid up a couple of inches. A clearly male hand reached in to grasp the bottom of the window. The thundering in Emma's chest made her ribs hurt. She raised the cane and swung, striking the man's thumb.

"Hell and fire," the voice hissed.

She froze. "Michael? Is that you?"

Her brother peered through the opening. His face ashen.

"You all but scared me to death," she scolded, shoving the sash up. "What's going on? Who is Mr. Wolf, and why do you owe him money?"

Her brother climbed through the window and grasped his injured thumb. "I'm in trouble, Em."

"Yes, I realize that. What have you done?"

He scrubbed his hands over his boyish face. "Gambled. Every cent I had and some I didn't."

Good Lord. Her temples began to throb. "And now you owe this Wolf fellow?"

Michael stared at the floor and rubbed the toe of his shoe against the dull and scratched wooden planks. He glanced up. Her brother's face flushed red. "Yes. Some call him the Devil of Danbury Street."

Emma clutched the bodice of her dress. She now recognized the name. Owing a merciless creditor was frightening enough, but the Devil of Danbury . . . Oh heavens. She'd read about the unsavory man in a recent article in one of the daily papers. It proclaimed him ruthless. Two days after the newspaper published the article, a suspicious fire caused extensive damage to the publisher's offices. Even the police were leery of the moneylender.

"How much do you owe him?"

Without looking at her, Michael rubbed at his thumb. "Three hundred pounds."

Her heart skipped several beats. A king's ransom as far as they were concerned. An unattainable amount.

Fast-moving footsteps charged down the stairs. Lily rubbed at her heavy-lidded eyes and squealed, "Michael! I thought I heard your voice." The child ran to their brother and wrapped her slender arms about his waist.

Emma took a deep breath and fought the urge to wrap her hands around Michael's neck, or grab his shoulders and shake him until his eyes rolled in his head. What had he been thinking, gambling such a staggering amount of money? Obviously, he'd not been thinking at all. They didn't possess such a sum.

"Hey, poppet." Michael returned Lily's embrace and kissed the top of her golden head.

"Lower your voices." Emma stepped into the morning room and pulled the front shutters closed. The two thugs might still be lurking around out front.

Holding Lily's hand, Michael followed.

"What's the matter?" Lily frowned.

Mrs. Flynn appeared. Wiping her hands on her apron, the housekeeper stepped into the room. Her gaze volleyed from Michael's pale face to Emma's, which was most likely even paler. "What's wrong?" she asked, a nervous pitch to the older woman's voice.

Everything. Emma paced. "Lily, please go upstairs for a bit."

Lily set her hands on her hips. "Why?"

"Because I need to speak to Michael. Alone."

"But I want to know what's going on. Why is he home from school again?"

"Come, dearie." Mrs. Flynn grasped Lily's hand. "Let your sister talk to your brother in private."

Grumbling about how unfair Emma was acting, Lily allowed Mrs. Flynn to pull her into the entry hall. The housekeeper closed the double doors behind her.

Emma spun toward her brother. "How long do you have, to get the three hundred pounds to this money-lender?"

Michael shoved his hands into his trouser pockets and stared at his shoes. "I was supposed to pay him yesterday. I came home to warn you that he might send a couple of his thugs here."

"Indeed, he already did." She rubbed her arm, which still stung from where the little runt had scraped his metal toothpick down her sleeve.

"Blast it! Did one of them hurt you, Em? I'll kill them!" Michael rushed to her side.

She stepped away and strode to the other side of the room. "No, I'm fine. I bumped my arm this morning." She spun back to face him. "Do they know where you attend school? Are you safe there?"

"I believe so."

Thank God. But the two men would return here. She was sure of it. Then what would she do? Her knees wobbled. Emma sank into a chair and momentarily buried her face in her hands, frightened not only about how she would get the money, but terrified of the harm this wretched Mr. Wolf could inflict on her family.

"I'm sorry, Em," Michael said, drawing her from her tumultuous thoughts.

She glanced up. "When did this happen? Did you go to a gaming hell?"

"I stopped there on my way back to school after Easter break. My friend . . . you know the one I told you about, Ernest Montgomery. He told me of a pub on St. George Street in Stepney. There's a back room where one can play cards."

Goodness! Emma had known Michael getting mixed up with some highborn lad would cause problems. Boys like that lived off their father's wealth. They didn't worry where their next coin would come from.

"I thought I'd try my hand at it," Michael continued. "I did well at first. Doubled my money. Then my luck changed . . . ran dry. A tall man approached me; told me he could see I was a fine player and offered to give me a loan. Said his boss did that for those he thought a good bet. Like him, I was sure my luck would change. Em, if I could have twenty-five pounds, maybe I could win it all back."

Emma clenched her hands. It appeared Mama had dropped all three of her children on their heads. She stood and jabbed her finger against Michael's chest. "Promise me you will never gamble again. You were set up."

Her brother shook his head. "That's not true. I tell you, I was winning every hand. I-I . . ." He scrubbed his hand over his face and slumped onto the ottoman. "Dash it all. I fell right into their hands. Didn't I? The perfect pigeon."

"Is that why you came home over a week ago? To gamble again?"

"I thought I could win some of it back, but I only fell further into debt. When I saw your neighbor outside, I thought one of the Devil's thugs had found out where I live."

Now everything made sense. "You must return to school."

Michael stood and set his hands on his lean hips. "I'm not going, Em. I must take responsibility for my actions. I will go and talk to Mr. Wolf at his place of business on Danbury Street in Spitalfields."

Her heart slammed against her ribs. She couldn't allow Michael to go to this wretched man, or his thugs, without the money. She would figure something out. "You will do no such thing."

"But—"

She slipped her hand behind her back and crossed her fingers. "No. I have nearly enough to pay him, and in a day or two, I'm to receive a commission from a nobleman," she lied.

Wide-eyed, Michael's mouth gaped. "God blind me, really?"

"Yes." She stepped up to the tall secretary desk, stood on the chair before it, and removed a key from the top of the piece of furniture.

As she stepped down, Michael grabbed her elbow to steady her.

She opened the desk, unlocked the small door centered between a series of drawers, and removed her bank passbook. She tried not to frown at the amount. She'd spent all the money from Mrs. Naples. And used a substantial amount of the money Simon had paid for the painting of the family walking in the park. What was left would have lasted them several months until she found another commission, but it didn't come close to the amount Michael owed.

Forcing a smile, Emma waved the book in the air. "I sold one of my paintings to a wealthy gentleman, and he's commissioned me to do his portrait, so I shall have the full amount shortly. You need not worry."

"Thank God." The relief in Michael's voice was almost tangible.

"Yes, and the gentleman is so pleased with my work, he intends to send more clients my way shortly." Lying wasn't her best skill, but since Lily's escapade at Simon's residence, Emma believed she might have perfected her duplicity. "And I've sent a note to an art dealer, Mr. Bishop, asking him if I might show him some of my work, so he might send some new clients my way." At least this was true.

Michael slumped against the wall. His blue eyes shone with unshed tears. He rubbed the heels of his hands against them and looked back at her. "I'm sorry, Em. So sorry. I will pay you back. I promise."

"Just promise on Mama's and Papa's graves that you will never gamble again."

Standing up straighter, he nodded.

"Good. Now, you must head to Victoria station first thing before daybreak tomorrow morning and return to school."

He squared his shoulders. "No, I will bring the money to Mr. Wolf."

"You can't be serious. It is dangerous. I will wait for his men to return here." Emma turned away from her brother and slipped the bank passbook back into the secretary desk and locked the small center door. She couldn't allow Michael to see her balance and know she lied. "I must go to the bank tomorrow, and you must return to school before the headmaster realizes your absence. When the two men return, I'll give them the funds."

Emma opened the doors and stepped into the entry hall. "Mrs. Flynn!"

The woman rushed down the stairs.

"Will you pack Michael a small satchel with food? He is to return to school at daybreak."

The housekeeper's gaze volleyed between Michael and Emma.

"Please, Mrs. Flynn," Emma said.

The older woman wiped her thick fingers on her white bibbed apron and nodded.

Emma dashed up the stairs so fast the toe of her shoe caught on her hem. She stumbled and fell forward at the first-floor landing. Her knee rammed against the hard wood. Tears blurred her vision.

Lily stepped out of the drawing room. "Are you hurt?"

"I'm fine." She battled to keep her voice calm. "I just tripped." Emma avoided her sister's direct gaze and swiped at the tears trailing down her cheeks and righted herself. "Michael must return to school first thing in the morning. You may spend some time with him before you go to bed."

"What is wrong, Em?"

"Nothing."

"I'm not a fool. I know something is wrong."

"It shall all be taken care of. You needn't worry yourself about it. Now go see your brother." She gave Lily a quick hug and moved up the steps. Emma closed the door to her bedchamber and swiped at a fresh batch of tears.

After allowing herself to cry for a minute, she dragged the cuff of her sleeve across her wet eyes. Crying would not solve this problem. She needed to do something. But what? She glanced down at her aching arm. Several specks of blood spotted the fabric. That little runt had not only meant to frighten her, but hurt her. And he'd succeeded. What would those two thugs do if they caught up to Michael, who didn't have the funds he owed the money-lender? Too dreadful to think about. On her deathbed, Mama had asked Emma to take care of her siblings. And she would.

She lit the gas lamp on her dresser and flipped open

the lid to her mother's jewelry box. Her fingers brushed against the ruby necklace. The stones might be paste, but if genuine they would be worth a great deal. She removed the necklace, along with Mama's cameo and gold wedding band.

As soon as Michael left tomorrow, she'd go to the pawnbroker and see what the pieces were worth. Perhaps if she gave the moneylender some of what Michael owed the man, he wouldn't harm her brother. She undid the top buttons of her dress and touched Simon's gold signet ring. It weighed quite a bit. How much was it worth? Most likely more than any of the other pieces.

She slumped on the bed and curled her fingers around it. She could pawn it, and when she had enough money, reclaim it. It was wrong, but she couldn't weigh her moral convictions against her brother's life.

Chapter Twenty-Six

The following morning, right after Michael snuck out the back door to make his way to Victoria station, Emma dashed up the stairs and into her bedchamber. She unfolded a linen handkerchief with a lily of the valley flower embroidered in the corner and spread it out on top of her dresser. Mama had stitched it for her, stating the flower represented luck in love. Obviously, it hadn't worked.

Emma gathered up Mama's ruby necklace, cameo, and wedding band. She set them onto the pristine linen, removed Simon's signet ring from around her neck, and placed it with the other jewelry. As she gazed down at his ring, guilt made her eyes sting with tears. Pawning it was wrong. So wrong, but she needed to protect Michael. Shoving aside her guilt, she gathered up the ends of the handkerchief, tied the blue ribbon around it, and dropped it into her reticule. She rubbed away the moisture blurring her vision. She would not, could not, question her actions. Not now.

Downstairs she found both Lily and Mrs. Flynn in the morning room. Emma looked about, hoping to spot something of value. But there was nothing worth more than a pittance left. "Mrs. Flynn, I need that silver tray you have been using."

"You need money, dear? Is Michael in trouble?" The housekeeper nervously twisted her hands together.

Emma glanced at Lily's anxious face. "No, all is fine. He just needs new clothing. He fears he looks the pauper compared to the other lads."

The expression on the housekeeper's face betrayed her doubt. "I have twelve pounds, dear. I can give it to you."

Mrs. Flynn used nearly all of her pay, the measly amount Emma gave her, to buy some of the ingredients she needed to bake her decadent desserts. "I cannot take it, but if you don't mind, I will borrow it from you."

"No need, child."

"I insist. With interest."

Mrs. Flynn nodded. "I shall get the money and tray." Grabbing her skirts in her pudgy fingers, the housekeeper dashed from the room.

Lily grabbed Emma's hand. "Something is wrong, isn't it, Em?" Without waiting for a response, she added, "I have a threepence, and you can sell my Inspector Whitley books."

Teary-eyed, Emma pulled Lily toward her and hugged her tight. Maybe she wasn't a complete failure at helping raise her siblings. Whatever their problems were, they did love one another, especially if her sister was willing to give up her prized books. Drawing in an unsteady breath, Emma kissed the top of Lily's head. "Everything will be fine. Don't worry." Though her voice sounded calm, her knees wobbled under her skirt.

Mrs. Flynn returned and handed Emma a green carpetbag with worn seams and frayed handles. "Here is the tray. I put it in my carpetbag so that nosy Mrs. Jenkins doesn't see you leaving the house with it. She'll know what you're about, and she'll tell the whole street before tomorrow."

The heavy weight alerted Emma to the fact that it not

only held the money and tray but something else. She peeked inside to see two brass candlesticks.

"They were my mother's. I never use them," Mrs. Flynn said.

"Thank you, but I can't pawn them." She reached inside to remove the candlesticks.

The housekeeper stilled Emma's hands. "Now, don't you worry about it, dearie. You, Lily, and Michael are like my own flesh and blood."

Pedestrians, drays, and hackneys clogged the streets of Bloomsbury as Emma made her way to Mr. Morgan's pawnbroker shop. She touched the flowered hat she wore, regretting purchasing it. The proprietor would give her very little compared to what she'd paid for it.

She turned the corner and onto a narrow street. Up ahead, the three gold globes of the pawnbroker's shop projected from a wrought iron hook.

Guilt over Simon's ring made her steps slow as she made her way to the entrance. A woman with a green dress of finely spun linen stepped out of the place while another woman, who looked less regal, entered with a bundle of clothes in her hands.

Inside, Emma waited for Mr. Morgan to help the other customer. He examined the woman's bundle of clothing and dropped a few coins into her hand and the pawn ticket. The amount so small, the proprietor waved off the half-penny for the ticket, causing the customer to smile and bless his soul.

As the woman chatted with the proprietor, Emma glanced around. Clothing, pots, and pieces of furniture crowded every inch. Her stomach clenched when she saw one of Papa's suits hanging near the front bow window and a familiar rose-colored glass bowl. The suit had been pledged to the pawnbroker only a couple of months after Papa died. The bowl over a year ago. The jangle of the bell over the door drew Emma from her thoughts. She turned to see the bedraggled woman exiting the shop.

"Can I help you?" Mr. Morgan smiled. He probably hoped she was here to collect her belongings and pay him the interest.

Though the shop was empty of other customers, she wished to conduct her business in one of the small rooms that afforded more privacy. "Can we go to a box, sir?"

"Follow me," he said in a businesslike voice.

They stepped into a tiny room with a single window. A pendant fixture with a milk-glass shade hung above the square table. The proprietor turned the lamp up, and Emma placed the carpetbag down, removed her hat, and set it on the table.

"I've my hat. It's all but new, and"—she opened the bag, pulled out the silver tray and the two candlesticks, and set them down—"I have these items."

The proprietor brought the jeweler's loupe that hung from a gold chain around his neck to his eye and peered at the silversmith's marking on the bottom of the tray. He inspected the candlesticks. "I'll give you twelve pounds for the lot. And you know my rates. Plus a halfpenny for the ticket."

Twelve pounds? Tears burned the back of her eyes. A pittance compared to what she needed. She opened her reticule, withdrew the linen handkerchief and untied the satin ribbon, and placed Mama's cameo, ruby necklace, and wedding band on the table. The jewelry caught the light from the gas lamp.

A smile lifted the corner of the man's lips. He held the necklace up to the window. The sunlight reflected off it, sending shards of muted red light around the room. He made a noise as if intrigued. Did that mean the stones were real or paste? She didn't wish to ask him—make him aware of her naïveté regarding the jewelry.

He withdrew a small pin from the lapel of his wool coat and ran it over the largest of the three red stones. Without saying a word, he placed it back on the table and picked up the wedding band and cameo. He angled the ring to the light.

"I'll give you thirty-five pounds for everything."

Disappointment swirled within her. "Can't you do better? I should go to a jeweler instead." Something she didn't wish to do, since she'd not be able to reclaim the items at a later date should she be fortunate enough to get the funds.

"Thirty-seven pounds. Not a penny more."

Her heart sank. Even with Mrs. Flynn's twelve pounds and what Emma had left in the bank, that wasn't enough. Her fingers flexed around Simon's ring. She set it on the table.

He cocked a brow and lifted his monocle and examined it. He glanced up at her with narrowed eyes. "Where did you get this?"

"Um, my father won it at some gaming hell years ago."

The proprietor nodded and slipped it onto his own pinkie. "Very well, seventy-five pounds for the lot."

Emma's heart sank. Not enough. Fighting her tears, she outstretched her hand for Simon's ring and gathered her belongings.

"Good day, sir." Setting her hat on her head, she strode from the room.

"Seventy-nine pounds," Mr. Morgan called out.

Still not enough. She needed another plan and knew just what she had to do—visit that blackguard the Devil of Danbury Street and barter with him. The thought of dealing with such a man made a shiver crawl up her spine, but what other choice did she have?

* * *

Mrs. Flynn set her hands on her hips and frowned. "Dear child, you cannot go running willy-nilly to the rookeries all by yourself. I'll accompany you."

After returning from the pawnbroker, she'd told Mrs. Flynn about the trouble Michael was in. Emma shook her head and glanced at the mantel clock in the morning room. She needed to leave. "No, you must remain here with Lily."

"But there are vagabonds, thieves, and even murderers there. And this moneylender they call the Devil of Danbury Street is the worst of the lot."

The anxiety already making Emma's palms sweat, amped up as the woman spoke. She knew the rookeries could be a dangerous place. She'd read articles about the crime. Even some policemen were leery of several areas in the East End, but she needed to protect Michael, and she could see no other way around it.

"I'll bring that blackguard what Michael owes him," Mrs. Flynn said, breaking into Emma's thoughts. "Not safe for a sweet thing like you to venture into the dark part of London, but no one shall mess with me." The housekeeper fisted her hand and shook it in the air.

What would Mrs. Flynn do if she realized Emma didn't have all the money Michael owed the moneylender? That she intended to barter with the man? The older woman would suffer an apoplexy. "Mrs. Flynn, you know I love you dearly, but I need to handle this—"

"You can't go there!" Lily said, stepping into the room.

What had her sister heard? Too much, by the tears shining in her eyes. "Lily, you shouldn't be eavesdropping. And there is nothing to be concerned about. I shall be fine," she said, feigning bravado.

Lily knotted her fingers into the skirt of her dress. "Why did you send Michael away? Why didn't you make him go with you?"

Because Emma had promised to care for her siblings, and she would not break that pledge. And hopefully her plan would work. She stepped up to Lily and hugged her. "Everything will be fine." Thankfully her voice remained steady, even though her heart beat erratically.

Sniffling, Lily rubbed her tear-streaked face into the bodice of Emma's dress. "Why don't you have Mr. Radcliffe . . . Lord Adler go with you? I bet he's not frightened of anyone. He'd take care of this dastardly character, Mr. Wolf. I know he would."

The thought of seeing Simon again—of having him accompany her—held great appeal, but she wouldn't be indebted to him. "I cannot do so, Lily. Now, I will be back shortly."

God willing.

Chapter Twenty-Seven

Surely, there was a demented woodpecker in Simon's head striking his brain. It seemed the only explanation for the constant pounding filling his skull. He opened his eyes to find everything upside down. It took him several painful minutes to realize he was supine on his bed in his Curzon Street residence. His feet were on the pillows and his head teetered over the edge of the mattress.

What was he about? Wincing, he sat upright. The agonizing tapping in his head slowed, but didn't cease. He swallowed in an attempt to remove the bitter taste coating his tongue.

Bugger it all. Had he drunk himself stupid last night? He had a slight memory of Huntington and Caruthers helping him into his house after he'd gotten himself soused at their club.

Moaning, he set a hand to his throbbing skull and jumped when he noticed both Baines and Harris standing in the room, frowning at him.

Simon sighed. "I know I look a bloody mess. You don't need to lecture me."

Without a word, both servants walked out of the bedchamber, reminding Simon that Baines and Harris had barely spoken a word to him since they'd all returned from Bloomsbury, over a week ago.

They thought him a deceptive cad. Simon should have told them the truth about Emma—that she was a thief and a liar and more duplicitous than he. He had half a mind to go over to Emma's and demand she reveal the name of the blackguard who'd hit him.

Yes, by God, I'll do that as soon as my head stops pounding.

His gaze shifted to the painting Emma had done of the family strolling through the park. Harris had tasked a footman with hanging it in Simon's bedchamber. The fact that Simon had taken it with him from Bloomsbury instead of leaving it or giving it to Westfield confounded him more than anything else.

He strode into his bathing room. The large copper tub contained clean, glistening water. Baines might not be talking to him, but the man wouldn't neglect his duties. Simon brushed his teeth to remove the wretched taste from his mouth, stripped naked, and slid into the tepid water. After washing his hair, he rested his head on the back of the tub, and closed his eyes.

A memory of him and Emma making love flashed in his mind.

Rot it. Even a night of excessive drinking didn't stop thoughts of her. Grumbling, he crawled out of the tub and wrapped a drying towel about his hips.

Inside his dressing room, he found his clothes pressed and laid out for him. With sluggish movements, Simon dressed, walked into his bedchamber, and set his shoes next to the bed. He glanced at Emma's painting again. No wonder he couldn't stop thinking about the woman, with that deuced thing staring him in the face.

Tomorrow he'd have it sent to Westfield's.

Or next week. Or next month.

He must be going mad because not only did he miss Emma, he missed her hoyden sister. He would even swear he heard Lily's voice. Obviously the liquor he'd ingested was still affecting him.

Yet the voice grew louder, along with fast-moving footfalls.

"I told you, Miss Lily, I would fetch him," Harris said. "You must remain in the drawing room and stop following me. His lordship might not be decent."

"I don't care. I must speak with him right now. It's a matter of life and death!"

Lily. Had something happened to Emma? Heart pounding, Simon wrenched his bedchamber door open to see the child trailing Harris up the corridor, tears streaming down her pale face. Several feet behind them stood Mrs. Flynn and Baines. The older woman looked as distraught as Emma's young sister.

Something *had happened* to Emma. For a moment, Simon thought he might retch. Lily ran up to him and wrapped her arms about his waist. She talked so fast, he couldn't make out what she was saying.

Heart still hammering a steady tattoo, Simon bent on one knee and looked the child in the eyes. "Lily, dear, take a breath and tell me what has happened."

"Emma's gone to Spitalfields, my lord," Mrs. Flynn interjected. "She went to pay off her brother's debt to the moneylender they call the Devil of Danbury Street. But after she left the house, Lily found everything Emma intended to pawn in her bedchamber. She doesn't possess the three hundred pounds to pay him. I don't know what she plans to do."

"Wolf?" Simon asked, his body tense.

Mrs. Flynn's head bobbed up and down. "Yes, my lord. We're frightened what that vile man will do to her when she shows up without the money owed him."

"Will you help?" Lily asked. "You love her, don't you?"

As much as he'd like to deny it, he did. Simon squeezed Lily's hand. "Don't worry. I'll go and find your sister. Harris, have my carriage brought around and put three hundred pounds in an envelope." Simon dashed back into his bedchamber to collect his shoes.

Lily ran after him. "May I go with you?"

"No, poppet, you must stay here with Mrs. Flynn."

"But I need to explain about your ring," Lily said.

Simon's gaze jerked to the child's pensive face as he dashed out of his bedchamber.

"Emma didn't take your ring. I did," Lily said, trailing him down the corridor.

For a moment, Simon's head spun. He rubbed the back of his neck. What was the child talking about? He'd kissed Emma, so did that mean . . . "You're the blackguard who hit me?"

A tear trailed from the corner of Lily's eye, and she nodded. "I did. I thought you were going to harm Emma."

"You, young lady, are going to tell me the whole story during the carriage ride to Spitalfields. Are we clear?"

Lily nodded again.

"Mrs. Flynn, I wish you to accompany us."

Fifteen minutes later, settled in the interior of Simon's carriage, Lily nibbled on her index finger and said, "And that's the whole story."

Good Lord, was the child telling the truth? Simon recalled how Lily had mumbled the word *murderer* the first time he'd met her. The child was telling the truth. He would have laughed out loud, if not for the fear over Emma having gone to Spitalfields.

"I didn't know, sir. Um, I mean, my lord." Mrs. Flynn twisted her hands in her lap. "Lily just told me the whole story on the way over here."

"Do you forgive me?" Lily asked in a small voice.

"I shouldn't," Simon said sternly. The tears that trailed down Lily's cheeks made that damnable ache near his heart start again. "Yes." He patted the child's hand and peered at the housekeeper. "Mrs. Flynn, when we get to Spitalfields, will you make sure Lily stays in the vehicle? She is not to enter Mr. Wolf's place of business. He has some rather unsavory characters working for him."

Mrs. Flynn grasped Lily's hand and held it tightly. "She's not going anywhere, my lord. I'll sit on her if I have to."

"You won't have to do that, Mrs. Flynn. I'll behave. I only want Emma home, safe and sound."

So did Simon. If Emma married him, he was going to set rules for Lily. His heart stuttered in his chest. *Marry?* Good Lord, had he just thought that?

Yes. If she'd have him.

At one time, the grand town houses that lined Danbury Street in Spitalfields would have housed prosperous Huguenot silk weavers, but now they were mostly overcrowded lodging houses. Children in threadbare clothing played on the pavement. A woman in a sweater and dirty skirt plucked a chicken while a bald man sat on a step smoking a pipe, his fingers gnarled with age. Emma strode by a house where two men stood awaiting admittance.

One of them tugged on the tips of his wide moustache and leered at her. "You coming here, my sweet, for a bit of slap and tickle?"

She wasn't sure what the man meant, but the way he leered at her made her stomach knot.

The other man set his hands on his rounded belly and laughed. "She looks a bit too high-and-mighty for the likes of you, Clark. Best stick to one of Mrs. Greyson's whores, if she ever answers the bloody door."

Pulse racing, Emma pulled her shawl tighter about her

shoulders and hastened her steps. She stopped at number fifteen—a brick Georgian with green shutters. A big brute of a man stood in front of the door, his thick arms folded over his wide chest, barring anyone's entrance.

"Sir, I'm here to see Mr. Wolf," Emma said, forcing her voice to remain calm.

The man's gaze slid a blatant path down the length of her body, then made its way back up, slowing at her bosom, before settling back on her face. "You've a fine-looking face, lass, but if you're 'ere to peddle yer flesh, best save yourself the trouble and 'ead home. Me employer likes his women with a bit more meat on them."

Why, she'd never . . . Anger momentarily replaced her fear. Emma straightened her spine and tipped her chin in the air. "I'm here on a matter of business, sir, and it has nothing to do with my body."

One corner of the man's mouth twitched. He stepped aside and opened the door, motioning with a jerk of his chin to follow him.

Emma wasn't sure what she'd expected to see, but surely not such opulence. The entry hall sported a black and white marbled floor, scrubbed to a near mirror shine. The polished mahogany woodwork was buffed, and the scent of beeswax filled her nose. It was a dichotomy to the world bustling about outside. She followed the big fellow up a winding stairway with wrought iron spindles, to the first floor.

As they strode down a long corridor, she thought of the two thugs who'd come to her residence. Would either of those slimy fellows be here? Would she have to deal with them? She ran her hand over her arm where the little runt had scraped her skin with his metal toothpick. Swallowing down her fear, she squared her shoulders, but couldn't halt the queasiness in her stomach or the rapid beats of her heart.

Emma passed a room where a maid wearing a mobcap, navy uniform, and white pinafore dusted the wood of a massive billiards table. It looked like what Emma imagined one would see in some grand residence or a gentlemen's club.

They strode through a doorway and into an office where three men sat at counting desks. A fourth man with spectacles perched on his razor-thin nose sat at a more substantial desk with ledgers stacked on it. He peered up at the bulky man standing next to her and shoved his glasses up his nose with his index finger. "Shouldn't you be at your post at the front door, Douglas?"

"I brought this little peach in to see the boss, Wimple."

The man called Wimple, who looked to be a secretary, sighed. "What's your business here, miss?"

Emma wet her dry lips. "I-I wish to speak with Mr. Wolf."

"In reference to?" Wimple sniffed and drew a white handkerchief under his thin nose.

"Repayment of a loan."

Wimple flipped open a ledger and dipped his pen into an ink jar. "No need to speak to him. Just give it to me along with your name."

The rapid pace of her heart escalated. She couldn't give him what she didn't have. She peered beyond Wimple into an office where a man with dark hair, a square jaw, and sizable shoulders sat at a desk. His white shirt was crisp and bright and his waistcoat a maroon damask. His clothing appeared as costly as Simon's. From this distance, he looked no more than thirty years old. Could this man, who looked like a wealthy merchant or barrister, be the moneylender?

"Is that him?" Emma asked, pointing at the well-dressed man.

The bespectacled man nodded.

"I will only give the funds to him."

"That's not how it works." Wimple inhaled deeply as if his patience was running thin. "Now—"

Swallowing her fear, Emma dashed by the man's desk toward the office where Mr. Wolf sat.

"You bloody fool, Douglas, grab her," the secretary hissed. "Or you'll have the devil to pay."

Emma felt her shawl being grabbed. She released her hold on it. The garment slid off her shoulders and into Douglas's grasp. Pulse echoing in her ears, she ran into the office, closed the door, and leaned her weight on it while turning the lock.

A dog's growl rent the air.

Every muscle in Emma tensed. Cold sweat prickled her skin as she slowly turned around.

A massive black dog crept up to her, looking as if he wished to tear out her neck.

Chapter Twenty-Eight

The dog hunched low, as if ready to pounce, and bared incisors sharp enough to chew through a sizable branch, or worse, human bones.

Heart pounding, Emma clasped her neck and fought a scream.

"Lucifer, heel!" Mr. Wolf stood and braced his palms on his desk.

Without blinking an eye, the massive beast sat, yet his nostrils flared as if deciding whether she'd be a tasty afternoon treat.

Emma swallowed the scream still grappling for purchase in her throat.

"To your bed, Lucifer," the moneylender said in a firm voice with a trace of cockney accent.

The dog walked through a pair of open pocket doors into an adjoining room furnished with tall bookcases and a sofa. The animal settled his powerful body on a large brown velvet pillow with gold-colored tassels.

"Stay," Mr. Wolf commanded. He turned to Emma and motioned to the pair of chairs facing his desk. "You, come here and sit." He spoke like a person used to having his orders followed. There was a hard, almost ruthless edge to his voice.

She contemplated turning tail and running, but the men on the other side of the door were banging on it as if intent on breaking it down. She needed to either deal with the devil or his minions. She'd come this far, she'd not turn back. On wobbly legs, Emma moved to the chairs the man indicated and sat in the closest one.

Mr. Wolf strode to the door and flung it open. Emma couldn't see his face, but by the way Wimple and Douglas cowered, she realized the moneylender's expression must be lethal.

"S-sorry, boss. She's a slippery one. I'll toss her out right now." Douglas's eyes narrowed to slits as he stared at her.

The moneylender held up a halting hand. "Never mind. I might as well learn what this is all about." Leaving the door open to the anteroom, the man walked back to his desk.

"Should I pat her down, boss?" Douglas asked.

Pat her down? Did he mean touch her person? Her fear shifted to anger. She would kick him if he tried.

"No need. She looks rather harmless." Mr. Wolf pinned her with his green eyes. "Do you carry a weapon?"

"A weapon?" she echoed.

"Do you have a knife? A pistol? Are you intent on blowing my head off?"

"Of course not. I only wish to talk to you."

He waved the men away and folded his exceedingly tall frame into the chair behind his desk.

Trying to relieve the tightness in her chest, Emma released a tense breath. "My brother—"

"Of course, it's always a brother, or father, or a lover. How much does he owe me?"

She swallowed. “Three hundred pounds, but I have a-a proposition.”

“You don’t say. If I took on all the women who offered their bodies in lieu of payment, I’d never get out of my bed. Sorry, love, but I’m not interested.”

Her face heated. “That’s not the type of proposition I meant,” she said stiffly.

One side of his mouth hitched up. “Then what is it you have to barter?”

“I have nearly seventy-five pounds, and to settle the remainder of the amount, I could paint you. I’m a portraitist.”

He leaned back in his chair, scrubbed his hand over his jaw, and contemplated her with astute eyes. “That’s a damn heavy price to pay for a painting. And how do I know you’re any good?”

“Right now I’ve been commissioned to paint a nobleman.” It wasn’t a lie. Simon *had* commissioned her.

As if that held little weight, he frowned.

“I could paint you, and if you’re pleased you could accept the portrait as payment. You have nothing to lose.”

A commotion in the anteroom drew their attention.

“Let me by,” a man demanded.

Emma sucked in a startled breath. *Simon. Goodness, what is he doing here?* Had he gone to her house to collect his ring and Mrs. Flynn told him what was going on?

The big, bulky fellow stood in front of Simon. “Crikey,” Douglas said. “If it ain’t the nob from Ferguson’s Music Hall. I ain’t never seen a man knock MacDonald out cold before. I should have known that woman in there was yours. She’s got a good set of bollocks, she does.” The man slapped his knee and burst out laughing at his own comment.

“Damnation,” the moneylender grumbled. “What type

of place am I running here? Why don't you just offer his lordship some tea and crumpets?"

Red-faced, Douglas stiffened. "Sorry, boss." He turned back to Simon. "He's busy right now. Have a seat and wait your turn."

"I have the payment Miss Trafford's brother owes you." Simon removed a thick envelope from his inside coat pocket and held it up for the moneylender to see.

"Let him by," Mr. Wolf said.

Simon strode into the room and tossed the envelope onto the desk. "That settles Michael Trafford's debt. Now come along, Emma. We are going home."

Lord knew she wanted to leave as quickly as her feet would take her, but Simon had no right to command her. What else would he demand of her for settling the debt? That she become his mistress? Emma squared her shoulders and stood. "I'm not going anywhere with you, Lord Adler. And I don't need your funds. I've got the matter in hand. I'm going to paint Mr. Wolf."

"You're what?" A nerve danced in Simon's jaw. Emma thought she heard his molars grinding against one another.

"You heard me." She turned to the moneylender. "Isn't that so, sir?"

The moneylender opened the envelope.

She knew by the look in his eyes that he'd rather have the funds. "I'm an excellent portraitist."

"Wimple, get in here," Mr. Wolf said. He handed the money to the bespectacled secretary. "Sorry, love, but payment on the loan has been rendered."

Though relieved she'd not have to return to this place, she didn't want to be indebted to Simon. "I'll pay you the funds as soon as I have the money, Lord Adler." She strolled out of the room.

Without saying a word, Simon followed her. She exited Mr. Wolf's residence and walked up the pavement.

"Emma, where are you going? Get in my carriage."

She glanced over her shoulder. The thought of returning home in Simon's vehicle instead of walking through the East End to the Liverpool Street station held immeasurable appeal, but being cloistered alone with him wasn't wise. Her mind seemed to forget propriety when they were together. Already her body grew warm.

"No, I'd rather take the rail," she lied.

"Your sister and Mrs. Flynn are inside my carriage."

Her feet faltered. She spun around. What were they doing in there? Obviously, they'd begged him to help her.

Simon opened the vehicle's door.

Lily popped her head out and waved.

Emma strode back to the carriage. "They shouldn't have involved you." She lifted her skirts and settled inside the vehicle.

Simon climbed in and sat next to her. As usual, he smelled like spicy soap and his skin sent out waves of tantalizing heat. The brush of his thigh against hers sent sparks fluttering in her stomach.

She narrowed her eyes at the turncoats sitting across from her. "I said I could handle it. You didn't need to involve his lordship."

"But you didn't have enough money," both Lily and Mrs. Flynn said in unison.

"And how did you know that?"

"I opened Mrs. Flynn's carpetbag and saw everything you went to hock still inside," Lily explained.

The child was incorrigible. "I had the situation well in hand. I didn't need to be rescued."

Next to her, Simon snorted.

She faced him. "Mr. Wolf would have let me paint him in lieu of some of the payment if you hadn't barged in."

Mrs. Flynn gasped. "You were going to paint that wicked man?"

"Wouldn't be the first wicked one I painted." She shot Simon a pointed look.

He leaned close. His warm breath touched her ear. "You did more than paint me, Em," he whispered sotto voce.

Her cheeks heated. She glanced out the window.

After weaving through the crowded streets of London, the vehicle pulled up in front of her residence. Simon stepped out and offered his hand to Mrs. Flynn and Lily.

Emma stood to exit.

Simon climbed back inside, closed the door, and locked it.

Her pulse quickened. "What are you doing?"

"You and I need to talk."

"There is nothing for us to converse about. I owe you three hundred pounds, and I've decided that is what I will charge you for your portrait." She waited for him to argue over the exorbitant fee.

"Fine."

Emma blinked. "You agree to that price?"

"Yes, fair enough." Simon pulled the curtains closed, darkening the space.

It took several seconds for Emma's eyes to adjust to the dim light, but even beforehand, she sensed how intensely Simon watched her. Being alone with him wasn't prudent. She reached for the door handle.

His warm fingers wrapped about her hand, stilling her. "I want you to explain why you lied to me, Emma." There was a dangerous undertone to his voice.

What had Lily told him? She swallowed. "I don't know what you speak of, sir. I've told you everything. I'm a thief who wished to profit off of ill-gotten gains."

His index finger traced the line of her jaw. "So it was your idea to break into my house?"

"Yes."

He leaned close and nipped at her earlobe. "Liar."

Her already erratic heartbeat picked up speed. "What did Lily tell you?"

"Everything. Now tell me why you lied to me."

Tears burned her eyes. Because he wanted a mistress, and she could not accept that role. If she spent too much time with Simon, she feared she might fall in love with him. Oh, who was she kidding? She'd already toppled head over heels. And his mistresses drifted in and out of his life like the seasons.

"The truth, Em," he said, breaking into her thoughts.

"Because I cannot become your mistress. If I had children they'd be bastards. I will not bear children that society scorns. I've decided I want more out of my life. I want a family and a husband who wishes to grow old with me."

"Do you care for me, Em?"

A warm tear trailed down her cheek. She nodded.

His grasp on her hand tightened. "Then say it."

"Yes. Damn you, I love you."

With the pad of his thumb, Simon brushed a tear off Emma's cheek. What a fool he'd been. He'd offered the one woman who loved him, not for his title or wealth, a position as his mistress. Why?

He needed to remember she wasn't Julia. Emma was kind and loving. Yes, she'd lied, but only to protect her sister. Even that act, in itself, said so much about her character. He didn't doubt Emma would have gone to jail for her sister.

He'd not realized how strong one's love could be. Well, that wasn't true. He saw it every time Westfield looked at his wife. Every time the man looked at his children. And if he was honest, he envied him—wanted what his friend had. Yet he'd allowed his distrust to mar his perspective. Emma had not kissed him because he was a member of the peerage. In fact, when she'd found out who he was, she'd been angry. She wasn't looking for a wealthy husband or protector. She was strong and independent, not manipulative and vindictive.

"But I still won't agree to be your mistress, Simon," she said, breaking into his thoughts.

"I apologize for even asking that of you. There are things in my past which have left me jaded." Holding her hands, he told her about Julia.

"Oh, Simon, that is horrid."

"I didn't tell you this because I want your pity. I need you to understand me. Can you see yourself with me for the rest of your life?"

A puzzled expression crossed her face. "What are you asking of me?"

"If you will marry me." The sudden silence seemed deafening. He understood her apprehension. She'd been ill-used, but he wasn't Charles Neville, just like she wasn't Julia. "If you say yes, first thing tomorrow I'll get a special license. Or, if you prefer a large wedding, we'll have the banns read."

"Why do you wish to marry me?"

There were so many reasons, but the most important one was easy. "Because I love you."

As if waiting for him to expand on his response, she said nothing.

He wasn't used to saying pretty words, but surely he could explain how he felt. "Emma, the thought of you not being by my side makes my future seem bleak. Unfulfilled. I want you to share my life. To bear my children. Our children." Good Lord, had he just said *children*? Indeed, and the thought of holding a child, their child, warmed his heart.

Her eyes grew shiny with unshed tears. "Children?"

"Yes. A whole cricket team of them."

"Eleven?" she squeaked.

"Well, perhaps that is a bit too many. But however many you want."

"And what of Michael and Lily?"

"They will be part of our family. I shall do my best to help you raise them, though I fear Lily will turn me gray."

"She, along with my brother, might turn us both gray."

"Then you'll marry me?"

She wrapped her arms around his neck and brushed her lips against his. "Yes, if you're up for the task."

In the dusky light of the vehicle, he saw the sparkle in her lovely blue eyes. "Oh, sweeting, I'm definitely *up* for the task." Simon opened the carriage door, clasped her hand in his, and pulled her across the street to his closed-up residence.

Mrs. Vale stepped out of her house. "Mr. Radcliffe! We have missed you."

Mrs. Jenkins exited her residence, as well. The gossip-monger's gaze dropped to Simon's and Emma's joined hands. She frowned. "People will talk if you two don't show better decorum."

"Madam," Simon said, keeping his expression bland. "You, of all people, should know that I don't always follow society's rules."

A puzzled expression settled on the woman's face. "Me?"

"Yes, indeed. Aren't you more aware of my actions than I am?"

The lines between Mrs. Jenkins's gray brows deepened. "I'm still puzzled."

"You don't recognize me? How could one forget a man one claimed to have seen rowing almost *naked*?"

The windbag's eyes widened. "Y-you aren't . . . ?"

"I am. The one and only Lord Adler. And once everyone

learns who I am, they will know you are a lying gossip and full of . . . balderdash."

Wide-eyed, Mrs. Jenkins slumped against her door and grasped her bodice as if her heart might cease.

"And as far as decorum, Miss Trafford and I are to be married." Without looking back, he pulled Emma inside his town house.

"That was wicked, Simon," Emma said.

"Admit it. You enjoyed that immensely."

She laughed. "I did."

"Now come into the drawing room and let me collect on your promise of repentance."

"Repentance?" she echoed.

"Didn't you promise it before your sister hit me with that dashed vase?"

"Ah, yes."

"Then for the rest of our lives, I shall collect it." Simon led her into the drawing room and locked the door behind them. With the shutters closed, only dim light filtered into the room. He sat on the settee and crossed his arms over his chest. "Remove your drawers, Em."

A flash of red colored her cheeks, but she reached under her skirts and slipped the garment off.

His manhood grew hard. He crooked his finger. "Come here, dearest heart."

Smiling, she stepped in front of him.

He slid his hands up her stockinged calves to her bare thighs, bringing the skirt of her dress upward, exposing her triangle of hair. His bollocks drew tight against his body. With her skirts lifted, he pulled her body atop his so she straddled him, and slowly slipped the buttons of her bodice free. This joining of their bodies would not be rushed, only savored like one of Mrs. Flynn's lemon tarts. He drew the garment off her shoulders and arms so it pooled at her waist, then removed her corset and shift until her breasts were bared to his hungry gaze.

God, she was lovely. Lightly he drew his index finger from her neck to her collarbone. His greedy mouth captured one perfect breast, sucking gently at first, then harder before his tongue lapped at the peaked nipple.

Arching, Emma moaned. Shifting backward, she worked loose the buttons on the fall of his trousers and slipped her hands into his drawers, freeing his hard manhood. Her cool fingers wrapped about his girth and slid down his shaft.

A guttural noise escaped his mouth. Perhaps they wouldn't do this slow. Already he felt close to exploding. "In this position, my dearest Em, you're in control. Slide your body over mine. Then take me in you."

She pressed her knees into the cushion of the seat and lifted herself enough to angle him at her opening, then slowly lowered herself, encasing him in her slick passage.

He sucked in a quick breath. She felt perfect. His hands clasped her buttocks, and he lifted his hips. "Move, love."

With her hands on his shoulders, she grinned and rose until she had a steady rhythm. Her lovely breasts jiggled in front of him, and he dipped his head to suck and lap at the hard peaks. He drew back and held her gaze. "I love you."

As if his words were a catalyst, she tensed as her pleasure took hold.

He cupped the back of her head, brought her mouth to his, and spilled his seed into his future wife—the woman he loved with all his heart.

Chapter Twenty-Nine

Twelve weeks later, Simon was tutoring his wife on how to engage in scandalous afternoon behavior when a knock sounded against their bedchamber door. "Go away," he snapped.

"Simon." Emma gave him a playful slap on his arm. "What will the servants think?"

He really didn't care. All he could think of was burying his hard manhood into his wife and bringing her to climax. "Yes, what is it?" he grumbled.

"A Mr. Bishop is here, my lord," Harris said. "He wishes to speak with her ladyship."

Grasping the blankets to her naked breasts, Emma sat upright in bed. "Did you say Lawrence Bishop?"

"Yes, my lady," Harris replied. A calling card flew under the door like a burst of air.

Emma's eyes widened. She clasped Simon's naked thigh and squeezed.

He wished she'd move her hand a little to the left.

"Simon, Mr. Bishop is the art dealer I told you about. His acquisitions sell for ungodly amounts at Christie Manson and Woods auction house. I sent him a letter months ago, asking if I could show him several of my portraits, hoping he might send some customers my way. He never responded."

Emma leapt from the bed, taking all the bedding with her, leaving Simon naked.

He sighed. Bishop had picked the most inopportune time to call on Emma. Sporting a heavy cockstand, Simon got up and pulled on his trousers.

Emma picked up the card and blinked. "Mr. Lawrence Bishop. Purveyor of Fine Art," she read aloud. "It is him. Simon, did you ask him to call on me?"

"Me?" Simon smiled as he slipped his shirt over his head. Emma's newest works were extraordinary and needed to be seen by more than her family.

She narrowed her lovely blue eyes at him. "You asked him to call, didn't you?"

"Perhaps. Harris, are you still waiting outside the door?" Simon asked.

"Yes, my lord."

"Tell Bishop her ladyship will be down shortly." Simon sat on the bed and dragged on his socks and shoes. "Don't keep the fellow waiting, darling."

"But I look horrid. I can't meet him now."

"Of course, you can. And as always, you look beautiful."

Blushing, she opened the door, still clutching the blankets around her naked body.

"Emma?"

She spun around.

"Though I think you look absolutely fetching, I suggest you get dressed first."

"Oh my!" She slammed the door closed.

Not even fifteen minutes later, Simon watched his lovely wife fidget as Bishop walked about her studio on the top floor of their Curzon Street residence.

The rosy color Simon had put on his wife's cheeks, mere minutes ago, was gone, and she was twisting her hands nervously together. She appeared completely unaware of the talent she possessed for doing genre and landscape scenes. Bishop would be a fool not to snatch up all the paintings Emma had recently completed. Lately, she painted scenes of London and the countryside at a fanatical pace, stating Simon was her muse.

Bishop tapped a finger to his pursed lips and stared at a painting Emma had done last week, of the front of Mrs. Flynn's new bakery shop. Simon smiled. His investment in the shop would pay off if Mrs. Flynn could keep Baines out of its kitchen.

Lifting her shoulders slightly, Emma glanced at Simon.

Relax, he mouthed. *They are fabulous.*

You're biased, she mouthed back.

He was also eager to get her back to their bedchamber and continue his lesson on debauchery. His wife was a very adept pupil.

Bishop removed his gold-rimmed pince-nez off the bridge of his nose. "Hmm. You did this?" He pointed at the painting with his glasses. His voice held a tone of authority, along with a note of accusation.

Did the art dealer think it unworthy? Simon would toss him out on his arse if he hurt Emma's feelings.

"Yes." Her voice came out on a barely audible whisper. But she squared her shoulders. Simon could tell she was quite proud of the painting. "I did," she replied more forcefully.

Good girl. Never back down.

Setting his glasses back on his nose, Bishop once again studied the artwork.

"Mr. Bishop, I'm a bit confused as to why you're here," Emma said. "Do you know someone who wishes to have their portrait done?"

"No," was the man's succinct reply. The art dealer walked about the studio, and every once in a while he'd stop before a painting and make a little noise, which seemed to originate from the back of his throat. At present, he stood before a landscape with a field of flowers.

Bishop made that odd noise again, glanced over his shoulder at Emma, and returned his attention to the painting. "You've never displayed your work?"

"No."

For the first time since entering the room, Mr. Bishop smiled. And the concern in Simon melted away.

"I'd like to represent you, Lady Adler. Would that be agreeable to you?"

As soon as Bishop left, Simon grabbed a bottle of champagne and pulled his wife back into the bedchamber to engage in a private celebration. He'd just set two champagne glasses on the bedside table and popped the cork, when someone knocked on the door. He took a deep breath and counted to ten.

Emma giggled. "It's probably Lily. Last I saw of her, she was besting Harris in a game of chess. She probably wishes to tell us all about it."

Harris and Lily seemed an odd pair, but since Baines and Mrs. Flynn had announced their plan to marry, and Simon had sent Nick away to the same school Michael attended, Lily and Harris had grown close. "I think it about time we ship your sister off to some private school. Perhaps in Switzerland."

"That's too far away, and you'd miss her as much as I would."

He *would* miss the little hellion, but he gave a noncommittal grunt, and called out, "Yes, what is it?"

"What are you two doing?" Lily asked.

"We're playing twenty questions." Simon smiled.

Emma's eyes sparkled and she chuckled. "Lily, we'll be downstairs shortly. We're getting dressed."

"You two change clothing more than anyone I know." Lily's heavy sigh filtered through the door. "Hurry. I want to tell you how I trounced Harris at chess."

Simon poured the champagne. "I think Switzerland is too close. Perhaps we could send her to America."

His wife smiled and slipped out of her gown.

Simon's gaze settled on the slight swell of Emma's abdomen. As usual, that place next to his heart ached. He was going to be a father. He pulled his wife to him and kissed her gently. "Thank you, Em."

"For what?"

"For loving me and allowing me to be part of your family."

Emma pressed her lips to his. "Our family, Simon. Now and always."

Love these scandalous lords?
Keep reading for a sneak peek at
the next book in the series,

NEVER KISS A NOTORIOUS MARQUESS,

coming soon.

And be sure to read

NEVER DARE A WICKED EARL,

available now from
Renee Ann Miller
and
Zebra Books,
wherever books are sold!

Helmsford, England
April 1878

The carriage hit a rut as it sped down the road. With an unladylike curse, Caroline Lawrence grasped the seat to stop herself from toppling to the floor. She'd obviously hired the worst hackney driver in all of London to convey her to the Essex countryside.

"Whoa," the cabbie called to the horses. The ill-sprung vehicle slowed and jerked to a stop.

Caroline peered out the window. Under the cloudy April sky, a crowd of mostly women stood before a stone barn to listen to Beatrice Walker speak in favor of women's rights.

A bolt of excitement shot through Caroline. She lowered the black mourning veil of her widow's weeds—the perfect disguise. She couldn't afford to have some gossipmonger inform Father they'd seen her here when he returned from his diplomatic meeting in Paris. He wouldn't approve of her attendance, nor her intention to write an article about Miss Walker for the *London Reformer*.

Ha! An understatement. Father detested the progressive

newspaper. What would he do if he discovered she was C. M. Smith, the paper's most notorious journalist? Everyone believed Smith was a man.

The cabbie flung open the door and flashed a gap-toothed grin.

Caroline alighted the vehicle. "You'll wait for me, sir?"

"Indeed, miss."

Clutching her folded umbrella, she lifted the hem of her plain black dress and strode up the dirt drive to the rear of the crowd.

Miss Walker, a sturdy woman of tall stature, stepped onto a crate to address the group. The suffragist thrust out her pointy chin and cleared her throat. The chattering in the crowd lowered to a hum. "Today, I will speak about the inequalities women must contend with."

A short man standing next to Caroline shouted, "'Tis a bunch of rubbish."

Caroline turned to him. "Sir, do you mind? I wish to listen."

He harrumphed. "To this hogwash?"

"Go home, you dried up ol' spinster!" a beefy man wearing a crumpled brown suit yelled at Miss Walker from where he stood near the front of the crowd.

"Go find yourself a husband," a third man shouted.

In all her twenty years, Caroline had never seen an orator treated so shabbily. As if used to this type of abuse, the suffragist continued speaking without blinking an eye.

The rude man next to Caroline pulled an egg from his coat pocket and pulled his arm back.

Oh, the audacity of the little weasel! Caroline lifted her umbrella and cracked it down on the man's head.

The egg flew out of his hand, sailed to the right of Beatrice Walker, and struck the fellow wearing the brown suit.

Red-faced, the man with yolk spattered on his coat uttered several obscenities. He removed his soiled garment, tossed it to the ground, and stormed toward the egg-thrower with his fist raised. "McAlister, that's me best coat. You were supposed to hit her. Not me, you bloody sod!"

A handful of women chastised the man for his profanity. Then all hell broke loose. A cacophony of raised voices filled the air. Men and women argued. The rude weasel and the beefy fellow rolled on the ground in a cloud of dust, while Beatrice Walker continued speaking in an elevated voice as if nothing were amiss.

A petite, gray-haired matron, who looked to be a century old, batted her umbrella at every male in sight. She swung it at a rotund man in front of Caroline.

The man ducked.

The nib of the umbrella caught Caroline's veil and her hat took flight like a lame bird—tumbling and twirling to the ground. She glanced around. God help her if there was anyone here she knew. Shielding her face with her hand, she crouched and reached for the hat.

Someone kicked the rim, and it sailed several yards away.

Drat! On her hands and knees, she weaved between the feet of the unruly mob. Her fingers were a mere inch from the hat when a foot landed on the gauzy veil. She peered up—past knee-high boots, past thick muscular thighs, and past a wide chest and broad shoulders.

The gentleman, dressed in black trousers and a cutaway riding coat, set his fisted hands on his lean hips and peered at the melee.

His dark eyes, straight nose, and high cheekbones gave him a stern countenance. The silky waves of his black hair softened his features, but the tight set of his jaw added to his severe appearance.

"What's going on here?" he demanded in a loud, authoritative voice.

As if the devil rose to stand before them, several women gasped, as did a few men.

Caroline stood and stepped back.

The gentleman's dark glower settled on her.

A spark exploded in her stomach and a bead of sweat trickled down her spine.

Everyone stood quiet and still, even Beatrice Walker.

With a scowl, the newcomer moved to where the wiry, egg-throwing weasel sat atop the larger man on the ground. He grabbed the weasel by the scruff of his coat and lifted him as if he weighed no more than a babe. "McAlister, what's this about?"

The weasel's mouth opened but nothing came out.

"I'm waiting," the gentleman said.

"'Tis not me fault, m'lord." The scoundrel jabbed a finger toward Caroline. "'Tis hers."

She squared her shoulders and swallowed the lump in her throat. "It is not, sir."

"'Tis too!" the weasel insisted. "You struck me with your umbrella."

The stern-faced gentleman cocked a dark, slashing brow at her. "Did you?"

The low, menacing timbre of his voice made her legs weak. She tilted her chin up. She was an independent woman. Well, not yet, but if all went as planned, one day she would be, and independent women didn't cower to men, even ones with broad shoulders and muscular arms and legs.

"Indeed I did, but he was about to toss an egg at Miss Walker."

His piercing gaze swung back to McAlister. "Is that true?"

"Y-yes, m'lord, but 'twas a very small egg."

The gentleman motioned to a thin man standing behind him, a constable of some sort by the look of his black uniform and top hat. "Ingles, I think McAlister needs to spend a night in jail, contemplating his actions."

Having made his pronouncement, he returned his attention to her. "Your name, madam?"

Caroline nibbled her lower lip. Mentioning Father might get her out of this mess, but when Papa found out, he'd be so vexed he *would* banish her to that Anglican convent in Oxfordshire—his favorite threat when displeased.

The gentleman took a single step toward her. With his long legs, it brought them face-to-face. Well, really, face to chest.

"Madam, you try my temper."

Nervous energy coursed through her. She stepped back. Her feet tangled with the man still lying on the ground. Arms flailing like a whirligig, she tumbled backward. Her bum, then shoulders, hit the hard, compacted dirt, followed by her head. The impact of her skull hitting the ground resonated in her ears. Flashes of light danced with splotches of black.

The gentleman knelt beside her, his face almost obliterated by the dark patches that floated before her eyes. He spoke. Muffled words she couldn't grasp. Strong arms lifted her. The spicy scent of shaving soap filled her nose, then darkness enveloped her, dragging her into a sunless pit.

James Trent, the Marquess of Huntington, braced his hands on his desk and tried to hold his temper in check as he stared at Dr. Clark. Did the physician seriously want him to keep the injured woman here at Trent Hall? "Why can't you take her to your residence?"

The doctor blushed like a debutante with a randy suitor's hand up her skirt. "My lord, I am a bachelor."

What the bloody hell did the doctor think James was? His wife had died two years ago. The physician was new in Helmsford, but surely the village biddies had shared the wicked gossip about Henrietta's death—that James had played a role in his wife's passing. He arched a brow at the man.

The doctor nervously shuffled his feet, confirming the tattlers had. "As . . . as are you, my lord, but you have your siblings residing with you, whereas I live alone."

Siblings. That might have made things better in society's eyes, but not in reality. Yesterday, Anthony arrived home from Cambridge, and already the rascal was down at the Hog and Thistle probably bedding one of the serving girls. And now James would have to worry whether the young buck would attempt to bed this woman while under James's protection.

Would attempt? Hell and fire, once his brother set eyes on her, he'd salivate like a dog after a beef joint. The chit was too lovely by half with her extraordinary green eyes, delicate face, and light brown hair with threads of gold.

"How long must she recover?"

The physician tapped a finger to his chin. "Hard to say. Injuries to the head are unpredictable. Perhaps a week."

"A week!" He snapped his nib pen in two.

The doctor paled.

"Did you find out if she has family? Where she hails from?" James asked.

"When she regained consciousness, she inquired about her veil. I presume it was lost in the scuffle. Then she mentioned she needed to return to London posthaste. She was most insistent it be today. When I told her she must not travel, she became overwrought. So much so, I felt compelled to give her a tincture. She is sleeping now."

James tossed the broken pen on the desk. "Send me your bill."

The physician nodded and left without another word.

Releasing a heavy breath, James picked up a financial

report that had arrived this morning from his business partners, Simon Marlton and Hayden Westfield.

The office door swung inward and Georgie walked in.

"Aren't you supposed to be in the schoolroom?" he asked the youngest and least troublesome of his three siblings.

His eight-year-old brother sat in one of the chairs facing the desk and swung his legs back and forth. "Mr. Harkins dozed off right in the middle of my math lesson. He's snoring so loud I'm getting a headache."

James leaned back and ran a hand over his jaw. Harkins was obviously getting too old to tutor, but James disliked the thought of pensioning the man off. The tutor had no family, and he feared the scholar would be lost without the employment. Harkins had served them well, having been both his and Anthony's teacher. The latter having caused the tutor's gray hair.

No, he'd not send the man away.

"What arithmetic function were you working on?"

"The multiplication of fives." Georgie wrinkled his nose.

James stood and ruffled the lad's hair. "Very well. Go get your paper and pencil. We shall work on them together."

A moment after Georgie darted from the room, the door to James's office flew open again. Anthony swaggered in with easy, loose-limbed strides. His brother's disheveled clothes implied he'd been up to no good. The reprobate would be fortunate if he didn't end up with the French pox or shot by some outraged husband before his twenty-second birthday.

His brother sank into the leather chair Georgie had vacated. "James, you have to hear the rubbish people are spouting at the Hog and Thistle."

Sitting, James kneaded the back of his neck. He didn't

wish to learn what the local gossips were saying, since it usually revolved around him.

"They say you lost your temper at Wickham's grange, where that suffragist Beatrice Walker spoke. Pushed some chit down and knocked her right out. It's outrageous what the denizens of this backwater whisper."

Pushed? Of course they would accuse him of such a villainous act. He should be used to their prattle. He'd gone there to make sure law and order prevailed. Beatrice Walker had a right to civility, but as always, he now found himself the center of gossip. He'd left London and come to the country to escape all the malicious talk about his wife's death, hoping for a small measure of peace and quiet. Was it too much to ask for? Apparently, yes.

The door swung open again, and Nina fluttered in. His sister's fair cheeks were high in color. "Who's that woman in the blue drawing room sleeping on the chaise longue? And why didn't anyone tell me Dr. Clark was here?" She touched her temple. "I'm sure I feel a headache coming on. He could have attended me."

James gritted his teeth. Nina's fascination with the doctor and every other male disconcerted him.

Anthony's eyes grew round. His brother sprang to his feet. "A woman? Good God, James, it's not true what they're saying, is it?"

"Blister it, Anthony. You know I would never harm a woman."

His brother's face turned red. "Yes, I apologize. I don't know what I was thinking."

James took a deep breath. "I have work to do, so if you'll both be on your way."

"But who's that woman?" Nina repeated.

Standing, James set a hand on his sister's back and ushered her to the door, motioning Anthony to follow. "It appears she is our houseguest. Tell Langley to task one of the footmen with relocating her to the bedchamber next to mine." It would be the best way to ensure Anthony didn't visit her. He shepherded his siblings over the threshold.

"The room next to yours," his siblings said in unison.

"Yes," he replied, closing the door on their gaping mouths.

Connect with
Us